A ⠀⠀⠀⠀⠀⠀ ila

THE CECILIA SERIES

Cecilia—The Last Croilar Tier
Cecilia—The Order of Terefellian
Cecilia—The Caladium

BOOK
2

CECILIA

THE ORDER OF TEREFELLIAN

SANDRA L ROSTIROLLA

Pinkus Books

www.pinkusbooks.com

Sandra L Rostirolla

www.slrostirolla.com

Cecilia - The Order of Terefellian
The Cecilia Series - Book 2

Library of Congress Control Number: 2020925736

ISBN 978-0-9991891-2-2
ISBN 978-0-9991891-3-9 (eBook)

Cover Design by Ivan Cakic
Map by Matthew R. Hinshaw
Interior Text Design by Phillip Gessert

Printed in the United States of America

For Mum

ESJAN RANGE

Katlahn Village

...ND

Horga River

Forbidden Pool

Nian Temple

Bayton

Lava Fields

KORFKAHN MOUNTAINS

*"In the absence of good, there can be no evil.
For there can be nothing at all."*

St. Augustine (354-430 AD)

CHAPTER

1

CECILIA LAY ON her back, staring at a puffy, one-eared elephant huddled within the fluffy white clouds decorating the sky. The green expanse of Vitus's southern headlands had fast become her favorite place to soak in the world's beauty. In his basket beside her lay Alistair, her son, peacefully asleep. The sounds of joyous children running around and squealing with delight fluttered through the air. A laughing child meant a happy child. A happy child meant Siersha's light shone bright. At least, this was the lie Cecilia told herself. She sat up and hugged her knees to her chest. Each day, the unsettled rumble in her belly grew. Her friends, Noah and Analise, had been gone for far too long. They had trekked off six weeks ago on a mission to spread Siersha's light to the uncharted lands south of Vitus. Not knowing where they were and when they would come back stoked her worry. She placed her hand to her brow and gazed south, hopeful to see their silhouettes returning in the distance, but the horizon remained empty.

"Hi, Brassal!"

The sweet call of a little girl's voice drew Cecilia from her thoughts to Brassal, a former Blind Prisoner, walking her way. The round cups he wore over his eyes to hide the hideous scars from where the Soldiers of Vitus burned out his eyes had become popular eyewear for all the former Blind Prisoners.

"Hello there," he called back to the little girl.

By Brassal's side walked Oisin. No longer a wiry twelve-year-old, the former Ground Boy had sprouted at least five inches in the past two years, and the sunlight had turned his once waxy, underground complexion a golden brown. He was still slender, but that had more to do with his slight frame than lack of food. The kid could eat half a horse if he put his mind to it.

"Cecilia, I'm glad we found you," said Brassal. "The little one, he is with you?" His silver-haired head bobbed as if trying to see over and around Cecilia—a thoroughly strange act considering he literally had no eyes. "Ah, yes, there he is."

"Brassal, how on earth did you know I was here?" Cecilia asked.

"I asked Tomkin, 'where's Cecilia?' and he told me out by the Freedom Tree."

"No, I mean just now. How did you know I was sitting right here, and that Alistair was with me?"

Brassal tapped a grassy spot with his cane, presumably to determine the area's suitability for sitting. At ninety years of age, the spry old man required minimal help from Oisin as he lowered himself into a cross-legged position. "I told you when we first met, I can see your light. And Alistair's. His is very tiny, so I can only see it when I'm up close. The Light of Siersha within him, though, grows stronger every day."

Cecilia sat up and cuddled her knees to her chest. Alistair exuding Siersha's light made sense. The Goddess glowed within Cecilia during his conception, creating the Ceannaire Fis—the Visionary Leader. Brassal still seeing light within Cecilia, however, troubled her. She'd done her job, delivered Siersha's goodness to Vitus. Why, then, did the Goddess continue to use her as a vessel?

"We have wonderful news," said Brassal. "The Tower clean-up crew found a library on the forty-ninth floor."

After Cecilia's army defeated the Senators of Vitus, the new leadership council set about relocating the Tower Folk and cleaning out the enormous structure. No longer would rulers reign from its immense height. Instead of letting the building sit idle, the council voted to convert the monolith into a hub for knowledge, research, and creativity. Because of the structure's sheer size, the process had been ongoing for the past two years.

"A library?" Cecilia repeated. "I thought the Senators had burned all the books."

"Show her," Brassal said to Oisin.

Cecilia's eyes widened at a photo of Siersha's statue on the front cover of the book Oisin handed to her. She had seen this alabaster carving inside what she and Amalardh referred to as the Temple Cave. The book's title, *Exploring the Gaussian Tuetin Cave,* suggested the actual name. Her hands held the answers to the Prophecy that Amalardh had seen, but she hadn't. After the Battle for Freedom, Cecilia had asked him how he knew they would have a child. He told her he saw their son in the Prophecy. Rather than explaining what he had witnessed, he said one day, he would take her back and show her. Between rebuilding the city and raising Alistair, that one day never came. Now, she didn't need to make the trip. The book's picture-perfect replicas of the cave's paintings and statues were as good as looking at the real thing. Well, maybe not exactly as good. The miniscule images paled in comparison to the life-sized murals. She turned from page to page, squinting at the various images, looking for a clue.

She arrived at a photo of the mural depicting children sitting under a Freedom Tree. A toddler of possibly eighteen months of age (six months older than Alistair) wore a Croilar Tier knife attached to his waist belt. She squinted, trying to get a closer look.

"Do you need this?" said Oisin. He held up a magnifying disk.

Cecilia placed it on top of the toddler and the hairs on her arms stood on end. The wolf on the knife's handle was missing its right, red ruby eye. This wasn't just any Croilar Tier knife. This blade was Amalardh's. Not only had he seen their son in the Prophecy, he'd seen his own end; Croilar Tier knives only passed down to the eldest child upon their father's death. Sometime between now and this moment of the children sitting under the Freedom Tree, Amalardh would die.

Cecilia snapped the book closed.

SANDRA L ROSTIROLLA

"What is it, dear child?" Brassal asked.

"It's getting late," she said. "Let's head back in."

The wind whipped her long skirt as she followed Oisin and Brassal along the worn path back to the city. Even though the social classes within Vitus no longer existed, Cecilia wore clothing reminiscent of the previous groups. Her skirt was made of taupe Citizen-hessian, which she topped with a white cotton Plocktonian blouse. Her buckled corset featured black Soldier-leather fashioned in the vein of the fitted Tower Folk outfits, and her cropped fur jacket resembled the Ground People's pelt-based attire.

With the revelation of Amalardh's impending death consuming her thoughts, Cecilia hadn't noticed Oisin stop. She stumbled into him and apologized. Standing still with his eyes locked forward, he seemed not to notice.

"Why have we stopped?" Brassal asked.

Cecilia followed Oisin's gaze to a bizarre person standing just outside Vitus's enormous, open gates. A thick, woolly beard hung to the man's chest and his head-to-toe, tan leather outfit was capped with a skinned brown bear cape, the head of which he wore like a hat. He stood rock solid, seemingly unwilling to step beyond the city's threshold.

"May I help you?" Cecilia asked.

"I had to come and see for myself," he said in a throaty voice. "Is it true? The Senators are dead?"

If this man had only recently heard of the Senators' downfall, then he'd probably remained in hiding. This would explain his strange attire. "Yes," she replied. "You are free to enter."

The lines on his face deepened as he scanned the city's threshold. "I'm good right here."

"Well, when you are ready, our gates are always open. My name is Cecilia." She waited for him to respond. When he didn't, she added, "And you are?"

"Here to see the one they call Amalardh."

4

Amalardh? She narrowed in on a collection of hatchets tucked into his belt. "What business do you have with him?"

"I'm his uncle."

Her spine straightened. This bear-cape-wearing man was Amalardh's uncle? Impossible. Amalardh didn't have any relatives. Then again, why would he lie about something like that? Only a crazy person would proclaim to be a relation of the Senators' former assassin if they weren't.

"Forbillian?" Brassal asked.

Cecilia blinked at the blind man. "You know this person?"

"I prefer Forbs," the man replied. His bushy brows rose as he wiggled his finger at Alistair. "So, who do we have here?"

"That's Alistair," said Oisin. Cecilia flung him a stern look, but her attempt to warn him not to say too much failed. "He's your great nephew."

The color drained from Forbillian's rosy cheeks. "That child is Amalardh's son? This darn Prophecy is true." He glanced down at his mud-splattered boots. "Thirty bloody years. I promised myself I'd never step foot back in this place. You need to take me to Amalardh, now."

CHAPTER
2

BROTHER WYNDOM'S HEART thumped as he gripped his rope and inched toward the edge of his buhleycob. In two weeks, one of two things would happen: his queen would arrive and deliver him and his people to the Sworn Province of Vitus, or he would face his Rite of Quinquagenary. Either way, his crippling fear of heights would be a thing of the past. He peeked over his cave's opening and the ground below spun in dizzying circles. He stumbled backward and clutched his sickened belly. "If our queen truly is meant to arrive before my Rite, she's cutting things a bit close."

"There, there," said his wife, Sister Rudella. She placed her craggy palm on his cheek. "Ethreet fofiel willmeco." In Terefellian, that meant, "The tree of life will come."

As a general rule, Wyndom found Rudella's touch unpleasant. Climbing close to one hundred feet up and down a rope every day for almost fifty years had given them both calloused palms as rigid as goat hooves. But since his graying beard acted as a softening layer, he stifled his desire to flinch.

"Brother Wyndom!" called a youthful voice from below. "The lookout requests your guidance."

Wyndom exchanged a perplexed look with Rudella. Guidance? The lookout had never needed help identifying Soldiers of Vitus. Blackened silhouettes riding across the open fields in broad daylight should be as obvious as white clouds in a blue sky.

His eyes grew wide. Whatever the lookout had spotted must clearly not be Soldiers.

Hushed chatter rumbled into his hollow home. Those on the

valley floor wanted to know what they should do. Return to their buhleycob? Those in transit dangled from their ropes and shared similar concerns. Rudella motioned for Wyndom to get to the edge of their cob and address his worried people. His stomach flipped as he crept forward. Loyal to the hilt, Rudella covertly clung to the back of his tawny tunic. Her brawny strength helped settle his nerves. No other Terefellian wife would offer such support. They would sooner shove their pathetic excuse for a husband to his deserved death. A Terefellian afraid of heights—a leader, no less—was an embarrassment to the tribe.

Dressed in earth tone tunics, climbers dangling from the caves mottling the opposite side of Terefellia's narrow canyon blended seamlessly with the rocky wall. "Settle all," Wyndom said. "While we are in uncharted waters, we must not expel undue energy. With the time of our queen drawing near, I urge restraint. An over-exerted climber could lose their grip and fall. And anyone who dies before their Rite is not saved." Knuckles blanched as those clinging to their lifelines tightened their grip. "Those of you traversing, climb to the closest cob and rest up. Everyone else, remember, our lookout can see far and wide. You will have plenty of time to retreat to safety."

As his people quietly went about obeying his order, Rudella, still clutching his robe, guided him back into the shadows. He doubled over and clasped his hands to his knees to support his weak body. Maintaining the appearance of a fearless commander drained him to the core. The very sight of his own rope made him want to rip the damn thing from its anchor and toss it away.

Rudella placed her steely knubs either side of his beard and forced him to look at her. "Brother Wyndom, you must not lose faith."

Easy for her to say. She wasn't the one staring forced retirement in the face. What if whatever the lookout spotted wasn't a sign from their queen? Maybe Rudella could embrace her Rite of Quinquagenary with her head held high, but Wyndom couldn't. He planned to run kicking and screaming from the horrid event.

He shrugged her away and shoved his hands into a basket of climbing powder.

Rudella sighed and straightened out their animal pelt bedding. "Do you think I stayed with you because of love?"

Thrown by the question, Wyndom absentmindedly wiped his dusty hands on his tunic. Of course she loved him, didn't she? Why else would she help him hide his shameful debilitation?

Rudella frowned at the chalky smear marks on his chest and wiped them with a damp cloth. "What you need to know, my dear Brother, is that I never cared for your love. I cared for your destiny."

His shoulders straightened. Rudella truly believed he would lead the Terefellians to Vitus? "How can you be so certain of my future?"

"A Terefellian afraid of heights is either a cruel joke or a sign he will lead us from our heights to the Sworn Province." She looked down her nose at him, an easy feat with her almost six-foot stature to his piddly five-foot-two. "I'd like to believe I didn't spend thirty years of my life protecting a joke. Tell me, my Brother. Is that what you are?"

"No, dear Sister, I am not."

She flicked his shoulder with the damp cloth. "Then stop behaving like one."

His pulse thumped at her brazen honesty. All this time, Wyndom had thought Rudella had blindly loved him. Hearing that she didn't, excited him. He went to kiss her, but she pulled back. "Rudella. I want you."

"The lookout is waiting."

"But I mean it."

A hint of sadness flashed through her eyes. "Yes. This time, you actually do."

A deep ache resonated in the left side of Wyndom's chest. He pressed his hand to the area. Was this what people meant when they talked about having heartache? After all these years, had some part of him fallen in love with his wife?

"Brother Wyndom," said Rudella.

He glanced up, hopeful. Had she changed her mind? Did she want him now, too?

"The lookout," she reminded him.

"Yes, of course," he replied.

The Terefellian Valley ran parallel to the Epona Ocean. Caves known as buhleycobs dotted either side of the narrow canyon's steep walls, which rose one hundred feet above sea level. Wyndom's cob sat on the valley's ocean side, and at fifty feet above the valley floor, it was the highest cave. The rocky peak above his home housed the lookout. He had visited the spot only once, about thirty years ago, during his induction as leader. The promotion came with a required orientation of his homeland's operations. Back then, he had started at ground level and scaled the valley wall's somewhat forgiving southern slope to the high pinnacle. From his cob, the fastest way to the top meant clambering out through a tight hole at the back and scaling the ocean-facing bluff—a simple task for most Terefellians. Not so much for someone with Wyndom's condition.

The lengthy drop to the ocean sent a dizzying rush to his head. As much as he despised his rope, he wished he had one at the rear end of his cave. The location, however, did not allow for such a convenience. A rope hanging out of a buhleycob can be pulled up and out of sight. One tethered from the back side of his cave to the rocky pinnacle needed permanent anchoring to the height above, and even though the chances of a Soldier exploring the waterfront cliffs were slim, Wyndom couldn't take the risk.

Sweat poured from his brow as he made the arduous climb. Several goats dotted the cliff face. The tiniest of the lot, a young kid, seemed to ridicule him with its incessant bleating and sure-footedness. If the feast for Brother Lasair's Quinquagenary had not already been set, Wyndom would've for certain ordered up a serving of tender goat cutlets for his evening meal.

His depleted muscles quivered as he neared the pinnacle. Because Terefellian society frowned upon requesting help to complete the final few steps to a destination, Wyndom employed an alternative tact. He stretched forth his hand and said, "Brother Stilton, show me your strength."

Seizing the opportunity to prove his worth, fifteen-year-old Stilton scuttled to the edge and hauled Wyndom up. He stood at attention, awaiting his leader's appraisal.

Wyndom took a moment to catch his breath. "Your might is not bad," he said, "but less than impressive for someone your age." A complete and utter lie. The kid's muscles felt made of steel, and this made Wyndom jealous of the youth's brawn.

Stilton's blond head lowered as he apologized for his failings.

Wyndom placed his hand on the kid's shoulder. "What say we keep this between us?"

Stilton's face lit up. The boy's expression reflected the loyalty of a servant forever indebted to his ruler, and this delighted Wyndom. Crippled with self-doubt, he needed to know his followers revered him. Manipulation was the only way he knew to gain their admiration.

A team of teenagers comprised the lookout, one working a solitary four-hour shift at the peak while another served as a runner on the valley floor to transport any messages. Each was young enough to still have perfect sight and old enough to grasp the magnitude of their role—the lookout was Terefellia's only defense. Lacking the weaponry and numbers to fight the Soldiers of Vitus, Terefellians survived by hiding. Between a handheld telescope and the sprawling northern savannah lands, the lookout could spot a scouting Soldier up to one hour's ride away, time enough for the Terefellians to remove evidence of their presence and scuttle up to their cobs.

"You were right to call for my advice," Wyndom said as he peered through the telescope. The travelers—a teenage boy and girl on horseback—were certainly not Soldiers. Their loose, fawn-colored clothing and casual posture made him certain of such.

They did, however, hail from Vitus. Wyndom recognized the scripted "V" branded on the horse rumps. Could they be the sign he longed for? "I must head out and greet them."

"Sir," said Brother Stilton, "send me instead. What if this is a trap?"

Wyndom patted the boy's shoulder. A brave soul indeed. Far braver than Wyndom ever was at his age, when his smarts prevented heroic stupidity. Only an idiot offered their life to protect their chief. Normally, he would have jumped at Stilton's foolish proposal, but the two smiling faces in the distance looked far from dangerous. "I should not forgive myself if harm befell you. As your leader, it is my duty to protect my subjects. Keep a close eye. I will signal with a raised arm if in danger."

Stilton's awed expression made Wyndom feel brave. A rare sensation indeed. *Please let these youngsters be a sign from our queen.* The queen's arrival meant peace, which meant no more living in caves, no more hiding from Soldiers, and no more frantic subjects needing his guidance. The concept of being a leader was far more appealing to Wyndom than the actuality. He trotted off with a skip in his step. Not only did the possibility of a new life lay ahead, the path from the lookout to the savannah lands involved no climbing. Just a leisurely downhill stroll.

CHAPTER
3

ANALISE SAT TALL on her horse. "Noah. Look." She motioned to a man dressed in a beige, knee-length tunic walking their way across the open savannah field. She and Noah had pledged to spread word of the Citizen uprising and the end of the Senators' dark reign. They had been on the road for weeks and had planned to give their mission another hour before giving up and turning back to Vitus. In the vast lands surrounding the city, the Soldiers must have killed everyone, or folk remained too terrified to show themselves, for they hadn't seen a living soul, until now.

"Greetings," said the man.

Analise and Noah offered their greetings back.

The man's dark, short, curly hair didn't have a lick of gray. If he shaved his salty beard, he'd look closer to forty than Analise's guess of about fifty. He introduced himself as Brother Wyndom, leader of the Terefellians, and offered his hand. His eyes lit up when his palm intertwined with Noah's.

"So soft," he said.

The comment perplexed Analise until she made her introduction. Her father had his share of callouses from working the fisheries, but his thickened palms were nothing compared to Wyndom's rock-hard skin. He seemed entranced and wouldn't let her go. She tugged free with more vigor than she probably should have.

"My apologies," he said. He turned his palms upward, exposing the cruel extent of his damaged skin. "I have not experienced such satin touch in... well, never."

Guilt jabbed her. She shouldn't have been so harsh. Her purpose was to spread Siersha's light, not indulge Eifa's dark hostility. She dismounted from her horse. Noah followed.

"We have news which, if you have not yet heard, I'm sure will be welcome," she said. "You no longer need fear Vitus's dark shadow. The Senators' villainous reign has ended. In their place sits a new queen."

Noah leaned close. "You know how much Cecilia hates you calling her a queen," he whispered.

Analise brushed him away and took hold of Brother Wyndom's coarse hand. "The life that has caused you this torment is over."

His face lit up and a film of water glazed his eyes. "Ethreet fofiel willmeco," he said.

Analise shared a confused look with Noah.

"The tree of life will come," Wyndom clarified.

Analise's confusion remained. Only when Noah nodded to her chest did she remember the replica of Cecilia's Freedom Tree pendant pinned to her top. She placed her hand on the symbol and smiled. "Yes. The tree of life has come."

A sea of Terefellians dotted the narrow valley into which Wyndom led Analise and Noah. Everyone wore similarly styled, muted tunics. Combined with their short hair and mid-forehead fringe, Analise struggled to tell man from woman, boy from girl. How had this group remained hidden from scouting Soldiers while other villages had fallen? The distance from Vitus and the densely covered trail leading into the valley probably helped. Still, they seemed so exposed in the slender canyon. Where could they possibly live? Heads popping out from a myriad of holes on either side of the steep walls provided the answer. Ropes dropped from the caves and bodies big and small began scaling down. No wonder Wyndom's palms felt like rocks.

"Ethreet fofiel sahmeco!" Wyndom called to his people.

14

Arms lifted as the Terefellians cheered.

A tall, broad woman with prominent facial features rushed over. "The tree of life *has* come," Wyndom said to her, then introduced her as his wife, Rudella. She studied Analise and Noah, and her joyous expression fell.

The saddened look jolted Analise, but she remembered her own intense swing of emotions when Cecilia had arrived in Vitus and announced her intent to free the Citizens. In a matter of seconds, Analise had flipped from excitement to apprehension to overwhelming sorrow that her people had needed saving in the first place. The tears Rudella swiped from her eyes were surely ones of joy.

Curious Terefellians lined up to touch Analise and Noah's hands. Analise couldn't fault their fascination. The feel of a little girl's coarse touch equally astounded her. As she pondered the hapless child's misery, a jittery fellow with silver temples and thin eyebrows scuttled up to Wyndom. Brother Lasair was his name. He prattled on about some rite. The man seemed adamant that since the Tree of Life had come, his rite had been abolished.

"There, there," Wyndom said to the man. "This is neither the time nor place for worry. Let us celebrate." He waved his arm to the crowd. "Come, my people. We have much joy to indulge."

He led everyone south through the narrow valley to where it opened into a desert-type landscape littered with sparse palm trees and shrubs. To the left, waves from the Epona Ocean crashed against a stony shore. Four men dusted an area, exposing a stone slab about six feet long and two feet wide. They slid the dense mass to one side, revealing a pit filled with rolled seating mats and clay eating ware for three hundred.

"We use our firepit to store our dining items," said Wyndom. "The less we lug up and down from our buhleycobs, the better. When we are done, we cover the hole back up, sprinkle it with sand, and voila! No one would ever discern a cooking station lay beneath their feet." His eyes sparkled as he watched his people unrolling mats and setting them with plates, cups, and eating utensils. "We never usually start a fire before sundown. We couldn't risk scouting Soldiers spotting our smoke. But thanks to your glorious news—" His voice cracked as he swallowed back his emotions.

Analise wrapped her arms around Noah's waist. Their weeks of doubt as they continued their southern trudge had most definitely been worth it.

They sat down on a woven mat with Wyndom and Rudella and listened as Wyndom spoke about their day-to-day existence. Wild orchards provided plenty of fruits and nuts; the local goats produced milk, from which the Terefellians made cheese and yogurt; and their hunters caught rabbits and the occasional deer or boar. Considered sacred for their climbing prowess, Terefellian law forbade the killing of the local goats unless absolutely warranted for survival.

"Does your respect for goats explain your ring?" Analise asked. She nodded to a silver piece of jewelry on Wyndom's left hand, featuring a goat's skull with curled horns, black pits for eyes, and an infinity symbol etched into its forehead. Its gaping mouth with no teeth looked ready to suck out her soul. She would normally find the imagery garishly threatening, but Amalardh's Croilar Tier knife with its snarling wolf teeth, one red ruby eye and black pit from where the other jewel had fallen out looked as unsettling the first time she saw it, and Amalardh had turned out to be Cecilia's protector and a thoroughly honorable man.

Wyndom studied his silver band as though never really giving the imagery much thought. "I guess so, although, prior to the Great War of two centuries past, our people lived on the flat lands on the other side of the Terefellian Valley. We moved to the caves to hide from Vitus's Soldiers. Why our great ancestors would revere goats for their climbing would be strange, as they had no need for the skill."

Rudella made a slight upward eye roll. She seemed accustomed to his lack of knowledge. "A goat's climbing prowess is not the primary reason Terefellians revere the animal. We do so because they are curious, independent creatures who do not follow the masses, and they don't let their harsh environment hinder their ability to survive."

Wyndom patted the top of her hand. "I must confess, my dear wife is far more attuned to our history than I am."

"Why the infinity symbol?" Noah asked.

Wyndom hesitated. This time, he seemed to know the answer. He glanced at Rudella as though deferring to her expertise and what they should divulge.

"It means eternal life," Rudella said. "As Terefellians, we believe our souls never die."

Analise's concern that maybe Wyndom was trying to hide something evaporated. She understood his reluctance to expose his inner belief. The former Senators of Vitus forbade Citizens to believe anything beyond what the Senators told them. Even a discussion about the possibility of life after death would've led to a Citizen becoming a Blind Prisoner. "You're in good company," she said. "We, too, believe our souls never die."

"All this talk of death and dying," said Wyndom. "This is a merry time. For years, our people have been waiting for our queen to arrive and deliver us to the Sworn Province of Vitus." He clapped his hands together and beamed. "I simply cannot believe that the time of our queen is here."

"Oh my gosh, did you hear that?" she whispered to Noah. "They have been waiting for a sign that their queen has arrived, and that sign is Cecilia's Freedom Tree symbol." She flashed him a smug look. "See, I'm not the only one who thinks of Cecilia as a queen."

Noah laughed. "I never said I disagreed with your description. Only that Cecilia hates it."

After the Battle for Freedom, Brassal had referred to Amalardh as the white knight of the Prophecy, and Cecilia, their queen. Although Cecilia had insisted that she was no one's queen, Analise often called her "my queen" because she believed Cecilia deserved the designation (and she enjoyed getting a rise out of her friend). For years, Analise's father had faith that two centuries after the Great War, the Flower Princess would come and free them from the Senators' oppressive reign. This fabled savior was Cecilia. Since a princess naturally progressed to a queen, Analise justified her continued use-in-jest. She couldn't wait to watch Cecilia squirm when the good folk of Terefellia tried to crown her for real.

As the sky darkened, the celebrations moved into full swing. For a group of people living in caves, these folks knew how to party.

"A Rite of Quinquagenary is normally a solemn event," Wyndom said. "Because of the threat of scouting Soldiers, we don't usually have the luxury of making unfettered noise. But with your good tidings, I gave the order for everyone to let loose."

The Rite of Quinquagenary. Analise recognized the phrase as the term the jittery man from earlier had quibbled about.

"Is something wrong?" Wyndom asked.

"This rite you are celebrating, that other man..." She looked around for the silver-templed fellow.

"You mean Brother Lasair?" He rotated her to their right and pointed out the man from earlier, drinking from a ceramic mug and laughing uproariously. "Everyone has a mild panic about their retirement."

"Retirement?"

"Yes. The Rite of Quinquagenary is a celebration of... well, reaching a milestone."

Retirement didn't exist in Vitus, at least not for the Citizens. Under the Senators' rule, Analise's downtrodden group had toiled the fields until they dropped. In contrast, when a work horse reached a certain age, the head farmer removed its harness and let the loyal animal roam the fields. Analise applied the concept of being put out to pasture to Brother Lasair's earlier misgivings and nodded to herself. No one wanted to be thought of as a forgettable member of society. Even the old horses still meandered to the fence line and watched as younger equines received the attention they once had. "I like your Rite of Quinquagenary," she said. "We should celebrate our elders."

The four of them chatter further about Analise and Noah's journey and how they were ready to give up and turn back, when Brother Wyndom had called out to them.

Wyndom grew pale. "Oh my. That would not have been good at all."

Analise agreed. Had she and Noah returned to Vitus, it could've been months, years, before anyone ventured this far south and freed these people from their existence. Her stomach growled as the cooking pit's delectable aroma wafted over.

A half-dozen young folk walked to the pit, placed a woven basket on the ground, and began dancing, making wide scooping motions with their arms as they cupped the smoke in their palms and thrust it at the basket. Wyndom described the display as the Tenococill Olus, which loosely translated to soul collection. "A soul floating the universe is viewed as lost," he said.

The explanation reminded Analise of Cecilia's belief that all souls were precious and the Plocktonian tradition of praying over a dead animal. Despite their harsh lives, the Terefellians had a culture rich with tradition. She squeezed Noah's hand and leaned close. "Thank you for insisting we give our journey that additional hour. These people deserve a new start away from their horrid caves."

He lifted their grasped palms to his lips and kissed her knuckles. "After my life of privilege as a Tower Folk, I am just so grateful to be in a position to help others."

"Will you all excuse me," Wyndom said. "I'll be back in the shortest of moments."

As he trotted off, Rudella sidled over to Analise and asked about her and Noah's relationship. Analise explained the Senators' ban of Citizen and Tower Folk unions, and how until the Battle for Freedom, she and Noah had to meet in secret. "We plan to marry once we return from this trip," she said. "Then we can, well, you know."

"So, you and Noah haven't?"

Analise blushed and shook her head. With Wyndom return-ing, she quickly whispered, "We're saving ourselves."

Rudella's posture sunk. "The tree of life truly has come," she uttered, more to herself than anyone else.

Why the sudden melancholy? Had Analise and Noah's youth-ful love evoked a wisp of envy? Although Rudella and Wyndom appeared friendly with each other, Analise couldn't imagine much passion between them. Beyond their extreme physical dif-ferences, their personalities seemed completely mismatched.

Wyndom handed them a goblet. "Shhh," he said. "Don't tell anyone." He explained that the offering held ceremonial brew, and the rules limited consumption of the short-in-supply bev-erage to the person of honor. "Since you're both our honorable guests... well, what's the point of being a ruler if you can't pull a few strings?"

Analise crinkled her nose at the liquid's acrid scent. Noah downed his drink in one chug. His face soured as he gagged. Rudella and Wyndom drank theirs. Possibly because they'd grown accustomed to the taste, neither so much as winced.

"Come on," said Noah to Analise. "Live a little."

Easy for him to say. In his previous Tower Folk life, he proba-bly drank similar brew every day.

She studied the brownish liquid. Maybe Noah was right. Maybe she should live a little. With curiosity getting the better of her, she took a sip and retched at the bitter flavor. "Yuck. I don't think so."

Noah laughed. "Wuss," he taunted.

Analise grimaced at him. She was the daughter of Finn, a rugged sailor, and her family had no namby-pambies. She tossed the objectionable stuff back and slammed the goblet to the mat. Noah and Wyndom cheered. Rudella's smile seemed forced. She probably disapproved of Analise's buckling to social pressure.

Analise felt the same way, but then a warm sensation traveled down her chest, bringing relaxation. Oh. Wow. No wonder people drank this foul-tasting gunk.

Fresh-faced Terefellian children delivered meat from the fire pit on handmade clay plates.

"Eat up," said Wyndom.

The tender meat's aromatic flavor entranced Analise's taste buds. "Oh my gosh! This is the most delicious meal I've ever had." Noah agreed. Considering he'd grown up with access to an array of scrumptious flavors, his delight in the dish said something. She looked around the cross-legged gathering for the man of honor. "Where's Brother Lasair?" she asked.

"You're eating him," Wyndom replied.

CHAPTER
4

THE AWE ON Forbillian's face as he took in Amalardh's glorious residence mirrored what Cecilia imagined her own must have looked like when she first saw the giant vines snaking up the pillars and along the walls, the silver-bladed grass growing in and around the broken floor tiles, and the enormous tree at the far end, whose broad canopy filled in a blown-out section of the roof. In the many months since Cecilia's arrival, Amalardh's sparse furnishings had grown to include a dozen more chairs, a dining table, a playpen, and a bunch of children's toys. They had also built out a nursery for Alistair and a bedroom for Oisin, who had surreptitiously adopted Amalardh and Cecilia after losing his father, his only living relative, during the Battle for Freedom. Excited about Forbillian's arrival, Oisin had broken away from the walk back home to share the news of Amalardh having an uncle with Cecilia's brothers.

Cecilia placed Alistair in his pen and left Forbillian and Brassal to their chatter while she searched for Amalardh. She found him in his basement workshop, exactly where she expected, curled over his bench reading a book. Probably *Veracid Donalino's Human Anatomy*, since an open space sat where its prominent spine usually did on the bookshelf.

She stood at the bottom of the spiral staircase and stared at the man who was only a few feet away, but may as well have been on the moon. After Alistair's birth, Cecilia and Amalardh's relationship had unraveled. Where she could once penetrate his stoic outer shell, the growing effort left her drained. She had hoped his new life with her would inspire him to abandon his brown robe, but he seemed more reliant than ever on the hood to shield him from the world. He looked up from his reading. His unwavering blue eyes still sent a flutter to her belly. The rest of his handsome face disappeared under his growing beard and dark, shaggy hair.

"There's a man upstairs who says he's your uncle," she said.

Amalardh's expression stunted. "I don't have an uncle."

"Brassal seems to think you do. He remembers your father mentioning a younger brother called Forbillian. Your uncle—this man—correctly identified his and Culloden's age difference of eighteen months and knew of a butterfly-shaped birthmark on your dad's right inner thigh." While Brassal's blindness prevented him from observing the discoloration, he had recalled a macabre comment Culloden once made—if anyone found a male, headless body with a butterfly birthmark on the right inner thigh, then the decapitated corpse would be his. The off-color comment suggested that Senator Culloden suspected the other Senators wanted for his death. And they did. At barely six weeks of age, Amalardh lay in his crib while the Senators' then assassin made a bloodied mess of the innocent baby's father.

"We may have overthrown the Senators, but do not believe for one minute we are safe," Amalardh said. "Uncle or not, I am not familiar with this man. You should not have let him into our house."

Cecilia's blood chilled as she followed him up the basement's spiral staircase. Had she incorrectly assessed Forbillian's sincerity? Surely, once Amalardh met the quirky man, he would see his reaction was unwarranted. She raced with him from the altar end of their cathedral home to the living area in the front section. Her breath seized at the sight of Alistair's empty play pen. Brassal lay strewn on an armchair, his head tilted back, his mouth gaping. "Brassal!" she called, shaking him.

He woke with a snort. "Yes. What? Oh, dear, I must have nodded off."

Although relief washed through her that Brassal had not

passed, concern for her son remained. "Where are Alistair and that man?"

Brassal sat forward. "They're gone? Oh, dear."

The front door opened and in walked Oisin and Cecilia's brothers, twenty-six-year-old Eideard and twenty-five-year-old Rabbie. Other than proving themselves worthy warriors in the Battle for Freedom, not much else had changed since their Plocktonian days. Eideard still wore his shirt loose, like his hair, and Rabbie remained tightly buttoned and neatly coifed.

"Hey, sis," said Eideard. "Tell us it isn't true. Amalardh can't possibly have—" His expression dropped. "What's wrong? What happened?"

"Alistair's missing," she said.

Amalardh dashed to where several swords hung on the wall. Eideard and Rabbie followed. Since fighting together in the Battle for Freedom, the three had become tightly synced. Amalardh tossed them both a weapon and grabbed one for himself. "Oisin," he said. "Give the order to close the gates."

Oisin stood motionless. His crestfallen expression reflected a hesitance to believe that the woolly man with the bear cape posed a threat.

"Now!" demanded Cecilia.

Oisin raced off.

"What does this person look like?" Amalardh asked.

"You know how the Ground People wore capes of sand and branches to disguise themselves? Well, this man uses a bear," Cecilia said.

"A bear?"

"Trust me. Once you see, you'll understand."

With the efficiency of a seasoned leader, Amalardh divided up the search area with Eideard and Rabbie, and the three of them exited in different directions.

Cecilia went to follow Amalardh, when Brassal latched onto her arm. "Dear child, this is madness. Alistair is Forbillian's blood. He would never harm the boy."

"Amalardh was Senator Akantha's blood, and she drove a knife through his belly. Blood is capable of killing blood."

As though acknowledging the gut-wrenching possibility of Forbillian possessing ill intent, Brassal released his grip. "May Siersha's light keep Alistair safe," he uttered.

Cecilia ran off in the same direction as Amalardh.

With the Seventh Division not as populated as the other areas of the city, Amalardh quickly picked up a solitary set of tracks leading down to the beach. Cecilia's breath quivered. Had the devilish kidnapper already fled by boat?

The trail ended in the beach's loose sand.

Rope moorings connected several canoes to a short pier ahead. Inside one of the narrow boats sat Forbillian. He may have removed his outlandish cape, but Cecilia still recognized his broad shoulders and woolly hair. She dug her fingers into Amalardh's arm and pointed him out.

Sword drawn, Amalardh sprinted at the kidnapper. As Cecilia followed, some oddities struck her. If this stranger intended to steal Alistair, why did he rock the still-tied-up-to-the-pier canoe, and why did he sing a lullaby?

"Amalardh! Wait!" she called, but his sword was already swinging down.

Forbillian's right arm flew up, halting Amalardh's blade with a stubby ax. "Stone the crows," he said. "I'd be right now looking at a ghost if I thought it possible. You sure have your father's looks. And your mother's temperament."

For a man his size and age, Forbillian possessed deceptively sharp reflexes.

"My name is Forbs," he said. "I'm your uncle."

Amalardh remained motionless, as if processing the unimaginable.

"If you still be insisting on popping my clogs, I'd ask you to do so quietly. It was, if you excuse the pun, a bear to get this little one settled." Wrapped in the furry arms of Forbillian's cloak lay Alistair, peacefully asleep. Forbillian scooped him up in one arm and offered Amalardh the other. "A little helping hand wouldn't go astray. I'm not the sturdiest in one of these things, and you wouldn't want the little one dunking headfirst into the ocean while asleep. Speaking from experience, I don't recommend waking up that way."

Amalardh still didn't move. Cecilia had never seen him this rattled. Understandable. The last thing anyone expected was Amalardh having a living relative, let alone one as offbeat as Forbillian.

She crouched by the canoe. "Why don't you give me Alistair?" she said to Forbillian. "That way you can steady yourself with both hands."

"Ah, yes. That's a smart way to go." He handed over the sleeping bundle, then hauled himself onto the pier. "I must beseech your deepest forgiveness. I never intended to scare anyone. While I waited for you to return with my nephew, the little one became grumbly. Brassal had dozed off, and since I didn't know where you were, I picked Alistair up and tried to walk the grumbles out. One step became a thousand, and I found myself on the beach. Remembering the soothing nature of a rocking boat, I tried the same on the little one." His eyes sparkled as he smiled. "It worked like a charm. The grumbles stopped in under three rocks."

Even though Forbillian shouldn't have taken Alistair, Cecilia appreciated that his heart was in the right place. She nodded and accepted his apology.

"Whatever you have come here to discuss, I trust you will make your visit short," said Amalardh. He stowed his sword and walked off.

Forbillian's eyebrows rose. "Looks like someone else needs the grumbles rocked out of them, too."

Cecilia sucked back her grin. The little that she knew of Forbillian, she already liked. "Don't mind him. He's going to need more than a moment to process all this. You may stay as long as you wish."

Back in Cecilia and Amalardh's living room, Cecilia, Eideard,

Rabbie, Brassal, and Oisin sat forward on their chairs, eagerly listening to Forbillian explain how he had left Vitus a little over thirty years ago, a few weeks after his brother, Culloden—Amalardh's father—had become a Senator. Sitting off to the side, Amalardh remained flat. What must be going through his mind? After all these years, discovering he had an uncle? Cecilia wanted to reach out, hold his hand, ask him how he felt about Forbillian's unexpected arrival, but she knew Amalardh well enough to know that until he fully processed the situation, he would need his space.

"I hope you believe me, dear boy," Forbillian said to Amalardh. "I had no idea Akantha had her claws in Culloden. And I certainly didn't know about you."

"Why did you leave?" Cecilia asked.

Forbillian's shoulders sagged. "Let's just say that once the pudding has been over-egged, there's no saving it." Deep pain etched his face as he rubbed his brow. Whatever had caused him to flee couldn't have been trivial.

After leaving Vitus, he headed to the northern Wynn Forest and took up residence in an abandoned shack nestled at the bottom of a difficult to climb valley. The Soldiers and their preferred path of least resistance, never once ventured down the steep incline. Besides the black vermin—Forbillian's term for the Soldiers of Vitus—his only contact with the outside world was the rare spotting of a Ground Person out hunting. After two years without sighting Soldiers or Ground People, he inched closer to Vitus.

"A few weeks back, I encountered a group traveling in broad daylight, some on horses branded with Vitus's scripted "V," he said. "In all my years, Citizens had not the freedom to roam the lands outside the wall. Something had to be up. I approached them and spoke with a charming fellow; Gildas was his name. He said he was heading west to his hometown of Plockton. He told me about the rise of the Citizens under the leadership of the Treoir Solas, otherwise known as Cecilia, and the slaying of the

Senators by their former assassin, who turned out to be a Croilar Tier called Amalardh, whose mother was, of all people, Senator Akantha. This news rocked my world. Our father told us, Culloden's line would hold the last of the Croilar Tier. For one to exist called Amalardh, meant my brother was dead. This was the first I knew of having a nephew."

He seemed hopeful Amalardh might say something. Possibly realizing he wouldn't, Forbillian continued. "When I asked Gildas why he was leaving, he said that he missed his homeland. But I'm not so sure. Something about the empty look on his face made me wonder if maybe his pudding had also been over-egged. Anyway, each to their own, I say."

Cecilia's cheeks flushed as she side-glanced at Amalardh. While the two of them had never spoken about it, they both knew the real reason why Gildas had left. Since the Battle for Freedom, her awkward relationship with the man she'd grown up with had intensified. Where Amalardh had failed to step up and father Alistair, Gildas had filled the gap. He'd changed diapers, fed, and burped Amalardh's son. Unable to remain a second fiddle in Cecilia's life, he decided to move back to Plockton. The part Amalardh didn't know about, but possibly sensed was Gildas's request for Cecilia to come with him. For the smallest moment, she'd considered saying yes.

Forbillian's eyes locked onto the *Exploring the Gaussian Tuetin Cave* book sitting on Oisin's lap. "May I?" he asked. Oisin happily handed it over. As Forbillian flicked through the pages, his expression soured as if experiencing a foul taste. "I'd never placed much stock in this damn Prophecy. Until now. Too much has happened for it not to be true. My father"—he glanced at Amalardh—"your grandfather, believed there was more to it than what's in here."

Cecilia clutched the arm of her chair. Forbillian had confirmed her worst nightmare. Siersha's light still burned within her because the Prophecy held further secrets. "What do you mean 'more to it'?" she asked.

"Do you have any paper?"

Oisin removed some loose sheets from a side cabinet and brought them over.

Forbillian flipped to the picture of the last Croilar Tier slaying the Senators atop the massive Tower of Vitus and slotted the blank pieces between this image and the next, depicting the children sitting under the Freedom Tree—the Prophecy's supposed end—and presented it to her.

"I still don't understand," she said.

Amalardh sat forward. Forbillian's story may not have piqued his interest, but the stomach-churning Prophecy certainly had. "Whatever has started between the Goddess of Light and her Dark Shadow is far from finished," he said.

"Ah. He speaks," said Forbillian. He tapped the picture depicting the Croilar Tier slaying the Senators. "This moment has happened." He turned to the Freedom Tree. "This one has not. Before we get to this moment"—he flicked through the blank pages—"these unknown events must first happen. The question is"— he placed his hand on the Freedom Tree—"has anyone seen a tree like this? Because in all my life, I haven't."

"After the Battle for Freedom, I planted a seed for a tree like that in the southern headlands," said Cecilia. "At the moment, it's barely a sapling. It would need another ten years to grow to that size. There is, however, a similar tree in my home village. The problem is the one in Plockton is within a forest. In that picture, water backdrops the tree." She turned to Amalardh. "If the Freedom Tree in the Prophecy matches the seed I planted near the Epona Ocean, then this little boy"—she pointed to the toddler with the wolf knife around his waist—"can't possibly be Alistair."

Amalardh's ill at ease eyes seemed troubled about this revelation. He had told Cecilia that he'd seen their son in the Prophecy. The boy with the wolf knife could be the only image he'd seen. "If this child in the painting doesn't represent Alistair, then who does he represent?" she asked.

He didn't respond.

Cecilia exhaled and sat back. As always, whenever Amalardh had no answers instead of saying, "I don't know," he said nothing.

"When we were boys," said Forbillian, "our father took me and Culloden to an island about a week's sail from here. The tiny speck of a place hosts one building—the Ezekian Castle. Inside is the Croilar Tier Archives. I'd say that would be the best place to find answers to our questions."

"Surely the Senators would have destroyed everything in that castle years ago," said Eideard.

"Vitus was known for a strong foot army and cavalry unit," said Brassal. "Trawling the seas did not interest the Senators."

"Even if they had found the island," said Forbillian, "discovering the hidden archives is one thing. Getting inside is another." He placed his hand on Amalardh's knee and grinned. "So, nephew. Fancy a sail with your long-lost uncle?"

CHAPTER
5

ANALISE CHUCKLED. "DID you hear that, Noah? We're eating Brother Lasair!" The young guests burst out laughing and quipped about how funny it was to be a cannibal.

Cannibal? Wyndom abhorred the word. As far as he was concerned, Terefellians were no such beasts. Cannibals ate their own and others indiscriminately. Terefellian law barred the killing of a tribe member purely to provide food. Since a Rite of Quinquagenary resulted in death, what better way for the retired to offer thanks to the tribe than giving their flesh for consumption? He sipped his goblet of water and shrugged to himself. What had he expected? He'd given the two youngsters Quinquagenary brew for this very reason—to induce laughter as opposed to screams of horror at the idea of eating Brother Lasair.

Wyndom may have often been cruel, but he wasn't completely heartless. His father had taught his younger self that outside folk would look upon the Terefellian proclivity toward human flesh as repulsive. "Offering someone a delicacy they are not accustomed to would be tantamount to me forcing you to eat worms," his father had said. Confused by the notion, young Wyndom dug up a handful of the slimy critters and shoved them in his mouth. Their vile texture made him heave. Out of a desire to share Brother Lasair's Quinquagenary, Wyndom had plied Noah and Analise with mincelase tea. Made by brewing buds from the Yetope cactus, the psychoactive drink was used to calm Quinquagenary recipients.

As much as the Terefellian belief system instilled an accep-

tance of one's Rite, when the moment actually came, the benefi-
ciary would certainly struggle against being bound, gagged, and
roasted alive, if not for mincelase's sedative effects. Whether the
young couple truly believed their bellies digested Brother Lasair,
Wyndom didn't know or especially care. His sole focus was on
their relaxation and surrender to the moment, for if devouring
human flesh didn't freak Noah out, then maybe the stroking of
Wyndom's knuckles down the handsome young man's firm thigh
wouldn't either.

Noah whispered something to Analise. They both giggled.
Wyndom smiled to blend in with their amusement. "What, pray,
is so funny?" he asked.

A sharp pain stung his ear. Rubbing the smarting spot, he
turned to see Rudella's ominous glare. What was her problem?
Married or otherwise, the rule of Terefellia allowed consenting
adults to be with whoever they chose. While Wyndom hadn't
clarified Noah's age, he surmised that if the lad was old enough
to roam distant lands with a young woman, then he was old
enough to determine who he may or may not want to be with.
Rudella should be supportive of Wyndom's bravery. She knew
of his attraction to males and his inability to act on his desire.
His insecurities ran so deep he didn't believe another male would
find him enticing unless the calming effects of mincelase coursed
through their veins. Since consumption of the liquid was primar-
ily reserved for Rite of Quinquagenary recipients, this moment
with Noah presented a rare chance for Wyndom to test his the-
ory.

He pulled his wife close. "Dear Rudella, you have always
encouraged me to face my fears, and now that I do, you are jealous?"

"My dear Brother Wyndom. Jealousy is the last thing on my
mind. If I had not intervened earlier, you would've blurted out
the true meaning of our infinity symbol and sent our young guests
running. And if I don't intervene now..." She shook her head at

him. "I sometimes wonder about the weakness of your will. To come this far and ruin it all for a bit of flesh."

Ruin it all? What was she talking...? His brow rose. "Dear Sister, may our queen bring you affluence beyond your imagination for bestowing such wisdom in my time of weakness."

With "the Tree of Life will come" as Wyndom's only source of comfort in the lead up to his own Rite of Quinquagenary, he'd forgotten the second part: "bearing a fruit so pure, it must not be eaten." During dinner, he had overheard Analise tell Rudella that she and Noah were "saving themselves" for their wedding day. Such an archaic concept, but if the Terefellian queen required unsullied sacrifices, then she would have them. He tucked his desires away. "Come," he said to the young couple.

"The party's not over, is it?" Analise asked.

"Quite the contrary. We're moving it indoors." He turned to his people. "The time has come to welcome our queen."

Analise gasped. "Is Cecilia here?"

"Pardon?" Wyndom asked.

"Our queen. Is she here?"

Wyndom smirked. The giddy girl didn't realize their conversations centered on different queens. "Not yet," he said. "But she will be soon. Come, let me take you to where we'll meet her."

Wyndom and Rudella helped the woozy young couple to their feet and guided them to the Terefellian Temple. Analise's mouth fell open at the immense stone structure.

"Whoa," said Noah with a long drawl.

The first time Wyndom had visited the Terefellians' most sacred place, his astonishment matched that of his young guests. A massive, ornate facade was carved into a sandstone ridge. Banded into two stories, each about sixty-five feet high, broad pillars etched with leaping goats decorated both levels, as did a repeating infinity symbol along the top and bottom borders. The enormous door was forty feet high, sixteen feet wide, and made entirely of rock.

"If I lived here, I'd stay in that," said Analise. "Why do you live in those tiny caves?"

"Beyond our temple being sacred, coming and going from this structure is not as easy as one might think," Wyndom said.

Because of the need to hide from Vitus's Soldiers, the Terefellians had permanently removed the ladder they had once used to access the temple door's unlocking mechanism. Wyndom nodded to Brother Jovian, a blond waif about seventeen years of age and their best climber. The lanky teen appeared all arms and legs as he scaled a pillar to the left of the door. The delicate goat carvings provided scant hand and footholds. When he reached the second-floor landing, he continued up a central pillar. Since the upper supports lacked carvings, he deployed what the Terefellians referred to as the inch worm technique. His thighs clamped the round surface while his arms reached up and pulled. The process required incredible upper body strength and was a skill Wyndom had never mastered.

At the top of the second column, Jovian held onto the rim and shimmied around to the back, where he disappeared into the shadows. The sound of grating stone meant he had pressed his weight against a stone lever and unlocked the entrance. Three men pushed the door's right side. For its imposing size, the stone slab required a relatively minor force to make it rotate on itself.

Wyndom waved his people in. When the last Terefellian stepped inside, the same three men closed the door, cutting the light. The blackness constricted Wyndom's chest. Along with his fear of heights, he suffered from nyctophobia. With his buhleycob lacking a frontal closure, even on the darkest, cloudiest night, the scant moonlight meant Wyndom was never in complete blackness. His pulse spiked as he fumbled for Rudella's hand and squeezed it tight.

A spark of light offered immediate relief. He quickly flicked Rudella loose and stood tall. He couldn't let his people detect any fear.

A knee-high flame sped along the periphery of the massive

temple. Light danced off Analise and Noah's eyes as they turned in a circle, following the blaze. Wyndom envied the young couple. The racing flame must have looked amazing under the influence of mincelase.

Even though the outside facade depicted two levels, the inside was one vast, open space. Shelves containing rows of woven baskets, like the ones used for Brother Lasair's Rite, lined the walls. The newer containers at the bottom stood tall compared to the crumpled, centuries old ones at the top.

"What are those baskets for?" Analise asked.

Wyndom rubbed his beard. He honestly didn't know. His father had attempted to teach him Terefellian lore and what his ultimate role as leader would be when the queen came, but the dull topic made Wyndom's mind wander. Thankfully, his father had allowed Rudella, who had displayed an abundant interest in the material, to sit through the lectures. As long as Wyndom's loyal wife understood what to do, he held utter confidence that the Brisqueneth Ceremony would move ahead swimmingly. "What now?" he whispered to Rudella.

"Order your people to kneel in a wide circle," she told him.

Wyndom gave the command and his people obeyed. Under Rudella's direction, he sat Analise and Noah just inside the circumference and offered them another sip of mincelase, which he'd earlier poured into a drinking pouch. As Wyndom had already noted, he may be often cruel, but he wasn't completely heartless. While he didn't know exactly what would happen to his guests, he surmised that the less connected they were to reality, the better.

"My Terefellians," he said, "the time has come. After years of suffering, our queen will bring us to salvation and everlasting life." He flung his arms in the air and said the words that Rudella fed to him, "Meco ymquene oivigeyu hebtare!"

The Terefellian crowd repeated the phrase, which translated as, "Come, my queen, I give you breath."

They repeated the words over and over, building in volume and speed.

A dollop of thick, black ooze landed in the center of the circle. Silence filled the room.

Wyndom clutched his arms to his chest as he looked up. Large, viscous tendrils writhed from the rocky ceiling like tentacles of black molasses. The air chilled, turning his warm breath into a misty haze. More globs fell, landing in random spots within the circle. As if drawn by some invisible force, each drop raced along the stone floor to an ever-growing, central mass.

His people turned their gaping faces to him. Since the Terefellians had never performed this ritual, no one knew what to expect. Wyndom's every instinct urged him to run. But where? The door was locked. Judging from Noah and Analise's calm, wondrous looks, his only salvation was the mincelase. He grabbed the pouch and downed the last few drops.

In the circle's center, an immense cylindrical form took shape. The last glob landed, and the tentacles retracted into the ceiling. The group sat quietly as all eyes locked onto the shiny, black column. Like a curious child, Analise went to poke the shimmery mass when it vibrated, sending a multitude of ripples fluttering up its surface. In their wake, a black deity appeared.

Tears of happiness welled in Wyndom's eyes. The ritual to birth Eifa—the Terefellian queen—had worked. He craned his neck at the towering entity. "Our queen! Oh, how I've longed for this day. I am your faithful servant, Brother Wyndom. Tell me your will, and it will be my command."

Rudella leaped to her feet. "If you do not know our queen's will, then you are as stupid as I thought." She ripped his Terefellian ring from his finger and placed it on her own.

Wyndom blinked. What was going on? Why had Rudella just embarrassed him like that? Surely, the silly woman wasn't attempting to take over as leader. He stood and made a calming motion with his hands, his way of telling his people, "Everything's okay. This is all part of the act."

"Sister Rudella," he said under his breath, "give back my ring and your transgression will be forgiven. Your mind is clearly clouded with confusion."

"No, my dear Brother. It is you who are confused." She turned and leaped, disappearing into their queen's slick, black substance.

Wyndom pressed his hands to the sides of his head.

Rudella! What had she done?

CHAPTER

6

FORBILLIAN CLAPPED HIS hands together. "It's decided, then. We sail to the Ezekian Island."

"I'm coming, too," said Oisin.

Amalardh shook his head. "Not this time."

"But I know how to sail. And you can't stay awake twenty-four seven."

Since losing his father during the Battle for Freedom, Oisin had adopted Amalardh as a surrogate father. Mostly, Amalardh didn't mind Oisin's company. Beyond the kid enjoying long stretches of silence, he was a quick study. For a child who had grown up underground, Oisin had become a worthy sailor in a matter of months. Still, Amalardh couldn't allow him to take part in a trip where they would be together twenty-four seven for two weeks. He needed to keep his bond with Oisin at arm's length. He'd foolishly let Cecilia into his heart, and that act had caused more pain than he could bear. "My word on the matter is final," he said.

Oisin's fists clenched. "I hope you drown," he said and dashed off.

Amalardh ignored the comment. He prefered Oisin's anger because then he wouldn't have to witness the look of disappointment—the same look he'd seen on Cecilia's face multiple times—when he would inevitably let the kid down.

"I see you inspire much love," said Forbillian. Having devoured the roasted chicken Cecilia had offered him, the slovenly man sucked the grease from his stubby fingers. "I wouldn't be too concerned with drowning, though. I'm not completely useless on a boat." He burped loudly. "Excuse me." He chuckled and patted his round belly, then wiped his mouth with a cloth napkin, which only pushed the bits of chicken deeper into his beard. "I've done my fair share of rigging. I mean, how do you think your grandpa, dad, and I got to the island in the first place? I'm not going to lie, it's been a good many years since I've stepped foot on a bucket with sails, but if I stopped walking for several decades, do you honestly think I'd forget how to place one foot in front of the other?"

From where Amalardh sat, he would've said yes. Forbillian had better prove him wrong. Amalardh couldn't sail the boat day and night without help. He enlisted Finn—the best angler in Vitus— to test Forbillian's seaworthiness.

"He'll hold up," said Finn, after concluding his battery of tests. "To be honest, though, I'd feel better about the whole thing if I came, too."

Amalardh respected Finn a great deal. The hardy man spoke frankly and understood Amalardh did not care to trifle more than necessary. He needed only to look at Finn for the burly sailor to follow with, "But of course, I know you'd feel better if I didn't."

Amalardh had moved into his massive cathedral because he needed his space from others. *Vitus I* may have had bedding for four, but for Amalardh, that was three bunks too many. As long as Forbillian had the strength to literally pull his weight, having half a sailor sat better than the prospect of adding a third.

As Amalardh packed his bag, Cecilia lingered with Alistair perched on her hip. He knew she wanted to talk about the Freedom Tree painting and the confusing notion of how the seedling on the southern headland could not possibly be the Freedom Tree in the Prophecy, unless the boy in the painting wasn't Alistair. But the boy in the painting was Alistair, Amalardh knew this for a fact, which meant the Freedom Tree depicted in the

Prophecy had to be the fully grown tree in Plockton, not the seedling on the southern headland. As for the discrepancy regarding the Prophecy tree depicting water and Cecilia's tree sitting in a forest, Amalardh couldn't explain. Because he lacked answers, he didn't want to talk about it, which was why he changed the subject before Cecilia could start it.

"How is Oisin?" he asked, without looking up from his packing.

"He'll be fine. You know how he can get. After spending some time with Brassal, he'll calm down and come back."

Amalardh zipped up his bag. The only reason Oisin 'got the way he got' was because of him. Hopefully the kid would realize that Amalardh was doing him a favor by not letting him tag along.

"You'll be back before Alistair's Hinge Celebration, won't you?" Cecilia asked.

A Hinge Celebration honored a child's first birthday. Alistair's special day was a little over two weeks away. With the trip to the Ezekian Island estimated at a week's sail each way, barring any unforeseen circumstances, Amalardh expected to be back in time and told Cecilia as much. He flung his bag over his shoulder and took a deep breath. He would have rather snuck out in the dead of night than face this moment of saying goodbye. While he loved Cecilia and Alistair with all his heart, Cecilia wanted—deserved—more than he could give. He knew he should hug them, but an impenetrable wall of his own design stopped him.

On the day of Alistair's birth, a vision Amalardh had locked away had rushed back. After the Battle for Freedom, when Senator Akantha—his mother—had stabbed him in the belly, he woke up in the Pass-Over Zone. Next to him stood the Goddess of Light, shrouded in silken ribbons and glowing white, just as Cecilia had described. Several feet away, a man wearing clothing unique to the Village of Plockton—sandals, beige linen pants, and a toggle-buttoned, loose-fitting shirt—lifted a giggling toddler of about eighteen months of age in the air. The act prevented

Amalardh from seeing the man's face. As the stranger lowered the child, he simultaneously turned, revealing dark, closely cropped hair.

A Croilar Tier knife missing its right-sided red ruby eye hung from the child's waist.

"Who is that boy?" Amalardh asked.

"He is your son," said Siersha. "You and Cecilia will name him Alistair."

Amalardh's breath escaped. The boy in this vision matched the same age as the infant Amalardh had seen in the Prophecy painting. He *had* been correct in seeing his son in the Prophecy, which meant, he was also right about his other supposition. Because the toddler possessed Amalardh's Croilar Tier knife, Amalardh would never live long enough to see his child grow up beyond about eighteen months of age. "That man is the one who will raise Alistair, isn't he?"

"Yes," Siersha replied.

"What is his name?"

"Deep in your heart, you know his name. Only when you accept what is best for Alistair will you be free from your torment, and the man who was supposed to die today will finally face his death."

Amalardh woke up with a bandage around his abdomen and Cecilia clutching his hand. He suppressed the vision as a dream and for the next nine months, tried not to think about the fact that another man would raise his son. With Alistair's first cry, the memory came flooding back. If destiny ordained a man from Plockton as Alistair's true guiding light, then Gildas, Cecilia's lifelong friend, seemed the only possibility. The man represented everything Amalardh was not—kind, loving, friendly. Amalardh's Pass-Over Zone vision was why he knew the Freedom Tree in the Prophecy was the tree in Cecilia's forest. Gildas was on his way back to Plockton, where, upon Amalardh's death, Cecilia would join him, and the final moment of the Prophecy, with the children sitting under the Freedom Tree, would live out.

Cecilia had been a bright light in Amalardh's otherwise dark world. He had hoped that he could start a new life with her and put his damaged past behind him. But what was the point of deepening their love when he was only going to die? By creating a barrier between him and the two loves of his life, he was sparing them future pain. He placed his hand on Alistair's warm, silken head, kissed Cecilia on the cheek, and walked out the door. Even if Amalardh wasn't destined to die—which he was—what kind of father would a former assassin make? Certainly not a good one. Either way, Alistair was better off without him.

"Wind's picking up nicely," said Forbillian as he boarded *Vitus I.*

Amalardh glanced up from where he stood winding up the bow anchor rope. Did his uncle really have to bring that absurd bear cape?

Forbillian grinned. "Don't mind him. He doesn't bite. Just so we're clear, I was talking to Edgar." He patted the bear's paw and laughed.

Ignoring the antics, Amalardh made his way to the stern.

"Me and Edgar don't go nowhere without each other," Forbillian said. "He's more friend than a best friend will ever be. Sure, your closest pal will hold your hand while you're dying, but will they lay down their life for you?"

Down on the pier, Finn uncoiled the anchor rope from the docking cleat and tossed it to Amalardh.

"Okay," said Forbillian. "Maybe my spear was the reason Edgar gave his life for me, but he's saved me countless times since. When I've been out hunting and Soldiers have come by, we just drop to our knees and whammo. What once was a man is a vicious bear." He dropped to his hands and knees and growled.

Amalardh took a deep breath as he coiled the rope. This trip was already feeling long, and they hadn't yet left the dock.

Forbillian glanced at him. "What? Not even a smile?" He grabbed the railing and hoisted himself to his feet. "There, there, boy," he said to the bear. "It's a tough crowd out here today." He draped his cape over the back of a chair and sighed. "Your dad would've had a chuckle."

"I'm not my father."

"Clearly."

Talk of his father—a man he never knew—unnerved Amalardh. He had spent most of his life despising the weak, drunken, morally corrupt version of the man the Senators had painted, only to find out that almost all of Vitus had revered him. From what he'd heard, Citizens, Tower Folk, and the odd Soldier had wept at Senator Culloden's funeral. Sometimes, Amalardh wished he'd never learned the truth. Despising a weak man was far less burdensome than living with the constant doubt that he would never be the man his father was. No matter how many times Cecilia told him, "Your past as an assassin is not who you are in your heart," Amalardh still worried—or possibly sensed— that more of his mother's tainted blood gushed through his veins than his father's.

Finn scanned from Amalardh to Forbillian. "Can't say part of me isn't relieved that my services are neither needed nor wanted," he said. "Seems like there's a right party going on up there."

"I'll see you in two weeks," said Amalardh. "If I come back alone, you'll understand."

Finn laughed. "Safe sails, my friend."

Amalardh had a sense of humor, albeit dry, but only shared it with people he knew and trusted. Uncle or not, Forbillian was still a stranger and someone he needed to keep at a distance. He settled behind the wheel and gave the order to hoist the mainsail.

"HOISTING THE MAINSAIL!" replied Forbillian with far too much gusto.

The silken sheet ballooned and the sturdy vessel crept forward.

Forbillian seated himself and nodded at Amalardh's woolen robe. "Did you know those who lived in that place you call a home wore that get-up and swore a vow of silence?" He waited for Amalardh to reply. When Amalardh didn't, he continued.

"I'm not worried about the no chatter thing happening between the two of us because they also swore a vow of chastity and clearly you've broken that." He winked and waved to Cecilia, who stood at the far end of the dock with Alistair.

A handful of other early morning well-wishers stood with her, including Marion, a Citizen helper who had delivered Amalardh's food and cleaned his house for more than a decade. Even though her wind-blown shawl hid her face, Amalardh recognized the shape of her generous hips. Notably missing from the group was Oisin. An unexpected pang twinged the spot where his ribs met. His brow furrowed as he rubbed the area. Why should he care if the boy waved him off or not?

"So, nephew," said Forbillian. "We've got thirty years of catching up to do. Where shall we start?"

Idle chit-chat was not Amalardh's forte. He had spent his life focusing on goals and achieving them. Right now, his fixation was on finding answers to the missing portion of the Prophecy, not bonding with a long-lost uncle. To derail the peppy man, he nodded Marion's way. "Maybe you can start this catch-up of yours with that person over there?"

Forbillian's head tilted as though unsure whom else, beyond Cecilia, he'd know. The wind blew the hooded section of Marion's shawl off her head. The portion of his cheeks that his woolly beard left exposed turned white. As she quickly covered herself up, he shot to his feet. His eyes remained fixed on her as *Vitus I* slowly edged beyond the wharf.

Last night, Marion, who had cooked and cleaned for Amalardh since he'd moved into his home, had arrived at the side courtyard door with a basket of fresh-baked rolls. The moment she spotted Forbillian chatting with Cecilia through the window, the basket fell from her hands. She picked up her mess and rushed off. Unlike Cecilia, who would've turned every stone to learn why Marion had reacted the way she had, Amalardh let it be. Secrets were for the holder to keep, not for the overly curious to expose. After Forbillian's "over-egged pudding" comment, it wasn't a huge leap to figure out that Marion was Forbillian's pudding. Amalardh hadn't pointed her out as a way to bond with his uncle over a tale of lost love. He had done so to shut him up.

"Misery loves company" was Senator Akantha's favorite quote. She had once stood with Amalardh on the Tower balcony used by the Senators to address their people and spied with glee at the expressionless Citizens as they went about their business on the shadowed streets below. "Misery is a self-infecting virus that spreads of its own accord," she had said. "Never doubt its power to subdue even the heartiest of souls."

An ache crept into Amalardh's chest as he took in his uncle's long face. He hadn't meant to hurt him.

Who was he kidding? Of course he'd meant to inflict harm. He'd calculated his options and had decided his peace was worth more. Only, upon seeing the depth of Forbillian's pain, regret had inched in. He sat back and pressed his hand to his forehead. While Amalardh may have struggled to understand the forward repercussions of his actions on others, in this situation, he had no trouble understanding the irony of the results of his actions on himself. The silencing of his uncle's chatter had heightened his awareness of the boat's monotonous rocking. Combined with the water's repetitive slap against the hull, Amalardh slipped into a place he didn't want to be—inside his head with his own troubled thoughts.

He had imagined leaving Cecilia and Alistair would be easy, but as the boat edged further away from shore, the hook tethering his heart to his greatest loves tore deep into his flesh. He may not have been the best soulmate to Cecilia or the best father to his son, but he was their best protector. At least, he had been. Now, he was nothing. Just an empty man running away from the only people in the world he truly loved.

CHAPTER
7

SILENCE HUNG IN the Terefellians' vast temple. The young visitors from Vitus were supposed to be the sacrifice to their great queen, not Rudella. Wyndom dropped to his knees. Why had she leaped into their queen? And why had she taken his ring? As much as it drained him to do so, he had to remain strong in front of his people. He pushed himself to his feet.

"My Terefellians, have no fear—"

He stiffened at a loud rumble coming from inside the queen. Pockets within her belly expanded and contracted as if something inside tried to escape. A long striation protruded forward, mimicking the shape of an arm. Then came another. And then a hideous, goat-like head with long, curved horns. The creature's mouth gaped as if straining to birth itself from its queen mother. Its long snout burst through and roared as it pushed a muscular torso and hulking, cloven legs from the muck.

Wyndom craned his neck at the eight-foot-tall beast, part human, part goat, that seemed made from the same black, wet-looking substance as the queen. It threw its head back and roared. The circle of Terefellians dropped and bowed low. The beast's slow shoulder roll gave the impression that it appreciated the respect. It scanned the circle of arched backs until its gaze fell upon Wyndom, who stood frozen, too confused to even consider the fact that he, too, should bow.

As Wyndom scanned the hideous beast's features, he stopped short and its familiar brown eyes. This could not be. "Rudella?" he uttered.

The beast stepped forward and sniffed. Its upper lips curled as if displeased by a sudden recognition.

The Terefellian ring on the creature's finger heightened Wyndom's suspicions. He cleared the ball lodged in his throat. "Rudella, if that is you, please answer me."

The beast placed one hand on their queen and pointed the finger of its other hand at Wyndom. Beads of sweat formed on Wyndom's brow as a worm-like tendril grew from the beast's finger and snaked over. "Rudella. Please. I... I love you."

"We shall see." The beast spoke with a low bass rumble.

The black worm shot into Wyndom's ear. He tensed as his eyes rolled to the back of his head. In a flash, he knew everything the beast wanted him to know, and just as quickly, the beast knew Wyndom's deepest, darkest secrets, even the ones he didn't want to share.

Yes, Rudella inhabited the beast. And, no, Wyndom didn't truly love her.

Wyndom now understood that the coming of the queen would bring forth the Maddowshin, the Shadow Mind. Created from the Terefellian ring wearer's soul, the Maddowshin possessed the power to see all and perceive all about anyone it infected with the queen's blackness and telepathically communicate with an infected individual's mind.

So, now you know.

Wyndom's knees buckled. Instead of the beast's guttural tone, Rudella's voice rang inside his head. This power. This ability to see and know all should've been his. He was the owner of the Terefellian ring. Destiny dictated that he be the Maddowshin. "You stole what was rightfully mine!"

I did what needed to be done. Her tone remained composed, as though suggesting she did what they both knew Wyndom wouldn't have been able to do.

He shuddered as the black, wormy thing shot out his right ear. With his eyes still rolled back, he couldn't see anything. His mind's eye, however, saw the Maddowshin's field of view.

"Rise all!" said the beast in its gravelly voice.

The circle of Terefellians stood.

The black worm entered Brother Sisco's ear. He stilled as his eyes rolled back, exposing the whites. The worm flew out of his other ear and into Sister Eliza's. It weaved around the circle until it connected every Terefellian.

The Maddowshin stood tall and recited the Birthing Prayer. "Hotrohugyu, twohiyu, e ceebom woyu, yu ceebom osu," which translated to, "Through you, with you, we become you, you become us."

Monotone, Wyndom and the Terefellians repeated the prayer over and over. As dreary as this was, Wyndom had no choice but to comply. While in this state, the collective conscious overrode his ability to act on his own will.

The black connective worm liquefied and splashed to the ground. Wyndom's eyes rolled back down. He looked up at his queen. He should've been happy. Ecstatic. After all these years stressing about whether she would arrive before his Quinquagenary, here she stood. Alive and in the...? What exactly was that slick, rubbery substance? Not flesh, certainly. In any case, his two-faced wife had sullied the joy he should've experienced. The sniveling old bi—

WHACK!

The back of the Maddowshin's hand connected with Wyndom's cheek, sending him stumbling sideways.

"You will not disrespect your Maddowshin!"

Wyndom pressed his palm to his throbbing face. He would have to remember to limit his thoughts.

"Yes, you will," the beast said. It's—Rudella's—eyes bore into him. "You'd best be careful, dear Brother, or I will do to you what I am about to do to them." The beast jabbed its gnarled finger at Analise and Noah. The intoxicated young ones still seemed oblivious to the fact that rather than sleeping through a vivid dream, they were living an actual nightmare.

The breezy look in Analise's eyes sent a pang through Wyndom's chest. She reminded him of his daughter, Saffron, in the rare moments when she wasn't angry at the world. Angry at him. Two months ago, Saffron and her birth mother, Sister Esme, had fled Terefellia the night before Esme's Rite of Quinquagenary. He had known they would leave. Saffron had told him as much. He didn't stop her because... well, she told him if he tried, she would kill him. Every fiber of his being believed she would. The sound of the Maddowshin's clomping hooves as it strode to the youthful couple pulled Wyndom from his thoughts. The substance comprising the beast seemed to possess a consistency ranging from malleable to rock hard.

Analise's mouth went slack. "Is this real?"

"Yes, dear child," said the Maddowshin. "And so is this."

Analise's gasp seemed part fear, part excitement as the creature picked her up and held her high overhead.

"Dear Queen, I give you eyes so you may see the hidden light." With a harsh grunt, the Maddowshin tossed Analise into the queen.

Noah staggered to his feet and shook his head. "What's going on? Where is Analise?" His wide eyes locked onto the Maddowshin as he drew his sword. "Stay back!" he yelled. "Analise! Where are you?"

"Noah!" came a muffled cry. "Please help me!"

A blackened arm reached out from within the queen.

Noah grabbed the extremity's hand. "Analise! I've got you!"

He yelped as the blackness from Analise's hand began swallowing his own. He tried to shake free, but the rubbery stuff held firm. His agonized yell reverberated painfully through the temple.

Wyndom pressed his palms to his ears. *Can't we just get this damn thing over with?* he said to himself.

The Maddowshin flung him a harsh glare.

Wyndom winced. Rudella hearing his every thought was a violation of the worst kind.

It is our queen's stance that only through terror can a soul truly appreciate life, echoed her voice in his head.

The screaming abated as the black ooze sucked Noah into Eifa's towering form.

"Dear Queen," said the Maddowshin, "these souls are pure and filled with knowledge of the one you seek to destroy."

The queen's belly ballooned. As with the birthing of the Maddowshin, multiple arms and legs protruded from the black mass. Wyndom cuddled his sickened stomach.

The head of a beast poked out from within the queen and roared. The body that followed cloned the Maddowshin's in three-quarter size. From the beast's flecked, hazel eyes, Wyndom suspected Analise's soul inhabited the creature. A second one lumbered out, possessing Noah's deep green eyes.

The Wirador Wosrah will cleanse infidel souls. The Maddowshin pushed the words into Wyndom's mind.

Wyndom scratched his temple. *Wirador Wosrah?* The name sounded familiar, but because of his lack of interest in the scriptures, the translation escaped him.

Shadow Warrior, came Rudella's unimpressed voice.

Shadow Warrior. Of cour—

Wyndom's breath sucked in. The queen needed an army of Wirador Wosrah to fight Vitus. The Terefellians, Wyndom included, represented the only source of souls. The idea of following Rudella's lead and rebirthing as a beast sent a chill to the base of his neck. He liked his flesh. "My gracious Queen," he said. "I am your ever-faithful servant. Please. You must not—"

The Maddowshin whacked him across the face. "No one speaks to the queen unless it's through me."

Wyndom rubbed his smarting cheek.

"Let him speak," the queen said. Her voice held the creaminess of whipped butter.

"My wise, powerful Queen," Wyndom said. "We have lived your praise for generations, awaited your coming with the promise that you will bring us eternal life. We are your believers, not your warriors." He pointed to Analise's spirit creature. "Is this to be our destiny? Eternal life as a"—he wanted to say "beast"—"Wirador Wosrah?"

"You doubt your queen's promise?" Her silkiness held a deadly edge.

Wyndom faltered. Doubt was the very reason he'd spoken up, and the queen knew this because whatever Wyndom thought, the Maddowshin heard, and so did she. He pressed his lips together. Better to remain a silent fool than an audible liar.

The queen sized him up, then lifted her arms. "My Terefellians. You are my chosen people. I will give you everlasting life and deliver you to the Sworn Province. But first, we must cleanse Vitus of the non-believers."

"Rudella," Wyndom whispered to the Maddowshin. "I still don't understand. Are we to become warriors or not? Because if we are, I'm not sure that's the best plan. Vitus's current regime had a force mighty enough to bring down the former Army of Vitus. As powerful as Wirador Wosrah seem, will three hundred be enough?"

You really are a fool, said Rudella in his head.

He was? Why?

"Good souls of Terefellia," said the Maddowshin, "for centuries, we have obeyed the Rite of Quinquagenary. Our forefathers and foremothers have given of themselves so you can have everlasting life." The beast directed the room's attention to the hundreds of woven baskets lining the temple. "I give you your Wirador Wosrah army!"

The basket lids flew off. Wyndom blinked wildly as hundreds of misty souls swam through the air.

SHOOM! A single spirit darted into their queen.

SHOOM! SHOOM! SHOOM!

Their black queen expanded, her features disappearing, as soul after soul dove into her.

Wyndom inched back. With the temple door locked, he had

no escape from the queen's ballooning mass. "What do we do?" he asked.

"What Terefellians are born to do," replied the Maddowshin.

Wyndom's gulp caught in his throat as he scanned the looming shelves. Climb? Really?

The Terefellians, Maddowshin, and two Wirador Wosrah scaled the wooden shelves like a troop of scurrying monkeys. Wyndom joined the scuttle. Halfway up, panic set in. His jelly legs stopped moving. The queen's expanding black mass steadily rose. How big was she going to grow? With the conglomeration of souls still waiting to dive into her, she was certain to expand beyond where Wyndom huddled. He whimpered. The second the queen's essence touched his skin, it would suck him in and spit him out as a beast. "Rudella! Please!" he yelled.

The Maddowshin stopped and gave him an irritated look.

"Please! Help me climb. I'm no warrior. You know that."

The queen's coagulated bulk inched closer. As Wyndom scuttled to the next shelf, one of his wet palms slipped. "Ahhh!" His legs flailed as he dangled. "Rudella! Plea—"

A vice-like, rubbery grip snagged Wyndom's free arm. With the strength of an elephant lifting a twig, the Maddowshin flung Wyndom onto its back. For its size, the beast moved with surprising agility. It scaled the remaining shelves to a ten-foot-deep stone platform that bordered the temple's top rim.

Wyndom slid off the Maddowshin's back and shivered at the ghastly pool of blackness below. "Now what happens?" he asked.

"We wait for our army to incubate," said the Maddowshin. "Birthing a Wirador Wosrah from a soul encased with flesh is faster than from a bodiless spirit."

"So? We wait here? How long will that take?"

"We leave and let the process take as long as it needs."

Wyndom sagged. Leaving meant exiting the same way Brother Jovian had come in and scaling down the slippery facade. "Brother Jovian," he called in a trumped-up authoritative tone. "Lead the way."

Everyone followed the blond Terefellian to the small exit hole, except the Maddowshin. The beast's eyes remained locked onto the blackness below. "She's terrifying, yet strangely beautiful, isn't she?"

Wyndom traced the Maddowshin's angular profile with his vision. "Yes. She is." As monstrous as the creature was, a particular feature drew his fascination. Fur-like texturing covered the beast's face, except for a portion around its eyes, nose, and mouth, which remained smooth.

The Maddowshin glowered at him. "What?" it demanded.

Wyndom kept his voice light. "I've just noticed this smooth section around here, and here." As he mapped out the area with the back of his hand, the tip of his knuckle touched the Maddowshin's springy skin. What an appealing sensation. He'd been in such a state when he'd earlier clung to the beast's back that he hadn't noticed how delectable the firm-yet-pliant substance was. Everything about Terefellia was rock hard: their hands, their caves, their bodies. He yearned to touch the Maddowshin again. Thinking better of the impulse, he pulled his hand back. "Around your eyes and nose, the smooth outline looks like a heart," he told the beast.

The living, breathing, human part of the beast—Rudella's eyes—softened.

"I should have been a better husband," Wyndom said.

"I would've preferred a better lover."

Wyndom couldn't blame Rudella for resenting his lack of affection. Beyond his limited attraction to her, he begrudged her for not bearing him an heir, requiring his bedding of Sister Esme to produce an offspring. One grudge begot another. Wyndom blamed Rudella for everything, including that Saffron—his successor—was of all things a girl who grew up to outperform him at almost everything.

He sighed. After everything Rudella had done for him, he could've at least tried to fulfill her needs. He held the Maddowshin's broad, rubbery hand. "Will you give me a chance to make things up?" A crazy notion indeed. But now that Rudella was gone, Wyndom wanted her more than ever.

A grunt, probably from some fool hitting their head on a low-hanging rock, drew the Maddowshin's attention to the exiting Terefellians. When its gaze returned, the softness in Rudella's eyes had disappeared. It pulled its hand from Wyndom's grasp. "I will not trifle with such foolishness."

Wyndom nodded and joined the Maddowshin in staring at the mass below. As a child, watching porridge cook over the firepit fascinated him. He sat next to the pot, entranced as bubbles rose and settled back into the mush. Some grew so big, they burst. The blackness below looked the same, only the bubbles didn't pop. Lumps slowly rose and shrank as the Wirador Wosrah army took shape within.

"It's very peaceful," said Wyndom. "Just you. Me. Our queen. And five thousand brewing Shadow Warriors."

The Maddowshin side-eyed him. "You stay because you need me to carry you down from here."

The statement was partly true. Wyndom could never climb down the temple's formidable facade without help. But that wasn't the only reason motivating him to stay. He'd meant what he'd said about making up for his past failings. If he sat with Rudella long enough, she might reconsider his offer.

"Your heart is thumping. Why?" the Maddowshin asked.

Wyndom tilted his head at the beast. "I thought you could only read my thoughts."

"I can feel everything if I care to." Its gravelly voice mellowed. "I felt your terror when we climbed the shelves."

The Maddowshin sat down and leaned against the wall just as a human would. Wyndom sat next to it. They both stared ahead as Rudella fed her voice into Wyndom's mind. She confessed to not understanding his affliction. How could she? Very little terrified her, least of all heights. She'd attributed Wyndom's issue to laziness, assumed he couldn't be bothered climbing. Resentment had grown at her end because he made her complete any additional trips to retrieve something they'd accidentally left behind. Experiencing his blood race as she climbed the shelving had confirmed his debilitating fear.

"Which do you think is better?" the Maddowshin asked. "Living an eternity as a terrified little man or being a beast that fears nothing?"

Wyndom rested his chin on his bent knees. A fearless beast sounded pretty good right now.

"You can still jump in," said the Maddowshin.

"But if I did, along with losing the ability to fear, I would lose all feelings, correct?"

"You would."

"But you still feel?"

The corner of the Maddowshin's eyes twitched ever so slightly. "I have calm and I have rage. Anything else, I experience from others at my discretion. That is the joy and curse of the Maddowshin."

Wyndom had lived with Rudella for thirty years. He may not have loved her as he should have, but he did know her every nuance, and lying wasn't in her. The part of her that remained human seemed in conflict with the part that embodied the Maddowshin. "My heart was pounding just moments ago," he said, "because you excite me more than you ever have."

The Maddowshin sat rock solid.

"But you already knew that, didn't you?"

The beast's breath seemed strained. "It's time to go." It stood and motioned for Wyndom to climb onto its back.

Wyndom locked eyes with Rudella. "I'd rather climb onto your front."

His passion was genuine and intense. He no longer saw a beast, only his darling wife. Always stronger. Always more powerful. And always taller. She stepped up close. Did she feel the same, too? She bent down to him, her oily lips moving closer. As his mind locked on to the image of Rudella's silky satin kiss, the Maddowshin squeezed Wyndom's arms. He may have been looking into Rudella's eyes, but all he saw was the beast's black soul. It picked him up and swung him over their queen's pulsating mass.

"No one tempts the Maddowshin!"

"Please. No, Rudella. I don't want to stop feeling. If you don't want to experience my temptation, then all you have to do is shut me out."

The Maddowshin growled.

Terror dripped from Wyndom's brow. Was the beast going to drop him into their queen's blackness?

It snarled and tossed him against the temple's stone wall.

He flopped to the ledge's hard surface and his world went black.

CHAPTER
8

"CECILIA," SAID TOMKIN, "are you still with us?"

The former Death Train captain was helping Cecilia and her brothers sort out the logistics for Alistair's Hinge Celebration. Questions about Analise and Noah's failure to return, and Forbillian's arrival and subsequent travel to the Croilar Tier Archives with Amalardh had hijacked her focus. She looked up. "Sorry, did I miss something?" she asked.

"We were talking about the Lighting Ceremony," said Eideard.

A knock at the front entrance provided a welcome excuse for Cecilia to stretch her legs. She opened one of the large, double doors to three men, dressed in gray, knee-length tunics and leather slippers. Their bowl-shaped haircuts with a mid-forehead fringe weren't very flattering. If not for their individual blond, dark brown, and red hair, they would have been almost identical—that and the blond man's one blue and one green eye.

"Please excuse our intrusion," said the redheaded fellow. "My name is Brother Skylark, and this is Sister Darna and Brother Atlas." Cecilia did a double-take. The dark-haired one was female? "We are from Terefellia," continued Brother Skylark. "We were told the Treoir Solas and Croilar Tier live here. Is this correct?"

"Yes. My name is Cecilia."

"May we come in? We have important tidings."

Because her two brothers and Tomkin were with her, she felt comfortable welcoming the three strangers into her home. "What are these tidings you bring?" she asked.

"The Dark Goddess has returned," said Brother Skylark. "And she is determined to win."

Cecilia shared a concerned look with her brothers.

"We came because of two very special people," Brother Skylark said. "Analise and Noah."

Cecilia's breath sucked in. "You've met them? Are they all right?"

"We met them. Briefly."

The dip in his tone concerned her. "What happened to them?"

"There are those among our people who wish great harm to you and yours." He handed her Analise's Freedom Tree brooch. "I'm sorry, but your two young friends are no longer with us."

Cecilia keeled forward. Eideard's hand shot out, offering support. Analise and Noah were gone? How was this possible? Tears crept down her cheeks.

"You grieve the loss of your friends," said Sister Darna. "As you should. Do know, they brought much joy. Hearing your story, learning that the Treoir Solas and last Croilar Tier were real, meant our beliefs were real, too." She grabbed Cecilia's arm. "You and your son are in great danger. You must let us protect you."

Cecilia flinched at the Terefellian's coarse touch.

Sister Darna withdrew her hand and held it to her chest.

"You must forgive our dear Sister," said Brother Skylark. "Her passion runs deep." He presented his palms for all to see. "Our methods needed to evade the Soldiers of Vitus have..." His voice trailed as he rubbed his thickened palm with his thumb. "Well, we sometimes forget how repugnant our touch feels."

These poor people. The suffering they must have experienced. "Thank you for risking your lives to warn us," said Cecilia. "I am very familiar with Eifa and her destructiveness. I have no fear of the Dark Goddess."

"Maybe you should," said Brother Atlas.

Because his mismatched eyes seemed laced with arrogance, Cecilia couldn't decide if his tone reflected concern or indignation.

Brother Skylark lifted his hands and stared at Brother Atlas. "Now, now. Calm heads. Calm hearts."

"I meant no disrespect," said Brother Atlas to Cecilia.

Cecilia nodded. She would take him at his word. For now. "I appreciate the warning," she said. "When Amalardh returns, we can—"

"Returns?" said Brother Skylark. "You mean, he is not here?"

"He is out to sea. He left yesterday and will be back in two weeks."

Apprehension etched Skylark's face as he exchanged looks with his companions. "Please pardon my impudence, but I don't think you understand the gravity of the situation."

Cecilia stood tall. "Do not tell me what I do and don't understand. I have been in danger from the moment the Soldiers of Vitus massacred my village, Amalardh has been in danger from the moment he learned who he was, and my son has been in danger since the day he was born."

"Forgive us if our zeal seems extreme," said Brother Skylark. "We know our people well and what they are capable of. We understand that the Croilar Tier is skilled, but we fear him being on the open water. Will you indulge us with this one request and send a boat out after him? We must warn him of the army Eifa is building before it is too late."

The Dark Goddess was building an army? Where would she find the fighters? The former Senators of Vitus had destroyed all the villages and townships within a hundred-mile radius. Their army—which now sided with Cecilia and Vitus's new council—was the greatest force in the lands. What army could Eifa build that Cecilia would fear?

She pulled her brothers and Tomkin aside and discussed their thoughts. They agreed that while the three strangers projected some bizarre quirks, they seemed earnest, and provided the perfect excuse to get Finn in the water. None of them had liked the idea of Amalardh making the long journey with only one deckhand.

Cecilia turned to the Terefellians. "I will arrange a boat to Amalardh's destination with our city's best sailors."

Brother Skylark offered his thanks and asked if Brother Atlas could stay behind. Apparently, the idea of floating on water terrified him. Cecilia understood. During her first trip on *Vitus I,* the rocky swell had drained the blood from her core and the contents from her stomach.

Finn welcomed leading the expedition. He, too, had not liked the idea of Amalardh making such a long sail, aided only with Forbillian's rusty knowledge. He recruited three of his top sailors and had his sturdy fishing vessel, *The Epona Dreams,* stocked and ready to go within a matter of hours. He patted his ship's hull. "She's not as fast as *Vitus I,* but she's just like my daughter— smooth, yet feisty, and doesn't back down when the seas get rough."

A heaviness dragged on Cecilia's chest. How could she possibly break the news of Analise's passing right before such an important trip? She hugged Finn and wished him a safe passage, then pulled Skylark and Darna aside. "Finn is Analise's father. I have not told him about her and Noah's fate. He is the only one I trust with your lives, and I'm not sure the news is best for his ears at this moment."

The two Terefellians nodded their understanding.

By the time Cecilia, her brothers, Tomkin, and Brother Atlas arrived back home from seeing the search party off, the sun had set, and dinner, courtesy of Marion, waited for them on the dining table. Brother Atlas's wide eyes scanned the vast array of delights. As he dug into his food with the eagerness of a starving child, Cecilia let go of his earlier brusqueness. She had no idea what he'd been through or the risks he'd taken to flee Terefellia to warn her.

She looked around. Oisin still hadn't returned since running off after Amalardh had refused to let him go on the trip to the

Croilar Tier Archives. In the past few months, Oisin's relationship with Amalardh had become as frayed as Cecilia's. Her way to cope had been to stop trying. Oisin, however, continued to force the relationship head on, which usually played out like it had yesterday. He would get hurt and run away, usually to Brassal's home. If he wasn't back by morning, Cecilia would go get him, and remind him that now, more than ever, he needed to give Amalardh his space.

Unable to stomach much in the way of food, she checked on Alistair. She had moved his bassinet from his adjoining nursery to her and Amalardh's bedroom so she wouldn't have to sleep alone. Her chest cramped as she stroked his satin soft hair. She'd always known Alistair would be a target for Eifa. She just hadn't imagined the Dark Goddess would threaten him so soon. *Siersha*, she said in her mind. *Please give me the strength to protect my baby boy.*

She picked up a real-looking doll lying next to him and cuddled it. During her pregnancy, she'd made an offhanded comment to Rabbie about how the thought of dressing a newborn sent her stomach into knots. "They have such tiny arms. How is anyone meant to thread such wee things into clothing without breaking them?" Rabbie, a gifted artisan, had made the toy, complete with human hair, to help her practice. Even though he'd given her the doll in jest, Cecilia adored the gift. She kissed its forehead and tucked it back into the bassinet with Alistair.

Drained from the day's events, she lay down on her bed to rest her eyes.

"Wake up, sweet one. It is time to go." Brother Atlas's voice crept into her consciousness. "We mustn't dillydally."

Cecilia forced her lead-laden eyes open and startled at Brother Atlas's inky silhouette seated on the bed. His smile seemed to mock her.

"I'd been against Brother Skylark's 'calm mind, calm heart' approach," he said, "but I will give credit where credit is due. If we'd done things my way, we may not have learned where your son's father was. So"—he shrugged—"all things considered, my idea to barge in and slice everyone into ribbons probably wouldn't have been the best plan."

Cecilia's blood surged. "Where are my—"

He placed his hand over her mouth. "Right now, I am maintaining a calm mind and a calm heart, and so should you." He lifted a sharp blade to her face. Moonlight reflected on its shiny surface. "Unless, of course, like me, you crave the sound innards make as they drop to the ground. Then by all means, scream bloody murder so we can get this party started." His head tilted expectantly. "No? You would prefer your brothers' entrails remain intact?"

She nodded.

"Such a shame." He removed his hand from her mouth and stood. "Get the kid. Keep your mouth shut. And no one gets hurt. Understood?"

"I will do anything you ask. Please, don't hurt anyone." She climbed off the bed and walked across the shadowy room to Alistair's crib. *Sweet precious*, she said to him in her mind. *May Siersha's light keep you brave. Whatever happens, please, baby boy, don't cry.*

With her back to Brother Atlas, she curled forward as if to scoop Alistair, but instead grabbed the handle of a knife attached to the outer side of his crib. Throughout their home, Amalardh had placed various knives and swords, some on display for all to see, others hidden like this one.

She spun around and swung the knife at Brother Atlas's throat.

His arm shot up and deflected the blade, rendering what should have been a death cut through his artery into a superficial wound.

Cecilia sucked in her breath. This man had skill.

Brother Atlas touched the side of his neck. His tongue lolled at his bloodied fingertips. "Thank you. I'd been hoping for an excuse to roast your brothers and suck their tender flesh from their bones." His face hardened. "Bring her and the child. Unharmed."

Who was he talking to?

She stiffened at the sound of hooves.

A beam of moonlight illuminated a pair of flecked hazel eyes and another set of deep green hovering a foot taller than Brother Atlas. Cecilia had seen nothing more horrifying than the Soldiers of Vitus on the day they rode into her village with their spiked gloves and thorn-covered boots. Until now. As the eyes moved forward, the moonlight exposed two blacker-than-black creatures—part goat, part human. Their horned heads, human-like upper torsos, and cloven legs were exact replicas of each other. The only distinguishing features were their eyes, which looked creepily human.

Cecilia jammed her knife where she assumed the green-eyed beast's heart lay and shuddered. During the Battle for Freedom, she had speared many Soldiers. The beast's unexpected creamy texture felt more like firm butter than resistive muscle. Its almighty cry seemed angry as opposed to pained. The back of its hand connected with her cheek, sending her smashing into the wall. She pressed her palm to her smarting face. Spearing the creature with a knife had been as effective as jabbing it with a toothpick. Were these things unkillable?

The beast pulled the knife from its chest, studied the blade, then shoved it into its own side as if placing it into a hilt. Only, it had no hilt. Just jelly-like flesh.

Hearing the commotion, Rabbie and Eideard burst in. Their expressions stunned as they stopped in their tracks.

"The Terefellians have betrayed us!" Cecilia yelled.

The beasts lifted their chins and roared.

"Kill them," ordered Brother Atlas.

The beasts lunged.

Sure-footed, Eideard and Rabbie spun out of the way and back into the main living space.

"Don't bother spearing them," yelled Cecilia. "Cut off their heads."

She ran to help them, but Brother Atlas held her back. "You are far too precious a commodity to get involved out there."

Swords drawn, Rabbie and Eideard guarded each other from the crazed beasts galloping around them at breakneck speeds, their human hands now morphed into hooves.

The green-eyed beast charged at Rabbie. The creature's flesh may have felt like butter, but its horns were rock hard. Rabbie's blade clunked loudly upon contact. The beast turned and roared at the sword. It stood on its hind legs and curled its nose at the knife it had shoved into its side.

Brother Atlas's face lit up. "Marvelous." He turned to Cecilia. "They're just like babies. Learning. Figuring things out. Memories of their former skills are all jumbled up. Seeing what they once knew helps piece things together."

The beast's hand, now human, pulled the knife and swung it at Rabbie.

CLANK. Metal hit metal.

The beast roared as though pleased with its new discovery.

The hazel-eyed beast's head tilted at the other beast's knife. It galloped to the back, plucked two swords from Amalardh's display wall, raced back, and handed one to the green-eyed monster.

"What one learns, they all learn," said Brother Atlas.

They? How many of these horrid beasts were there?

CLANK. CLANK. CLANK. Metal against metal as Rabbie and Eideard fought the beasts.

"None of my people have ever used a sword before," said Brother Atlas. "But I hear young Noah was quite the fighter. Those memories are coming back."

Cecilia froze. Did he just imply the green-eyed beast was Noah? Did that mean the hazel-eyed one was Analise? Agony ripped through her. What wickedness was this? Turning her own people into monsters and using them against her.

Eideard swung. His perfect aim sent the hazel-eyed beast's head rolling along the bumpy cobble-stones. Its sword clanked to the ground as its body collapsed into a black clump.

One down. One to go.

Brother Atlas beamed. "Wonderful. Now our Wirador Wosrah know how to behead. But I'm sure young Noah already knew how to do that."

Cecilia glared at him. Why did he not seem worried that one of his beasts was dead?

The hazel-eyed creature's severed head formed into a ball and started rolling toward Eideard.

"Eideard! Watch out," yelled Cecilia.

He turned and swatted the head with his sword like one would a ball.

THUD!

Cecilia recoiled as the black slime engulfed Brother Atlas's face. His muffled cries were barely audible as he struggled to pull it off. Pawing at the stuff only worsened his situation. It swallowed his hands and began traveling along his arms and down his body.

As Eideard joined Rabbie in fighting the remaining beast, the blackness from the decapitated monster's body and the one devouring Brother Atlas formed into cylindrical columns.

When Amalardh had held Cecilia prisoner, he told her a story that left her cold. Before the Senators sent him in search of her, they summoned him to their chamber. When he arrived, an ornate symbol, similar to Cecilia's Freedom Tree pendant, was burned into their desk. "How did this get here?" Amalardh had asked. The frightened leaders told him that an inky molasses-type substance had dripped from the ceiling and formed a tower of jelly. Ripples had shot up from the bottom, revealing a black entity, who Cecilia later learned was Eifa. Upon her departure, Eifa collapsed into a pool of sludge and burned the Freedom Tree symbol into the desk. The beasts seemed made of the same substance Amalardh had described. If the tower of jelly had formed into the Dark Goddess, might these two columns convert back to monsters? If so, Cecilia needed to hide Alistair.

She dashed to his crib. Her heart thumped. Where was her boy?

Worry etched deep on Marion's face as she peeked through a crack created by the slightly open door connecting the bedroom to the nursery. In her arms, she cuddled Alistair.

Cecilia pressed her hands to her chest. Thank goodness. "Take him far away," she whispered. "Go to Tomkin. He will help."

Wide-eyed, Marion nodded.

Heavy pounding came from outside the living room's side door. Her brothers must have battled the Noah beast into the courtyard and locked it out. The powerful vibrations as it rammed the door with its horns suggested it would break through any minute.

Eideard appeared in the bedroom doorway. "Cecilia! We need to go."

The black column that was once Brother Atlas rippled at its base. From Rabbie's aghast look, the one in the living room must also be transforming. Cecilia's fingers fumbled as she fashioned a carry sling and tucked the doll inside with its front facing her chest. The exposed human hair should be enough to make the bundle seem like a real baby. If she fled without Alistair, the beasts were certain to split up and search for him. At least this way, their focus would remain on her.

The ripples shimmied up the black column by the bedroom doorway, morphing into a beast with Brother Atlas's mismatched green and blue eyes. It opened and closed its fists as if needing a moment to understand its new form.

"Cecilia! Hurry!" called Eideard.

As she sped past the creature, its black arm shot out, grabbing her.

"Run, Rabbie. Run, Eideard," she yelled. "They can't hurt me."

Probably because a portion of its substance, in the form of its head, had been used to create the Brother Atlas counterpart, the newly formed Analise beast stood a foot shorter. The beast picked up its previously dropped sword and threatened it at Eideard.

The Noah beast smashed through the side door and readied its blade at Rabbie.

The Brother Atlas beast scanned Cecilia and her bundle. Satisfied that it had what it needed, it swung her onto its back and dropped to all fours, its hands turning into hooves. Strips of black separated from its flanks and strapped her legs to its torso. The other two beasts sheathed their swords into their flesh and converted their hands to hooves. The trio released a guttural cry and galloped off.

"Quick," Cecilia heard Rabbie say. "To the horses."

The beasts dashed through the empty, shadow-cast streets, exited the open gates, and turned south. Cecilia had no idea where she was going, other than, she was on her way to meet the beasts' maker—Eifa.

CHAPTER
9

A CRACK OF thunder woke Amalardh with a start. He grabbed the side of his cot and steadied himself against the lurching cabin. The rise and fall of the bow reflected a heavy swell. The storm must have raged for more than just a moment. Why hadn't Forbillian woken him? As a light sleeper, Amalardh normally jumped awake at the first hint of rain hitting the hull. He sat up and rubbed his throbbing temples. He knew better than to consume Finn's *Seaman's Sleep Aid*. Amalardh never drank, but with his racing mind cutting into the limited time he'd allotted himself to sleep, he figured the elixir would help knock him out. The stuff seemed to have worked a little too well.

The boat lurched sharply, forcing him to grip both side rails as he climbed the cabin's narrow stairs. He opened the galley door to roaring wind and stinging rain. Black clouds smothered the setting sun's rays. What were the chances that on the first day at sea, a storm would hit during the small window when his barely seaworthy uncle was at the helm?

Light from the exterior lanterns exposed an unmanned wheel. The lowered sails and locked-off rudder angled slightly windward blunted Amalardh's concern. He leaned over the railing and caught sight of a taut rope attached to the bow that disappeared into the water. His uncle might not be as useless as he assumed. The man had the sense to deploy the parachute anchor while keeping the bow directed into the oncoming waves.

Intermingled with the wind's howl came a deranged cry. On

the bow, Forbillian's husky silhouette clung to the railing and screamed to the heavens. What was the foolish man doing?

Amalardh negotiated his way along the side decking to the front.

Forbillian threw his arms in the air. "Dear nephew! Come join me in this fine weather."

A wave crashed down, knocking him into Amalardh. They tumbled toward the edge.

As the surging swell rose, Amalardh seized hold of both his uncle and a nearby rope.

Another wave bucketed down.

Forbillian's laughter held a crazed edge. "Isn't this amazing?" he yelled.

"Get the hell below deck before this storm sucks you into the sea," said Amalardh.

Forbillian's eyes turned wild. "Let it try!" He freed himself from Amalardh's grip and stumbled back to the bow's pinnacle. "Here I am, you miscreant harpy," he yelled to the sky. "Come and get me!"

"Old man! Do you want to die?"

"What I want is irrelevant. It always has been. If I die, then so be it. Death is what I deserve." He turned back to the storm. "Is that all you've got? I've had better in a bathtub."

Amalardh reached out, but Forbillian flicked him away. "I left her!"

Was his uncle crying? With the rain, Amalardh didn't know if Forbillian's red eyes spilled tears.

"I left her with those animals!" Forbillian fixated on the wild, black waters. "The Dark Goddess took everything. And now she's come for me. Well, I'm here for the taking." He spun to Amalardh and pulled him close. "You know what I'm talking about. You know my pain because you have your own. I can't live with it anymore. I'd rather die."

Amalardh reeled from the stench of Finn's *Seaman's Sleep Aid* on Forbillian's breath. "Get below, now!"

"Or what?"

THUD! Amalardh's right hook knocked Forbillian unconscious.

He dragged his limp uncle into the galley and hauled him onto a cot. He probably should remove Forbillian's wet clothes, but the overexertion from lugging his uncle's deadweight combined with his hangover caused his head to pound. He draped a dry blanket over Forbillian's damp body and let him be. He dried himself with a towel, sat on the opposite mattress, and stared at his snoring uncle. He should never have pointed Marion out the way he had.

He flopped his head against the wall. More than anyone, Amalardh understood the pain of an unscratched itch. At the Battle for Freedom's conclusion, he had planned to saddle a horse and go. Life without Cecilia would have been far less painful than watching her fall in love with another man—Gildas. He had seen the way the good-natured man from Plockton looked at her. He had also noticed her uncertain glances toward her fellow Plocktonian. If Amalardh had never come into Cecilia's life, the two long-standing friends would surely have ended up together. Leading up to the battle, Amalardh had planned to keep his feelings for Cecilia to himself, but on the night before the bloodied assault, everything changed—Cecilia confessed her love. With his painful itch finally scratched, his protective walls came crumbling down. Because of his vision in the Pass-Over Zone—Gildas raising Alistair—his itch returned and his defensive shield shot back up.

He took in the torment on Forbillian's unconscious face, and affinity gripped his soul. If his own heart's itch remains unscratched, he, too, will probably look just as disordered, smell just as stale, and have a stomach just as unfitting thirty years from now.

The boat lurched. Forbillian woke. He looked around as if wondering how the hell he got down there. His cheeks puffed as he placed his hand on his belly. Amalardh thrust a basket under

Forbillian's chin just in time to catch the retched contents of his uncle's innards.

"Son of a monkey's testicles," said Forbillian. "What happened?" he sat up on the edge of his cot and rubbed his face.

"Nothing a long sleep won't fix," said Amalardh. He didn't know which version of his uncle raked his insides the most: the jolly chatterbox or the sullen, foreboding man sitting before him. He supposed he preferred the happy-go-lucky version, because he hated seeing Forbillian in so much pain. "You should know," he said, "I dispatched Marion's Night Husband."

Forbillian's expression held surprise, then morphed into relief. "I hope you made him squeal like the pig he was." His head dropped. "You spared her the pain that I couldn't. Tell me everything."

"Marion's story is not mine to tell."

"The pain, the torment, of wondering what that animal was doing to her. Every minute, of every hour, of every day, I imagined the worst. It has been eating me alive."

"If you have been imagining the worst, then you have been imagining correct."

"That's it? That's all you're going to tell me?"

Amalardh remained silent.

"If the same happened to Cecilia, you would want to know everything."

Amalardh didn't want to tell Marion's story because revealing hers meant exposing his own. But Forbillian was right. If anyone ever harmed Cecilia, Amalardh would want to hear every detail. He leaned forward and rested his elbows on his knees. "I was fifteen when I started killing for the Senators," he uttered.

Forbillian's expression softened.

"They were all I knew. Their lies were my only truth. Back then, I wore the clothes of Tower Folk, and every day, my skin crawled. At night, I would jump awake drenched in sweat. Maybe my subconscious understood that I was doing wrong. I got to where I could no longer breathe in that place. The Tower. So, I left. Since I was neither Citizen nor Tower Folk nor Soldier, I moved to the Seventh Division and took on these clothes." He regarded his sodden robe.

Amalardh rarely talked about his past, even with Cecilia. The calm washing over him from speaking openly with Forbillian surprised him. Was he experiencing the bond of family?

He had chosen the Seventh Division because the region's sparse population and its hilly landscape gave him the perfect overview of the Tower and the Army Base below. Senator Akantha, while not especially thrilled with Amalardh's decision to branch out on his own, set him up with a Citizen housekeeper—Marion, who did not know Amalardh's connection with the Senators. "I had assumed her scars and bruises had come from working the fields. But then one day, she arrived with a split lip, which she tried to hide by sucking into her mouth."

Forbillian's knuckles whitened.

Amalardh didn't ask Marion who hit her. He didn't need to. Citizen husbands rarely struck their wives. The law of the land sided squarely with the women. The perpetrator of any obvious contusion faced death by guillotine. Citizen husbands did not own Citizen wives. Vitus did. And the city did not tolerate visible abuse. As Senator Akantha once explained, "Nobody likes to take a bite out of a bruised apple." With a Citizen wife's role foremost that of a Night Wife to a Soldier, the Citizen husband must keep her body free of blemishes. And while the law also banned Soldiers from hitting their Night Wives, many still did. Most were wise enough not to leave obvious marks.

After spying Marion's lip, Amalardh retired to his basement workshop, where he began work on his very first wire sculpture—a three-foot-tall, thorny Tower replica. When night came, he followed Marion to the Nocte Deversorium Uxorem, the central locale in each division where Night Wives spent their allotted fifty minutes pleasuring their assigned Soldier, who because of pledging their lives to Vitus, were forbidden to marry.

The pinched-faced Tower Folk staffing the sign-in desk thrust his hand at Amalardh's young chest. "Boy," he said, "you can't be in here. Now go before a Soldier finds you and makes you leave."

"My name is Amalardh. I answer only to the Senators."

By the clerk's blunted expression, the stories floating around about the Senators' new Dark Shadow did not align with the teenager in front of him.

Cries of muffled pain echoed up the hallway. As Amalardh stepped toward the sound, the clerk blocked his path. "I don't care who you are. A Soldier's time with his Night Wife is not to be distur—"

Amalardh's arm shot forth, shoving the spindly man in the chest. The clerk flew backward and crashed into the wall. His wide eyes locked onto Amalardh as though finally believing the brawny teenager was the mythical Dark Shadow of the Senators.

"Dear boy," he said, "surely even you understand that Soldiers will be Soldiers. So what if some are a little more aggressive with their passions than they should be? They are closer to beasts than men. Even a friendly cat in the throes of a loving cuddle will scratch its—"

The flick of Amalardh's blade across the clerk's throat had been as reflexive as slapping one's skin upon the sting of a mosquito. His intent had been to stop the lies, not inflict death. As blood pulsed from the clerk's severed artery, Amalardh's heart rate spiked. He had not maimed another outside of the Senators' orders. Would they dispatch him because of his recklessness?

Marion's pained cry brought him back. He strode down the hall to her room and planted his foot against the locked door. The wooden slab flew open, revealing a muscular Soldier attacking Marion.

Forbillian buried his face in his hands.

"She saw me and terror shot through her eyes," said Amalardh. "I can only imagine she feared the Soldier might harm me."

His roundhouse kick sent the hulking predator to the ground. As the Soldier shook out his head, Amalardh drove his knife through the man's chest. This time, he had every intent to kill.

Of the several slayings he had made at the behest of the Senators, this was the first where Amalardh had felt nothing. No guilt. No remorse. No uncertainty. The Soldier was a pig. He deserved his death. Amalardh kept this moment sealed in his heart. Every subsequent kill evoked the same detached state. That evening, his night terrors left, and he became the Senators' perfect killing machine. Devoid of doubt. Bereft of any emotion.

Forbillian's drained expression remained locked on Amalardh. He seemed just as horrified to hear Amalardh's story as he had Marion's. He rubbed his brow. "Thank you for ending her suffering. I should never have left her."

"Part of me is thankful that you did," said Amalardh.

Forbillian scowled at him.

Amalardh shook his head. "You are worse than Cecilia for imagining the darkest possible meaning of my comments. If you had stayed and witnessed Marion's bruises, you would have tried to kill her Night Soldier. If you had succeeded, you would have been dispatched. If not by Aetus"—the former army leader, who performed the Senators' dirty work before Amalardh—"then by me. I would not have known I had killed my uncle."

"If I'd stayed, I would've known about you. I could have helped."

Amalardh leaned back against the wall. "The past is the past," he said. But was it? While he was thankful that Forbillian had left, resentment bubbled for the very reason Forbillian had stated—an uncle could have saved Amalardh's young self from the Senators' clutches.

Most emotions, Amalardh could bury with ease before they surfaced. Since Forbillian's arrival, he struggled to settle the confusing sensations swirling inside. Moonlight glowing through a porthole exposed a starry sky—the perfect distraction from his unwanted state. "The storm has cleared," he said. "I guess I should give credit where credit is due."

Forbillian began stripping off his wet clothes. "What credit would that be?"

"You did a good job stabilizing the boat."

"I did? I don't remember." To say Forbillian stood as naked as the day of his birth would be incorrect, unless, like a bear cub, a full coat of fur had covered his newborn self. Thankfully, his rotund stomach shielded from view whatever dangled below. He motioned to Amalardh's robe. "You got a spare one?"

Amalardh flung him a dry blanket. Even if he had a spare robe, which he didn't, he wouldn't let his uncle's sweaty body near it.

Forbillian grinned. "There's the nephew I know and love."

"Get dried off. I need help with the parachute anchor."

"The what?"

"The anchor you launched off the bow."

"I did?"

Amalardh took pause. Something about Forbillian's nautical knowledge seemed askew. "During a storm, what's the protocol for stabilizing a boat?"

Forbillian scratched his head. "Lower the sails?"

"And?"

"There's more?"

"If you don't know what you're doing when you are sober, how the hell did you figure it out drunk?"

Forbillian rubbed his wet hair with the blanket. "The mind works in mysterious ways."

Unsatisfied with his uncle's answer, Amalardh glanced around the cabin. On the ground outside the back cabinets lay a pool of water. Neither he nor Forbillian had stood in that area, so the puddle had not dripped from their clothes.

"Do you think we got a stowaway?" Forbillian whispered.

"No," said Amalardh. "I know we do." And he knew exactly who.

He whipped open the cabinet door. Wet and shivering sat Oisin with his knees cuddled to his chest.

Amalardh's jaw tightened. The kid had betrayed his order. He should be furious, but Oisin's purple fingers and chattering teeth muted his anger. "Get a fire going," he said to Forbillian.

He guided Oisin out of the cupboard and directed him out of his wet clothes. As he wrapped the shivering boy in a blanket and bundled him next to the kitchenette's small potbelly stove, another unexpected rush of emotion flooded him. His head spun. His breathing hitched. Were the cabin walls closing in? They couldn't be.

He shot up the stairs. He needed some fresh air.

"Let me come help you with that parachute thingy," said Forbillian.

"No!" Amalardh snapped. "Stay with the kid."

He burst out from the galley and sucked in the salty breeze, but no matter how deep he breathed, he couldn't seem to fill his lungs. The moonlight dancing on the rippling water compounded his spin. He closed his eyes. What was happening? What was going on? Amalardh could fight Soldiers, dispatch enemies, slay intruders without so much as a blink. He could handle any physical challenge thrown his way. Why couldn't he handle this moment?

His knuckles turned white as he grasped the railing. He was breaking down because he wasn't facing a material threat. By exposing his soul to his uncle and opening his heart to Oisin, his emotional defenses had collapsed. For the first time in his life, Amalardh was experiencing a panic attack.

CHAPTER
10

CECILIA'S LEGS CRAMPED. Did these Terefellian beasts never tire? The day dawned and still they had not rested. She looked behind. Rabbie and Eideard were nowhere in sight. She whacked her beast's neck, demanding for it to stop. It didn't.

"If you do not allow me a rest break, then I will be forced to pee on your back."

Her threat went unheeded.

She grabbed the beast's horns and yanked back. The creature squealed and slid to a stop. The gooey straps around her legs retracted. The creature stood up, sending Cecilia sliding off its back. Her numb legs gave way, and she collapsed to the ground. She tried to stand, but her lower limbs remained devoid of blood. The three creatures surrounded her, growling and snorting.

She looked around. The sunburned landscape seemed deadly foreign compared to the Wynn Forest's lush greenery north of Vitus. In the distance, the Epona Ocean offered comfort. If Cecilia escaped, she could follow the coast back home. Not that she would need the ocean as a guide. The beasts' hooves left the perfect trail. Rabbie and Eideard could find her. She needed to figure a way to slow the beasts down and give her brothers time to catch up. She wiggled her toes. Her legs were coming back to life. She pointed to a cluster of bushes.

"I am going over there. I have to relieve my bladder." She spoke slowly, hoping doing so would help them understand.

She took a step toward the bushes and all three growled like rabid dogs.

She paused and reevaluated the situation. The Terefellians may have understood that she and Alistair were not to be harmed. Did their creature counterparts know the same? Rather than test their limits by insisting on using the bushes, she hitched her skirt, pulled down her underclothing, and squatted. These beasts would have to learn for themselves about human toileting needs. Their noses curled as they sniffed the wet patch. When she finished, she settled her clothing and made a drinking motion.

"Water. I need water. Do you understand?" She frowned. The beasts didn't seem to. "No water. I die. And if I die, baby dies. I don't think your queen would like that."

The beasts silenced. Their eyes glazed over. What on earth was going on? Their eyes came back to life. The Noah beast ran off. Sometime later, it arrived back and presented its hand, except the beast had reshaped it into a mug. Inside was water. It pushed the offering to her mouth. Cecilia grimaced. She really didn't want to drink from it, but what choice did she have? With her goal to slow the beasts down, every delay helped. Plus, she truly was thirsty.

Its rubbery skin felt smooth and cool on her lips. She gulped a mouthful of the refreshing water and smiled at the beast. "Thank you." It offered more. She downed the last of the liquid and wiped her mouth with the back of her hand. If these beasts really were like children with malleable minds, maybe she could train them. She had turned Amalardh from the dark side; maybe she could do the same with these things.

She pointed to her mouth. "Food," she said, then mimicked a chomping motion. Once again, the beasts' eyes glazed over. They were learning. Their expressions came back to life and the Noah beast dashed off and returned with a rabbit. Cecilia curled her nose. On her journey with Amalardh, a long, rainy night had rendered any potential firewood too wet to burn. Driven by practical needs, Amalardh sliced the rabbit he had caught and presented the raw meat to her. Dubious, Cecilia tried a sliver, but the stringy, gamey texture made her spit it out. She took a calming breath. If eating raw rabbit meant gaining time for her brothers to catch up, then she would do what she had to do.

The meal left her stomach churning.

The Brother Atlas beast motioned for her to get on its back. Cecilia had to keep stalling. She pressed her hands together and placed them to the side of her head. "Sleep," she said. "I must lie down and slumber." The beasts' eyes glazed. When they came back to life, they formed a circle around her. Cecilia's spirits lifted as she lay down. Her plan was working. They let her rest a solid three hours, during which she didn't sleep a wink.

Over the next few days, the beasts let her stretch her legs, brought her food and water, and allowed her sleep. As long as she pretended to feed and hydrate her baby doll, her ruse remained solid. Even though Cecilia's worry bubbled at the exhaustive number of miles covered during the traveling phases, hope held strong in her heart that the more the beasts learned, the more they would understand that she posed no threat. Maybe then, she could convince them to set her free. The creatures, however, plateaued in their learning.

During a rest break, Cecilia gently placed her hand on the hazel-eyed creature's shoulder. "Analise," she whispered, "I know you're in there. Please. Find the light and come back to me." For the smallest second, she thought she saw a flicker of humanity in the beast's eyes.

"C-e-c-i-l-i-a." The slow, hissing voice came from within the beast.

A chill shot to Cecilia's toes. She knew Eifa's voice.

"We meet again," said the Dark Goddess.

Cecilia's fists clenched. She should've known Eifa had been watching. Listening. The creatures hadn't followed Cecilia's orders, they'd been obeying their queen. Their eyes had glazed over because they were receiving commands, not learning a new skill.

"You will not win," Cecilia said. "I will defeat you like I did during the Battle for Freedom."

The voice cackled. "My defeat was my win. You chose love. Love always loses."

The beast opened its mouth wide and roared in Cecilia's face. Its rancid breath smelled of death.

"Come," said the voice from the Brother Atlas monster. "I await your arrival."

In the southern distance, a plume of smoke shot into the air. *The Dark Goddess.*

The Brother Atlas beast lowered to all fours. Sweat prickled along Cecilia's skin. Her next stop would be Eifa's lair, a place where escape would be near impossible. She needed a plan. But what?

A small light flickered from a patch of dense shrubbery a few feet away. The creatures didn't seem to notice, or if they did, they didn't react. Cecilia, however, knew the light came from her brothers. Months ago, Rabbie had found a compact mirror. The reflective surface fascinated him. He enjoyed shining a beam of light on a wall and moving the dot around. He especially relished flicking a beam into Eideard's unsuspecting eyes.

As Cecilia puzzled over how to create a diversion, the creature with Analise's eyes grasped her arm and led her to the awaiting Brother Atlas monster. She needed to act now. She grabbed the sword from the Analise monster's hip and pulled. The weapon didn't budge. The monster roared, as did the other two.

Fueled by panic, Cecilia yanked harder. The slime stretched, stuck to the blade like sticky dough.

An arrow pierced the Analise monster's head. It squealed. As it pulled the arrow from its skull, its substance relaxed. The sword broke free. Cecilia spun out from under the beast's grasp and held the blade at the ready. "You are not Analise!" she yelled and drove the sword through the beast's hazel eye. The creature expelled a screech unlike any other. It writhed back and forth as if experiencing genuine pain.

Cecilia bit down. She had found a vulnerable spot.

She rammed the blade through the other eye.

The creature liquefied and splashed spectacularly at her feet. "Their eyes!" she yelled to her brothers. "Spear them in the eyes!" By the time she finished imparting her discovery, the wet ground had dried.

Armed with bows and arrows, Rabbie and Eideard leaped up and began firing. With them came Parlan—a wiry former Citizen. By his side raced... Feltor? The former Citizen who had betrayed her? Cecilia couldn't believe her eyes. With his sword thrusted high in the air, Feltor bellowed and charged at the Brother Atlas creature. The man who almost unraveled Cecilia's efforts to inspire the Citizens of Vitus to revolt against the Senators seemed hell-bent on redemption. He swung his sword.

"Feltor! No!" she yelled. But his sharp blade's momentum continued to slice through the beast's midsection.

Just as with the beheaded creature back in Cecilia's house, the two separate pieces collapsed into globs. The top half formed into a large ball and rolled toward Cecilia. She turned and ran, tripping on a rock. If the doll strapped to her front were Alistair, she would've flattened her baby boy.

Her heart pounded as the ball drew near.

Inches from connecting with her feet, it stopped. Like a curious cat, it rolled forward a half rotation, then sprung back as though afraid. Interesting. Cecilia moved her hand toward it. The ball shuffled back. She inched her fingertips closer. The same thing happened. A force within her seemed to repel it.

Siersha's light. Of course! The Goddess must have left her glow within Cecilia to protect her from Eifa's muck. Relief flooded her. Her soul was literally untouchable. Possibly realizing the same, the glob rolled away in search of another victim.

With the body of the Atlas monster still reforming, Rabbie, Eideard, Parlan, and Feltor focused on the green-eyed Noah creature. Swords clanked as the skilled beast battled hard. It rammed Rabbie in the chest, sending him to the ground.

The black death glob raced at him.

"Rabbie! Watch out!" yelled Cecilia. But he was too winded to move.

She ran and dove at the ground, sliding between the ball and her brother.

The ball spun on itself and rolled away.

"Parlan! Run!" she yelled.

SPLAT! Too late. The large ball engulfed Parlan's legs. He yelped with fear.

Cecilia pulled Rabbie to his feet. As he rubbed his pained chest, Parlan's agonized cry drew his attention.

"We can't let him go through this misery," Cecilia uttered.

Rabbie's face filled with regret as he nocked an arrow in his bow. He aimed at Parlan but seemed hesitant to release it.

"End it for him! Please," Cecilia said.

"Then we'll still have that stuff to deal with," said Rabbie. "If we wait, we can get him right as he changes."

As the muck steadily consumed Parlan, he flung his head side to side and wailed.

"Please," insisted Cecilia.

"No!" said Parlan. His face reddened as he sucked in a pained breath. "If you stand a better chance another way, then do it."

Cecilia's stomach folded. Brave Parlan, who had once thrown his shoe at Vitus's formidable army leader, remained defiant to the end. "Parlan, I'm so sorry," she said.

"Fight hard—" His words cut as the blackness wrapped around his cheeks and into his mouth.

Cecilia wiped her eyes and sucked back her emotions. Rabbie was right. The stunned moment after a monster woke up was the perfect time to jab its eyes. She spun to where the black cylinder representing the Brother Atlas monster had stood. In the commotion, she'd forgotten about it. She should've been waiting by the formation, ready for the beast's eyes to open. But now, her opportunity to destroy it had passed. The newly formed creature looked hideous. Because it had lost half of its composition, what it lacked in height, it made up for with oversized, muscular arms. Its one blue and one green eye locked onto her.

Feltor ran to her defense.

"Stop slicing their bodies," she said. "Go for their eyes!"

While Eideard battled the Noah green-eyed monster and Rabbie waited for the Parlan monster to form, Cecilia and Feltor took up arms against the Brother Atlas creature. The beast knocked Feltor's sword from the stout man's grip, then head-butted Cecilia backward with his curled horns, knocking the wind from her.

She turned toward the sound of a wet gasp.

Feltor! The man determined to redeem his honor coughed up blood. The Brother Atlas creature had straightened its horns and speared them through Feltor's belly.

Sword drawn, Rabbie pulled Cecilia to her feet. "I have this," he said. "Check on Feltor."

With the Parlan monster still yet to reform, Cecilia rushed to Feltor's side, leaving Rabbie to battle the Brother Atlas beast.

"I failed you again," said Feltor.

"No. You were brave. Your father and children will be proud."

"You truly are a precious light. Save this world from Eifa's darkness," he said and fell limp.

She kissed the back of his hand. "Rest in peace and feel guilt no more."

The Noah beast flung back its head and squealed. Eideard had climbed onto its back and stabbed out an eye. "May your soul now be free, my good friend," he said and thrust his knife into Noah's remaining eye.

SPLAT! The creature liquified, dropping Eideard to the ground.

Ripples shot up Parlan's black column. Just as with the original version of the Brother Atlas monster, the Parlan monster stood as tall and dangerous as the original Noah and Analise beasts. This suggested that so long as Eifa's muck had flesh and blood to consume, the resulting monster would be full-sized. Thankfully, they all died the same way. Cecilia snatched a knife from Feltor's belt.

As the Parlan beast took in its fresh world, she bounded onto its chest.

JAB! JAB! She fell to the ground as the blackness splashed to the grass. "Go, Parlan," she whispered to the evaporating liquid. "May your soul now be free to join the many that take comfort in Siersha's light."

Eideard yelped and rocketed through the air. He smashed against a tree trunk, crumpling into a heap at the bottom. With its hefty arm, the stocky Brother Atlas beast knocked Rabbie to the ground. It had taken up Parlan's fallen sword and was about to ram the sharp blade into Rabbie's chest.

"Nooo!" cried Cecilia.

WHOOSH! An arrow speared the creature's eye. Its head jerked as it screeched. Cecilia spun around but saw no one.

Another arrow pierced the beast's other eye.

SPLASH! Rabbie coughed and spluttered as black liquid gushed onto him.

He scrambled to his feet. "Get it off me! Get this stuff off me." He scuttled out of his wet clothes, underpants and all.

"If you're trying to impress me, it might just have worked," came a flat-sounding female voice.

Cecilia turned to see a teenage girl with a bow and quiver flung over her back and ash-brown hair pulled into an elementary ponytail. Her mottled-green canvas pants and matching mottled top blended seamlessly with the shrubs. Rabbie's face turned crimson as his hands shot in front of his nakedness.

The girl's face scrunched at Cecilia's mid-section. "Is that a doll?"

The scuffed and beat-up Alistair decoy dangled from its carrier blanket. Cecilia tossed the toy aside. "Thank you for saving my brother's life. Who are you?"

The girl's eyes followed the doll, then flitted momentarily to Rabbie. "Don't you think you should take care of him?"

Rabbie remained crimson. He always was the more private of Cecilia's brothers. If a strange young woman had encountered

Eideard naked, Cecilia doubted he would bother covering up. She strode over to Rabbie and wrapped the carrier blanket around his lower half. "Their black water won't harm you." She picked up his shirt and shook it out. Dusty particles from the desiccated liquid filled the air. "Get yourself dressed."

Still crumpled at the base of the tree, Eideard woke and rubbed the back of his head.

"Are you okay?" Cecilia asked.

"Nothing feels broken." He glanced at Rabbie. "Why is our brother naked?"

"I'll explain later." She helped him to his feet, then walked over to the stranger. "My name is Cecilia and they are my brothers, Eideard and Rabbie."

"Saffron," said the girl. "I'm told it means yellow flower. But... yeah... whatever."

Cecilia stretched out a welcoming hand. "It's a pleasure to make your acquaintance." Saffron's fist clenched. Cecilia considered withdrawing her hand when the girl took hold and shook.

"Likewise," she said with a shy smile.

The girl's thickened skin made Cecilia's chest heave. She swept Saffron's legs out from under her and pressed her knife to the stranger's throbbing neck. "Your people have fooled me once. You won't fool me again."

"Cecilia! What are you doing?" said Rabbie.

"She's one of them. She's a Terefellian."

"Wait. Please. You don't understand," said Saffron.

"No. You don't understand," said Cecilia. "I know your mind games. Your penchant for manipulation. No word that exits your mouth will ever be the truth."

CHAPTER
11

THE MADDOWSHIN LIFTED its head to the sky and roared. Something had angered the beast. Wyndom grinned. Maybe Rudella would now understand the challenges a ruler faced. He sat on his resting mat under the shade of a broad palm tree and relaxed against its rough trunk. In the several days since the Maddowshin had tossed him against the temple wall, Wyndom had laid low. He despised violence, especially when it involved him.

Rather than return to their valley, the Terefellians had made camp in the open land outside their temple. The queen had birthed close to four hundred Wirador Wosrah. With the warriors standing guard, the Terefellians no longer needed to hide away in their cobs.

If the queen birthed at a rate of just under thirty warriors a day while, over the years, the Terefellians had collected about five thousand souls, then how long would it take for their army to march on Vitus? Unable to figure the math in his head, Wyndom picked up a stick and began writing in the sand.

Six months. Rudella's voice rattled in his head.

Wyndom flicked the stick away. The woman had always been good with numbers.

The Maddowshin lumbered over. Wyndom feigned interest in a hangnail. Regardless, the beast pushed its thoughts about the Treoir Solas (a young woman called Cecilia), the last Croilar Tier (a former assassin known as Amalardh), and the Ceannaire Fis (Cecilia and Amalardh's child) into his mind. Wyndom pressed his hands to his face. Was there not some sort of helmet or clay cap he could shove on his head to block her out?

"Yes. I can make one out of molten steel," said the Maddowshin.

"If my thoughts displease you, then don't listen to them," said Wyndom.

The Maddowshin's eyes narrowed.

Wyndom stood and brushed himself off. "Yes. You've told me before. With one squeeze of your hand, you can crush me like the bug I am. Yet... you haven't."

After everything that had happened between them, Wyndom doubted the creature would kill him. Although the Maddowshin embodied their queen's raw, calculating resolve, it also held Rudella's spirit. And whether because of codependency or the remaining ounce of love she'd once had, the woman needed him. Why else would she continue to push her troubled thoughts into Wyndom's mind? He took a seat on a rock and waved permission for the Maddowshin to offload its concerns. Apparently, the plan to capture the Treoir Solas, Ceannaire Fis, and Croilar Tier had not gone as expected. While the news surprised him—after all, the Terefellian team had two Wirador Wosrah with them—his shock did not match the Maddowshin's.

"I told you sending Brother Atlas was a mistake. The man has the tact of a—" He cut himself off before saying "Maddowshin," not that that made a difference. His musings still betrayed him. But the beast simply sneered and continued to push forth its thoughts—this time, though, with visuals. A terrified, intoxicatingly pretty young man flooded Wyndom's vision. The beasts' collective memories of the failed kidnapping and Cecilia's attempted escape became Wyndom's own, along with the fact that the pretty young man's name was Rabbie. Wyndom's point of view came from the Wirador Wosrah with Brother Atlas's soul, who stood over Rabbie, its oversized arm held high, readying its blade to jam into the frightened young man's chest.

Something flew at Wyndom's face. He squealed as his left field of vision went blank.

"Calm yourself," said the Maddowshin. "The arrow hit the warrior, not you."

The arrow had blinded the beast's left eye. The other eye scanned some shrubs directly ahead, locking on the tip of an arrow poking from the greenery. Unable to stop himself from doing so, Wyndom shrieked and flung his arms over his face. His mind's eye went black. "What happened?" he asked.

"The Wirador Wosrah is dead," said the Maddowshin. Its nostrils flared. "Our queen is not happy. The girl knows everything about us."

Wyndom massaged his pounding chest. The arrows had felt far too real. "What girl?"

"Your daughter."

His hand stopped rubbing. The figure in the bushes was Saffron? She was alive! She was safe! His relief curdled as his blood boiled. What in all that was good in Terefellia was she doing helping the enemy?

CHAPTER

12

"AYE, YOU'RE A stubborn bastard," said Forbillian. "I'm certain you get that from your mother. Let the kid do it."

Amalardh grit his teeth. He detested Forbillian for siding with Oisin, even if both of them were right. Oisin's eagle eyes could search for land from the mast far better than Amalardh's. But handing the task to him would be the same as telling him, "I'm no longer mad at you for going against my word and stowing away." But in the five days since discovering the boy drenched and shivering in the cabin closet, Amalardh remained annoyed. He needed his anger to maintain his wall. The last time he let his defenses down, the ensuing panic had terrified him.

Forbillian flipped down one of the mast's short, stubby climbing pegs. "Jizzipes! I'd never trust one of these with this." He jiggled a handful of his rotund belly. Normally, such antics would send Oisin into a fit of laughter, but the drilling down Amalardh had given him for going against his orders appeared to still sting. As though determined to get a smile out of the boy, Forbillian persisted. "You sure these aren't some sort of toothpicks or something?" He pretended to grind it between his teeth. Noting the flat response, he quit his act. "Geez. What's in the water you all drink in that city of yours? It must have some chemical that's washed away everyone's ability to have a laugh."

Amalardh had had enough. He jabbed his finger at Forbillian. "You. Behind the wheel." He turned to Oisin. "And you... the next time I give you an order, you follow it. Get below deck."

Oisin's fist clenched. "No. You and Forbs would be dead right now if I hadn't come. You and your stubborn way of thinking that you can get by on just four hours of sleep. The storm had been raging for an hour before you woke up. If I hadn't been here to anchor us off, the boat would've flipped over, and I would've never seen you again. You can hate me. And you can never talk to me. I don't care because your orders suck." He wiped an escape tear and shimmied up the mast faster than a lizard up a tree trunk.

Forbillian shook his head and chuckled. "You certainly have the most charming effect on people."

Amalardh glared at him. He didn't give a damn if Oisin and Forbillian hated him. He just wanted everyone to do their job.

"Okay. Okay," said Forbillian. "To the wheel I go." He gave an aye-aye salute and shuffled off.

Amalardh grabbed the boat's side-railing and squeezed. Of course he cared if his uncle and Oisin hated him. And that was the problem. Life was so much easier when he didn't care.

"You see anything up there, eagle eyes?" Forbillian yelled.

"Not yet," said Oisin.

Something wasn't right. According to Amalardh's calculations, the island should be within view.

"Wait! Over there!" Oisin called. "I see something."

Amalardh opened his handheld telescope and scanned in the direction of Oisin's pointing finger. On the far-off horizon sat the top portion of a tower. Damn it. The storm had pushed them further south than he'd realized. He adjusted the mainsail, took the wheel from Forbillian, and reset their course.

Forbillian lounged back. "You're too hard on the young lad."

Amalardh remained focused on his task. He didn't need a lecture.

"He idolizes you. And you're going to ruin him."

The word "ruin" jabbed Amalardh.

"You really have perfected that silent treatment, haven't you?" said Forbillian. "Honestly, I don't know how you've managed to keep Cecilia as long as you have."

Amalardh exhaled a constricted breath. Neither did he.

The Ezekian Island seemed not much bigger than a football field. A white stone barricade, about fifteen feet high, ringed the circumference, giving the island the appearance of a mini-fortress. At the apex sat a magnificent castle about the size of Amalardh's cathedral home, only higher. Tall pines, broad oaks, and an abundance of shrubs mottled the surrounding landscape in shades of green. The place seemed untouched by the Great War of two centuries past. Had Amalardh known of this island's existence, he would have moved here long ago.

He guided the boat around the border to where a twenty-foot gap in the wall opened into a docking bay. With the boat secured, he hooked a small oil lantern to his belt and followed Forbillian and Oisin onto firm ground.

Forbillian immediately stumbled sideways.

Oisin cradled his belly. "I think I'm going to be sick."

The poor kid looked almost green. Amalardh's own head swam. Getting his land legs back after a week at sea was going to take more than a moment. "Give me your hand," he said to Oisin.

Remaining guarded, Oisin lifted his arm.

Amalardh pressed a point an inch and a half below Oisin's wrist and held it for a minute. "Better?" he asked.

Without looking up, Oisin nodded.

He placed Oisin's finger on the spot and told him to hold it a few minutes longer.

Forbillian thrust his wrist at Amalardh. "Me next?"

Amalardh started walking. "The quickest way to right your head is to keep moving."

"Don't worry about me," said Forbillian. "I'll just be over here throwing up."

"We don't know who we are going to run into," said Amalardh. "Keep your eyes and ears open."

Forbillian placed his hands on his hatchets. "My axes are sharp and at the ready." He dry-retched. "Of course, I could just vomit on the enemy."

"I don't have a weapon," said Oisin.

Oisin aimed a sling-shot better than Amalardh waved a sword. The boy had killed an impressive number of Soldiers during the Battle for Freedom. "A sling-shot is as much a weapon as a sword or ax," Amalardh said.

Shame plastered Oisin's face. "I don't have it with me. I figured if we were mainly going to be on the boat, I wouldn't need it." His eyes met Amalardh's. "Go on. Say it. I'm a stupid kid who wasn't thinking. You were right for not wanting me to come along."

Amalardh went to give Oisin his wolf knife, when Forbillian's hand clapped down on his forearm.

"A Croilar Tier must never be without his blade. I know you see me as your foolish uncle. And that's okay. Life is too short to be an uptight draggard. But just remember, this foolish uncle of yours survived thirty years under the noses of Vitus Soldiers. You don't have to respect me. What you have to do is pull your arrogant head out of your ass so that your ears can listen."

Amalardh sheathed his knife and eyed Forbillian. He had not expected such a confident level of intimidation.

Forbillian untied a leather strap from around his waist and handed it to Oisin. A sheathed knife hung from one side. "Here you go. I rarely use the darn thing. I prefer my axes."

Unable to watch Oisin fumble with the ultra-long strap, Amalardh took the lengthy belt from him and completed the job. The three revolutions needed to wrap it around the boy's slender waist exposed Oisin's frailty. At the same age, the Soldiers of Vitus had beaten Amalardh countless times and locked him for days inside a dank cell void of any light except a solitary candle with a burn time limited to one hour. Imagining Oisin's tiny frame enduring such torment filled Amalardh with dread. But was his treatment of Oisin much better? He may not have been inflicting physical pain, but the emotional damage he was causing was probably just as bad. Forbillian was right. Amalardh was going to ruin Oisin.

Standing, he led the way along a cement path to a lengthy flight of stairs that snaked toward the castle. Except for the occasional lizard rustle and bird tweet, the island appeared abandoned. Halfway along, Forbillian groaned, propped himself against the side of a decorative brick archway, and dug his thumb into his wrist. The old fool didn't even know the correct spot to press. Amalardh relented and walked over to him. "Give it here," he said.

Gratitude filled Forbillian's face as he held out his hand. Amalardh found the point and pressed. The color returned to Forbillian's cheeks. He shook his head. "The deadly sting of a scorpion, and the tender touch of a kitten. You are an enigma."

Amalardh placed Forbillian's forefinger on the spot and motioned for him to press. "I'm just trying my best not to ruin you," he said, emphasizing the word *ruin*.

Forbillian's eyes twinkled. His mouth cracked into a grin. And then, out came his warm, uncomfortably comforting chuckle. "So, there *is* a funny bone buried deep within my nephew."

Amalardh turned from him and continued his trudge up the stairs.

Two golden doors marked the castle's entrance. Amalardh turned a metal ring attached to the mouth of a lion-head handle. *CLUNK.* The internal latch unlocked. He pushed open the heavy slab of wood and stepped inside to a scent of smoky vanilla and musk. The order and symmetry of rows and rows of books stacked neatly floor-to-ceiling on shelves made from burgundy rosewood appealed to him. About every ten feet, the shelving jutted out perpendicular to the main aisle, creating multiple U-shaped cubicles. The same repeated two floors above. It would take a man a lifetime to read all these books.

Forbillian's nose curled. "I remember this smell. It's worse down below."

Oisin turned in a slow circle. "You mean there's more to this place?"

"Where to now?" Amalardh asked.

The way Forbillian scratched his head as he looked around did not bode well. "I just need a bit to get my bearings." He lifted his finger. "This way."

He led Amalardh and Oisin down the central aisle to the end of the building, where a broad staircase spiraled upward around a wide central column. The stairs curved through the second and third levels and ended in the castle's tower.

Six-inch-wide, cream-colored tiles, mottled with miniature cracks, carpeted the circular room. Each featured a unique, hand-drawn, royal blue, leafless tree with an embellishment to either the left or right of a small shrub, a tombstone, or a rock. The trees were grouped into four basic designs: broad, tall and skinny, short and skinny, and L-shaped, as if wind-blown. Golden disks connected the tiles' corners, creating a striking design.

"Puffin root," mumbled Forbillian. His mouth twisted as he studied the room. "I think there's one there, there, and there." He pointed to various spots on the floor.

"One what?" said Amalardh.

"There are three tiles that we need to pull up and rotate in a full circle." He dropped to a knee and showed how the golden disks between the tiles rotated along a central axis, allowing his thumb and middle finger to grab the diagonally opposite corners of a tile. He lifted the ceramic square a few inches and pointed to a central rod attached underneath. "Every tile has one of these. Rotating the correct three, in the correct order, will unlock the stairs to the Croilar Tier Archives."

Oisin looked around. "What stairs?"

Forbillian set the tile down, hoisted himself to his feet, and stood in the middle of the room. "Right here. Once we figure out the combination, this section of floor will open, allowing us to climb down a small staircase inside the big column that the main stairs wrap around."

"I take it you don't know which specific tiles open the lock," said Amalardh.

"This was all about forty years ago. I don't remember there being so many of these darn things." He pointed to a tile with a broad tree design. "I know for certain that of the three motifs, that's not one of them."

"So, instead of the seven hundred tiles to choose from, we only have about five hundred," said Amalardh. "That should speed things up."

Forbillian gave him a look. "Some people believe sarcasm is the lowest form of wit. But if this wit is coming from my surly nephew, I'll take what I can get." He patted Amalardh's arm a little too hard. "Looks like we're off to plan B." He led the way back down to the third floor.

"What's plan B?" asked Oisin.

Forbillian leaned on the central railing and looked out over the mountain of overstuffed shelves. "It's 'B' for book."

"What book?"

Forbillian sucked on his lower lip. "Yes. Exactly."

"You better not be telling me this trip was a waste of time," said Amalardh.

"No. I'm not telling you that." Forbillian motioned to the vast expanse. "What I am telling you is somewhere out there is a book with a key to help us open the stairwell."

"And if I'm understanding correctly, you have absolutely no idea where this book is, which very much sounds like you telling me this trip is a waste of time."

Forbillian stood tall. His booming voice echoed throughout the vast space. "I was ten years old. Give me a break." He rubbed his beard and settled his anger. "I wasn't the one who needed to know about this stuff. Your father was. He was the one paying attention. I came along for the ride."

Amalardh took a deep breath. Stressing his uncle out wasn't helping. "Do you remember the general location of this book?"

Forbillian waved his arm to the distant left. "It's definitely on this floor somewhere over there."

A single U-shaped cubical had at least ten rows on each of the three sides, with a minimum of fifty books per row. Conservatively, this amounted to around fifteen hundred books. With Forbillian's general wave covering about four cubicles, that meant the group had about six thousand books to choose from. Amalardh kept this frustrating fact to himself. "Do you remember what the book looked like?" he asked.

Forbillian offered a weak shrug.

"Do you at least remember what it was about?"

"Like I said, I wasn't the chosen one. Your father was. I just know the two of them walked down in that direction." He motioned to the floor's left side balcony. "I hung out here playing with my spinning top."

As much as Amalardh wanted to be furious at Forbillian for dragging him on this useless mission, he couldn't fault a ten-year-old for not paying attention to something that didn't concern him. He had to find a way into the Croilar Tier Archives. If needed, he would look through every page of every book until he found something that sparked his uncle's memory. He went to walk off when Forbillian muttered, "Eight Croilar Tier to protect the vision."

"There's a rhyme!" Forbillian said. "Yes. I remember now. To help Culloden know how to find the book, our father taught him a rhyme." He tapped his fingers on his lips. "How did it go again?" He uttered the first line, but came up short with the next. He motioned at Amalardh and Oisin. "You two just... hang out here. I've got to think." He began pacing up and down the balcony.

Amalardh took a seat on a red velvet bench.

Oisin joined him. His mouth pursed as if he wanted to say something. Finally, he came out with it. "I'm sorry I yelled at you back on the boat."

The apology took Amalardh aback. Oisin was apologizing to him? Amalardh was the one who should be repenting. "Never be sorry for expressing your feelings," he said.

Oisin sucked on his lip as though processing Amalardh's words. "Okay. Then I guess what I really should say is, I hate that you made me feel like I had to yell. Like if I didn't shout, you wouldn't hear me."

Cecilia, too, had told Amalardh more than once that she shouldn't have to stir up a flurry to get his attention.

"When we get home," said Oisin. "I'll find somewhere else to live. I'll stop bothering you."

Refusing to acknowledge the sting in his chest, Amalardh kept his tone flat. "Where exactly will you live?"

Oisin's eyes thinned. "I'll find somewhere." He stormed to the balcony and slammed his foot on the railing's bottom rung.

Amalardh's brow knotted at Oisin's anger. What just happened? He'd been trying to engage in a "normal" conversation, yet somehow, he'd still managed to upset the kid. He sat back and rubbed his face. Confusing reactions like Oisin's were exactly why Amalardh didn't want to get involved.

Forbillian tossed his arms in the air. "I ask for a moment's silence so I can think, and what do I get? You two are worse than a rabbit in a snake's hole. You"—he jabbed his finger at Amalardh—"when the kid said he was going to move out and stop bothering you, he wanted you to tell him, 'please don't move out, you're not a bother.' And you"—he pointed at Oisin—"get it through your head that he will never be what you want him to be. The Senators saw to that a long time ago. There are no great mysteries in this world, only great expectations. Once you stop having them, life will be a whole lot easier. Now, come with me. I've figured it out."

CHAPTER
13

"Please, don't hurt us," came an older female voice. "We mean you no harm."

Maintaining her grip on Saffron, Cecilia turned to see a woman dressed in a beige tunic similar to the three Terefellians' who had arrived at her home, but with a red satin scarf around her neck. Something about the timid glint in her pale blue eyes and the nervous way she rubbed her hands made Cecilia's stomach twist. This woman reminded her of her mother.

"Your people killed my friends, turned them into monsters," Cecilia said. "They came to my city with lies. Why should I trust you?"

"We are no longer with them," said Saffron. "We are just as terrified of them as you. We ran because they were about to kill my mother. They know where we are. They will send more. We have to leave this place, now."

Cecilia removed her blade from Saffron's neck. "There are more of those things?"

"The last I saw, close to one hundred."

One hundred! Her mouth went dry. She stood and pulled Saffron to her feet. "Show me. And this better not be a trap."

"It's no trap," said Saffron. She nodded at the Alistair decoy doll splayed on the ground. "Are you going to leave that here?"

Even though Rabbie had made it for her, Cecilia did not intend to take the toy on an extended journey. "Do you want it?" she asked.

Saffron's eyes darted to Cecilia's brothers. She seemed wanting to say yes, but probably didn't wish to appear foolish in front of young men. "Of course I don't," she said. "It's just, leaving it there like that..." She shrugged. "Whatever. It doesn't matter."

Cecilia had been eighteen when she left Plockton. After experiencing the world outside her isolated forest, she realized she'd often acted more like a naive child than a mature teenager. At the start of her journey, desiring comfort, she had packed her doll. After an encounter with a mountain lion, she had realized that holding on to it impeded her ability to withstand the dangers ahead. Unable to leave it on the damp forest soil, she had tucked it in a tree. She glanced at the facedown doll and her shoulders sagged. Had she completely lost her previous innocence? She picked it up, brushed off the dust, and spoke directly to it. "How about we put you somewhere safe?" She walked to a nearby tree and sat it in the branches.

Saffron nodded lightly, as if in approval. "This way," she said.

"Wait up," called Rabbie.

He jogged to the bush he and Eideard had earlier hid behind and returned with Cecilia's sword. Cecilia held the precious gift to her chest. This sword once belonged to Amalardh. He had forged it himself and used it to train her to become a warrior. The weapon had seen Cecilia through the Battle for Freedom, and it would see her through this current mess. She flung it over her shoulder. "Thank you," she said to Rabbie.

As Saffron led the group through scratchy shrubs, Cecilia introduced her brothers to the two Terefellians. Saffron's mother introduced herself as Esmerelda. "But everyone calls me Esme," she said.

"Thank you for saving my life," Rabbie said to Saffron.

Her cheeks reddened. "It was nothing."

Maybe Saffron killing the Brother Atlas beast had been "nothing," but the awkward exchange between her and Rabbie immediately after was not. Even though Rabbie's nakedness probably heightened the moment, the glances between the two of them still spoke volumes. If a similar moment had transpired between Saffron and Eideard, Cecilia wouldn't have thought twice about it. Her eldest brother flirted as routinely as most people breathed. But Rabbie? Love had stolen his heart only once, with Cecilia's best friend, Lileas, who had died during her village raid. In the two years since, no other woman had caught his attention the way Saffron did. Even now, as Cecilia studied them, they shot side-glances each other's way.

"What?" asked Rabbie in response to her stare.

She wanted to tell him, "Don't you dare fall for this girl. We know nothing about her." But who was she to chide another about their heart's attraction? She had fallen for Amalardh, an assassin sent by the former Senators of Vitus to kill her. Rather than confessing her concerns, she shook her head and told him, "Never mind."

The shrubs gave way to trees with a dry, aromatic scent. The dehydrated layers of wilted leaves and bark crunched beneath Cecilia's feet, drowning out much of Saffron's voice as she spoke of her former home and her people's strange traditions. Apparently, she and her mother had fled because Esme faced an impending ritual called the Rite of Quinta-something. Cecilia didn't quite catch the phrase. She did, however, grasp the part about Terefellians killing their own on their fiftieth birth year. She'd not thought a society more heinous than the one created by the Senators of Vitus possible.

Saffron stopped at the base of a tall wooden tower with a central spiral staircase. "My mother and I come up here every so often to monitor what they're doing." She began climbing the stairs. Cecilia and Eideard followed.

"I'll stay here," Esme said. "After a lifetime of climbing, I can't do it anymore. I prefer the use of my feet and hands for walking and cooking."

Saffron stopped. "Mother. This is hardly climbing. These are just stairs." When Esme didn't relent, Saffron released a sharp exhale. "You can't stay by yourself. It's not safe."

"I'll stay with her," said Rabbie.

Saffron's frown made Cecilia suspect that Saffron found her potential attraction to Rabbie annoying. Cecilia had felt the same way when she'd first met Amalardh.

"Are you sure, Mom?" Saffron asked.

Esme nodded. "I'll be fine with this nice young gentleman."

Her mother's warmness toward Rabbie seemed to bother Saffron even more. Her boots stomped as she continued her climb.

Around and around the stairs went. Already dizzy, Cecilia foolishly looked down. Her stomach swooned. Heights had never been her thing.

The watch tower rose above the forest canopy. A top platform about ten feet long and wide capped the stairs. Cecilia placed her hands on the wooden safety guard and took in the grand view. Far north sat a gray splotch—Vitus. She followed the coastline south as it curved inland and then back out and around a peninsula. In the midmorning sun, the vast Epona Ocean twinkled like a blue velvet carpet. Somewhere out in those waters were Amalardh and Forbillian. Were they okay? And what of Alistair? Had Marion made it to safety?

"My people come from down there," said Saffron. She pointed to a dry, desert-type land pocketed with scant palm trees and shrubs, southeast of the watchtower. The curving coastline placed the area close to the ocean and almost directly south of Vitus. No wonder the Soldiers had never discovered these people. Once the scouts hit the savannah fields and noted the rocky landscape beyond, they would've decided not to waste time searching lands that appeared unfit to support life.

On each railing sat two silver devices with patterning that made them look like owls. Based on their positioning, they were probably visual scopes. Saffron grabbed a silver coin from a rusted box filled with them, dropped it into a slot of a machine, and pulled down a lever, eliciting a ticking sound. She placed her brows on the part of the owl that looked like eyes, rotated the device, then motioned Cecilia over.

"That's our valley," she said.

Through the viewfinder, Cecilia took in the desolate scape. The poor girl and her mother grew up down there? The place was the complete opposite of Cecilia's lush Plockton Forest.

Eideard pressed his face to a telescope and complained that it was broken.

"You need one of these." Saffron must have handed him a coin because Eideard's scope began ticking.

At the mouth of the valley's southern opening, Terefellians dressed in tunics styled the same as Esme's went about their daily lives. "Your people all dress the same," Cecilia said.

Saffron's scoff hinted at her annoyance about this very fact. The first thing she probably did after running away was ditch her useless clothing in favor of her more durable outfit.

"Where are the monsters?" Cecilia asked.

"Once you get to the opening of the valley's south end, keep going. You can't miss them."

Cecilia rotated her scope. The hairs on her arms stood on end at a black sea of beasts standing in perfect formation outside a towering, ornate facade. "Where are they coming from?"

"The rock carving with all the pillars is our temple," said Saffron. "They're coming from inside."

Cecilia pulled back from her scope and listened as Saffron spoke of her people's ability to capture the soul of the departed. After the Great War and the forced move to the Terefellian Valley, the group had faced a dilemma. Not only did the caves offer limited accommodation, with their height from the ground, how would the elderly make the daily climbs? The then leader rewrote the scriptures. The Rite of Octogenary became the Rite of Quinquagenary. He reasoned that after fifty years, a Terefellian's ability to climb plummeted. Why risk losing souls to a deadly fall? "Our people have been performing this ritual for centuries. In that time, we've collected about five thousand spirits."

Five thousand! When the Terefellians who had invaded Cecilia's home first spoke of the Dark Goddess building an army, she had wondered what army Eifa could build that she would fear? She had her answer. She leaned on the railing and dropped her chin to her chest. What was she going to do?

"The Terefellian queen is the goddess, Eifa," said Saffron. "She's in that temple birthing Wirador Wosrah from the souls we captured. And at the rate she's going, the army will be ready in under six months."

Cecilia rubbed the back of her neck. Would six months be enough time for Vitus to prepare? Even if they manufactured enough arrows, less than a dozen of their archers possessed the accuracy needed to kill a monster. "Other than putting out their eyes, is there any other way to kill them?" she asked.

"Not unless you can think of a way to destroy Eifa before she births them," said Saffron. "And even if you did, no one is getting within a hundred feet of the temple." Her eyes lowered. "I'm sorry. I know my people have done a terrible thing. I honestly didn't believe that the coming of the Terefellian queen was true."

"That big one by the broad palm tree," said Eideard, looking through his viewfinder. "Is that the beasts' leader?"

The ticking sound had stopped in Cecilia's scope. She fed in a coin and rotated it away from the temple toward a stout palm tree. A beast almost two feet taller and wider than the others and a wiry man half the creature's height stood under the tree's long fronds.

Saffron looked through Eideard's scope. "Bloody stars," she uttered. "That's my father."

"I hope you're not talking about that beast," said Cecilia.

"No. The pathetic man next to it. His name is Brother Wyndom. He's the head of Terefellia."

Saffron was the enemy ruler's daughter? This information pleased Cecilia. In her experience, children who defied their parental leaders had proved honorable allies. Oisin had gone against his father's orders of not allowing strangers into the

Ground People's home. Noah had turned on his grandfather, Senator Nuka, and fought with Cecilia against the Soldiers of Vitus. And Amalardh had disobeyed the only parental figures he'd known—the five Senators.

Saffron fed a coin into Eideard's scope and handed it back to him. "My father has a ring. According to our scriptures, when the time of our queen comes, the bearer of this jewel will bring forth the Maddowshin, a supreme being that will lead the Wirador Wosrah—those beasts we just fought—to victory." She glanced out over the valley and shook her head. "Typical," she uttered to herself.

"What?" Cecilia asked.

"The Terefellian leader is supposed to become the Maddowshin. My spineless father has clearly tricked some other poor unsuspecting soul into the role." She explained that Maddowshin meant Shadow Mind, because it could see and hear anything the Wirador Wosrah saw or heard. This was why she'd insisted they leave the spot where the fight had taken place. If other beasts lingered near, the Maddowshin would've known where to direct them.

Her expression flattened as she gazed in the direction of her valley. "When I first spotted those things gathering outside the temple, my mother and I contemplated returning home and throwing ourselves at my father's mercy. How could anyone defeat such power?" She turned to Cecilia. "But then I saw how that substance wouldn't come near you, and I knew you were special. If anyone can destroy my father, and the evil he has brought into this world, you can."

Her desperate look filled Cecilia with dread. Repelling a single soulless blob didn't equate to leading a victory against an entire Wirador Wosrah army.

"I can't go back to my people," Saffron said. "I won't. Their beliefs are wrong. If I hadn't left with my mother, she'd be one of those beasts. My father plans to destroy your city and take over. Only those who pledge their life to the Terefellian queen will be spared. My mother and I can't do that. I would rather fight and die than live under Eifa's rule."

Cecilia rubbed her hands across her hair and breathed deep. Even though she wasn't ready for another war, she would have to be. What choice did she have? "We will face Eifa in battle, but just so you know, chances of death are very high."

"Well, dear sister," said Eideard. His eyes remained glued to his viewfinder. "Since I don't fancy dying just yet, I suggest we leave."

Cecilia jumped behind her scope in time to see a dozen Wirador Wosrah disappearing into the southern end of the Terefellian Valley. From what Saffron had said about the Maddowshin's ability to see all and know all, this herd would head straight to where Cecilia and her group had killed the three beasts. From there, tracking their path through the dry forest would be relatively easy. "Eideard is right. We have to go."

"I know a place," said Saffron.

CHAPTER
14

AMALARDH FOLLOWED HIS uncle along the library's third story balcony.

"Eight Croilar Tier to protect the vision," Forbillian said, and counted off eight of the U-shaped cubicles. At the eighth one, he stopped. "Look to the right and scan with precision." The group stepped inside and faced the shelving to their right. "If red is blood, then white is bone. From father to son, our bond is sewn." He scratched his woolly chin. "Not certain I know what that means."

The colorful array of spines related mostly to animals.

"White is bone," said Oisin. He pulled out a book about mammalian skeletons.

From father to son, our bond is sewn, Amalardh repeated to himself. Did the line refer to the Croilar Tier wolf knife, passed from father to son? He took the book from Oisin and flipped to the section detailing a wolf skeleton. He showed it to his uncle. "Anything look familiar?"

Forbillian's eyes darted across the page. "Like I said, I never saw the book. Your guess is as good as mine with relating these images to those tiles."

Amalardh closed the hardcover and gave it to Oisin to put back.

"The last line is, 'Croilar Tier, what does it be? Inside one, there are three,'" said Forbillian.

"Croilar Tier are protectors," said Oisin. "But that doesn't make sense because most animals are predators or prey."

"Croilar Tier means wolf heart," said Amalardh. "The line, 'If red is blood, then white is bone,' is not just referring to a skeleton. We need to be looking at a wolf's anatomy. More specifically, a wolf's heart."

They scoured the shelves, retrieving all the books related to animal anatomy. After filtering out books that did not have a wolf, five remained. They each took one and flipped through pages. The first four books included pictures of hearts, but nothing clicked as clues for the tiles.

Oisin sighed at the fifth book. "This one's a dud as well."

The book featured anatomical sketches by Veracid Donalino, a name Amalardh knew from a copy of Donalino's human anatomy in his workshop. The scientific illustrator lived around the same time as Gaussian Tuetin (the seer who had written the Prophecy) and his sketches were as accurate as the newer photographs seen in the more modern books. Amalardh took the book from Oisin and studied each sketch until he found a detailed drawing of a wolf's heart complete with the main arterial feed. This sketch had to hold the answer.

"That's it!" said Forbillian. "You've found it. 'Inside one, there are three.'"

Facing Amalardh, Forbillian viewed the sketch upside down. He turned the book so Amalardh and Oisin could see what he had noticed. The arterial structure resembled a leafless tree with three major branches. Each branch looked like its own separate tree and each tree matched one of the four styles on the tiles: wind-blown, short and skinny, tall and skinny.

Forbillian pointed to each branch. "Tile one. Tile two. Tile three." He clapped his hands. "I knew I'd figure it out."

Amalardh cocked his brow at him.

"Well, you and the boy helped, too."

Book in hand, Amalardh led the way back to the circular tower room and they began hunting for the specific tiles. With hundreds to choose from, all with slight variations in the branches, the process took a while. Finally, Oisin found a tile that matched the arterial branch associated with the wind-blown tree. Amalardh slotted his thumb and forefinger in the tile's diagonally opposite corners and lifted. "Which way?" he asked Forbillian.

"Oh. Uhm. Clockwise. In a full rotation." His tone didn't sound confident.

"Are you sure?"

"Well, as sure as I can be, which would be to say, I'm fifty percent certain."

Amalardh set the ceramic square back in place and dusted off his hands. There were three tiles, each with two ways to turn. Whoever designed this locking system would have left nothing up to chance. He took a shelled peanut from his pocket and placed it on top of the tile to mark it. Once they found the other two, they could figure out the pattern of the turn directions.

Forbillian picked up the nut and popped it in his mouth. "You got some more of those? I'm famished."

Amalardh glared at him.

"What?" asked Forbillian.

"I think Amalardh put the nut there so we wouldn't forget which one it was," said Oisin.

"Oh! So you did. My bad."

Amalardh set another nut on the tile, then turned his attention to the heart sketch. Oisin's slight gasp made Amalardh look up in time to see Forbillian pop something in his mouth. The missing marker suggested this something was the second nut. Rage pulsed through his veins as he shoved his uncle against the wall.

"Whoa!" said Forbillian. "I was just playing around to lighten the mood." He opened his hand, presenting the nut.

Amalardh didn't need his mood lightened. He was tired and had little time for humor during a serious situation. "This may be fun and games to you, but not to me. You have no idea what I have seen, what I have done to protect the Prophecy. Protect Cecilia.

You may be blood but do not for one second think I would hesitate to throw you from this tower if you try to keep me from doing my job."

Forbillian's pupils grew wide. For all his lecturing to Oisin about the Senators messing Amalardh up, only now, it seemed, did he truly understand the extent of the damage.

"Stop it," begged Oisin. "Leave Forbs alone."

"It's all right, son," Forbillian said to Oisin. He fixed his stare on Amalardh. "I never need to learn me a lesson twice."

Amalardh released his grip, marched to a window on the opposite side of the room, and sucked in the cool air. If Oisin had played the same trick, would Amalardh have reacted the same way? He may have snapped at the kid, but the act wouldn't have incited the same level of rage. The more time Amalardh spent with Forbillian, the deeper his uncle's presence scratched at Amalardh's buried wounds. He liked Forbillian. A lot. And because of this, he resented him for leaving. Amalardh wouldn't be the mess he was today if he'd had his uncle's protection growing up. But Amalardh had had no one. Even his own mother had turned against him. As a consolation prize for the other Senators giving Akantha Culloden's senate seat, she had offered up six-week-old Amalardh to train as their assassin. When Vitus fell, she had revealed herself as Amalardh's mother and instead of hugging her son, she rammed her knife into his belly.

Back in the center of the room, Forbillian and Oisin were on all fours, searching for the other two trees. On the tile they had just found sat the nut Forbillian had only pretended to eat. Sinking to the ground, Amalardh joined the hunt.

Minutes later, Oisin matched a tall, skinny tree on a tile to the sketched image in the book. Amalardh placed three nuts on the find, clarifying its position as the third segment of the wolf heart arterial tree. He kept two more nuts in his pocket and handed the rest to his uncle.

Forbillian waved the offering away. "Give 'em to the kid. He looks famished. I'll settle myself with these when we're done." He motioned to the nuts already on the ground.

Amalardh handed Oisin the peanuts, then noticed Forbillian lingering. "Is there a problem?" he asked.

"I wanted to say, I know I can take the joking thing a little far and I'm sorry. To give credit where credit's due, you were right to mark the tiles."

Of course Amalardh had been right. He didn't require the acknowledgement.

Forbillian rocked on his heels.

"Is there something else?"

"Well, I mean, this is the part where you say, 'Thank you, uncle. I appreciate your apology. I'm sorry, too, for slamming you up against the wall and threatening to toss you out the window.'"

Apologies didn't come easily to Amalardh. He'd not uttered the words "I'm sorry" to anyone other than Cecilia, and he'd done so far less than he should have. "You should know," he said. "I rarely make threats. Most of the time, I simply act."

Forbillian's face morphed through an array of expressions, as though trying to figure out how to take Amalardh's statement. He settled with a slight head tilt. "So, I take it you not following through on a threat would be because the person you're threatening is pretty special to you."

"That's a possible interpretation," Amalardh replied.

The corner of Forbillian's mouth pulled into a grin. "If it's any consolation, as even-keeled as your father was, I used to annoy the bejeebies out of him, too." He patted Amalardh's arm, then groaned like a tired old man as he dropped to his knees and got on with the search for the last tile.

A lightness flittered through Amalardh. Forbillian's comparison helped dilute Amalardh's belief that more of Akantha's tainted blood flowed through his veins than his father's. He got back to the task at hand.

Minutes felt like hours.

"Well, butter my butt and call me a biscuit! I think I found it," said Forbillian.

Amalardh matched the tile with the sketch. Perfection. He set his last two peanuts on the find, then scanned the three tiles. Now, which way to turn them?

Oisin pointed to the wind-blown tree. "That one's branches bend off to the right. Maybe we're supposed to twist it clockwise and the other two the other way?"

A creative suggestion, but the arbitrary nature of assuming that the other two trees, which were mostly straight up and down, meant rotating their tiles to the left, just because the third tree bent to the right didn't satisfy Amalardh. He squatted and focused on the three images. What was the same and what was different? An additional embellishment decorated all three tiles: a tombstone. The tombstones belonging to the first and third tiles sat to the right of the tree. The second tile's tombstone sat to the left. He pointed to the second tile. "We turn that one counterclockwise. The other two, clockwise."

Forbillian rubbed the side of his beard with the back of his fingers. "Yep. That sounds about right to me."

"Wait," said Oisin. His eyes darted from tile to tile. "How do you know that?"

While Amalardh set about turning the ceramic squares, Forbillian explained the tombstones. The moment Amalardh set the last tile into place, a grinding noise reverberated.

"Stand back, everyone," said Forbillian. He lifted his arms and guided them to the periphery.

A three-foot-wide, square section of tiles dropped and slid under the flooring, revealing a narrow, metal staircase that spiraled down into blackness.

"Whoa!" said Oisin. "That's amazing."

His wide grin reminded Amalardh why he enjoyed the kid's company so much. Oisin held excitement and curiosity for most things, and this zeal rubbed off on Amalardh. He unhooked the small oil lantern from his belt, lit it, and descended to a small anteroom.

Forbillian lumbered up next to him. "I remember those stairs being far more fun." He leaned against the bottom railing and grabbed his head. "That's it. After this trip, no more boats or twisting things for me."

Oisin's eyes remained bugged as he glanced around the cramped space. "Where's the door?"

Amalardh pushed a rectangular cutout in the black-walled room. The wooden slab held solid. "How do we get in?" he asked.

Forbillian motioned to the same cutout Amalardh had just tried. "Through that door."

"I mean, how do we open it? There's no handle."

Forbillian surveyed the situation. "Hmm. Well, that's an interesting state of affairs. Now, before you go and get all annoyed, I was the last one down. By the time I got here, the door was already open." He tapped the side of his finger to his mouth. "I remember something about an Eternal Lock. Anyone with enough knowledge can open the stairwell door, but only a Croilar Tier can get into the archives." His eyes went wide. "And blood. I remember blood. Culloden—your dad—cut himself. I remember our father chiding him for being too overzealous."

"Your knife," said Oisin to Amalardh. "It's sharp and only a Croilar Tier has one."

Amalardh pulled his six-inch blade from its hilt. Even after all he had gone through—slaying the Senators and winning the Battle for Freedom against the Soldiers of Vitus—he didn't feel a worthy owner. He held the lantern close to the door, lighting the area. A hole sat where one would expect to find a knob. Holding the knife horizontally, he attempted to slot the top of the wolf head handle into the opening, as if it were a key, but it didn't fit.

Forbillian pointed to the ornate mask on the handle's wolf sculpture. "What's that?"

Amalardh snapped the mask off and handed it to him. "All the Croilar Tier knives once had one," he said.

"What's crazy is that it used to belong to Cecilia," said Oisin. "At the time of the Great War, one of her ancestors found it lying on the ground. See how it looks like a tree? He saw it as a sign to move as far away from the city as possible. That's how Cecilia and her people wound up in the Plockton Forest."

Forbillian studied the artifact, then handed it back. "Well, it wasn't on the knife when your father had it. Maybe try again without it."

Amalardh pressed the handle end of his knife to the keyhole and it slid in perfectly.

"To open a lock, the key must be turned," said Forbillian. "I must say, using a sharp blade as a type of handle is a strange and dangerous way to open a door. Based on the intricacy needed to access this stairwell, I would've expected something a little cleverer." He offered Amalardh a tattered piece of cloth. "Wrap it with this so you don't cut your hand like your father did."

"Hey, wait," said Oisin. "What are they?"

Amalardh shone the lantern to where Oisin pointed. Four black metal rods, as thin as matchsticks and about half an inch long, poked out to the side of the keyhole. They must have popped up when he put the handle in the hole. He removed his knife. Sure enough, the rods retracted. He pushed the knife back in; the rods reappeared.

"Could they have something to do with the mask?" asked Oisin. "Whatever attaches to those rods looks like it would be about the same size."

On the underside of the tree mask were four small indentations. Amalardh pushed the mask onto the rods and the indentations snapped perfectly into the holes, creating a miniature, two-inch wide handle. Amalardh turned the pendant-knob, and the knife rotated. The sound of a lock releasing reverberated through the anteroom.

"Clever enough for you?" Amalardh asked.

Forbillian's lower lip poked out as he nodded.

The hinges creaked as Amalardh pushed the door open. Stale

air with a musty, woody aroma wafted out. The lantern lit up a stone room about fourteen feet wide and twenty feet long, supported by three ornate, central pillars. Down the left and right walls stood similar pillars, only semicircular. Three round pedestal tables made of stone provided adequate reading space, and colorful, woven mats covered a half-dozen wooden stools. Scrolls and ancient-looking books packed floor-to-ceiling shelves.

"So," said Amalardh. "Where do we start?"

Forbillian rubbed his chin. "Oisin, dear boy. How about you run to the boat and fix us a bite to eat? We might be here a tick or two."

CHAPTER
15

WYNDOM FLOPPED ON a rock and buried his face in his hands. How could he have failed as spectacularly as he had? Rudella had stolen his place as the Maddowshin, and Saffron—his only child and heir to the Terefellian throne—had sided with the enemy. When Saffron had run away almost two months ago with her mother, Wyndom had put no effort into finding her because he worried that once he did, his fragile ego and misplaced sense of pride would call for her death. Although he may be a poor excuse for a father, Wyndom did care for his one and only child. Sure, his face had soured when he discovered his heir was a girl. And yes, he'd barely spoke to her during her childhood. What adult can deal with a needy, yappy little kid?

In the past year, though, Saffron had come into her own. She handled herself the same as, if not better than, most of the boys her age, and she didn't take crap from anyone, least of all her father. On the night she fled with Esme, Saffron told Wyndom, "Tomorrow is my mother's Rite of Quinquagenary. If our queen hasn't arrived by then and ended this ridiculous ceremony, then expect to wake up without a daughter or your vessel for another heir, because that's all my mother ever was to you: a fertile belly for your sad little seed. If you try to stop me, I will kill you."

Wyndom's few talents included the ability to read people. He deciphered a lie the second the deceiver spoke, and he analyzed the truth even sooner. Saffron's words flowed with bitter sincerity. His fear of her truth motivated the real reason he didn't seek her out. He worried that if he found her, she would find a way to live up to her threat and kill him.

He glanced at the temple and quivered. Beyond his fear of his daughter, the queen's arrival had exposed a deeper terror—his current purpose. With Rudella as the Maddowshin, what use did Wyndom serve? Until he figured out exactly where he fit amongst the hierarchy, he needed to act more than ever like the powerful, authoritative, decisive leader he struggled to be. "We must send more warriors to apprehend the Treoir Solas," he said to the Maddowshin.

"And what of your daughter and the girl's mother?" asked the grand beast.

A ball formed in Wyndom's throat. "Kill them."

He stood by the Maddowshin's side and watched as a dozen Wirador Wosrah raced off into the Terefellian Valley. Soon, his own flesh and blood would most probably be dead.

"Why did you just order your daughter's death when you don't want her to die?" the Maddowshin asked.

"How do you know what I want?" Wyndom had not specifically said as much to himself, so the Maddowshin couldn't have read his mind.

"The thought you just had about your own flesh and blood dying made you sad," said the Maddowshin.

The Maddowshin had felt that? Wyndom stood tall to project an air of detachment. "In order to make crucial decisions, a leader must put their emotions aside. This is something you wouldn't understand."

The Maddowshin's eyes bore into him as it inched forward. "I understand more than you know. As for your ability to put your emotions aside, we shall see."

Wyndom cradles his arms around his chest. What did that mean?

CHAPTER
16

CECILIA, SAFFRON, AND Eideard dashed down the watch tower stairs.

"What happened? What's going on?" asked Rabbie.

"They've sent more beasts," said Cecilia.

"This way," Saffron said.

Cecilia and her brothers followed Saffron and Esme on an exhausting sprint through the woods. Esme seemed just as nimble as her daughter as they leaped over logs and ducked under low branches.

"Why are we running?" said Eideard. "Those things are still many miles away."

Saffron stopped at a stream where the sweaty group took a moment to catch their breath. Cecilia splashed water on her face and rubbed her cramped chest. Since having Alistair, she'd performed little in the way of exercise, and from her heaving lungs, it showed.

"You thought the Wirador Wosrah were going fast when they had your sister," Saffron said. "Trust me, they were barely going a quarter of their speed. If the Terefellian queen wants to, she can feed them more energy, make their legs move so fast it's like they're flying. Right now, they might seem many miles away, but before we know it, they will be upon us. We have to keep going."

Cecilia puffed her cheeks and pushed herself to her feet. Her lungs had finally caught up with providing enough oxygen to her muscles, when she burst from the woods into a clearing and the end of the trail. Ahead lay a ravine. To the far right, the Epona Ocean sparkled under the sun's rays.

Behind, birds burst from the green canopy. The Wirador Wosrah had found their trail and were closing in. Saffron flashed Eideard a see-what-I-mean look. She waved for everyone to follow her along the escarpment to a rickety rope and plank bridge spanning approximately fifty feet across the deep ravine. On the other side stood a salmon-colored building with arched windows and a moss-covered roof. A narrow waterfall raged to the left, feeding a stream below.

"Hold on tight and watch your step," said Saffron.

Esme led the way, followed by Eideard, then Cecilia.

"You next," said Rabbie to Saffron.

"Go," Saffron said. "Make sure your sister gets safely to the other end."

From the way the structure rocked, she must have shoved Rabbie onto the bridge. For such a slight person, Saffron sounded and acted impressively authoritative.

A loud rustling noise made Cecilia look over her shoulder. A dozen hideous beasts burst from the woods into the clearing. They stopped and roared. She stiffened as their guttural cries reverberated through the valley. Her team could not possibly fight off that many attackers.

"Keep going," Rabbie told her. He then turned and negotiated the broken planks back to Saffron, who held her bow at the ready.

"Rabbie!" Cecilia said. But of course, he ignored her. Her frustrating brother was too heroic for his own good.

He reached Saffron and nocked an arrow.

Saffron let hers fly. A beast lifted onto its hind legs and shrieked as her sharp shot skewered its weak spot. Rabbie's precision aim to the beast's other eye sent it into a pool of mush.

"Cecilia! Get over here, now!" yelled Eideard, who waited with Esme at the other side.

She took a step.

SNAP! The rotten wood beneath her feet failed. As she fell, she clutched hold of a plank.

The decaying fibers crumbled beneath her grip. "Help!" she yelled.

"I'm coming!" Eideard called.

Her heart pounded. Eideard was all the way at the other side. He'd never make it to her in time. *This can't be it! Siersha. Please. Don't let this be it.*

The plank failed. Her yelp cut short as she dropped. Something rough had grabbed her. Saffron. Rabbie stepped to the other side of the hole and helped haul Cecilia up.

The black herd slid to a stop at the bridge's entrance.

Maybe they would be too fearful to cross.

Wishful thinking. Wirador Wosrah didn't know fear. They seemed, however, to understand caution. The rope creaked as a beast stepped onto the first plank.

"Let's go," said Saffron, and pushed Cecilia and Rabbie forward.

The three of them headed to the other side.

Cecilia's blood chilled at the sound of snapping wood. Rabbie hadn't fallen because she clutched his hand. *Saffron!?*

She spun to see the flailing arms and legs of a plummeting beast. The planks at the start of the bridge had given way. The beast hit the rocks like a paper bag filled with black custard. Slime splattered everywhere. Could a beast survive that? Blobs clustering together, like a magnet attracting iron balls, confirmed that it could. These darn things were near indestructible.

The bridged creaked as another beast stepped on.

"Keep moving—" Saffron's words cut as the planks under her feet gave way.

"Saffron!" Rabbie yelled.

She dangled from a horizontal length of rope strung under the bridge. "I'm fine." Get your sister to the other side.

Another beast edged forward.

The planks under Cecilia and Rabbie's feet splintered.

"Go!" yelled Saffron. "I will not have Cecilia die because of me."

The beast closed in and leaped. Cecilia and Rabbie scuttled back.

The already faulty planks disintegrated as the beast landed, sending it plummeting into the stream below. Its arms thrashed in the flowing waters. Cecilia doubted it would drown, but at least, it seemed, it couldn't swim.

Saffron's grip on the underneath rope remained firm as she steadily made her way to the other side.

"We have to go," Cecilia said. Clutching Rabbie tight, she ran. When she made it to firm ground, she turned to her brothers. "I have a plan. Once all the beasts are on the bridge we'll cut the rope." If they could send the remaining herd into the water, the flowing stream would sweep them out to sea where they'd stay for eternity, or until the tides washed them ashore.

Rabbie's desperate eyes locked on to Saffron as she inched along the rope.

As the rest of the herd traversed the bridge, they seemed to understand the centerline's weakness because they kept their step to the outer edge.

"Hurry Saffron!" Rabbie yelled.

"We have to cut," said Eideard. "They're getting too close. You've seen how far those things can leap."

Agony flashed across Rabbie's face. "No! Please. We have to wait."

"You will do what you need to do," called Saffron from under the bridge.

The beasts drew near.

"We can't wait," said Eideard.

Cecilia faltered. She couldn't bring herself to send Saffron to her death.

Esme gasped and pressed her hands to her mouth.

Rabbie turned white. "Saffron!"

What just happened? Cecilia followed Rabbie's gaze to the

bridge and horror stole her breath. Saffron no longer dangled from underneath. The stubborn girl had let go, no doubt, to take the pressure off. Although rife with heartache, Cecilia didn't have the luxury of freezing up. As Amalardh had taught her, grief held no place during a battle.

She lifted her sword. "Now," she said. Their sharp blades bit through the upper set of anchor ropes. The change in tension buffeted the bridge from side to side. One beast fell. The rest held firm.

"Again!" she yelled. Their blades sliced through the lower tension ropes.

As the bridge fell slack, the beast in front sprung, its powerful legs propelling it to the safety of the landing.

It grabbed Cecilia's forearm.

Eideard swung his sword, severing the creature's extremity at the elbow.

The beast turned to him and roared.

Holding a flat plank, similar to the ones used for the bridge, Esme clobbered the warrior across the snout. The beast punched back, sending her crashing into the building.

The severed arm formed into a ball and sped at Eideard.

Cecilia kicked it into the canyon. "Go back to your maker," she yelled.

Rabbie took the plank from Esme's unconscious grasp and whacked the beast in the chest. It stumbled back and slipped over the precipice, snagging Cecilia's foot with its intact arm.

She yelped and clung to a rock, halting her fall. The weight of the creature dangling from her foot felt as if it would tear her leg from her hip. It probably would've, too, if not for its hooves finding footholds to help bear the burden.

Eideard and Rabbie strained to pull her to safety.

Something tight clamped around her left thigh. The hideous beast had sacrificed its horns to regrow its arm and now used Cecilia as a type of rope to climb.

She startled at a moist, jabbing sound. The weight pawing at her instantly lightened. A chilly wetness soaked through to her skin.

"Sorry I was late," said Saffron. She held an arrow in each hand. Saffron! She was safe!

Eideard and Rabbie hauled Cecilia to flat land and the three of them collapsed onto their backs.

Saffron rushed to her mother, who was awake and rubbing the back of her head, and asked if she was okay. Esme nodded and pressed her lips tight, as if sucking back her emotions. The poor woman seemed to have also thought Saffron had met a tragic end. Although mother and daughter expressed tenderness toward each other, their lack of physical affection stood out.

"I'd thought you'd fallen," Cecilia said.

Saffron helped her mother to her feet. "I jumped for the edge and landed a little further down than expected. In Terefellia, it's not a fall unless you die."

Her torn trousers and scuffed arms very much fit Cecilia's definition of a fall. Saffron was far too humble. Did nothing send ripples of fear down this girl's spine?

A roar came from below. The beast that had splattered onto the rocks on the other side of the stream had reformed. All the others bobbed like chunks of driftwood as the flowing current washed them out to sea.

"Do your people not swim?" Cecilia asked.

"As climbers, we prefer land," said Saffron. "I take it your two friends, the ones you mentioned had been... you know, converted, didn't know either? Because if they had, any warrior hitting water should've remembered the skill."

Under the Senators' rule, swimming was a banned activity. After the Senators' downfall, Noah hadn't expressed any interest to learn. Analise had, but she wouldn't trust anyone to teach her other than Cecilia. With the stress of rebuilding Vitus and raising Alistair, Cecilia hadn't managed to find the time. Her head lowered at the memory. Who was she kidding? Because Analise was such an understanding friend, Cecilia had placed her in a lower priority. She could've freed herself up. How was she supposed to feel now? If she'd been a better friend, Analise would've learned to swim, and the hideous beasts below would paddle to the side of the ravine and climb up. She cuddled her arms to her chest. "Our friends didn't know how to swim either," she uttered.

Saffron nodded at the beast across the way. "Then we don't have to worry about that one crossing the stream and climbing up here. It will eventually climb its way out, but it has a long backtrack in order to cross the river. Even then, it will have to travel a fair way north to bypass another waterway and swing back around to us. For now, we can rest up and grab something to eat."

"Rest up?" said Eideard. "Those things know where we are. There will be a bunch more here in a matter of hours."

"More will come, but not as fast as those last ones," Saffron said. "The queen has five thousand creatures to birth. Every minute she spends offering additional energy to the ones outside her womb is hours lost from building her army. She cannot release herself from that temple until all her warriors are born. If you were giving birth to multiple babies, would you want to prolong your labor? So, unless your goddess has a way to keep us going, I'm heading inside, because I need something to eat." She strode off.

Esme and Rabbie followed.

"Come on," said Cecilia to Eideard. "We need to keep our energy up so we can figure this mess out."

CHAPTER
17

THE HOURS SEARCHING for an unknown inside the Croilar Tier Archives dragged late into the night. Amalardh rubbed his stinging eyes.

"Maybe we should pack it in for the evening," said Forbillian. "For the boy's sake."

"Don't use me as an excuse," said Oisin. "I'll go all night if I have to."

Forbillian yawned. "Fine. Then maybe we should pack it in for mine."

"You must have some idea what we are looking for," said Amalardh.

"Asking me that for the one-millionth-and-one time won't..." Forbillian blinked. "Well, knock me over with a duck feather. Your constant pestering has paid off." He walked to the corner closest to the door and held his hands out as if feeling the room's energy. "I was sitting here." He motioned to the diagonally opposite corner. "Father and Culloden were over there. Culloden was snippy, telling our father, 'Okay, okay, I think after the one-millionth-and-one time, I've got it.'" He tapped his temple. "The one millionth and one jogged the ol' cobwebs." He pressed his finger to his lips. "I believe they were talking about *The Flower Princess and the Wolf* fairytale."

He walked to the corner he had just motioned to, pushed some scrolls aside and beamed. "Aha! Yes! This is it!" He pulled out a brightly colored book, the glossy style of which seemed more appropriate for the newer library above. Amalardh immediately recognized it as an exact duplicate of the story, *The Flower Princess and the Wolf*, given to Cecilia by Danmar, the Citizen resistance leader.

Forbillian placed it on the nearest table. "Father had another book with this one." He turned back to the shelf, pushed some scrolls aside. "Blazing glory! It's still here." He removed an old, smooth-grained, leather-bound book. "Father kept hammering into Culloden the importance of the fairytale and how the story was a retelling of the Prophecy. He said Culloden's job was to keep the fairytale alive so that when the time of the Prophecy came, people would remember and hopefully choose to stand with the Treoir Solas—the fairytale's Flower Princess. That's when Culloden made his gripe about the one-millionth-and-one time."

Amalardh took the leather book from his uncle and ran his fingers over its satiny cover. "What is this?"

"That there is Gaussian Tuetin's diary."

Oisin's eyes widened. "That's the guy who wrote the Prophecy. His name is on the *Exploring the Gaussian Tuetin Cave* book we were looking at."

Amalardh's skin chilled. One of the original eight Gaussian Tuetin followers—the original eight Croilar Tier—included Amalardh's great ancestor. Touching the book that influenced his and Culloden's life evoked a profound connection to the father he had never known. How different their childhoods had been. At twelve years of age, Culloden had learned of his destiny as a Croilar Tier and his role as the Prophecy's protector. At the same age, Amalardh had trained to become an assassin.

He opened the diary's front cover. A sketched portrait of a bearded man possessing a discerning expression stared back at him. The text below read: *Gaussian Tuetin*. On the next page was a picture of an enormous mushroom-shaped cloud swirling high into the sky. Written underneath were the words: *A dark cloud will fill the sky*. A replica of this picture had been painted on the wall of the Temple Cave, as had the next picture of men on horseback torching a village and the text: *For two centuries, the shadow of Eifa will spread*; and the next one of a young woman surrounded by flowers, kneeling before a white entity with the inscription: *Siersha will offer her remaining light to the Treoir Solas (the Light Guide).*

Forbillian sat down on a stool. "The Croilar Tier who painted the cave where you and Cecilia first learned of the Prophecy would've based the artwork on those sketches."

Amalardh turned the pages until he came to a drawing of a walled city—Vitus. Siersha hovered over one side, Eifa over the other, and far below, a bloody battle played out. *The Treoir Solas will lead a battle to end all battles*, read the text.

"The Battle for Freedom," said Oisin.

The next sketch featured a man standing atop a tall building in the walled city's center, wielding his sword at five silhouetted figures. *The Croilar Tier will face Eifa's darkness*. The graphic represented Amalardh killing the five Senators.

The next page matched exactly to the original Prophecy. *In the end, only one side shall prevail.* A line led diagonally up and across to the opposite page, and another led diagonally down. The top line pointed to a sketch of a glorious Freedom Tree surrounded by children, all facing the young woman from the previous sketches. Written below the drawing was *Freedom for all*. The lower line pointed to text: *The end for all.*

Amalardh turned back to the sketch of the man standing atop the walled city. Between these two sketches bristled the remnants of torn-out pages.

"I was right!" said Forbillian. "There is more to Gaussian's Prophecy."

Amalardh slumped. He'd come to the archives to find the missing pieces of the Prophecy, not confirm its incompleteness. The people who had painted the Prophecy in the Temple Cave had probably not included the entire story because they based the artwork on this missing-page version of Gaussian's diary. He flipped back to the Freedom Tree sketch and eyeballed the toddler with the knife around its waist. "I don't suppose you brought that magnifying glass you're always playing with?" he asked Oisin.

The kid's palm opened, revealing the tool. "Like I said, I didn't think to bring a weapon because I figured we'd just be looking at books."

Gaussian's drawing was extremely detailed, all the way down to the tiny version of Amalardh's wolf knife around the toddler's waist, missing its right eye. While he hadn't expected the wolf knife to be any different, he'd hoped to discover that those who had translated the sketches to the Temple Cave had interpreted the Freedom Tree's location incorrectly. But even in a sketch format, the Freedom Tree clearly stood on a headland backdropped by an ocean, and not within a forest.

He placed his elbows on the table and pressed his face into his hands. Although the Freedom Tree location still didn't make sense, he'd seen enough to know for certain that sometime within the next few months, he would die.

"I know what you're thinking," said Oisin, "and it's not true. You're not going to die. I won't let you."

Amalardh tapped the drawing. "The child in this picture is Alistair, and he's wearing my knife. There's only one reason why that would be so. You know it, Forbillian knows it, and so does Cecilia." His uncle's head dropped, confirming his agreement with Amalardh's interpretation of the imagery. "And you can forget the notion that the reason the child in the painting is wearing my knife is because on that particular day, for some inexplicable reason, I'm going to let Alistair wear it. Forbillian has made clear, a Croilar Tier is never to be without their knife. You know me well enough to know I'm going to respect that directive."

"But that picture has an ocean," said Oisin. "In six months, Alistair will be that infant's age and the Freedom Tree on the southern headland will still be nothing but a twig. How do you explain that?"

Amalardh couldn't. "You can hope all you want for a different outcome," he said. "We can't change what was meant to be."

Oisin frowned and scuffed his boot to the ground. "Cecilia always says, 'What was meant to be will be if we let it.' You don't want to change what was meant to be, because for you, dying is easier than trying to fix the mess you made with Cecilia. And Alistair. And... everyone." He bolted from the room.

Amalardh rubbed his aching forehead. Even if he wanted to change what was meant to be, he did not possess the power. The Prophecy determined the outcome.

"Don't beat yourself up," said Forbillian. "Whatever needs to happen between this moment of us sitting here right now, and this moment here"—he pointed to the sketch of the woman and children under the Freedom Tree—"is anyone's guess. All we can be certain of is that there will be another battle, which means there's still the possibility of this." He dragged his finger down to the phrase, *The end for all.* "You're worried about if this darn tree is in a forest or on a coastal bluff, and what does any of it matter if none of us are alive to sit under the damn thing?"

Forbillian was right. The one outcome the Prophecy couldn't determine was the final one. Siersha would either win or lose; the world would either survive or fail. Amalardh couldn't waste time worrying about his own fate when a grander problem was at hand—how was he going to stop Eifa?

He picked up the diary. The next page had a sketch of the wolf head wearing Cecilia's pendant mask. The Temple Cave had a porcelain sculpture of this image with the same text as written in Gaussian's diary: *The Croilar Tier protects the Treoir Solas. The Treoir Solas is the Croilar Tier's savior. Together, they form the Ceannaire Fis (Visionary Leader).* Amalardh scoffed to himself. Some protector he'd been. The only person he'd been protecting lately was himself. Not wanting the reminder of his own failure, he flipped the page and furrowed at script written in an unfamiliar language. He showed the writing to his uncle. "What do you make of this?"

Forbillian scratched the back of his ear. "Can't say I've seen anything like it."

The foreign scripting covered the next couple of pages. The rest of the diary was blank except for a loose, folded piece of paper tucked in the back. Amalardh opened it. The neat handwriting matched Gaussian's.

"What is it?" Forbillian asked.

"A letter from the Prophet." He began reading it to himself.

"Don't leave me hanging," said Forbillian. "What does it say?"

Amalardh went back to the beginning and read it out loud. "If you are reading this, then you will do so for one of two reasons: pure curiosity after an accidental stumbling or your search for that which we most seek... the truth. Of course, I am pretty certain I know you are reading this because of the latter. I say pretty certain because predictions are fallible. We cannot account for the true nature of the human spirit. I must acknowledge the fractional possibility that something is awry, and you, my dear reader, have come across this note accidentally. If such is the case, I urge with all politeness that you return said letter and diary back to its rightful place, for if the eyes which this is meant for do not come upon this, well, my writings would be in vain, and you, dear reader, will have sidelined humanity's one chance at survival."

"This Gaussian fellow does like to prattle," said Forbillian. "Can't he just get to the point? I mean, geez, was all that blabber really necessary? Surely, he can just write what he needs us to do. Why all this filler stuff? Some people just don't know when too much is too much."

"Yes. Excessive chatter, either verbal or written, is tiresome," said Amalardh.

Forbillian feigned indignation. "Well. At least I don't break the spirit of a young kid who idolizes me."

Amalardh kept his tone flat. "Show me a child who idolizes you, and I'll show you more than a broken spirit. I'll show you someone with a broken mind."

Forbillian grinned. "Get on with the damn letter. If it provides some answers on how to save humanity, well... I want to make sure the end for all doesn't happen, so that I'll get to spend as much time with my nephew before whatever is going to happen to him happens." He cleared his throat as if to suppress his emotions.

Amalardh's chest cramped. How was he supposed to respond to such vulnerability? He wasn't worthy of his uncle's care. Rather than confront his own brewing feelings, he did what he did best. He ignored them and continued reading Gaussian's note. "Now, back to you, my latter reader. You are reviewing this note because you want to know what was in the missing pages, why they were removed, and by whom. I know the answer to all three questions. Since the shortest answer is to your third question, I will confess that it was I who removed the pages. As for why and what was on them, you will soon learn. You still have a choice. Return home and let what will be, be. Or search for the truth and let what is, be revealed. Yours in Full Authenticity, Gaussian Tuetin."

"What will be, will be, if we let it be so," Amalardh uttered to himself. Cecilia had the right perspective. And so did Oisin. If Amalardh went back to Vitus and did nothing, then everything he thought would happen probably would. This letter put forth the possibility of a different truth. One that "is," not the one that "was meant to be." In other words, maybe Amalardh could change what was meant to be.

"I take it we are not going back to Vitus," said Forbillian.

"Your take is correct."

"So, what do we do next?"

"Our great Prophet seems to believe you hold the answer."

Forbillian's forehead crinkled. "Me? Why would you think that?"

Amalardh handed over the note. Forbillian's scanning eyes froze as he came across Amalardh's meaning.

CHAPTER
18

FROM THE ROPE bridge, Cecilia and Eideard followed Saffron, Esme, and Rabbie along a cracked path to the building's royal blue, paint-chipped front door. Tall, thin windows, one of which was boarded up, framed either side of the entrance. Cecilia stepped through the door and paused. The building's understated exterior had not prepared her for such internal opulence.

"Have you ever seen anything so magnificent?" Esme asked.

Cecilia had. The gold-leafed walls and ceiling, marble pillars, and red satin-like carpet reminded her of the Tower's grand lobby. Because the former leaders of Vitus had tainted such grandeur with their greed, Cecilia's interest in the indulgent interior remained flat.

Saffron explained that she and her mother had found the building after fleeing their people. They had strung a thin line from the rope bridge to the building's interior and attached it to a bell found on the front desk. The moment anyone stepped onto the bridge, the movement set off the alarm. So far, the bell had rung twice, false alarms due to wind and a wild boar. The boar alarm had happened just yesterday, and Rabbie and Eideard hungrily scoffed down the plentiful meat that Esme had salted and smoked.

Cecilia paced the broad room. She probably should eat, too, but her tumultuous stomach wouldn't let her. They couldn't stay here forever. What were they going to do next?

Several long, plush, red benches adorned the center of the grand space. Bedding covered two. After living in a cave most of their lives, the runaway Terefellians must have felt this place was like stepping inside a dream. A teddy bear sat on one of the slumber benches. Saffron's, no doubt. Cecilia sat down and cuddled the plush toy. Her chest heaved as images of Alistair assaulted her mind. Was he okay? And Amalardh. She had foolishly organized passage for the other two Terefellians—Brother Skylark and Sister Darna—to Amalardh's location. She buried her face in the bear's soft fur. What had she done?

She tried to stay strong, but the image of Eifa's growing black army suffocated her thoughts. Two years ago, the idea of preparing for battle, while terrifying, had also thrilled her. Now? Hope slipped away. Vitus stood no chance against Eifa's Wirador Wosrah. Never in her wildest dreams had she imagined that going underground—hiding—would be the right thing to do. She had despised the Ground People for doing so. In this moment, she understood their fear. Wasn't it better to live than die?

Light shining through the narrow window by the entrance door hit a tall, shapely lamp and cast a shadow on the wall. If the teddy bear had been alive, Cecilia's clenched hand around its soft belly would've ensured its death. The shadow resembled Eifa. She marched to the lamp and with a sharp thrust of her foot, sent the thing tumbling. The noise echoed painfully in the vast room. Stopping mid-bite, her brothers glared at her, as did Esme and Saffron.

A rolling pin sat on a bench. From the dusting of flour, Esme probably used the area to knead bread. Cecilia may not know how to defeat Eifa and her army of monsters, but she knew someone who did. She picked up the cylindrical chunk of wood and presented it to Eideard. "Whack me on the side of the head with this," she ordered.

He coughed as he choked on his food. "Are you crazy? Why would I do that?"

"Because I asked you to. Now do it."

"There's no way I'm hitting you."

She thrust the pin at Rabbie. "If you trust me, and you love me, you will do what I ask."

Rabbie held his hands up at the offering. "I... I'm sorry. I can't. I can't hurt you."

Saffron snatched the rolling pin and swung.

A painful jolt rocketed through Cecilia's skull. Blinding light filled her vision.

She blinked several times. The bright light remained. She pressed her hand to the side of her head and noticed no lump. No pain. Darn it. Saffron mustn't have hit her hard enough.

"Let's try again. This time—"

Her breath caught. She was no longer standing, but on her back. She wiggled her fingers. Springy grass had replaced the ornate room's satiny carpet. She pushed herself into a sitting position and looked around. The bluer than blue sky and greener than green grass matched those of the Pass-Over Zone. She smiled. Her plan had worked. She had visited this place once before, only that time, her arrival had been unintentional. During her village's raid, Vitus's army leader had chased Cecilia through her forest to a precipice where she used broad vines dangling over the edge to escape. But the callous Soldier had cut her lifeline, sending her plummeting to what would've been her death, if not for a slight ledge breaking her fall.

"I have been awaiting your arrival," whispered a voice.

The bright light dulled. The same glorious, angelic creature clothed in woven ribbon Cecilia had spoken to while lying unconscious on the rocky outcropping stood before her—Siersha. The Goddess of Light. Souls reached the Pass-Over Zone by either dying or, as in Cecilia's current case, getting whacked across the head with a rolling pin to induce unconsciousness.

Cecilia stood. As with her previous visit, a calming warmth washed over her. She could happily spend the rest of her life here. "I need your help," she said. "How is it possible that Eifa is amongst the living?"

"How is it possible that I am in you?" the Goddess replied. "In the realm of gods, possibility is limitless. But there are rules, all of which are governed by the Law of Equity. For every action, there is a reaction. I broke a rule by swimming in the Forbidden Pool. As a result, the Great Father brought forth my dark shadow— Eifa. As her strength grew, my light weakened. To prevent my death, I poured my light into you. The act caused a transitory fracture between our worlds, allowing Eifa a taste of humanity's domain. And she liked what she felt."

"Do you mean the time she appeared before the Senators?"

"Yes."

"Why was she unable to stay back then, but now she is here building her army?"

"As I said, the Law of Equity governs all. For every one of my breaches, Eifa gains one of her own. My actions result in her reactions."

"What rule did you break that allowed Eifa to cross realms for more than just a few seconds?"

Siersha's glow dulled. "Amalardh."

Cecilia's pulse slowed. She knew exactly what the Goddess meant. After the Battle for Freedom, Amalardh had lain dying in Cecilia's arms. Siersha had saved him. The Goddess may have had the power to restore his life, but not the right to do so. "I forced you to spare Amalardh by threatening to kill myself. Eifa's arrival is all my fault." Feeling weak, she lowered herself onto a nearby rock.

Siersha sat next to her and placed her hand on Cecilia's forearm. A warm wave washed over Cecilia, erasing her anxiety. "This is no place for despair," said the Goddess. "You are not to blame. A god cannot be forced to do anything they don't want to do. You were never going to kill yourself. I did what had to be done."

Cecilia glared at the Goddess. Siersha had deliberately caused a tear between the worlds for Eifa to slip through? Why would she do that? As much as Cecilia loved Amalardh, the value of his life did not equate to the loss of thousands once Eifa's black army marched on Vitus. The Goddess had made the wrong choice in placing one life ahead of many. Cecilia wanted to yank her arm away from Siersha's touch, but the warmth flowing through her prevented the anger needed to perform the act.

"You must not bring such feelings into this world," Siersha said. She removed her hand from Cecilia's forearm. "I don't say this in negativity toward you. I say this to protect myself. I do not know anger or sadness or fear or revenge. Only Eifa knows these feelings—and humans. If you expose me to your anger, you expose me to her. You must go, but before you do, remember, in the end, only one side shall prevail. I hope for humanity's sake, my light triumphs. But such is out of my hands and in yours. When this is over, you will understand that in order to defeat Eifa, I had to save Amalardh. Continue toward the rising sun. The Final Battle will be fought. My wish is to be there, by your side."

Cecilia buried her brow in the crook of her elbow to protect against a blinding light.

Darkness fell. With it came a pained throb on the side of her head. She gingerly touched the area and found a tender lump. *Ouch.* She opened her eyes. Rabbie, Eideard, Saffron, and Esme's worried faces peered down at her. The feel of soft carpet under her fingers confirmed she lay on her back inside the waterfall building.

She sat up and pressed her hand to her throbbing head. "The next time I ask you to bash me over the head, please, don't listen to me."

Eideard glowered at Saffron. "I told you."

"I'm joking," Cecilia said. She lifted her hand. "Help me up."

Eideard's stern expression remained as he pulled her to her feet and guided her to a red couch. "What in the blazes were you thinking?"

"That if you knocked me out, I could visit Siersha in the Pass-Over Zone and get some answers."

"Well, that was stupid."

"Says you." She regarded Saffron. "Thank you for being better than these two and trusting that I knew what I was doing."

"Any time," Saffron said.

"Just because a woman says something crazy doesn't make her so," Cecilia said to her brothers.

Eideard shook his head. "Only in your world do we have to feel bad for not whacking our little sister into the next century."

"What did Siersha say?" Rabbie asked. "Does she know how to defeat Eifa's army?"

Cecilia kept the part about Siersha deliberately creating a void for Eifa to enter the human realm to herself. Even though she held annoyance for the Goddess's reckless act, she still trusted her. Others may not, and she didn't want to plant any seeds of doubt. "She said to continue toward the rising sun."

Rabbie frowned. "How are we supposed to do that? Directly east is the Epona Ocean."

The group sat in silence.

"There's only one solution," said Eideard. "We head back to Vitus, then sail to this very spot so that when we travel east, we'll hit the correct location on the eastern coastline."

Cecilia supposed he was right. While the journey to Vitus and back would waste more time than she liked, it would give her the opportunity to warn her people about Eifa and her black army. The council could decide if they wanted to stay and fight or run and hide. She wouldn't fault those who chose the latter. "Without horses, the journey to Vitus will take weeks," she said. "The beasts are certain to catch us along the way. Then what?"

"I agree," said Rabbie. "But we don't have any other choice."

"What if you did?" said Saffron.

Cecilia perked. "Do you have a boat?"

"I wouldn't exactly call it a boat. Maybe a ship."

"A ship?" said Eideard. "How big is this thing?"

"Well, it's really more a ship in the sense that a camel is also known as a ship of the desert."

Eideard huffed and rolled his eyes. "If you're not going to be serious, then you'd best leave the planning to the adults."

"I am being serious. It's just... I don't really know how to explain it. It's easier if you see for yourself."

What could be so difficult to explain about a boat? Then again, Saffron did say her people didn't like water. Did she even know what a ship looked like? She was probably having a hard time describing what she'd found because she didn't know the difference between a canoe and a trawler. Cecilia pushed herself to her feet. "Okay, then. Let's go see this ship of yours."

Saffron led the group out a side door into the bright sunshine. Daisies carpeted the ground like a white sheet covered in sunny polka dots. They walked along an overgrown path and through a wooded area.

"If we make it across the water—" started Eideard.

"When we make it," said Cecilia.

"When we make it across the water, what then?"

"Siersha didn't say."

"Great. So, we just head off without knowing where we're going and without a plan?"

She gave him a look. "At least no one's asking you to do so, alone."

He sucked in his lower lip as though realizing the feebleness of his complaint compared to what Cecilia had done for him and Rabbie. Back when she had embarked on an uncharted journey to save her brothers, she'd had to face the unknown by herself under Siersha's limited directive of, "Walk to the rising sun."

"I'm sorry," he said. "I guess I've never really understood what you'd gone through, until now."

She hooked her arm around his waist. "It's okay. I'm just thankful that this time, you and Rabbie are with me."

They exited the brushy forest and stepped onto a wide field that swept for miles along the coastline. Exposed brown cliff faces along the northern bluffs jutted out over the water. This ship of

Saffron's must be anchored at the cliff base. Hopefully, the climb down wouldn't be too torturous. Cecilia started toward the edge.

"Where are you going?" said Saffron.

"The ship's this way, isn't it?"

"Not this one." She tilted her head toward a red wooden shed about one hundred and fifty feet inland.

Cecilia exchanged confused looks with her brothers. How could a ship possibly fit in that small structure? It seemed only about as wide and long as Cecilia and Amalardh's bedroom. Sure, as bedrooms went, theirs was sizable, but not sizable enough to store a ship. A boat, maybe, but one no larger than a single-sail dinghy.

Saffron stopped outside the shed door. "Here we are," she said.

Eideard hooked his hands to his hips. "Okay. I've had enough fun and games. We're wasting time. We need to go back to Vitus."

Matching her brother's frustration, Cecilia folded her arms across her chest. She was ready to head to Vitus, too. Still, she couldn't leave until she'd satiated her curiosity as to Saffron's ship. "Putting aside that whatever is in there must be way too small to brave the rough ocean waters, aren't we too high to launch a boat?"

"In the traditional sense, probably," said Saffron. "But in this case, I think that's the point."

CHAPTER
19

WYNDOM GASPED AND sat bolt upright. He'd just finished watching Saffron battle the Wirador Wosrah on a rickety rope bridge. Her stabbing out the last warrior's eyes as it used a dangling Treoir Solas to climb up a cliff should've filled him with rage. Instead, pride swelled in his chest. His daughter had the makings of a Wrethun Lof, just like her grandfather. Wrethun Lof, which meant Wolf Hunter, were elite Croilar Tier assassins.

Our queen is displeased, said the Maddowshin in Wyndom's mind. *She finds your incompetence draining.*

Wyndom's throat went dry. Incompetence? What incompetence?

The Maddowshin walked over to him. *Don't feign ignorance to the slack handling of your duties.*

Wyndom wasn't feigning anything. His unsettled surprise was sincere. The Order of Terefellian had two goals: prepare for the coming of the queen, and hunt down and kill the Croilar Tier. "I did my part in preparing for our queen," he said. "I mean, she's here, is she not? As for killing the last Croilar Tier, you and I both know that task was impossible. My father had learned of the Croilar Tier's whereabouts and tried several times to break into Vitus. But the city is a secure fortress. The queen can hardly expect the Croilar Tier to die under my rule when my father had failed. After all, he was the Wrethun Lof, not me."

"I am referring to the mincelase," said the Maddowshin.

Wyndom's spine loosened. He knew what the beast hinted at. Because of its rarity and power, Terefellian Law limited the consumption of mincelase tea to Rite of Quinquagenary recipients and Terefellian leaders. The scriptures dictated that on the first of every month, the Terefellian leader was to ingest enough mincelase to place himself in a near-death state where he could talk to Eifa, their queen. As a boy, Wyndom observed his father perform his ritualistic duty. His eyes would roll back into his head and he would speak in a gibberish Wyndom didn't understand. Upon waking, his father mostly told Wyndom the same thing. "The time of our queen is drawing near. She will arrive in the months leading up to your Quinquagenary."

One day, Wyndom's father woke from his stupor with fresh news. Their queen had discovered the locale of the eighth Croilar Tier. His name was Culloden, and he lived in Vitus, the Terefellian's Sworn Province. Over the years, Wyndom's father (an elite Wrethun Lof) attempted to enter Vitus, but even his climbing prowess failed to breach the smooth, thirty-foot wall.

When Wyndom became Terefellia's leader, he shirked his responsibility to drink the mincelase. "Why dance along the line of death when I already possessed all the answers?" he said to the Maddowshin. "I knew where the last Croilar Tier was. I figured we could dispatch of him when our queen delivered us to the Sworn Province."

He sighed and rubbed his brow. The stupid mincelase. So what if he didn't drink the stuff? What was the big deal? His rubbing hand stopped. "Hang on a minute. If I recall correctly, my dear Rudella, you offered to partake in the communication sessions in my stead." He jumped to his feet and jabbed his finger at the Maddowshin. "If the queen is annoyed at anyone, it should be you."

The Maddowshin's eyes thinned, as though annoyed Wyndom had remembered this detail. "During my sessions, I never heard from the queen. I had assumed she had nothing to say. Since becoming the Maddowshin, I have learned that only the wearer of the Terefellian ring can communicate with her. The mincelase, while a pleasant escape, was otherwise useless."

Damn it. Wyndom had hoped to shift the blame. "I still don't see what the brouhaha is. How would've my drinking the mincelase changed anything?"

"If you'd not shirked your duties, you would've learned of Senator Culloden's death and that his son, Amalardh, had inherited the role of the Treoir Solas's protector. You would've also learned that during your reign, our queen would appear before the Senators of Vitus and instruct them to send their assassin, Amalardh, on a mission. You would've known the exact date and time he would leave the safety of Vitus and have our Wrethun Lof at the ready to kill him. Our hunters could've then traveled west, found the Treoir Solas, and brought her back to Terefellia. You would've recognized her pendant as the Tree of Life and started the Brisqueneth Ceremony. Cecilia represented the pure soul meant for the queen's sacrifice. Luckily, the two other young offerings still worked. But no one knew any of this because you took the path of least resistance. Your ineptitude delayed our queen's arrival by close to two years. And now, the Treoir Solas continues to evade our Wirador Wosrah."

Wyndom's breath hitched. He was the reason his queen had "cut things a bit close" regarding his impending Rite? He'd almost burned alive because of his own lack of action? Lightheaded, he lowered himself to the ground. If not for Noah and Analise's decision to travel south, the Tree of Life would never have come to Terefellia. The queen would never have arrived, and Wyndom's Rite would've happened. The image of his people sucking on his bones pounded his brain. He cuddled his knees to his chest. His queen was right. His incompetence was draining.

His pulse raced as two Wirador Wosrah grabbed him from behind and dragged him backward. "Wait. Stop. What are you doing?" He strained his neck around, confirming his worst fears. The warriors pulled him to their queen's lair. "No! No, you can't do this to me. Rudella! Please," he begged.

This is not my call, rang her voice in his head.

Wyndom fell limp. Finally, his purpose was clear.

He had no purpose.

He passed the last row of Wirador Wosrah, which meant the temple door stood only a few feet away. His breath quickened. He needed to prove his worth to his queen, and fast. But how?

Ymquene. Vorfeer won hafted tennodo mite, came Rudella's voice.

Wyndom furrowed at the Maddowshin. Why had Rudella fed him these words? They sounded familiar, but his Terefellian was rusty. What did they mean?

The Maddowshin repeated the phrase and gave him an encouraging nod.

Wyndom's eyes grew wide. Of course. The Covenant Prayer. "Ymquene. Vorfeer won hafted tennodo mite," he yelled. He stared hopefully at the Maddowshin for the next line. Although he knew how to say this devotion in the common tongue, he would impress his queen and his people if he said it in Terefellian.

Rudella's voice fed him the next line, which he repeated out loud. Liquid fear dripped from his temple as the Wirador Wosrah continued dragging him to his fate. He stretched his arms to the sky and said the prayer again.

Flat-faced, his people turned and stared at him.

At the temple entrance, the warriors spun him around to face their queen. Less than ten feet away, her blackness rippled with grace as the thousands of souls in her slowly transformed into beastly Wirador Wosrah. In a matter of seconds, his soul would become one of those ripples.

Why wasn't the prayer working? Wyndom repeated it one last time, then collapsed into a sobbing heap.

The two warriors pulled him to his feet. This was it. This was Wyndom's end.

Over by the campfire, a lone voice recited the prayer. Wyndom's wet eyes blinked at Brother Stilton. The sinewy lookout lad was on his knees with his arms stretched to the sky. Wyndom's manipulation of the innocent teen had paid off. Brother Stilton remained a loyal servant, indebted to his ruler.

Following Stilton's lead, the other Terefellians dropped to their knees and said the prayer. Glory filled Wyndom. If his queen wished for him to join the ranks of the Wirador Wosrah, he would do so knowing his people still trusted their leader.

The queen's voluminous black mass stilled. The warriors slapped their arms to their sides and stood rock still. Wide-eyed, Wyndom glanced around. Every Wirador Wosrah had followed suit. Even the Maddowshin.

A voice as smooth as liquid gold filled Wyndom's mind. *My children, my chosen ones. Your praise is my glory. Believe in me and no other and everlasting life shall be yours.*

The faces of his people looked radiant. They, too, must have heard the queen's voice.

Wyndom bowed low and spoke the Covenant Prayer in the common tongue. "My Queen. Forever now and until the end of time. I give you my heart, my soul, my life. I am yours for the eternal days."

The mass rippled as if with joy.

"Be well, my Queen," said Wyndom. "You have much work to do." He side-eyed the two warriors who had dragged him to the temple. Their lack of movement convinced him that his queen had withdrawn her order to dispatch him. His prayer had worked. Wyndom had forged his true purpose, his true worth. The jealousy, anger, and betrayal Rudella had ignited for taking his place as the Maddowshin evaporated. Becoming the Shadow Mind, however grand and strong, had never been Wyndom's destiny. He was who life dictated him to be—Terefellia's spiritual guide.

For thirty years, he wore the title of leader without fully understanding his duty. He had believed a true ruler should be capable of rising to the level of a Wrethun Lof, just as his father and grandfather had. Because he couldn't fulfill this responsibility, he shirked the others. Wyndom should have been drinking the mincelase tea to communicate with his queen. He should have used his hunters to pursue the last Croilar Tier. He should have prevented his daughter from leaving the second she had revealed her plan. And in the days since his queen's arrival, he shouldn't have let his anger with Rudella for upstaging him, prevent him from praying. Just as plants need water, and flowers need sunlight, Eifa needed praise and adoration from her people if she were to maintain her strength. He hopped onto his prayer rock, a three-foot high, ten-foot-long stone platform, and turned his hands palms up.

"My fellow Terefellians! Come, let us gather our love."

His brood immediately huddled at the base of the rock.

He thrusted his arms into the air. "My people, can you hear me?"

"We hear you," the Terefellians called back.

He pressed his hands to his chest. "My people, do you feel me?"

"We feel you!" they bellowed.

He strutted up and down his platform, spouting his sermon. The more energy Wyndom gave his people, the more they threw back at him, the more his elation grew. He spoke of their queen's love for her chosen people and denounced Siersha and her impossible ideals.

"Before the time of the Great War," he said, "the preachers who spoke of this false god were the true evil. Through one cheek they condemned greed, lust, and power, called these qualities Eifa's evil. Through the other, they built massive worshipping centers and became some of the most greedy, most lustful, and most power-hungry individuals ever to walk the earth. No wonder the world crumbled and fell to the Great War. It is the teaching of the insane to hold humanity up to a purist ideal. No wonder the people revolted, constantly hating themselves for their own natural thoughts and inclinations. Believers of Eifa are free to be who they wish to be. Free to love who they desire to love. Free to act how they wish, with the understanding that the will of the masses will ultimately dictate what is socially acceptable. Terefellians are free to take another's life, free to commit any injury to another, so long as you all understand that your actions are subject to all others responding in kind."

He turned to the temple, dropped to his knees, and bowed low. "My Queen, we are forever yours."

His people duplicated his action and words.

Wisps of black smoke slithered out the temple's open door and weaved over to the praying group. In unison, everyone kneeled tall and lifted their arms to the sky. "Eifa, we are ready to receive you. We say to you, we are yours!"

The smoke strands burst forth. Wyndom jolted as the willowy vapor impaled his chest. A euphoric rush shot from his fingertips to his toes, giving him a high unlike all others. He pressed his hands to his beating chest, flung back his head, and hollered. He preached not for the benefit of Eifa, but for himself. Although his people offered their worship to the queen, they did so through him, allowing him the fanciful belief that he was the true recipient of the praise.

With a spring in his step, he jumped down from the rock and felt a tug on his tunic. He turned to see a boy of about six whose name escaped him. Wyndom cared not for learning a child's name. Why bother when he rarely needed to converse with them?

"Brother Wyndom," said the boy.

"Yes, Brother Little One," he replied.

"How can our queen be both our queen and our god?"

Wyndom grinned. All too often, children asked inane or utterly nonsensical questions. This one, though, he appreciated. Mainly because his answer did not require a complete fabrication or the bending of his rubbery truth. He pointed to the sky. "When our queen is up there in her realm, she is our god. When she is down here, with us, she is our queen."

The little boy bowed. "Praise to you, Brother Wyndom. You are good and you are great."

"Indeed, I am," Wyndom uttered to himself as the tiny Terefellian dashed off. He wandered over to the Maddowshin. "I guess I should thank you." He scuffed the dusty ground with his leather slipper. "Why did you save my life?"

The Maddowshin's—Rudella's—glassy eyes were hard to read. "Your life is more important to the outcome of all of this than the queen realizes. My job is to protect her from her own passions. As much as I may welcome your death, I am not at liberty to allow it to happen—just yet."

As the cryptic beast strode off, Wyndom's euphoria flattened. His life was important to the outcome of all of this? What did that mean? He kicked a stone and in the process, stubbed his toe. Pain and frustration brewed as he limped back to his resting mat. He hated being on the receiving end of mind games. What did Rudella know that Wyndom didn't?

CHAPTER
20

FORBILLIAN LOOKED UP from Gaussian Tuetin's letter. "This can't be possible," he said. "This man, this Prophet, lived hundreds of years ago. How could he know who I am?"

"How could he know Cecilia would save my life as I dangled above a bed of death spikes?" said Amalardh. "How could he know we would find the Ground People, that they would initially refuse to fight but then ultimately come to our aid? How could he know anything about all that has happened? He was a Prophet. For whatever reason, he saw the future."

Oisin slunk back into the archives and over to the table. He'd run out because Amalardh had refused to fight for his own destiny. The kid cared more for the damaged assassin than Amalardh did for himself. Part of Amalardh's problem was that he accepted too much about his lot in life—like his own death. What will be will be, if one lets it be so. Amalardh had always let his life be so.

"What did I miss?" Oisin asked.

"I've decided not to let what will be, be," said Amalardh.

Oisin's expression brightened. "Really? What do we do? Where do we go?"

Amalardh motioned to Forbillian. "Ask our friend here."

"What is it, Forbs?" asked Oisin. "What does the letter tell us to do?"

Forbillian's pursed mouth affirmed that, yet again, he was completely lost, and had absolutely no idea what Gaussian's words meant.

"Come on, Forbs," Oisin insisted. "What does it say?"

Forbillian cleared his throat. "P.S. To the man known as Forbillian, the map to the truth flies on the wings of a plane."

Oisin's face scrunched. "What the heck does that mean?"

"Exactly," said Forbillian.

The three of them sat in silence.

Amalardh turned the note over. A bunch of strange markings and random, single-digit numbers written at different angles dotted the page. "Do you have any idea what these are?"

Forbillian shook his head. "I venture to say they're just doodles."

"If it says, 'the map to the truth,' then maybe that means we need to find a map," said Oisin. "What if we gather them all up? Looking at them might jog something with Forbs's."

Amalardh nodded to a section crammed floor to ceiling with scrolls. He had searched the paperwork earlier and discovered mostly maps. "Be my guest."

Forbillian and Oisin started rifling through the stack.

Oisin unrolled a scroll. "They're not all maps. This one shows how to open these archives."

"Fat good that does us now," said Forbillian.

Oisin chuckled. "I know, right?"

Forbillian unraveled a brownish-yellow document. "Well, I'll be a monkey's..." He swept the nearest table clear of paper and laid the scroll out flat.

"It's an airplane!" said Oisin. "You did it, Forbs! The map to the truth has to be somewhere on the wings."

Amalardh walked over. The randomness of this find did not align with the specific nature of all the other clues they had found.

"What's with the face?" Forbillian asked. "Does nothing ever excite you, offer a glimmer of hope?"

"I promise to skip with delight the moment you find what you are looking for on that paper," Amalardh replied. He sauntered back to his stool and sat down.

"There's no way Amalardh would've made that promise if he

thought for one second he'd have to skip with delight," whispered Oisin.

Forbillian scoured the schematic. "Yes, well, the man is just too darn smug and deserves a good skipping." He rolled the scroll back up.

"I gather I don't need my dancing shoes," said Amalardh.

"At least we're trying," said Forbillian with a sharp edge.

Amalardh let his uncle's tone slide. The night had been long and everyone was tired. "There's trying and then there is wasting time," he said. He hadn't intended his statement as an insult, but a fact. The answer to Gaussian's clue had to lie somewhere in the scribble on the back of the note, not in a random pile of scrolls.

Forbillian strode over. His face reddened as his fist pounded the table. "Do you think I wanted this? These blasted riddles? Why does this even involve me? I'm not a Croilar Tier."

Amalardh pulled back. What was Forbillian's problem? Amalardh had tried to keep things light with his "dancing shoes" comment. Why was his uncle jumping down his throat? Rather than taking the high ground, and assuming that Forbillian was simply expelling his frustration for not knowing the answer to the clue, Amalardh let his own irritation bubble forward. He'd spent weeks on the road with Cecilia listening to her complain about "not asking for her role as the Treoir Solas." Amalardh never asked to be a Croilar Tier and did anyone ever hear him complain? He pressed his hands on the table and leaned into Forbillian's stare. "You're right. You are not a Croilar Tier. Croilar Tier are protectors. They do not run from the people they love."

Forbillian deflated. "You leave Marion out of this."

"I'm not talking about her. I'm talking about you deserting your brother. My father. May you carry his death on your shoulders. And may it weigh heavy."

Forbillian blinked. His voice lowered. "Trust me, my boy. It weighs heavier than a thousand elephants on my heart." He strode with a low-hung head to the far corner of the room.

SANDRA L ROSTIROLLA

Oisin gave Amalardh a black stare. "Why do you have to be so mean?"

Amalardh dug his nails into his thigh. He hated himself for letting his emotions take over. "I didn't write the rules about the truth hurting," he said.

Oisin's lips pursed. "If we're talking about the truth, then I guess only one of two things is possible. You truly aren't a Croilar Tier, because you're continually running from those you love, or more likely, you are a Croilar Tier, and you don't love anyone."

The look of utter disappointment on Oisin's face stung. Amalardh pressed his lips into a slash. Didn't everyone understand he would give his life for them a thousand times over? What more did they want from him? His fingers rapped wildly on the table. He needed to find an outlet for his brewing turmoil or risk breaking inanimate objects.

A stack of old paper sitting in a crate should help settled his unrest. He tore several sheets into one-inch-wide strips and weaved them into a fibrous cord, malleable enough to bend and stiff enough to hold its shape. Inspired by the very thing that fed his frustration, he began fashioning a plane.

Forbillian rushed over. "That's it! That's it!" He patted Amalardh's shoulder. "One day you're going to realize what an excellent team we make." He plonked himself at the table and slapped Gaussian's note face down. "My annoyance with you aside, you are right. Everything we need has to be in this letter." He nodded at Amalardh's sculpture. "I see you building this thing and it hit me. What was my most favorite thing to build when I was a kid?" He beamed at Amalardh expectantly. When he got no response, he tossed up his arms. "Planes!" He began folding Gaussian's note. "But not fancy ones like yours. My specialty was the simple, good ol' fashioned paper plane." He made a final fold and presented the simplistic model to Amalardh. "The map to the truth flies on the wings of a plane." Down the center of Forbillian's paper replica, where the two wings met, certain symbols lined up to form a vertically written code: "M 11 8 3" and a sym-

162

bol of a human eye. "For what it's worth, I actually think better when I'm willfully aggrieved."

"Well then, if you ever need to think better again, I'm your man." Amalardh was not making light of the situation. He'd been wrong for suggesting Forbillian held blame for the death of Amalardh's father. Akantha—Amalardh's mother—had arranged Senator Culloden's assassination. His statement to Forbillian was the closest he could get to apologizing without opening the gates to a flood of emotions he was not yet ready—or possibly able—to deal with.

Forbillian seemed to understand. "Apology accepted," he said, then turned his attention back to the plane. Between the two of them, they figured out the code represented a location in the archive's filing system. The letter "M" denoted a shelving group made up of several square cubicles. "11, 8" referred to the cubicle eleven rows up and eight across.

Oisin climbed onto a stool and rummaged through the storage hole. "There are some books and a scroll." He peeked inside the rolled document. "It's a map!" He dashed with it back to the table and rolled out the narrow and uncharacteristically long piece of parchment. The map showed the Ezekian Island, and foreign lands east of the Epona Ocean.

"This proportion feels strange," said Forbillian. "Almost like it's about a third the width of most normal maps."

"Read a lot of maps, do we?" asked Amalardh.

"Actually, yes. I've quite the fondness for the geographical art of flattening our peaks and valleys into a melee of lines and swirls."

Amalardh raised an eyebrow. "Melee of lines and swirls?" Forbillian's grand flare for the dramatics outstripped Cecilia's.

"Well, not on this map in particular. This is what you'd call your standard graphical map. If you'd studied some with topography, you'd know what I mean."

"What's topography?" Oisin asked.

"It is where the relative depths of peaks and valleys are shown by a melee of lines and swirls," said Amalardh. He emphasized the word *melee*.

"What's a melee?" asked Oisin.

"A term used to describe confusion, turmoil, or jumble," said Forbillian. He gave Amalardh a smug look as if to show he hadn't just randomly used the word.

Oisin smirked. "I get it. A melee is a little like this trip."

"Indeed," said Forbillian.

Enjoying the banter in his own limited way, Amalardh returned his focus to the map. "You wondered why this involves you?" he said to his uncle without looking up. "Well, consider yourself the navigator of lines and swirls."

Forbillian scoffed. "The Prophet hardly needed me for that. It's not like you can't read one of these things."

"Yes. But I lack your stated enthusiasm in doing so."

"When are you going to admit that map or no map, the Prophet included me and Oisin on this trip because you need us?"

Amalardh glanced up. "So, you're saying I also need this throbbing ache in my head?"

Forbillian chuckled and shook his head. "One day you're going to laugh at one of your own jokes."

"Yeah. Right," said Oisin. "And one day we're all going to sprout wings and fly."

Forbillian laughed. Oisin cracked a smile. The two of them seemed to get a kick out of poking fun at Amalardh. Surprisingly, he no longer minded being on the receiving end of their playful digs. Not that either of them would know. Keeping his amusement to himself, he dropped his focus back to the map. With no "X marks the spot," they still needed to figure out where to go. From the code written on the spine of Forbillian's paper plane, the number three and the human eye symbol remained, neither of which made sense as coordinates.

"What if the eye symbol represents words like: see, look, stare, gaze, peek, glimpse?" said Amalardh.

"It's a thought," said Forbillian. "But as soon as we combine them with the number, they don't make sense. I mean, three sees, three looks, three stares, three peeks, three glimpses?"

Oisin slapped his hand on Forbillian's shoulder. "That's it, Forbs! Three peaks. Look." He pointed to a mountainous marking with three finger-like protrusions located in a northern mountain formation labeled *Esjan Range*.

"Well, shake my rump and call me a bell! Three peaks. Good lad." Forbillian measured out the distance to the destination and released a slow breath. "This hike will take several weeks, if not more."

"We told everyone we'd be back in a fortnight," said Oisin.

Amalardh pointed to a coastal landmark on the eastern side of the Epona Ocean, marked *Katlahn Village*. He estimated the distance to be about a week's sail. "You will drop me off here, then both of you will sail back to Vitus and explain to Cecilia and the others what we found."

Forbillian patted Amalardh's back. "You really do have a sense of humor because that's the funniest thing I've ever heard. Right, Oisin?"

The kid kept a straight face. "Yep. I'm belly laughing out of my butthole."

"We're tethered to you whether you like it or not," said Forbillian. "Now, if we need to use the proper stuff, I'm sure there's plenty of rope back in the boat."

Amalardh had expected as much, but he worried about Cecilia if he disappeared without letting her know why. As a compromise, he wrote a note explaining the extended journey. When *Vitus I* did not return within the expected arrival window, Cecilia would send out a search party. Finn would no doubt lead the charge. He would find the note and carry word back to her. Amalardh missing Alistair's Hinge Celebration would upset her, but she would trust he wouldn't have pressed forward without an important reason.

CHAPTER
21

T̶HE SHED'S HINGES̶ creaked loudly as Rabbie and Eideard swung the oversized, wooden door open. Cecilia stepped inside and frowned at a hodgepodge stockpile of crates, boxes, and cannisters. "I don't understand," she said to Saffron. "Where's the boat?"

"I never said there was a boat."

Cecilia exchanged a look with her brothers, then flung Saffron a ruffled glare.

"I said I have access to a ship. Of sorts."

Eideard folded his arms across his chest. "Fine. Where's this damn ship?"

Saffron motioned to the space. "Here."

Had the girl gone loopy? Nothing in the place remotely resembled a vessel capable of floating on the ocean. Eideard's impatient huff reflected Cecilia's annoyance. She readied herself to ask Saffron if this whole thing was a joke when Eideard beat her to the punch, albeit with a snarkier tone than Cecilia had intended to use.

"There's no joke," said Saffron.

"And there's clearly no ship," snapped Eideard.

Saffron once again motioned to the items in the room. "All this stuff here is that." She pointed to a large sketch pinned to the wall.

Cecilia blinked at an image of a bulbous balloon-type thing, shaped like a sideways teardrop. Attached to the pointy end were a series of fins and a fan-like contraption. A platform hung slightly front of center, atop which sat two metal cylinders and two chairs, like those Cecilia had seen inside the multitude of rusted cars littering the streets of Vitus. *Silverdrop Airship 2.0*, read the picture's label. "What on earth is this?" she asked.

"A ship," said Saffron. "Only, instead of floating on water, it glides through the air. At least, that's what it looks like to me."

Rabbie's eyes poured over the drawing.

"This is ridiculous," said Eideard. "We need to find our horses, get back to Vitus, and board an actual ship. One that floats on water, not this pre-Great War fanciful junk."

"It's not junk," said Saffron.

Eideard motioned to the various dust-covered boxes. "I guess for a cave dweller, this crap looks like something." His unkind tone was out of line.

Rabbie shoved him. "Leave her alone."

Saffron shoved Rabbie. "I can fight my own battles."

"Saffron!" said Esme, mortified.

Rabbie glared at Saffron and rubbed his arm. He'd experienced far worse trauma during the Battle for Freedom, so the act no doubt reflected emotional as opposed to physical pain.

Cecilia jostled between the three of them. "Stop it! Dissention and discord are just what Eifa wants. Now grow up, all of you, and let's figure this out." She turned to Rabbie. If anyone could make sense of how the surrounding pieces of equipment fitted together, he could. When the Ground People came to Vitus, he immediately gravitated to their core group of "thinkers," who had unlocked technology from before the Great War. "Does that sketch and this stuff mean anything to you?"

"Wait," said Esme. "Before you start anything. Saffron, apologize to this young man." She motioned to Rabbie.

Saffron's mouth fell open.

"It's fine," Rabbie said.

Esme's firm look remained on her daughter as she quieted him with her hand.

Saffron's face morphed from surprise to incredulousness. "But that's how I always—"

"Yes. I know. But we are not in Terefellia anymore."

Saffron's cheeks turned red. She hugged her chest and twisted awkwardly to Rabbie. "Sorry," she said.

Rabbie's face turned a similar shade of crimson. Unlike Eideard, he hated being the center of attention. "It's okay. I understand. Really."

A thick silence hung in the air.

"Where's my apology," Eideard uttered.

Cecilia kicked the side of his boot. Not hard. But enough to send a message. Ignoring his frown, she turned to Rabbie. "So, do we have a ship?"

"Uhm. Yeah. Let me figure it out." He muttered quietly to himself as he bounced from the drawing to various objects in the shed: four silver canisters; a large platform with two car seats; a big fan; and a ten-foot-wide spindle housing a roll of soft, silver material, a portion of which was patterned with repetitive squares. He rocked a canister back and forth. Its ease of movement suggested the depletion of whatever it previously contained. The dense noise made by rocking the next three, combined with Rabbie's pleased look, suggested they were full. He unscrewed the lid of a heavy-looking metal contraption that he referred to as a generator, sniffed, and scrunched at the odor.

"It looks like everything is here," he said. He pressed his hand to the silver material's patterned squares. "So long as this stuff works the way I think it does, and there are no holes, then we should be able to build Saffron's ship. There's only one problem. We'll never get it off the ground unless we have fuel for that." He pointed to the generator.

"What kind of fuel?" Saffron asked. Her tone had significantly subdued. While her mom's dressing down was probably partly the reason, the awe on Saffron's face as Rabbie flittered effortlessly around the room exposed an internal shift from unwanted attraction to unexpected respect. Cecilia knew the signs. She'd gone through the same emotions with Amalardh.

"Have you come across any liquid around here that smells like this?" Rabbie presented the generator cap to Saffron's nose.

She took a whiff and curled her upper lip. "Ick. No. I'd certainly remember that stench."

Esme took a small sniff and pulled back. "Oh yes. I know that odor. There's a container with that smell not far from here."

She led the group down an overgrown track to a long, oval-shaped metal tank propped on four-foot-high metal footings. A vine with lilac flowers blanketed the structure, making it almost imperceptible amongst the dense shrubbery and foliage. "I discovered this a few days ago while searching for berries and seeds. The displeasing stench from the spout made me move on."

Rabbie grasped the spout's handle, and after much grunting and cussing, the knob rotated. A pungent, golden liquid poured out, the fumes of which stung Cecilia's eyes. He turned the tap off, told everyone to wait, and darted in the direction of the shed. Minutes later, he returned with a knee-high red cannister and filled it with the liquid.

Under Rabbie's orders, the team laid out the *Silverdrop Airship 2.0's* various bits and pieces on the open field, positioning the wooden platform with the two attached car seats about sixty feet away from the shed. Rabbie put two of the full silver cannisters into their respective slots. He pointed to the wide spindle. "All right," he said. "Let's roll that thing out."

He and Eideard clutched the material's front end and walked the one-hundred-foot-long silken cloth forward, placing it up and over the platform. They then unfolded it outwards, revealing the massive cloth's seventy-foot width.

At the material's narrow tail end, Rabbie secured the propeller unit and plugged its cable into a socket in the centrally positioned, square-patterned section. He then disappeared under the material to attach the platform cables to the underside of the balloon. A few minutes later, he reappeared with a length of cylindrical silver material about twenty feet long and three feet wide, which he referred to as an umbilical cord. Eideard sat the fan inside the mouth of the silver tubing, while Rabbie fired up the generator's engine.

Cecilia pressed her hands to her ears to help drown out the loud noise. "Great!" she yelled. "If the monsters didn't know where we were before, they do now."

Rabbie flicked a switch on the fan, and the flat umbilical cord expanded into a long cylinder. Like the slow blooming of a metallic flower, the silver material grew and took on its teardrop shape. Rabbie's keen eye remained glued to the growing structure as though he'd overseen the building of this machine a thousand times before. If he harbored a hint of concern that maybe he'd put the contraption together incorrectly, he didn't show it.

The filling balloon lifted, exposing the platform. Rabbie jumped up and checked the cabling. Everything seemed to his liking. "Saffron," he called out. "This is your ship; you should do the honors." He waved a box of matches at her.

Saffron seemed too awed by the ever-expanding, massive horizontal teardrop to hear him. Cecilia poked her out of her stupor.

"What?" she asked.

"Rabbie wants you."

Saffron faltered, then walked over to the platform.

Cecilia followed.

Rabbie patted the balloon's silvery surface. "The cold air from the fan is filling this up, but we need hot air to fly." He placed his hand on a canister. "That's where these come in." He handed the matches to Saffron, then gripped a round knob on the canister. "When I turn this dial, you strike the match and put it here." He pointed to a circular spot on the canister's top. "You ready?"

Saffron nodded.

He turned the dial. A strange odor filled Cecilia's nose.

Saffron struck the match.

WOOSH! A flame burst upwards.

Saffron's face beamed. "That was cool."

They repeated the same for the second cannister.

"Good job," said Rabbie. His eyes met with hers.

Saffron's shoulders curled. She handed the matches back and jumped off the platform.

Rabbie maintained his composure. The only sign of his inner turmoil regarding Saffron was his shaking of the matchbox. He caught Cecilia staring. "What?" he asked.

"Nothing," she replied.

His eyes flinched the slightest bit at her. He knew Cecilia well enough to probably deduce that her constant "nothings" were becoming something.

He gave Eideard the "kill-it" gesture. The generator's clamor silenced. He stepped off the platform, rolled up the silver umbilicus and tied it off in such a way that it created its own seal within the structure.

The group stepped back and watched the giant silver balloon take on its final shape.

"There's only seating for two," said Cecilia. "Will it carry five?"

"Don't include me and Mom," said Saffron.

"You're not coming with us?" Rabbie asked. Everything about the way he shoved his hands in his pocket and scuffed the ground with his boot oozed disappointment.

"Eifa wants Cecilia, not me or my mother. Besides, you saw how Mom was with the tower. No offense to your skill, but I could never get her up on that thing. Your job is to protect your sister. Mine is to look after my mom."

Rabbie nodded. He pulled a piece of paper from his pocket, studied it a moment, then looked at the airship.

"What's wrong?" Cecilia asked.

"Saffron is right. Five will be too much weight. As it stands, three will be pushing the limit."

"You're not suggesting that only two of us go?"

"No. Of course not." He tucked the paper away, and although he tried to appease her with a smile, concern lingered in his eye.

Esme, who'd been back at the building preparing food and water for the journey, arrived with a basket full of goodies. Her mouth gaped as she took in the magnificent structure. "Saffron. Your ship really is real."

"It's not my ship," Saffron said. "It's his."

She nodded at Rabbie, who maintained a quiet poise. Had Eideard been the one to build this aircraft, he would've gloated incessantly about his successful feat. But unless Rabbie had just won in a head-to-head against his older brother, he never crowed about his achievements. He motioned to the entire group. "It's our ship," he said.

"Not for long," said Saffron. "If you don't get that thing anchored down, it'll be nobody's ship."

Cecilia gasped at the balloon's lifting platform.

"Oh, shoot!" said Rabbie. As he dashed off, his feet tangled in the fan's electrical cord, sending him flat on his face.

Eideard ran and leaped at the rising plank only to swipe thin air.

Saffron bolted forward. Using Eideard as a pedestal, she sprang from his shoulders, grabbed the upward floating platform, and swung herself up. "What do I do?"

"Turn down the burners," said Rabbie.

In her panic, Saffron turned the first burner off.

"No! Not off! You'll drop like a rock. Ease the second flame down."

Saffron did as instructed. The balloon lowered.

"Throw me the anchor rope," said Rabbie.

She kicked a coil of rope over the edge.

Rabbie and Eideard held it tight.

A gust of wind pounded the balloon's side, sending the huge contraption several feet down the field, dragging Rabbie and Eideard with it.

Another gust tipped the platform, digging its side into the grassy soil.

Saffron slid off the tilted plank.

The corner released. The platform righted itself and floated directly over her.

"Saffron!" yelled Rabbie. He dove to the ground, pulling her out of the way as the platform dropped the final couple of feet.

Terror stole Cecilia's breath. The airship's danger shot far beyond what she had imagined. She rushed to Saffron, who convulsed as if in dire pain. "Are you ok—" Noting laughter, Cecilia cut her concern.

"Wow! That was crazy," said Saffron.

She shared an awkward moment with Rabbie, who still had his arm over her chest.

His cheeks flushed as he recoiled from the embrace. He jumped up and immediately set to work with Eideard to anchor the ship's rope to the ground.

The group shook out their nerves, then started laughing about the insanity that had just happened. Life felt normal, as though Cecilia was back in Plockton reliving one of her brothers' hilarious antics. But she wasn't back in her village and life was far from normal. Esme's panicked scream made certain of that.

"Saffron! Cecilia!" Esme yelled. "They're coming."

Cecilia's blood turned to ice.

Across the open field bolted another dozen of Eifa's black monsters.

CHAPTER
22

FIVE DAYS AFTER Amalardh, Forbillian, and Oisin set sail from the Ezekian Island on their journey to the mountain with the three peaks, they anchored *Vitus I* in the chilly ocean waters several feet from the Epona Ocean's eastern shoreline. Unprepared for the brisk weather, Amalardh rummaged through the boat's wardrobe. The shirts he'd found offered minimal protection from the biting wind that blew down from the snowcapped peaks ahead.

Spray from the icy water numbed his hands as he lowered the small dinghy attached to the boat's stern into the water. Wrapped in a woolen blanket, Oisin shivered as Amalardh and Forbillian took an oar each and rowed to shore. Concern rarely rattled Amalardh, but the weather in these eastern lands did. With daytime temperatures this cold, how would they survive the subzero nights in the glacial peaks? The frosty temperatures didn't seem to bother Forbillian. He looked perfectly content in his bear shawl.

After a half hour hike along a muddy road, they came upon a small, abandoned township. A *Welcome to Katlahn Village* sign confirmed their arrival at the village marked on their map. They made camp inside the only fully intact building—a one-story sandstone structure called *Katlahn Post Office*.

Inside, cartons of envelopes provided the perfect kindling. Amalardh started a blaze in the fireplace and fed it with logs of old, dry wood. He found a thin blanket, wrapped it around Oisin, and sat him by the fire. "Stay here," he said. "I'll search the village for warm gear to help with the hike ahead." Oisin's teeth chattered as he nodded.

"As the melee of lines and swirls purveyor," said Forbillian. "I'll come too. I'd like to get the lay of the land."

Halfway down the compact town's dilapidated main road, Forbillian's gaze cut to the far-off snowcapped peaks. "It's going to be right chilly up there. Anything we find in this town won't cut it." He patted Amalardh's shoulder. "If I'm not back by nightfall, don't worry about sending out a search party."

"Where do you think you're going?"

"I have to go see a man about a goat."

"I'm not letting you walk around out here on your own."

Forbillian beamed. "I'm a mountain man. A place like this is my home. I've got things to do and someone"—he pointed at Amalardh—"needs to go hunting for salt."

"Salt?"

"Yes. And lots of it." He turned and walked off.

While Amalardh didn't like the idea of Forbillian roaming around these foreign lands alone, his exhaustion overrode his desire to stop him. He spent the rest of the afternoon scouring the town's handful of rundown cottages and collected three backpacks and a sizable assortment of salt. He found a few intact blankets, but otherwise, smashed windows and open doors had exposed interiors to the elements, rendering most items too rotten and threadbare to be of use.

The hour was late when Forbillian lumbered through the front door. "You can call off that search party I told you not to send," he said.

"Hey, Forbs, did you find the man with the goat?" asked Oisin.

Forbillian laughed. "As a matter of fact, I did."

"Really? How did you know he'd be here?"

"He's pulling your leg," said Amalardh.

"Oh." Oisin's head tilted. "So, there's no man with a goat?"

Forbillian ruffled his hair. "It's just a figure of speech. Don't trouble yourself about it."

Oisin handed Forbillian one of Amalardh's scouted blankets. "We figure we can make some jackets and pants out of these."

Forbillian motioned to the distant peaks, which glowed a frosty blue under the moonlight. "The wind up there is going to bite right through this stuff." He tossed the blanket aside. "Did you get the salt?" he asked Amalardh.

Amalardh nodded to an array of glass and ceramic containers.

"Very good. The key to staying warm in a freeze is to keep your body heat in and cold air out. Come on, lads. We've got some work to do." He opened the front door. On a makeshift, drag-gable stretcher lay a wolf and a spotted lynx. Forbillian rose his bushy eyebrows at Amalardh and Oisin. "Turns out, the man I went to see was out of goats."

Over the next few days, they dried and smoked the skins and meat. Oisin held a piece of feline jerky between his thumb and forefinger and eyed it dubiously. "I've never eaten cat before."

"As a general rule, I try not to eat anything that has a sharper bite than mine," said Forbillian. "But I'm not about to skin, stretch, dry, and sew together a couple hundred rabbit hides for you both, so kitty cat and big dog it is."

On the final evening of their week-long stay, a gale raged into the morning hours. Amalardh woke to see Forbillian sitting in the same spot as last night, still threading together bits of animal fur. "Did you sleep?" he asked.

Forbillian scoffed. "There'll be plenty of time to sleep when I'm dead." He glanced out the window. "The rain has stopped, but that wind is going to bite. You'd best hope we don't get too many storms like last night on our trip, because I can't guarantee the path I put us on will protect us from being blown off the mountain. What I can guarantee, though, is your warmth." He presented Amalardh with his ready-to-wear wolf cape, complete with grisly head and fluffy tail.

As ridiculous as Forbillian looked in his bear cape, the animal fur seemed to keep him warm and dry. Amalardh slipped the cloak over his shoulders and shimmied out the window.

"Where are you going?" Forbillian asked.

"If I'm going to trust my life to your fur covering, then I need to test it."

"There is such a thing as a door, you know."

Yes. But the window had access to a tree. The storm's power had stoked Amalardh's concern. He needed to check their boat. He grabbed a low-hung branch and scaled the tall pine. Even though the sharp wind stole his breath, he remained warm. The cloak really did work.

The tall tree offered an unobstructed view of the ocean. Amalardh's stomach folded at the sight of *Vitus I* laying half submerged on the rocky shoreline. A few weeks ago, he had lamented being tied down to Cecilia and Alistair. Now, all he wanted was to be with them. How would he ever make it back without a boat?

Forbillian responded to the news with a shrug. "Well, as they say, the only way through life is forward."

"But how will we get home?" asked Oisin.

"The same way we got here."

"Amalardh just told you, the storm sank our boat. We can't get back without it."

"If you think the boat is how we got here, then I guess that's true."

Oisin's face scrunched. "If we didn't get here by boat, how the heck did we get here?"

"With grit, determination, and a sprinkling of luck, and that's exactly how we'll get back."

Oisin groaned and slapped his hands to his head. Amalardh continued packing their bags. The kid should've known better than to leave the door wide open for Forbillian's nonsensical answer.

"Speaking of luck," said Forbillian. "I caught me some skunk and squirrel and fashioned these little beauties for everyone." He handed over a collection of mottled mittens, vests, and boot coverings.

A set of woven paddles hung from the sides of all three backpacks. "What are they?" Oisin asked.

"Snow shoes," said Forbillian.

"Shoes? They look like racquets. All we need is a ball."

"Trust me, when we hit thigh-high snow, the last thing you'll want to do is hit a ball. Powdery snow is a bugger to walk in. Those things will keep you from sinking."

Loaded with food and water, and wrapped in fur, the three travelers stepped out into the biting wind.

Oisin smoothed his mittened hands down the front of his lynx coat. "Wow, Forbs! I barely feel the cold."

Forbillian beamed at Amalardh. "And there you thought your uncle was just some crazed, wild man who wore a bear because he was *just* some crazed wild man."

Amalardh cocked his brow. "Was I wrong?"

Forbillian laughed. "Probably not."

Despite himself, Amalardh grinned.

The wet, spongy ground turned to icy slush as the grasslands gave way to snowy fields. With a smile a mile wide, Oisin stomped from one icy mound to another. He had not seen snow before and by the end of this trip would probably be glad to never see it again. When Amalardh had first seen snow, his awe had matched Oisin's. Over the years, his interest waned. While he appreciated its elegance when masking the rusty and rotten, he considered snow as fake and temporary as his own soul. Left in the heat too long, it would melt, exposing the underlying ugliness.

"Catch a flake and look at it up close," Forbillian said to Oisin.

Oisin held out his mitten and studied the tiny speck that had landed up close. Bright-eyed, he gaped at Forbillian.

"Pretty darn amazing, right? Here's the kicker. With the millions and millions of crystals that fall every day, you'll never find two that are the same."

Oisin spent the next several minutes capturing flake after flake, dumbfounded by their unique appearances.

Amalardh held out his gloved hand. A lone flake floated onto a black section of skunk fur. He had not intended for his breath to catch, but it did. He'd never bothered or even thought to study a flake up close. The symmetry and perfection of the crystal moved him. Amalardh's life had centered on excellence. He had to be the best at everything. If he wasn't, the Soldiers had struck him with a barbed whip. He wasn't used to failure, which was probably why he wanted to run the second his son was born. What if he wasn't a capable dad? What if Alistair grew up like Amalardh had, hating his father? In Amalardh's case, his hate for Culloden had been unjustified. The Senators had sold him a pack of lies. Alistair, however, would have every reason to resent Amalardh.

He balled his fist. When he opened it, the flake was gone. In its wake, a tiny droplet of water. No matter how beautiful or unique or perfect the flake had been, under enough pressure, it exposed itself for what it was: plain, simple, and ordinary. Snowflakes were fallible. And so was Amalardh. He stopped momentarily in his tracks at this alarming truth. Amalardh wasn't special. He was just as common as the next man. Maybe if he could let go of some of his manufactured perfection, he would be a better person.

The air thinned as they snaked their way up the mountainside along a narrow path. Forbillian joked about how instead of having a metaphorical rope binding all three together, an actual one would be better in the event that one of them slipped.

His foot did just that.

"Forbs!" called Oisin. He yelped as his own footing succumbed to the crumbling border.

Amalardh rushed to the edge. A few feet below, Forbillian clung to a rock while Oisin dangled from Forbillian's backpack.

"Don't worry about me," said Forbillian. "Get the boy,"

Amalardh removed a length of rope from his pack and dropped one end down. "Hold tight," he said.

The lightness of Oisin's slight frame made the going smooth.

A massive force jerked the rope, pulling Amalardh forward. His pulse spiked as his heels skidded to the edge. Planting his boot on a rock, he strained back. "What just happened?" he yelled.

"Forbs slipped and grabbed the rope," said Oisin.

A section of rope slipped through Amalardh's gloves.

Oisin yelped.

Amalardh anchored the rope to his belt. There was no letting go at his end. If he slipped, all three of them would plummet to their deaths.

He strained hard, but lacked the power to haul Oisin and Forbillian's combined weight. He needed another way to save them.

He glanced over the edge.

Oisin's frightened eyes bore at him. "I can't hold on!"

"Yes, you can." His attention dropped to Forbillian and his blood chilled. He knew what his uncle's flat expression meant. "Don't you dare! Don't you dare let go!" he yelled.

"Forbs! Please! Don't do it!" cried Oisin. "I'm not going to let go. You can't either. Amalardh will save us."

But could he? The weight dragging on him made his leg muscles quiver. At this rate, Amalardh would kill all three of them. Forbillian's unspoken words held the truth. For Amalardh to save Oisin, Forbillian would have to release his grip. The thought of losing his uncle shredded Amalardh's soul. He scanned for a way to save him.

"Forbillian," he said. "Below and to your left, do you see that rock?"

Forbillian rotated his head. "Aye, I see it."

"When you let go, you better bloody grab it."

The weight pulling on the rope lessened, sending Amalardh backward. He heaved Oisin up and over the edge, then sprung back to the precipice. Relief washed through him at the sight of what looked like a bear clinging to the cliff.

He tossed down the rope. Compared to Oisin, Forbillian felt like an elephant. Sweat dripped from Amalardh's brow as he hauled. Finally, his uncle's furry mitten surfaced. Amalardh hooked Forbillian's belt and heaved him onto the icy path. As Forbillian lay on his back catching his breath, Oisin threw his arms around him.

"Don't leave me, Forbs. Promise you won't ever leave me."

The show of affection stabbed Amalardh's chest. But why should he care? Amalardh had deliberately kept the boy at arm's length. He wound up the rope and shoved it into his pack.

"Thank you," said Forbillian to Amalardh.

"We need to get moving," said Amalardh dryly.

He flung his pack over his shoulder and led the way. The world could put as much pressure on Amalardh as it wanted. No matter what, he would not melt. He would not become as common as the next man because the next man cared far too much.

Caring meant weakness.

And weakness meant pain.

CHAPTER
23

As WYNDOM STROLLED from the toileting pit to his resting mat, words floated into his mind as if he, himself, held the paper upon which they were written:

Finn,

Relax your worries. Our discovery has expanded our journey to the eastern shores of the Epona Ocean. Send apologies to Cecilia and word that we are safe.

Regards,

Amalardh.

Because the Maddowshin fed him the information, Wyndom knew the letter was addressed to the man captaining Brother Skylark and Sister Darna's vessel. With his attention focused on the words, he tripped on a rock and fell over. If the Maddowshin had invaded Wyndom's thoughts a moment earlier, the fall could've been far more disastrous. And stinky. *You can't just drop in whenever you want,* he said in his mind to the Maddowshin. *It's dangerous.*

FLASH. The letter faltered and skipped to the image of Sister Darna from behind as she walked with purpose along an upward-sloping path to a castle with a round spire. Wyndom recognized her only because of her dark hair. With their loose-fitting tunics, all Terefellians had similar silhouettes. If he was seeing Sister Darna, then he must be in Brother Skylark's point of view.

Wait, Wyndom said. *I can hear birds chirping. And smell a bunch of scents that are not familiar.*

That is because beyond visuals, I can send you everything our Wrethun Lof or Wirador Wosrah feel, sense, taste. I am taking you slowly. Building up your tolerance to accepting stimulus that is not yours.

FLASH. The image of Sister Darna faltered and skipped to a sailboat on the far-off horizon. Wyndom's belly swooned as Brother Skylark's vision dropped to the grassy surface below. The man must be standing on the castle's pinnacle.

I am bringing you up to speed with all that has happened in the past couple of weeks, said the Maddowshin. *The boat you just saw is the Croilar Tier's. We had him in sight.*

Had? Wyndom asked.

FLASH. Finn and his men laid out a massive white, silken cloth on a grassy patch of land.

A torn mainsail and damaged mast prevented our Wrethun Lof's boat from leaving the island for a week.

FLASH. The mainsail ballooned, revealing a newly patched section. "I've locked in *Vitus I's* last known heading," said Finn to Brother Skylark.

Our Wrethun Lof were only a day away from the Epona Ocean's eastern shore, when a storm hit, said the Maddowshin.

FLASH. Brother Skylark and Sister Darna crammed below deck with the burley captain and his crew as heavy winds pummeled the vessel. Wyndom dropped to the ground and clutched a grass clump to steady himself from the boat's side-to-side rocking. A foul, acidic taste rose in his throat as the contents of Brother Skylark's stomach projectile vomited into a bucket.

Couldn't you have skipped past this moment? Wyndom said.

I could have, said the Maddowshin. *But until you see what your people go through for you and their queen, how can you truly appreciate them? Even when faced with the ultimate test, they persevere. You can learn a lot from them.*

Me, learn from them? With everything Rudella knew about

Wyndom's fears and his daily struggle, how could she possibly suggest that he didn't know how to persevere?

Your life has been a pathetic shamble of misery, said the Maddowshin. *That, I do not disagree. You may think you have already faced your greatest challenge. I assure you; you have not.*

Did the swirl in Wyndom's stomach come from the lurching boat or the Maddowshin's insistence that daunting days still lay ahead?

FLASH. While the blue, sunny sky and tranquil ocean helped calm Wyndom's nerves, the chilly air made him shiver. On the distant horizon—snowcapped peaks. Immediately ahead—a rocky shoreline and a sailboat called *Vitus I* half-submerged. Panic on Finn's face as he yelled at his crew to check the sinking boat for survivors.

FLASH. Wyndom slapped his hand to his mouth as a four-inch blade attached to Brother Skylark's hand sliced a crew member's throat. Skylark spun around and dispatched the other two. Agony engulfed Finn's face as he rushed to his fallen men. He turned to Brother Skylark. "You traitorous—" His words cut as the blade of Skylark's thrown knife impaled Finn's chest.

The Maddowshin cut the feed and walked over to Wyndom. "You are sending five thousand Wirador Wosrah to massacre a city and you shudder because of four deaths?"

Wyndom cuddled his chilled hands to his chest. "I'm fine," he said. But he truly wasn't. Even though he'd overseen many Rites, watching the life drain from another's eyes left him cold. "What?" he snapped in response to the beast's judgmental stare.

I am not judging, said the beast in Rudella's voice. *A Wrethun Lof is everything you are not. Cold, detached, ruthless. You are attracted to our male Wrethun Lof because of what they represent.*

Wyndom dropped his face into his hands. Even without the Maddowshin's ability to read his mind, Rudella had known of Wyndom's unrequited desire for Terefellia's wolf hunters. The thought of lying with a body as dangerous as theirs curled Wyndom's toes. He imagined the moment like a flower in a giant's grasp. One squeeze too tight and the petals would turn to mush. Only, in Wyndom's fantasy, this giant cared for the flower so much, it would go out of its way to keep the delicate blossom safe. "I'm not bothered by the deaths of non-believers," he said, maintaining his lie. "The killings simply came as a shock. I mean, how are Brother Skylark and Sister Darna supposed to come home?"

"Instead of sitting back and enjoying the ride, like Brother Skylark, Sister Darna learned everything about that ship. She could sail it single-handedly if need be." The Maddowshin's voice lowered. "You will be expected to get your hands dirty by the end of all this. It is good that you have experienced, at arm's length, so to speak, what it is like to kill."

Wyndom's throat closed. He would have to take a life, for real? He relived the moment of Finn's life draining and shuddered. He didn't want to see death take hold ever again. But if he had to, he would. He would do anything for his queen, if such act meant sparing his own life. "I will serve my queen in any way she requests," he said.

The Maddowshin stared at Wyndom, and a hint of what looked like empathy flashed through the part that remained human—Rudella's eyes. *You cannot let your thoughts linger on a lost life. Doing so... will ruin your soul.*

Rudella seemed to speak from experience. Could she be referring to the lives she'd taken—Analise and Noah's? But how could the Maddowshin experience the sensation of a "ruined soul" when it only possessed two states of being: calm and rage? Unless... had Rudella lied? Did she—her soul—continue to experience a broad range of emotions?

The beast's hooded eyes deepened. "You are best served not trying to analyze me. I was only trying to protect your mind from needless guilt. The crew had to go. We couldn't risk them following our Wrethun Lof."

The Maddowshin was worried about the Wrethun Lof being followed? Where exactly could Brother Skylark and Sister Darna possibly go that would warrant such a concern? Because of the torn sail, not only were they a good week behind the Croilar Tier, the storm would've washed away any footprints.

"Maybe this will help settle that thought," said the Maddowshin.

FLASH. Brother Skylark and Sister Darna passed a sign reading *Welcome to Katlahn Village*. Outside a stone building, a wooden frame stood next to a firepit that smelled of fresh ash. Wyndom recognized the setup as a stretching station for drying animal fur. Empty containers with salt residue littered the ground. Brother Skylark squatted by a set of footprints. His vision trailed the markings to a pine forest, beyond which stretched snowcapped peaks.

"Whatever time we lost because of the torn sail, we appear to have gained," said the Maddowshin. "Brother Skylark calculates the Croilar Tier to be less than a day ahead."

Wyndom shivered as a sharp wind whipped through Brother Skylark's thin clothing. "It would have been better if the Croilar Tier had died in the shipwreck. Terefellians are desert folk, not ice dwellers. Our two hunters will never survive this weather."

"You must pray that Amalardh does not die until our Wrethun Lof find him."

"But our queen wishes him dead. What should it matter if the death be by a Wrethun Lof's hand or a drowning at sea?"

"Our queen may wish for his death, but not before she gets from him what she needs."

"One can retrieve a knife from a corpse far easier than from living flesh, especially flesh, if rumors are true, that fights with unfettered abandon." Because of his conversations with Analise and Noah, Wyndom knew of Amalardh's impressive skill.

"The Croilar Tier's knife, while heavily desired by our queen, is of secondary consequence to her. What she desires most of him cannot be obtained from a corpse."

Wyndom stroked his beard. What could the queen possibly want with this man called Amalardh? His eyes widened. Of course. A breathing Croilar Tier would be the perfect bait to lure the Treoir Solas. The young woman had been slippery, especially since receiving Saffron's help. "But how will our Wrethun Lof even survive a night? They are not dressed for such a place."

"I have that under control." The Maddowshin motioned to the main campground. In the center, Terefellians hauled logs and dry branches onto a large firepit.

How could a fire in Terefellia possibly help Wrethun Lof thousands of miles away?

CHAPTER
24

AMALARDH GRABBED HIS knife and sat bolt upright, ready to slay anyone who drew near.

Forbillian stumbled backward. "Hold your horses there, laddie," he said. "I'm just getting some tea on."

Amalardh breathed deep and lay back down. The stone walls and frosty air jogged his memory—he was inside a snow-covered cave with Forbillian and Oisin, not battling an unknown entity. The moonless sky kept secret whether it was very late or very early. Forbillian making tea did not help with the answer. The hour could be three in the morning and Forbillian would find a reason to be "getting some tea on."

"What time is it?" Amalardh asked.

"Close to sunup." Forbillian handed him a steaming mug. "That was some nightmare you were having. Care to talk about it?"

Amalardh's silence dampened his uncle's curiosity. Even if he had wanted to talk about his worsening dreams, which he didn't, he couldn't explain why a dream about fighting another man evoked such terror. Possibly because the assailant wore a hooded robe, similar to his own. And whenever Amalardh tried to swing his sword down on his attacker, his arm would not respond.

Days blended into weeks as Amalardh, Forbillian, and Oisin made the long, cold, slow trek up the snowy mountain range. If not for Forbillian's insistence that they bundle up in fur cloaks,

Amalardh and Oisin would have frozen to death. Because Amalardh had spent minimal time in the alpine regions, he defaulted to Forbillian's knowledge. The gruff mountain man had spent an entire year atop Mount Wilson, the tallest peak of the Berwyn Mountains, which ran along the coastline north of Vitus, separating the Wynn Forest from the Epona Ocean. Mount Wilson was the farthest north Amalardh had traveled. Ten years ago, he had contemplated climbing the formidable elevation.

"Wait," said Forbillian. "You were going to climb Mount Wilson ten years ago?"

"I needed a challenge," Amalardh told him.

They chattered further and discovered that the exact year Amalardh had considered scaling the great height, a rare event occurred in the night sky involving a bright ball of light with a long, glowing tail. Both had since learned this phenomenon was called Kryton's Comet, and it passed by in the night sky about every seventy years.

"Blimey," said Forbillian. "That was the same year I committed to my Twelve Months of Frost." He chuckled. "To think, we could've run into each other a decade ago. That could've been an interesting state of affairs. Do you think both of us would've come out of that meeting alive?"

Amalardh's insides tightened. He could've met his uncle ten years ago? Amalardh had few regrets in his life. Right now, he regretted not making that climb. Back then, Forbillian would have been a bright light in Amalardh's otherwise destitute existence.

"What did you eat up there?" Oisin asked.

"The occasional snow rabbit, but mainly seeds, insects, and lizards," said Forbillian. "Raw bugs are tastier than you'd think. But unless you want your stomach erupting worse than an overblown volcano, I'd recommend boiling 'em first."

Thankfully, the menu during this trip did not include crunching on grasshoppers. A glacial lake provided a healthy supply of fish, which they smoked for later, and sporadic rabbit droppings exposed the location of the furry vermin.

While the adequate food supply kept Amalardh's belly from folding in on itself, Oisin's diminishing stamina sent his gut rumbling. "Show me the map," he asked his uncle. He matched a broad mountain with a stepped peak to a similar marking on the map's Esjan Range. Their destination was close.

They set up camp inside a cavernous hollow at the base of the mountain. Minutes later, they discovered the cave existed because of erosion from brutal winds channeling up the gulley. The freezing gust dumped buckets of snow. If they stayed, they would get buried alive. But where else could they go? The exposed outside was just as formidable.

Forbillian sat with his back to the cave's small opening and ordered Amalardh and Oisin to do the same. "Now plug any holes with your packs," he said.

The snow piled up behind them, forming a wall.

"Won't we run out of air?" Oisin asked.

"We most certainly will, which is why I was just about to make these." Forbillian drove his walking stick through the top of the snow barrier, creating air holes. "Now, we should happily survive the night. And if we don't, well, we'll be asleep, so we're not going to notice if we don't wake up."

Oisin huddled into a ball.

Amalardh lit his lantern. "Show me your hands," he said to Oisin.

"I'm okay," he replied.

Amalardh took hold of Oisin's trembling extremity and removed his mitten. His purple fingers were ice cold.

"He's nothing but skin and bone," said Forbillian.

"I said I'm fine," said Oisin.

Amalardh opened his wolf cape. "Come here."

Oisin stayed put, his look holding a wary edge.

Amalardh's brow flickered. Had he pushed the boy to the

point of no longer trusted him? "If you don't warm up, you will start losing limbs."

"He's not wrong about that," said Forbillian. "Got myself caught in an ice drift once. When you stop feeling the cold in your toes, that's when you need to worry." He pulled off one of his woolen boots and wiggled four toes. He pointed to where his little one used to be. "This little piggy got black and blue."

Horror washed over Oisin's face. "Did it fall off?"

Forbillian made a snipping motion.

"You cut it off!"

"Frostbite is no joke." Forbillian slipped his boot back on. "Once the flesh is dead, it turns poisonous. You get that poison in your blood and let me tell you, that's a slow, painful way to go."

Oisin seemed to reconsider Amalardh's offer. Possibly because of shyness, embarrassment, or continued distrust, he only half entered the protective space.

Amalardh wrapped his arms around Oisin's thin frame and pulled him close. As he gave in to the moment, his heart pained. In the almost twelve months Alistair had been of this world, Amalardh had held his son only once, and that one time, he did out of duty. When the Senators ruled Vitus, if a father did not acknowledge a child by holding it in his arms, then the law deemed the baby Erro Vitae (a Mistaken Life) and either the mother or a suitable sibling had to leave the infant outside for the Death Train. Although the new council had abolished this arcane practice, Amalardh was keenly aware of Cecilia's unspoken expectation that he embrace his child immediately upon its birth. He did so once, then never again.

He should have shown more love for his son. He should have held Cecilia more often. And he should have let Oisin know he truly does care about him.

Forbillian shuffled close. "You don't mind if I get some of that, too?"

*

192

Forbillian barreled through the snow partition, then stretched his spine backward. "That was certainly one of the rougher nights I've had."

Amalardh squinted in the bright sunlight. He turned to Oisin. "Did you get some sleep?"

Oisin shrugged. "A bit."

The goodwill Amalardh thought he had built up seemed to have fizzled.

"Well, I'll be," said Forbillian. He motioned to a distant mountain with three peaks. "There she finally is. So, when we get to its base, what then?"

Amalardh rubbed his frosty beard. He had no idea. They could spend days figuring out their next step. "How's your water supply?" he asked Oisin.

Oisin swung his pack onto his back. "You don't have to keep looking out for me." He regarded the peaks. "I guess this is the way then," he said, and trekked off.

"Don't worry too much," Forbillian said to Amalardh. "He's just feeling bad because he thinks he's becoming a burden."

Amalardh threaded his arms through the straps of his pack. "There was a reason I didn't want him on this trip."

"Aye. And there's a reason you didn't want me on this trip, either. The sooner you can be honest with yourself about what that reason truly is, the easier this whole thing will be for all of us."

Forbillian settled his bag on his shoulders and set off.

Amalardh had never lied to himself about why he didn't want Oisin and Forbillian to come. He knew they would become a burden. And they had.

They burdened his heart. A great deal.

CHAPTER
25

WYNDOM'S BLOOD PUMPED. His chest heaved. His useless legs fumbled as he dashed in terror. He didn't care where he went, so long as he escaped the enormous, silver wasp bearing down on him. He tried to scream, but no sound came out.

He startled awake and breathed with relief. The horror was only a dream... or was it? The gigantic silver creature still lingered, only it seemed more complacent as it hovered above a distant field. He wiped his sweaty brow. A Wirador Wosrah's vision had bled into his daytime nap, causing his mind to conjure the nightmare. As his warrior lumbered closer to the silver object, the outline of a wooden base and chairs attached to the metallic balloon's underside exposed Wyndom's silver wasp as a type of flying craft.

He scanned the enemy silhouettes and his spine straightened. Saffron! Her hardened expression seemed locked onto his; her arrow aimed right at him. Did she know he could see her? Surely not. Even so, the moment held the terrifying edge of an estranged daughter itching to kill the father she despised.

Her arrow flew. The left side of Wyndom's vision went black. The girl possessed too much skill. Blast that she chose to leave him and serve the other side.

Another arrow came flying. Blackness filled his vision. Saffron had rendered Wyndom's Wirador Wosrah dead.

Her image returned, though he now viewed her from a fresh angle through another warrior. He settled his paranoia. She clearly couldn't see him inside the Wirador Wosrah, because she would aim right back at him. Instead, her arrow flew at another beast.

He frowned. What was that look Saffron shared with the handsome young man called Rabbie? She'd never given Terefellian suitors the time of day. Now, she found a member of the enemy suitable enough to whisper intently into his ear? "Will it work?" he read on her lips. Rabbie nodded and offered her a similar look filled with affection and worry. Wyndom's fist curled. If left unchecked, that attraction would manifest into genuine love. How dare Saffron care for another man—an enemy, no less—when she never developed even a hair's breadth of admiration for her own father?

Rabbie dashed to a rectangular red cannister and tipped it. Liquid poured out. He then ran in a straight line, creating a trail of the watery stuff.

Wyndom's anger burned hot. He wanted to rip this young man limb from limb. He perked. Maybe his current beast would carry out his wishes. It galloped right for Rabbie.

"Kill him," he said through gritted teeth.

Rabbie lit a match and dropped it.

WHOOSH! A wall of flames flew up in Wyndom's face. He yelped and flinched back.

The Wirador Wosrah's ear-piercing squeals grated worse than metal scraping against rock as they slid to a stop.

"To the shed!" yelled Saffron.

"What? Why?" said the other chiseled young man. Eideard was his name. "We'll be trapped. We need to get on the airship."

"We don't have time," said Saffron. "You have to trust me."

It is only fire, the Maddowshin told the Wirador Wosrah. *Run through it.*

Wyndom's warrior leaped through the fiery wall in time to see Saffron disappear into a red, wooden shed. Why would she go in there? Surely the fool girl knows she'll be cornered.

His beast galloped at the structure. Wasn't it going to stop? He tensed as the door rushed at him. Oh no! His beast intended to ram its way in. He yelped loudly and buried his face in the crook of his arm.

The feed cut. What happened? Was his warrior dead? He opened his eyes. His worried people stared at him.

You must learn to stay calm when interacting with our warriors, said the Maddowshin. *You are scaring your people.*

The burn in Wyndom's cheeks traveled to his chest. As much as he didn't want the Maddowshin's lifeless state, he craved the beast's ability to remain calm while receiving a Wirador Wosrah's feed.

"Good Terefellians," Wyndom said. "I am okay. I just had a bad dream. Go about your work and ignore my outbursts." He smoothed the front of his tunic, then nodded to the Maddowshin to continue the feed.

A moderately sized crack in the wooden door filled Wyndom's vision. As old as the shed seemed, it remained sturdy.

His Wirador Wosrah's angry snarl ignited a notion. What if Wyndom could feel their strength? Right now, no matter what he saw or heard, he still felt like the same ineffective man that he was. If he could experience their inner power, maybe his own internal panic wouldn't rise. *Can I have everything?* he asked. *I don't just want to see, hear, and smell. I want to sense all that they experience.*

I can send everything, said the Maddowshin. *You must remain focused as you will be far more immersed. Remember, nothing can harm you.*

"I will not be afraid. I will not be afraid. I will not be afraid," Wyndom uttered to himself.

His Wirador Wosrah rammed the door. A section splintered. A bolt of sheer indestructibility ricocheted through Wyndom. He shuddered with pleasure. The beast head-butted again and its horns smashed through the wood. As it roared triumphantly, the vibrations echoing through Wyndom felt as though he, too, howled. Death and destruction consumed him like an insatiable hunger. He wanted—needed—to find these vermin—in particular, the audacious fellow who desired Saffron's heart—place his hand around his spindly neck and squeeze with the iron might he knew his Wirador Wosrah possessed. Unflappable courage poured from his core as his beast lowered its head and galloped at the bothersome door.

BAM! The wooden slab imploded. The warrior strode into the grim room, and unfamiliar smells assaulted Wyndom's nostrils. As the beast scanned the ramshackle space, its rage bled into Wyndom's bones. Where was the enemy? Surely Saffron and her foolish team didn't honestly think they could hide in this cramped space? The warrior picked up a wooden crate and hurled it. Sandbags spilled out. That crate seemed mighty heavy, yet the beast had flicked it away as effortlessly as Wyndom would a bug.

The warriors roared and began trashing the place. The crashing, smashing, and thrashing sent Wyndom's excitement into overdrive. He balled his fists and pounded the dusty ground. This. This was what he wanted. This power. This utter lack of fear. This unrelenting belief that he was the mightiest man alive. Men, women, children, even the stoic Wrethun Lof, would fall at his feet. His mere presence would send the enemy to their knees, begging his mercy. With this power, he would be the pinnacle of dominance. All would love, fear, and adore him.

While basking in the thrill of his primal fantasy, a thought struck him. How could five people hide in this limited space? He thumped his thigh. Idiot! How could he be so reckless? He should never have allowed his boundless sense of power to sideline logic and reason.

Rudella, he said to the Maddowshin. *Tell our warriors to stop.*

In unison, the Wirador Wosrah quit their destruction and stood at attention. The sudden silence brought awareness to a strange hissing sound. Amongst the various odors that had earlier attacked Wyndom's senses, a particularly strong smell stood out. *What is that stench?* The hiss drew his warrior's vision to a silver canister. It stepped up close and sniffed. A stream of cold air, rife with concentrations of the pungent scent, tickled the beast's— and Wyndom's—nostrils. Wyndom's belly knotted. Something was wrong. He should have known better than to think his daughter a fool. Saffron would never have entered such a compact space without a plan.

A flaming bottle tumbled through an open window. Although Wyndom didn't understand the danger of the exposed flame, he had seen and smelled enough to know something was very wrong.

"RUN!!!!" he yelled.

But his Wirador Wosrah couldn't hear him. "Rudella! Tell them to get—"

BOOM!

Red and yellow flames filled the air. A force more powerful than a thousand storms ripped Wyndom's flesh apart while scorching it with heat hotter than the surface of the sun.

"Arrrgh!" he screamed. "Help me! Help me!"

He writhed like a crazy man, attempting to roll out flames that weren't there.

Stop it! said the Maddowshin. *It's all in your head. Control yourself.*

The pain and intense heat didn't exist. Wyndom's mind had manufactured the sensation. He slapped his hands over his body, checking that everything truly remained intact. The rush of relief mixed with his previous terror set off a chain reaction of uncontrollable emotions. He curled into a ball and whimpered.

Settle yourself, said the Maddowshin. *Your people cannot see you like this.*

Horrified Terefellians stared at him.

Young Brother Stilton rushed to his side and placed a comforting hand on his shoulder. "Brother Wyndom, are you all right?"

Wyndom threw his arms around the boy and cried harder than a newborn. Reality had finally hit. No matter how hard he tried, he would always be everything he hated about himself: small, weak, and pathetic. His mind—the only part of his being that he believed held strength—had let him down. He should've been able to separate the real from the hypothetical. But his fear—as always—had won. A true leader, a real warrior, should not fear death. Wyndom always had. He had abhorred Brother Lasair for not facing his destiny like a man and despised Sister Esme for fleeing the tribe when her Rite drew near. How could Saffron have aided her mother in such a disloyal act?

Saffron.

He whacked the ground with his clenched fists. Seeing her strength and ingenuity ripped his soul to shreds. Why did she leave him? Wyndom would be a better man, a better ruler, with her by his side. He should've secured her loyalty and allegiance back when she was small. How could he have known the skinny, annoying child would grow into such a formidable warrior? Saffron was everything Wyndom wanted to be: strong, fearless, and capable. She wouldn't have freaked out like he just had. When the flames came, he'd been unable to shake the horror of burning alive.

His insides folded at the fear and panic his people must have felt during their Rite of Quinquagenary. The mincelase would have done very little to squelch the agony of their searing flesh.

Brother Stilton's gentle coddling settled Wyndom's sobs. He sat up and wiped his wet face. He needed to come up with a story to help restore his good name with his people. "Because our journey to the Sworn Province draws near, I am engaged in important work for our queen," he said to Stilton. "As you can see, this work drains me. I do what I do to protect Terefellia from our enemy's horror. You believe me, don't you?"

Wide eyed, Stilton nodded.

"Good lad. Go now and spread this news with our people."

As Stilton sped off, Wyndom flopped against the trunk of his palm tree and pressed his hands to his face. *Rudella, please. No more. I do not want to see, hear, or feel anything from our warriors or Wrethun Lof.*

I cannot honor that wish, the Maddowshin said.

Wyndom groaned. *But my presence in their head is not helping anyone. Unless...* He glared at the beast as it strode to him. *That's why you're doing this! You enjoy watching me crumble, don't you?*

The Maddowshin stepped up close and looked down its snout at him. "After hiding your fears for thirty years, I admit, part of me derives a certain pleasure from watching you fail."

Rudella confirming her deep contempt for him stung his heart. Wyndom had spent his life deriving pleasure from another's pain. And now, here he was, a helpless victim on the receiving end.

The Maddowshin's tone softened the way it does when Rudella's humanity takes over. "As much as I crave your failure, indulging my dark desire will be my undoing, because, in the end, you cannot fail."

Wyndom stood. "My dearest Rudella, you see what these feeds are doing to me. Why won't you stop? What purpose do they serve?"

"They serve as education and training."

"Education and training for what?"

"For when the day comes where you will need to control a vessel to precise perfection."

Wyndom's throat tightened. "You want me to take over a Wirador Wosrah?"

"As a starting point, yes."

"A starting point? Rudella, what are you planning?"

"The queen has her needs. You will help her get what she wants."

"Stop hiding things from me. What does our queen want?"

"The queen's secrets are hers and hers alone to divulge."

Resentment rumbled through Wyndom. An image of him ramming two blades into the Maddowshin's eyes flooded his mind. He knew better than to let the thought seep into his consciousness, but the fantasy of sending the beast into a pool of black sludge was too delicious not to indulge.

"Shall I hand you two knives so you can try?" the Maddowshin asked.

Wyndom sighed. He couldn't very well pretend the daydream hadn't happened. "You know how much I despise secrets. Allow me my feeble fantasies. We both know I lack the wherewithal to act on them."

Confidence brimmed on the Maddowshin's brow as it sized him up. *If only you knew how deep the deception goes.*

"What deception? What do you mean?"

The Maddowshin stiffened, as though not intending Wyndom to hear what it presumably thought had been a private quip to itself. Its harsh tone returned. "You will learn what you need to know when you need to know it and not before. The next time I place you in control of one of our warriors, you better figure out a way to stay calm." It snorted at him and strode off.

Wyndom cradled his belly as he lowered himself into a crossed legged position on his resting mat. What did the queen want and why did she need his help to get it? He eyed the Maddowshin as it strolled the line of Wirador Wosrah and made a face. "Need to know basis," he grumbled to himself. He flopped back against his tree's trunk and picked up a fistful of sand. Watching it flow steadily to the ground helped settle his frustration.

He glanced back at the shining mass of warriors. Full control of a Wirador Wosrah was truly possible? Now that would be something. He could experience the thrill of marching into battle without fear of death. Sure, his mind might still play tricks on him, but no matter what, he wouldn't die. Could that be the queen's intent? Allowing him to partake in the fight for their Sworn Provence in such a way where he wouldn't get physically maimed? But why would she need him to fight as a warrior? Why waste time training him to overcome his fears when the kill instinct came innately to a Wirador Wosrah's blackened soul?

He sat forward. Of course. The beasts, while powerful and courageous, lacked critical thinking skills. When the battle starts, the queen would need a lead soldier. Pride welled in his chest. The queen must think Wyndom more capable of leading her battalion than the Maddowshin. Which made sense. Wyndom possessed far better analytical skills than Rudella.

He hugged his knees to his chest and smiled. His mind in control of a Wirador Wosrah body would make Wyndom the warrior he was meant to be.

CHAPTER
26

THE FORCE FROM the exploding shed rocketed through Saffron. If not for the tree trunk that she and the others were hiding behind, it would've knocked her to the ground. Because the queen had programmed the Wirador Wosrah to do one thing—kill the enemy—Saffron had predicted the single-minded beasts would follow her into the shed. Once inside, she had directed everyone out the back window. She had shared her idea to use the gas in the third cylinder to burn the warriors with Rabbie. By the current look on his face, he hadn't expected such a massive explosion either.

"We must hurry," she said.

"What's the rush?" said Eideard. "We killed those things."

"The only way to kill them is to destroy their eyes," said Saffron. "Wood splinters or debris may have ripped some eyeballs apart, but don't kid yourself that we destroyed all of them. As you make your way to the airship, keep close to your sister." She motioned to the open grasslands. "That field will be covered with hundreds of black balls looking for new hosts."

Eideard flung his arms in the air. "Brilliant. Our situation is worse now than before."

Saffron accepted his contempt. Even though she hadn't intended to spread Wirador Wosrah pellets everywhere, her actions had created a new challenge. "Your sister repels them," she said. "Just stick close to her and you'll be fine."

"I really wish you and your mom could come," said Rabbie.

Saffron sucked on her lower lip. Why was he looking at her

like that? "I guess you're lucky you forgot to anchor the ship down earlier, and that the wind blew it down the coast. That blast could've destroyed it." Her attempt to find a positive aspect didn't allay the concern on Rabbie's face. Maybe in another place, another time, she might have had the opportunity to grow close to him. But she couldn't let her unexpected attraction to him cloud her judgement. Cecilia's safety was what mattered.

She spun to the sound of rumbling leaves. Her eyes went wide as a blob the size of a man's fist rolled Rabbie's way. "Watch out!" she yelled, shoving him aside.

The blob skidded to a stop, then rolled to Rabbie's new location.

She pointed to a tree directly behind him. "Quick! Climb up!"

He grabbed a branch and swung his legs into the air. The glob bounced against the trunk repeatedly, as if wanting to climb but not able to do so.

"Arrrgh!" yelled Eideard. While everyone focused on Rabbie, another ball had found Eideard's boot.

Her mother gasped and dropped to Eideard's side.

"Mom! Don't touch it," said Saffron. "Cecilia will get it."

"What do you mean?" Cecilia asked.

Saffron hooked Cecilia's arm and led her to Eideard. "You repel that stuff. Whatever force is in you should push it off." She placed Cecilia's hands on either side of Eideard's knee. "Now, swipe down."

Cecilia moved her hands as directed. As her palms neared the black slime, her muscles quivered as though experiencing resistance. The muck seemed to fight against her repelling force.

"Get it off me!" pleaded Eideard.

"I'm trying," said Cecilia. "Just... stay calm."

The ball at the base of Rabbie's tree rolled Saffron's way. She snatched up a hefty stick and batted it. The ball landed in an outdoor tub filled to the brim with rancid water. Unable to gain traction, the ball spun on itself. She turned back to Cecilia. "You can do it," she said. "Just concentrate. You're stronger than it is. You have to believe that."

Cecilia's arms shook. Her face turned red.

The black muck rolled back on itself.

"That's it!" said Saffron. "You're doing it."

Cecilia took a deep breath and threw her weight into it. "Get off my brother!" she said through gritted teeth.

PLOP! The blob bounced onto the grass. Cecilia kicked it with her boot then flopped against a tree trunk, exhausted.

Rabbie jumped down from the branch and placed his hand on Eideard's shoulder. "Are you okay?"

Eideard managed a weak nod.

The three siblings hugged.

The moment felt strangely uncomfortable. For as close as Saffron was to her mother, they didn't hug. Displays of affection were not the norm in Terefellia.

As the balls in the open field rolled around and collided into each other, their growing size made a sickening display against the otherwise spotless green grass.

A team of balls ranging in size from a mouse to a small dog bounded their way.

"In the trees! Now!" said Saffron.

Cecilia stood her ground while everyone fled to safety.

"Cecilia! What are you doing?" said Eideard.

Saffron eyed Cecilia's planted stance and resolute brow. Her ability to repel one or two rolling balls didn't mean she possessed the power to withstand the force of dozens. Before she attempted to guide her brothers to the airship, and place their lives at risk, she would need to know for sure. As brave as her firm posture seemed, her opening and closing fists revealed uncertainty.

"You can do it!" said Saffron. "They will not harm you!"

"Our sister is not some kind of experiment," said Eideard. "Cecilia! Get up here now!"

"I believe in her and you should, too," said Saffron.

Cecilia's fists clenched as the collection of balls thundered toward her. The mass showed no signs of slowing down. A chill settled in Saffron's bones. Had she made a mistake in supporting Cecilia in this crazy test?

A gush of wind from below kissed her cheeks. Her jaw slackened as the black herd split and curved around either side of Cecilia's feet.

"Holy heck!" said Rabbie. "Did you see that?"

Saffron jumped down from the tree. "You know what you have to do now, don't you?" she said to Cecilia.

Cecilia nodded. "Thank you for believing in me."

As Eideard climbed down from his tree, the color remained drain from his face. What must it be like having a sibling to worry about? A younger sister, no less?

"You better get started," Saffron said to Cecilia. "We need those things gone before they form back into warriors."

Cecilia dashed off.

"What exactly is she doing?" Eideard asked.

"She's going to round those things up and drive them into the ocean," said Rabbie.

Saffron watched in awe as Cecilia cut back and forth, corralling the black globs toward the cliff edge.

"All those hours we spent back in Plockton training sheepdogs when we could've just used our little sister," said Eideard.

Rabbie jabbed him. "Don't be mean."

Eideard smirked. "What? I'm just saying."

A wistfulness overcame Saffron. What wouldn't she give for a relationship like theirs? Earlier that day, the two brothers had been at odds. Now they shared a laugh. Beyond not having a sibling, Saffron had never had a friend. All the girls shunned her (or maybe she shunned them), and all the boys feared her. As they should. She had sent the message more than once that if any of them came too close, she'd punch them in the face. She wanted to like the boys in Terefellia, but she couldn't abide by their mindless lapping up of her father's drivel. If they were stupid enough to believe him, then they deserved Saffron's wrath. She raised her arms and cheered as Cecilia drove the last of the globs over the edge.

Eideard and Rabbie rushed to their sister. Feeling like an outsider, Saffron hung back with her mother. She wanted more than anything to go with them on the flying machine, but even if the ship could take five passengers, Saffron could never convince her mother to fly. Persuading her to leave Terefellia had been hard enough.

Maybe the lack of room on the airship was a good thing. Saffron and her mother could help the cause by pressing forward to Vitus and warning Cecilia's people of the impending battle. Inspired by Cecilia's closeness with her brothers, she wrapped her arms around her mother's waist and held her tight. Her mother returned the hug. The moment felt so comforting. Why hadn't Saffron done this before?

"Saffron! Esme! Behind you!" yelled Cecilia.

Saffron spun around just as a death glob latched to the back of her mother's leg. Her heart seized. She'd forgotten about the ball that she'd batted into the rancid tub. The horrid thing had escaped.

"Mother!" She dropped to her knees and reached for the stuff.

"No, don't—" yelled Cecilia.

The second Saffron touched the gunk, she pulled back. But it was too late. A thin layer of slime had adhered to her palms. Her breath came in sharp spurts. What had she done? She knew better than to touch Eifa's muck.

While her mother cried out in pain, Saffron felt no discomfort. The thick callouses she despised were protecting her. The black filth spread to the smooth skin on the side of her fingers and the burn of a thousand tiny needles bit at her flesh. Her poor mother! The stuff covered her entire calf. The pain must be unbearable. Saffron sucked in her breath. Any hint of her own agony would only make her mother's torment worse.

"Don't worry about me," she said to Cecilia. "Help my mother."

"No!" said her mother. "You make sure my daughter is safe first."

"Mom! No!"

"You have less on you," said Cecilia to Saffron. "You'll be fast."

She swooped her hands down Saffron's arm. A few years back, Saffron had accidentally spilled liquid beeswax on her leg. The pain of the hardened wax ripping her leg hair from their roots as she pulled it off felt similar to this moment. But instead of tiny hairs shedding from her skin, minuscule black tendrils tore from her flesh, leaving tiny dots of blood from where they'd burrowed in.

Cecilia had been right. The small amount of muck on Saffron's palm popped off with ease. So that it wouldn't try to reattach itself back to Saffron or seek out either of Cecilia's brothers, Cecilia guided the glob to the larger mass attached to Saffron's mother. She repeated the same on Saffron's other hand.

"It's okay, Mom," said Saffron. "Cecilia will save you."

Her mother wailed as her body seized.

Cecilia placed her hands at Saffron's mother's upper thigh and moved her open palms down. Her muscles tensed as the resistance started. She sucked in her breath and pushed. Her face turned crimson as she grunted.

Saffron's knuckles turned white. Why wasn't the stuff budging? Then again, her mother did have twice the amount of gunk stuck to her as Eideard had, and his boot and trousers had offered an added layer of protection. Her mother's tunic stopped at her knee. The soft, unprotected skin would be the perfect surface for the muck's burrowing tendrils.

"Please, don't give up," Saffron said to Cecilia.

"I've trekked over mountains, crossed deserts, and battled the Army of Vitus into the early hours of the morning," Cecilia said. "Trust me, I have no intention of letting Eifa win."

Saffron's mother writhed and released an anguished cry.

Cecilia strained.

The substance folded back on itself.

Saffron's heart skipped. "It's working! Stay strong," she said to her mother.

Beads of sweat dripped from Cecilia's brow. "I beat you once," she said through gritted teeth. "I'll beat you again!"

The muck rolled down Saffron's mother's calf, leaving dots of blood in its wake.

Happy tears formed as Saffron squeezed her mother's hand. "We've got this, okay?"

Her mother's chin quivered as she nodded.

Cecilia paused and caught her breath. "Sorry. I just need a second. This is way harder than with Eideard."

Saffron might not be able to touch the blackness, but she could touch Cecilia. If the Treoir Solas needed physical strength, then Saffron had plenty. "Let me help you," she said. She placed her hands over Cecilia's. "Okay. On the count of three. One. Two. Push."

They both pressed down hard.

The muck rolled at least an inch.

"Oh, my gosh!" said Cecilia. "That... that helps!"

The two of them heaved again. The blackness rolled all the way to Esme's ankle.

Joy flooded Saffron. Just a couple more pushes and her mother would be free.

She pushed down with all her might.

Her palm slipped.

Cecilia yelped as Saffron's ghastly callouses sliced the top of Cecilia's tender hand.

With the power of a compressed spring, the blackness shot to Esme's mid-thigh.

Saffron's blood chilled as her mother cried out. What had she done? As ugly as her hands were, they'd always been the one thing that had never failed her.

"No!" yelled Cecilia. She immediately got back to work.

Rabbie joined her. Surely his firm muscles and cottony hands would fare better.

"I'm so sorry, Mother," Saffron said.

"Please. No. It's not your fau—" Her pained cry sent tears streaming down Saffron's cheeks.

The deeper the black muck ate into her mother, the stronger it became.

For every inch Cecilia and Rabbie pulled it down, it sprang forward another three.

"Cecilia. Rabbie," Esme said. "It is time."

"No. We can do this. I know we can," said Cecilia.

Saffron held her mother's hand. "Don't give up. You must hold on. Cecilia. Rabbie. Don't you dare stop!"

"We won't," said Rabbie.

The blackness hugged all the way to Saffron's mother's ribs and sprawled halfway down her left thigh. "You must stop," her mother said. "Save your strength. You have so much more work to—" Her face contorted as torment sucked the words from her mouth.

Cecilia grunted. Her face turned crimson as she collapsed. "I'm sorry," she said between gasping breaths. "I'm so sorry."

Saffron yanked her to her feet. "What are you doing? Why are you giving up?"

Esme placed her hand on Saffron's shoulder. "It's happening, my darling. Let me go."

Saffron's heart wrenched. As much as she knew her mother was right, she didn't want her to be.

Shimmery water filled her mother's eyes as she smiled weakly. "Because of you, every day since my fiftieth life day has been a gift. You have shown me a world that in my wildest dreams I could not have imagined existed. Knowing that you have found these wonderful people fills my heart with so much joy." She turned to Rabbie. "Promise me you will find room on your machine for my daughter."

Sadness swam on Rabbie's face. "We will. I promise."

Saffron gasped at the blackness swarming her mother's neck.

"When the time comes," her mother said, "you know what to do. I love y—" The muck slid into her mouth, muffling her words.

Saffron screamed. She had risked everything to spare her mother's soul from becoming an unearthly monster. And she had failed. As the stuff moved down her mother's arm, Saffron's tears flowed. She held her mother's hand, then fingers, then their tips until she finally had to let go.

She stepped back and swallowed her grief. This glob of black was no longer her mother. She wiped her face dry and pulled her knife from its holster. Her fingers massaged the grip as she readied herself for the small window she would have to strike.

A touch on her arm infiltrated her senses. Wild with rage, she spun, ready to spear the offender. She locked onto Rabbie's wide eyes. What did he want? He presented her with his knife. Two eyes. Two weapons. Make the act swift and as painless as possible. She nodded lightly and accepted his offer.

A ripple rushed up the black column and the blackness morphed into a Wirador Wosrah, complete with snarling teeth, grisly brow, and curled, spiked horns.

Saffron's breath caught as its eyelids popped open, exposing her mother's deep brown eyes.

Mother? Maybe Saffron could talk to this beast. Convince it—

She startled at its mighty roar. Her grip on the two knives tightened. This beast held no humanity. Killing it would free her mother's soul from an eternity of misery. She lunged forward and jammed her shiny blades into her mother's eyes, sending the creature into a pool of liquid black.

She dropped to the ground and sobbed. Any love Saffron had left inside turned as dry and powdery as the dirty particles wafting up from the evaporating puddle.

CHAPTER
27

CECILIA'S HEART CAVED. If Eifa's darkness ever turned either of her brothers into a monster, would she have the strength to stab out their eyes with the same unflinching resolve as Saffron? If it did ever happen, Cecilia would have to follow the brave girl's lead.

Mist rose from the dead beast's pool of black. Was anyone else seeing this? Rabbie and Eideard held their heads low and Saffron remained face down on the ground, sobbing. Cecilia's skin tingled as the mist formed into an ethereal figure that looked very much like Esme. Cecilia wanted to call out to Saffron, tell her to look up, but except for Esme's wafting spirit, time seemed frozen. A tear rolling down Saffron's cheek had stopped, Rabbie and Eideard remained motionless, and Cecilia couldn't utter a sound.

A shimmering cloud formed in the sky. The speckles of sparkling dust took Siersha's shape. The Goddess of Light's slender arms wrapped around Esme's spirit. Together, they floated upward.

Dark wisps rose out of the black puddle and swirled into long, thorny, tentacles. They shot out and ensnared Esme's spirit. As Siersha continued to pull Esme with her, the thorny black tentacles tightened.

A serpent face with sharp teeth and wicked eyes burst forward from a tendril and hissed. "You know the rules," Eifa said. "This spirit is mine."

Cecilia's stomach swirled. She couldn't let Saffron's mother linger for eternity with the Dark Goddess. If the force within her repelled Eifa's black slime, maybe she could do the same with the smoky form and help the Goddess of Light free Esme's spirit from Eifa's dark clutch.

She strained to break from her frozen state. Her skin prickled as her fingers wiggled. *Come on, you can do this.* She set her focus on moving her legs. Her foot slowly rose as though moving through molasses. She took a step. *Keep fighting this resistance. You have to save Esme's soul.* She took another step, and another. Once at the celestial tug-of-war, she placed her hands above the evil mass and pushed down. Just as with the black gunk, the closer she moved to the smoky tendrils, the more force she felt pushing back. Eifa had destroyed Esme's life. The Dark Goddess would not take the innocent woman's spirit. Gritting her teeth, Cecilia shoved with all her might. The tentacles discharged an ear-piercing screech.

"You cannot do this," Eifa hissed to the Goddess of Light.

"Do what?" Siersha replied.

"Use your vessel to break the rules!"

"Unlike you, I do not control my believers. The Treoir Solas does what she does out of love. And love trumps all rules."

Like the failing fibers of a crusty rope, one by one, Eifa's smoky tentacles squealed and snapped back into the black puddle.

Eifa's gravelly voice echoed in Cecilia's ears. "Ask her the truth about who I am."

Cecilia looked up at Siersha. "What did she mean?"

A crystalline tear dropped from the Goddess's eye as she floated upward with Esme's spirit. The world unfroze.

"Who are you talking to?" asked Rabbie. He glanced to where she had been standing. His stare shot back to her current spot. "How did you get over there?"

Cecilia looked up. The Goddess and Esme were gone. "Did you not see what just happened?" she asked.

Saffron dried her eyes and stood up. "I saw very well what happened. You let that stuff swallow my mother and turn her into a monster."

Eideard stepped forward. "That's not fair—"

Cecilia's terse hand gesture cut him off. "Saffron," she said. "Please trust that I did everything I could. I know your pain."

"You know nothing," Saffron snapped.

Eideard's mouth tightened. "She watched our own mother die at the hands of Vitus's deadliest Soldier!"

Saffron faltered.

"Eideard, please," said Cecilia. He relaxed his stance and stepped back. She turned to Saffron. "You may not believe me, but I saw Siersha come for your mother and ferry her to the Pass-Over World. She is safe and happy. I know it in my heart. One day, you will see her again."

"I don't want to hear about your stupid god and your stupid beliefs. I'm a fool for leaving my people and an even worse fool for believing that if I did good and protected the one who serves the Goddess of Light, then this god would protect me. Protect my mother. If your god is so wonderful and virtuous, why does she let innocent people die?"

Cecilia had no answer.

Saffron pounded her fist in the air. "The god of my people may be fearsome, but at least I know what I get with her. If I praise her, honor her, and live by her will, then she will not forsake me. Instead, I turned from her and look what happened. I lost my mother because I believed in the wrong person. My father is right. There is only one true god, and her name is Eifa." She turned and stormed off.

Rabbie ran after her. "Saffron! Where are you going?"

"Away from here."

He grabbed her arm.

She flung his hand away. "Don't touch me."

"I'm sorry... it's just, you can't leave."

"Really? Watch me." She spun on her heels and marched off.

"Wait!" he called.

She maintained her stride.

"You have my knife."

Saffron glared at him. She pulled a knife from her belt and handed it over. "I hope your stupid airship flies."

As she stomped off, Rabbie went to follow.

"Rabbie," Cecilia said. She motioned for him to let her go. Right now, Saffron was like an overexcited cat, puffing up at an unwanted intruder. In such a state, a wild feline will swipe at both friend and foe.

Rabbie's head hung low as he returned. "We can't let her leave on her own."

"She's not leaving."

"You can't be certain of that."

"True. But I am certain that she needs time to process her hurt and anger."

"What if she goes back to her people?"

"That is her right. We can't stop her."

Rabbie glowered at her. "You're meant to turn people to Siersha's light, not drive them toward the Dark Goddess."

"My job is to show people Siersha's light. I cannot force them to see it. And as for driving Saffron to Eifa, she grew up embraced by such blackness. You would be well warned to avoid her."

"That's precious coming from you."

"What does that mean?"

"Amalardh took you prisoner. Shouldn't that have been warning enough to stay away from him?"

Cecilia's cheeks burned hot. "How dare you?"

"When you met him, he was no more corrupted by Eifa's influence than Saffron. He became the love of your life. Are you that arrogant to think that you're the only person who can sway a darkened soul?"

His words hit like a stake through her heart. Did her brother not realize how awful things had become between her and Amalardh? "How can you possibly think me arrogant? Unless you're that ignorant to not even notice what's become of me and the supposed love of my life?" Angry tears formed. "If I'd swayed the darkness from his heart, then why am I barely within his sphere? Or are you that uncaring that you haven't noticed how miserable I've been?"

Rabbie's expression fell. "I'm sorry," he said. "I never meant to hurt you."

Her arms remained folded as he hugged her. "I love you more than anything in the world. You know that, right?"

She nodded. She'd never doubted Rabbie's love.

"For the record," he whispered. "I have noticed a rift between you and Amalardh. I should've talked to you about it. Part of me wanted to pretend that everything was fine because if you and Amalardh, with the deep love you have for each other, can't make it, then what chance do I ever have of finding and keeping love?"

Cecilia dropped her arms and wrapped them around his waist. Poor, dear, sweet Rabbie. He was far more of a romantic than she would ever be. She'd been wrong to project her insecurities about Amalardh onto Rabbie. "Go after her," she said.

"Go after who?" asked Saffron.

The stealthy Terefellian stood beside them.

Rabbie startled.

Braking from her embrace with him, Cecilia threw her arms around Saffron and gave her the hug she should've given her earlier. Her rigid response only made Cecilia squeeze tighter. "I'm heartbroken about all that you've been through. Please know, you'll always have a family with us."

Saffron held out a knife to Rabbie. "I gave you the wrong knife," she said.

Cecilia stepped back. Saffron had only returned to collect her blade? She wasn't staying? The rejection hit hard.

Rabbie fumbled for Saffron's possession in his waistband. As he handed it to her, their fingertips touched. Interesting. If Saffron truly didn't have any feelings for Rabbie, why did she retract her hand so fast? And why had her cheeks turned beet red? Cecilia's lips pursed as she sized Saffron up. Had she handed Rabbie the wrong knife on purpose?

"Before you go," Cecilia said. "I would like to show you one of our beliefs that doesn't involve a god. Would you let me do that?"

Saffron's skeptical expression held an edge of relief that she didn't have to leave right away. "Fine. Whatever."

"More of those beasts will come," said Eideard. "We need to go."

"We will go, but not before we lay Esme to rest. If our enemy makes us run with such fear that we stop being who we are, then what is the point of running at all?"

She held Eideard's defiant stare.

He relented. "I just won't feel safe until we get away from this place."

"I know. But we must do this."

Cecilia led Saffron to a sturdy bush with cylindrical flowers that looked like brushes. "This is a pretty tree, don't you think?"

Saffron gave a non-committal shrug.

"In Plockton, we plant a seed over the buried. We choose a plant that's representative of the departed. This tree with its delicate, red flowers is a mix of softness and strength, just like your mom." She looked at Saffron expectantly.

"If you say so," Saffron said.

The tree's pods had a hard shell, and like a pine cone, opened during extreme heat. Scorched from the shed blast, some pods had opened. Not letting Saffron's dry reply deter her, Cecilia tapped a seed into her hand. "Your mother's body may no longer be of this earth, but we can still plant something in her honor. I was thinking we'd lay her somewhere with a view of the water so she can see the sunrise. I love sunrises, don't you? Especially over the ocean."

Saffron remained detached.

"Or we can plant her... wherever."

"Why do you keep saying 'her'? My mother is gone. And if you expect me to believe she's going to become some shrub, I won't."

Cecilia drew in her breath. Did Saffron have no imagination at all?

"We're not suggesting that the seed is your mom," said Rabbie. "It's a symbol. Because a seed grows, it represents life. The plant it becomes reflects the life that's gone, but not forgotten."

Saffron's rigidity softened. His words seemed to affect her.

"So, overlooking the ocean? And sunrises?" asked Cecilia.

"Whatever you think is best."

"Sunrise it is. Your mom would've liked that idea."

Saffron's gaze dropped. "I wouldn't know," she uttered. "I've never seen one."

Eideard guffawed. "You've never seen a sunrise? How is that possible? Must be nice to grow up in a place where you can sleep in to all hours of the morning."

Hurt flickered through Saffron's eyes.

Cecilia wanted to punch her stupid brother for his ignorant comment. Thankfully, Rabbie took the liberty. He palm-shoved Eideard's shoulder. "You really are a toad bucket sometimes."

"Why? I was only stating the obvious."

"If you would listen to anyone other than yourself, you'd know Saffron grew up in a narrow valley. What bloody sunrises was she supposed to see?"

The red from Eideard's cheeks spread down to his neck. He jabbed the toe of his boot into the soil.

"I'm sorry about my brother," said Cecilia. "He was dropped on his head as a baby."

Genuine surprise replaced Saffron's hurt. She seemed almost saddened by the revelation. Cecilia immediately felt bad for expecting Saffron to understand her family's dark humor. "Eideard wasn't really dropped on his head," she said. "The comment is just a family joke." She cocked her brow at him. "Sadly, my brother has no excuse for his thoughtlessness."

"Other than the affliction of being born a toad bucket," said Rabbie.

Eideard folded his arms and didn't fight his siblings' good-natured abuse. What choice did he have? Whenever he dished on Cecilia or Rabbie, if they tried to complain, he would always remind them of the golden rule—anyone who dished it out needed to also take it.

Saffron smirked and shook her head. "You guys are weird. I like that. Let's go plant a tree."

As Rabbie and Saffron strode off, Cecilia turned to Eideard. "I know what your problem is," she said. "You're jealous."

He burst out laughing. "Hardly. I have zero attraction to Saffron."

"Oh, I know. You feel zero attraction for most women. Your stunted self has yet to appreciate all that we offer. What you crave is our attention, which Saffron is giving to Rabbie."

Eideard twitched uncomfortably.

"Tell me I'm wrong."

"I don't know what you're talking about."

"I'm sure you don't. But for your own sake, I suggest you try to figure it out. You've always had a big ego. It's part of your charm." She poked him in the chest. "Just so we're clear, I will not let that ego come between Rabbie and Saffron. Tell me you at least understand that much."

Eideard shoved his hands in his pockets. "I'm not a toad bucket."

"I know. Which is why you need to stop acting like one."

He breathed deep. "Fine. I'll make sure not to speak ever again. Then no one will get hurt."

Cecilia rolled her eyes. Such a drama queen. "That sounds like a splendid plan." She hooked her arm under his. "Come on. Help me find something to dig with."

Among the shed's rubble, Cecilia found a blackened trowel and used it to dig a small hole in the open field. She buried a seed and remained kneeling as she recited her people's prayer.

Tears welled in Saffron's eyes. "You do this for your dead? You bury them this way? Take this much care?"

Cecilia stood. "Of course."

Saffron wiped her wet cheeks with the back of her hand. "You told me earlier that I'd always have a family with you."

"And I meant it."

"You say that now. If you knew the truth, you wouldn't want me to be part of your family."

"Amalardh, the one I love, was once an assassin for the Senators of Vitus. Your truth cannot be worse than that of a murderer's."

"You would think so, but tell me this. You all might sleep comfortably by this man's side, knowing he won't slit your throats. But would you rest just as easily next to me knowing that while your people revere the dead, my people eat them?"

Rabbie didn't flinch.

Cecilia hoped her swallow wasn't too audible.

"I'm sorry," said Eideard. "Your people do what?"

Cecilia looked daggers at him.

"What?" he asked.

So much for her brother never talking again. "It's okay," she said to Saffron. "We heard what you said."

"That may be so," said Eideard, "but I need clarification. To be clear, you don't specifically kill your people to eat them, do you? I mean, they die of natural causes first, correct?"

Saffron closed in on herself. "It's part of the Rite of Quinquagenary."

This time, Rabbie flinched.

And Cecilia's gasp was most definitely audible.

"I guess I'll be on my way," said Saffron.

"Wait." Cecilia's mouth opened, but she didn't know how to say the awful thing that she wanted to ask.

Saffron's upper eyelids drooped as she exhaled. "If you're wondering if I desire to eat any of you, the answer is no."

Cecilia bit back her desire to suck in air. "Your people are led by Eifa. Her influence wrapped this tradition of yours in so many layers of false logic that no one considered challenging this ceremony. You left Terefellia for a reason. You shouldn't feel shame for finally seeing a truth hidden under a blanket of lies."

Saffron threw her arms around Cecilia. "Thank you," she whispered. "You truly are who I hoped you would be."

The moment held an undercurrent of dread. Rabbie had promised Esme that he'd find room on the airship for Saffron, but would there be? He'd already expressed his concern about the vessel's ability to take three passengers. Could they risk adding a fourth?

Saffron trailed Cecilia's gaze to the awaiting balloon and must have sensed her concern. "Don't worry about your promise to my mom," she said. "We all know the airship can't afford the additional weight."

"We're not leaving you behind," said Rabbie.

"Yes. You are. Someone needs to warn your people about Eifa and her black army. Let me do that for you. Now come on, we've wasted enough time." She waved for them to follow.

As Cecilia walked across the open field toward the airship, her spirit sagged. Saffron was right. Cecilia couldn't leave and not warn her people. "As much as it grieves me to say this, we have to split up."

"We are splitting up," said Saffron. "I'm going north and you three are going east."

"That's not what I mean."

Eideard stiffened. "No. Rabbie and I are not leaving you."

"You will travel east with me," she said to him. "And Rabbie will head to Vitus with Saffron."

Saffron's eyes flittered to Rabbie. Her look bordered on terror. "I don't need a babysitter."

"I don't doubt your ability to get to Vitus," said Cecilia. "What I doubt, is my people listening to you. In their eyes, you'll be another deceitful Terefellian."

Saffron's mouth twisted. She seemed to know Cecilia was right. "Rabbie has the most skill with the airship," she said. "I will not have you risk your life by not flying with the best." She glanced at Eideard. "No offense."

"None taken," he replied. And he was probably serious.

Eideard knew his limits. He never proclaimed himself a better sculptor than Rabbie or smarter with technology.

"It's not that hard to fly," said Rabbie. "I've already explained everything to Eideard."

"Then the decision is made," said Cecilia. While her straightened spine may have projected confidence; inside, she crumbled. The last thing she wanted was to separate from her brothers.

The group set about readying the craft.

Eideard handed Rabbie a container to store his and Cecilia's weapons. "You know why Cecilia doesn't want me traveling back to Vitus with Saffron, right?"

Rabbie eyed him cautiously. "If you say anything mean—"

"Geez. I can't even have any fun anymore. Let me at least have one laugh before I plummet to my death on this thing."

"Fine. I'll indulge you. Why doesn't Cecilia want you to go to Vitus?"

"Because she's worried Saffron would realize how irresistible I am and fall in love with me instead."

Rabbie burst out laughing. "Now that really is funny."

Saffron arrived with heavy duty blankets made of a waterproof material to keep out the wind and rain. "Fall in love with you instead of who?" she asked Eideard.

Rabbie occupied himself with something at the other end of the platform.

Eideard attempted to sidestep his embarrassment with a flutter of incoherent mumbling.

"Is this one of those, 'don't mind Eideard because he was dropped on his head' moments?" Saffron asked Cecilia.

"I believe it is."

Saffron leaned close to Eideard. Her expression remained flat as she said, "If I were your sister, I would've been more concerned that you'd get under my skin so much that I'd end up eating yours."

Cecilia choked back her laughter. Even Eideard seemed impressed by the clever quip. Saffron truly was part of the family.

Rabbie's gaze locked onto the balloon.

"What's wrong?" Cecilia asked.

"We know this thing can go up and down, but it's the rear engine that pushes it forward. If it doesn't turn on, this ship won't fly."

Cecilia stiffened. He waited until now to divulge this not-so-little tidbit?

Oblivious to her concern, he clapped his hands together. "No time like the present to figure out if we need a plan B." He flicked a switch on the platform's front panel. A whirring noise emanated from the balloon's tail. Relief flooded his face.

"What's making them spin?" Cecilia asked.

"The patterned squares on the uppermost strip are made of a special material that converts sunlight to electricity."

"Are you sure you want me to captain this thing?" said Eideard. "Our brother knows far more about this stuff."

An element of doubt crept in. Maybe Eideard wasn't the best choice.

Rabbie sat in the driver's seat and demonstrated how two tall rods on either side of the chair controlled the steering through cables connected to the rear engine. "Think of the propellers like a rudder. Just like with a sailboat, you turn the propeller sideways to counter the force of any cross winds."

Cecilia's apprehension settled. Eideard enjoyed sailing far more than Rabbie and had spent considerable time commanding *Vitus I* with Amalardh. Maybe her eldest brother was the better choice after all.

Rabbie patted one of the silver canisters. "The only other thing we don't know is how long the fuel will last." The metal fabric provided something he called Thermal Solar Heating. During the day, the metallic skin would supposedly use the sun's rays to keep the air warm while maintaining much of the heat at night. "We turned the burners on earlier to provide the initial warmth," he said. "You shouldn't need to light them again until the early morning."

The vessel's manual suggested that in calm weather, the balloon could fly for up to a week on one tank. Conservatively, Rabbie proposed a week to mean five days. "If you're not where you need to be in ten to twelve days..." His lips compressed.

"Then, I guess we'll be swimming," said Eideard.

"Ten days on this thing?" said Cecilia. "Surely we'll reach land sooner."

Rabbie retrieved an old map from a slot within the machine's control unit and smoothed it out. Based on the airship's stated cruising speed, and barring any unforeseen weather, he estimated that Cecilia and Eideard should hit land in about ten days.

Cecilia gripped the back of the seat. Having "about" ten to twelve days of fuel for a trip "about" ten days long weakened her knees.

Rabbie tapped the ship's compass. "Just keep this thing pointing east, and you'll be fine."

"We should get going," said Eideard.

With the time to leave upon her, Cecilia's stomach knotted. She kissed Rabbie and squeezed him tight. "When you see Amalardh, tell him I'm sorry, but I had to move forward without him. He'll understand." She hugged Saffron and asked her to look after Rabbie.

Watching her brothers embrace caused even deeper pain. Even though they poked fun at each other and called each other toad buckets, Rabbie and Eideard were best friends and almost inseparable. Where one was, the other was always close. Eideard broke from the hug and wiped his eye. Seeing his tears made Cecilia's flow. Why did life have to be like this? Why did she have to separate from the ones she loved?

"Come on," Eideard said. He took hold of her hand and led her onto the platform.

Rabbie untied the anchor rope and handed it to Eideard. "Safe travels," he said.

As the ship slowly lifted, Rabbie startled. "Oh, shoot." He

shoved his hand into his pants pocket. "Eideard. Catch." He tossed him the box of matches.

Eideard hooked his hand to his hip and shook his head. "You're the smartest one among us, and you almost forgot to give us these?"

Rabbie grinned and gave a palms-up shrug.

Eideard smiled and switched on the electric motor.

The ship glided forward.

Cecilia waved her last goodbye, settled back in her chair, and kept her eyes on the horizon. She felt unsettled enough and didn't need her stomach swimming from the fifty-foot-height, which according to the altimeter (a device Rabbie said measured elevation) was her current distance from the water. "You will want to cruise at about two-hundred feet," he'd said. "Climb to that height slowly, so your ears don't hurt."

A trill squeak from below made Cecilia look down. She gaped at a dolphin tossing its snout back and forth. "Look Eideard. It's waving good-bye."

The warmth inside her belly expanded—Siersha. The friendly creature had to be a sign from the Goddess that Cecilia traveled the correct path. She opened their food bag, unwrapped a freshly steamed fish meant for their lunch, and dropped it in the water.

"What the—" said Eideard. "That's our food. It's got an entire sea of fish down there."

"And we have plenty of smoked boar up here." She smiled and placed her hand on his knee.

His sour expression settled.

When Cecilia had left Plockton to search for her brothers, she'd come across a bear. Even though the grizzly creature had a forest full of food, Cecilia gave it her fish. Okay, so maybe she'd done so because she'd feared for her life. In any event, the next morning, the bear saved her from a mountain lion. Because of this previous experience, the fish offering to the dolphin had felt like the right thing to do.

CHAPTER
28

THE FROSTY WIND tore at Amalardh's face like a wild cat infected with the Rage—Cecilia's term for what very much sounded like rabies. They neared the base of the three-peaked mountain and, as Amalardh had feared, had no idea where to go next. Forbillian led the way, followed by Amalardh, then Oisin. As much as he disliked the idea of Oisin trailing, the situation required it. Even with the snow paddles Forbillian had made, this section of soft, powdery snow had proved too challenging for Oisin's short legs. The path cleared by Amalardh and Forbillian's paddles offered the boy easier navigation. He glanced over his shoulder to check on Oisin's progress. His frozen brain took a moment to comprehend the splayed lynx lying face down in the snow.

Oisin! Amalardh dashed over and rolled him face up. The boy was alive, but barely.

Forbillian bounded to his side.

"We have to find cover," yelled Amalardh over the howling wind. He placed his hand to his brow to protect against the blinding snow and scoured the harsh surroundings. If he didn't find cover soon, Oisin was certain to die.

Forbillian tapped Amalardh's arm and motioned to three stone pillars about fifteen feet tall.

"This is no time for games," Amalardh said. "I need to get Oisin out of this weather before he freezes to death."

"I'm not suggesting we huddle under them, ya daft fool." He

pointed to the mountaintop. "Three peaks." And then to the columns. "Three pillars. It could mean something."

Forbillian's clarification carried weight. Amalardh hoisted Oisin over his shoulder and marched to the landmark. His hope fizzled. The smooth stones appeared devoid of any further clues.

Forbillian stepped up to the central pillar and pulled his bear cape tight. "Rotten goose clover. I really thought these darn things meant something. What do we do—Ahhh!" He disappeared into the snow. Seconds later, one of his shoe paddles poked up through a hole in the frosty ground. "Ahoy up there," he said, waving the paddle. "Seems those three beauties mark an entrance of sorts. Come on in."

Amalardh cradled Oisin close and skidded through the icy hole into a spacious ice tunnel. The frosty walls glowed blue, lighting the space with a soft hue. The quietness and protection from the biting winds offered immediate relief. He took a step and almost lost it on the slippery ground. Snow paddles were perfect to maneuver in powder, not so much on a hard surface.

"Let me get those," said Forbillian. He dropped to his knee and unclipped Amalardh's paddles.

Stepping free, Amalardh walked to a nearby rock and sat. He closed his eyes and held Oisin tight. *Stay with me*, he said in his mind.

"He's got a fighting spirit," said Forbillian. "He'll pull through."

After what felt like an eternity, Oisin's eyes opened. "What happened?" he asked weakly. "Where are we?"

Amalardh exhaled his relief.

"We're inside the mountain with the three peaks," said Forbillian. "If you hadn't passed out where you had, we would've missed the entrance to this tunnel."

"I passed out?" Oisin's head lowered.

The poor kid probably dreaded facing more of Amalardh's wrath. Cecilia had once told Amalardh, "I know the Vitus way is to dispatch those that have no purpose. The Plockton way is to find purpose in everything." Just because Amalardh had failed to even look for Oisin's purpose didn't mean the skinny four-teen-year-old didn't have one. "Forbillian's right," he said. "If you hadn't dropped where you had, all three of us might have frozen to death. You shouldn't feel bad."

Oisin's posture remained hunched as he unclipped his snow paddles and crawled off Amalardh's lap.

"Here. This will make you feel better," Forbillian said. He handed Oisin a piece of jerky. "Mark my words. You were meant to be on this journey just as much as me and Amalardh."

From Oisin's lackluster response to his usual ravenous approach to food, he didn't seem convinced.

The ice tunnel opened into a vast, glowing blue atrium. Ripples of frozen water undulated down the walls as though stilled mid-flow by a sudden frost.

"What next?" Forbillian asked.

Amalardh didn't know. The place seemed like a dead end. "Look around," he said. "Maybe there's another clue."

The three of them scoured the place.

"This might go somewhere," Oisin called from the far corner.

A horizontal crevice, not more than about eighteen inches high, stretched about ten feet, exposing more blue ice on the other side. Oisin volunteered to shimmy through. Even though the idea didn't thrill Amalardh, letting him go first made sense. In the event of an unexpected drop-off, his light frame would be easy to support with the rope.

Forbillian studied the narrow area as Oisin scuttled through. "Are you sure we're supposed to climb through this? I mean, it's a wee bit tight, don't you think?"

Amalardh eyed Forbillian's ample stomach. "For some of us, maybe."

Forbillian hoisted his trousers. "I'm like a cat, you know.

Whatever my head and shoulders can get through, so can the rest of me."

"I hope so, Forbs," said Oisin from the other end, "because this end definitely leads somewhere. Wait till you see this!"

Amalardh slid his sword and their three backpacks into Oisin's awaiting grasp. He flopped onto his stomach and belly-crawled to a small atrium at the other end. He followed Oisin's excited gaze to an ice slide that dropped almost vertically for about twenty feet, then disappeared into darkness.

Forbillian took off his bear cape and pushed it through. "Last, but not least," he said. He poked his head and shoulders into the crevice and wriggled forward on his belly. Halfway in, he stopped.

"What's the hold up?" Amalardh asked.

"It's just a slight bit tighter than expected," said Forbillian. "Toss me the rope so I've got something to grab on to."

Amalardh resisted his urge to scoff. So much for Forbillian being "just like a cat." He slid the rope in and held firm as his uncle pulled.

The rope went slack.

"What now?" Amalardh asked.

"Maybe I should just hold and you pull," said Forbillian.

Amalardh set his grip and strained, but the mountain man didn't budge.

"His butt's too big," said Oisin.

Sure enough, the crawl space's top lip had snagged Forbillian's rear end.

"Go back out," said Amalardh.

Forbillian wiggled like a legless lizard. "I appear to be stuck."

Why was Amalardh not surprised? Thankfully, the narrow crevice's width provided enough room for him to slide back past Forbillian and return to the large atrium.

Forbillian's rear end and dangling legs provided quite the sight. He took hold of his uncle's ankles. "So much for being a cat," he uttered.

"Well, at least I'm not a sarcastic pri—"

Amalardh yanked and freed Forbillian from the tight space.

Forbillian dusted ice specks from his chest. "I guess we have a bit of a pickle," he said. His lips compressed as he placed his hand on Amalardh's shoulder. He wasn't going to cry, was he? "It was an honor meeting you. I will cherish the days we spent together. Look after the boy for me, will you?"

Amalardh shook his head at Forbillian's dramatics. He was hardly going to leave his uncle behind. "First, it would help if you took this thing off." He unclipped Forbillian's waist belt. "Second, we need to remove some excess material." He grabbed an ax from the belt.

Forbillian cuddled his belly and inched back. "What in the ferry-glades are you gonna do with that?"

Amalardh's brows lifted. Forbillian didn't honestly think Amalardh was about to slice his stomach off, did he? And what's with the constant blurting of random phrases and words? "Ferry-glades?" he said.

Forbillian shrugged. "When one lives alone for thirty years, one has the freedom to make up their own lexicon." His gaze shifted back to the hatchet in Amalardh's grasp. "You still haven't explained what you're going to do with that."

Amalardh rammed the ax into the lip of the passageway's ceiling. A chunk of ice about six inches thick broke off, exposing the rock roof. As expected, ice had rendered the space tighter than it should be.

"Right. Yes. Of course," said Forbillian. "I was just about to suggest we try to clear some of that there ice."

Amalardh flopped onto his back and chiseled a groove wide enough for Forbillian's sizable rump.

Forbillian's rosy cheeks glistened as he shuffled out of the expanded opening. "Like I said. Just like a cat."

Oisin smirked. "I think for this next part, Forbs, you might need to be more like a penguin."

Forbillian caught sight of the ice slide and his expression dulled. "Are you sure this is the way?"

"You tell me," said Amalardh. To the right of the slide stood three stone pillars, each about a foot high. He jabbed them with his foot. "You seemed to think the three pillars outside were a sign."

Forbillian leaned forward to inspect them, then dropped to his knees. "Give me my ax," he said to Amalardh.

Using the corner of the ax's blade, Forbillian chipped away the build-up of ice around the base of the small columns. "Well, I'll be darned. Aye. I would say this is definitely the way." He stepped back, allowing Amalardh and Oisin a closer look.

The base of each pillar displayed an etching of a wolf, a bear, and a lynx. The temperature in the chamber seemed to drop a few degrees as a chill creeped down Amalardh's back.

Oisin's round eyes remained focused on the find. Destiny truly had wanted him on this journey.

"Do you still feel bad about passing out?" Amalardh asked.

Oisin offered a weak shrug. "If your only purpose on this journey was to collapse face down so the rest of the team could find a marker, would you feel worthwhile?"

Oisin's long face affected Amalardh. "You locked off the boat during the storm. You saved my and Forbillian's life. I think that's purpose enough, don't you?"

Oisin shrugged.

Tell the kid your truth, he told himself. "For what it's worth, I'm glad you stowed away."

Oisin's face lit up. "Really?"

Amalardh nodded. "Really."

Oisin threw his arms around him. As Amalardh returned the hug, the deep ache gnawing at his heart lessened the littlest bit. Factual admissions came easily to him. Honesty related to exposing his vulnerability didn't. He'd always known how to physically fight for the ones he loved. Now, he was beginning to understand the emotional battle he needed to fight with himself if he wanted to keep his loved ones by his side. If he wasn't willing to clobber his stubborn self, and allow himself the freedom to express his feelings, then chances were high that he'd end up just like his uncle—living the next thirty years alone, wrapped in a shaggy wolf cloak, and spouting random words like "ferry-glades."

"I'm glad you both are having your bonding moment," said Forbillian. He eyed the steep slide. "I heard it's good for one to make peace before they die." He opened his arms wide. "Come in for a hug, nephew."

Amalardh picked up Forbillian's bear cape and thrusted it into his uncle's open arms. "No one's dying. Just follow my lead." He held his backpack and sword to his chest and sat on the slide's top edge. "Just lean back. And let go."

Down Amalardh shot. What a thrill. Until he reached the pitch-black shadow. The sudden inability to see made his pulse race. He burst into light and slid to a stop inside another ice tunnel about twice as wide as the first one.

"Can you hear me?" he called up the slide.

"Yes," came Oisin's distant voice.

"Just remember to lie flat and—"

"Yeahhh!" Oisin's excited cry cut Amalardh off.

A few seconds later, he slid to a stop.

He jumped to his feet. "That was so cool. I want to do it again!"

The kid's infectious energy spread a smile across Amalardh's face. This was the Oisin he knew and loved. "Your turn, Forbillian," he called.

Forbillian's whimper echoed down.

"Come on, Forbs. It's awesome," said Oisin.

Amalardh folded his arms. He went to ask about the hold up when—

"Ahhh!" Forbillian screamed.

Pale-faced, he slid to a stop.

Oisin bounced up to him. "Hey, Forbs, wasn't that the best thing ever?"

"Blimey. You could've warned me about the dark spot. I nearly shat my pants."

Oisin burst out laughing. "That was the best part."

Amalardh hoisted his uncle to his feet. He reset his backpack and the three of them pressed forward along the blue, glowing tunnel.

"What do you think's down here?" asked Forbillian.

Nothing living, surely.

The tunnel opened into a majestic ice chamber. A stone bridge arched over a narrow, crystal clear stream. Small fires burned in wrought iron pits, casting a dazzling light on the stalagmites above. At the far end, on the other side of the stream, a long stairway carved into the rock climbed up and out through a tall arch. A man wearing a royal blue hat that was broader at the top than the bottom and a long robe of similar color sat on a red, velveteen chair. The pointy collars of a white undershirt protruded from the robe's neckline. While his thick, auburn beard lacked any gray, the wisdom etched on his face made him seem to have lived more than a lifetime of experiences. He set his rose-patterned tea cup onto a similarly patterned plate and stepped toward them with outstretched arms, as if greeting dear old friends.

"Amalardh," he said, "I've been expecting you."

Amalardh's brow twitched. This man looked weirdly familiar.

"Do you know him?" whispered Forbillian.

"And Forbillian."

Forbillian's spine straightened at his own name.

"You and your bear look more thrilling than I could've dreamed. Literally." He turned to Oisin and pressed his hands to his chest. "And Oisin. My little lynx with the eagle eyes."

Oisin's jaw gaped.

This man knew things he could not possibly know. "Who are you?" Amalardh asked.

The man bowed. "Allow me to introduce myself. My name is Gaussian Tuetin."

Amalardh's shoulders tightened. Gaussian Tuetin was the original Prophet, the father, so to speak, of the Croilar Tier.

Amalardh now recognized him from the portrait sketched in the diary they found inside the archives.

"Gaussian Tuetin?" said Forbillian. "Impossible. Eifa worshippers known as the Order of Terefellian murdered the Prophet Tuetin over fifteen hundred years ago. Now, who are you, really?"

Gaussian pressed his fingertips together. "I know this all seems very strange, and I wish I had time to explain. Alas, after many centuries, time is no longer on my side. If you will bear with me, I have a message for each of you."

He stepped over to Oisin. The kid's eyes shot at Amalardh, who returned an "it's okay" gesture. Gaussian placed his hands on Oisin's shoulders and whispered into his ear.

Forbillian leaned into Amalardh. "Do you believe he's the Prophet?"

Dressed in clothing more fit for Vitus's temperate climate, the man should have perished in the frost long ago. "I'm just following the signs," Amalardh replied.

Apprehension stole Oisin's face as he glanced at Amalardh again. He then nodded at the Prophet.

Gaussian stepped left as if moving down a production line. He smiled and turned his hands palm up. "Forbillian. The pleasure is most definitely all mine."

Forbillian stiffened as the Prophet leaned close and whispered in his ear. He tucked a rolled scroll, about the same size as the map from the archives, into Forbillian's front pocket. As with Oisin, Forbillian offered Amalardh a perplexed stare, then acknowledged his understanding of whatever directive the Prophet gave.

"And Amalardh." Gaussian stepped over.

Amalardh pulled out the Prophet's diary. "Why did you remove the pages from this?"

"A man who knows his destiny is less likely to listen," Gaussian said. "Sometimes, we need to allow the true nature of the human spirit to do what it will, not what it believes it must." He glanced over Amalardh's shoulder as if expecting someone. Amalardh turned to follow the man's gaze, but the Prophet stopped him.

He placed a rolled parchment in Amalardh's hand, similar in size to the one he'd given Forbillian, then projected his voice at an unnatural volume, as if addressing a room full of people. "Here are the answers to life eternal." He leaned close to Amalardh's ear and whispered. "May the Light of Siersha stay with you."

He shoved Amalardh sideways and gasped as a spiked metal disk about three inches wide impaled his forehead. For a slight second, he stood frozen, then crumpled to the icy floor.

CHAPTER
29

HEAVY WINDS BUFFETED the airship. Beneath the howl came a guttural whisper. Eifa. During Cecilia's journey from Plockton to Vitus, the Dark Goddess had appeared many times as gloomy tunnels, raging waterfalls, and deadly storms. Her singular goal: to instill fear. Right now, Eifa was succeeding. Today marked day ten, with no land in sight. At least, none that Cecilia could see. The downpour and blackened sky limited visibility to the choppy water two hundred feet below. Rabbie's calculations for the airship's hot air burners had proved pretty spot on. With the cloudless sky offering the sun's rays unfettered access to the balloon's thermal heating material, the first cannister had lasted five days.

The altimeter began clicking down. 200. 195. 190. The lack of sunlight, combined with the wind and rain, meant the balloon lost heat fast. Eideard dialed up the burner's flame to max and exchanged a concerned look with Cecilia. He grabbed her hand and squeezed tight. If land did not appear within the next twenty minutes, they would be in the water. If only they hadn't used the additional cannister as a weapon against the monsters. Then again, if they'd saved it for the airship, they wouldn't have survived the Wirador Wosrah raid.

They floated dangerously close to the choppy waters. Cecilia's nails dug into her chair. Had she made the wrong decision in letting Rabbie go with Saffron instead of captaining the flight? Her brothers had their strengths. Eideard ran faster. Rabbie's wits were sharper. No matter the situation, Rabbie could always figure a way out. Like the time they got lost in the forest and he used a needle, his woolen sock, and a floating leaf to make a compass. She looked around the airship. What would Rabbie do if he were here?

She picked up the empty cannister. "Throw off anything not anchored down. The less weight we carry, the less fuel we'll use."

"Damn it. Why didn't I think of that?" said Eideard.

He tossed the blankets and remaining food and water. He went to pick up the plastic container housing their weapons. Cecilia placed her hand on his arm, stopping him. Her sword's sharp blade and resilient steel had saved her life countless times. She couldn't toss it into the frosty abyss like a useless artifact just because its purpose didn't match her present needs. "Leave them," she said. "You never know."

He turned his attention to the seats. "Do you think we can unscrew these?"

A bright flash of light followed by a thunderous roar made Cecilia jump. She looked up at the silver ball above. When she and Amalardh ventured through the Dead City on their trip to Vitus, a bolt of electricity had connected with a crumbling building's exposed support rod, creating a spark so big, the structure lit up. "This balloon is metallic," she said.

"So?" Eideard replied.

"So? Metal attracts lightning!"

Eideard's eyes widened.

Thunder cracked. A bolt of lightning ripped through the sky.

"Nothing bad is going to happen to you," Eideard said. "I won't let it."

As brave as his words seemed, he was powerless against the wild storm's might.

He tugged her arm. "Look!"

She followed his pointing finger.

In the distance, a ray of silver sunlight broke through the angry clouds. Land!

Cecilia's excitement plummeted. The bluffs matched the height of the ones they had flown from. With the burner already on high, they couldn't lift the balloon up and over. "If we don't drop into the water now, we're going to smash into that rock wall." Both options seemed as bad as each other.

"Wait!" said Eideard. "There's an inlet."

As the airship drew closer, what had looked like a continuous cliff face revealed itself as dual headlands separated by a waterway. If they made it to the opening, the waters might be calmer. Eideard dialed down the burner. The more fuel they saved, the better their chances of traveling down the inlet to a place where the steep rock might flatten out. At thirty feet above sea level, Eideard leveled off the ship.

Cecilia steadied herself against the winds and kept her focus forward. *Siersha will not forsake me.* But did she really believe her own words? If she did, why did terror still rage through her bones? Brassal once told her that maintaining faith amid danger challenged even the heartiest souls, whereas succumbing to Eifa's darkness proved easy. The storm had made Cecilia falter. To calm her soul, she repeated her people's prayer. When she got to the last line, her terror was all but gone. *Never more will darkness dwell, nor fear within our—*

A bolt of lightning connected with the balloon. The smell of burning metal assaulted her senses as the entire structure lit up.

BEEP. BEEP. BEEP. The altimeter's alarm signaled their rapid descent.

The choppy water rushed closer.

"Jump!" yelled Eideard.

They leaped from their respective sides.

Coldness sucked the oxygen from Cecilia's lungs. She swam for the surface, but the flattened balloon blocked her escape. *Don't panic. You're a fish. You can hold your breath longer than anyone.*

She swam further. Still more material.

Her pulse quickened. It was one thing to hold her breath underwater for two minutes while stationary. Doing so fully clothed while swimming was completely different. She needed to get out from under this cover, and fast. She pressed her hand up. More material. Was this it? After all that she'd survived, her one natural skill—holding her breath underwater—would fail her? Images of Alistair flashed through her mind. His dimples, just like his father's. His deliciously long eyelashes. His stubby toes. She had to keep fighting.

She pushed forward and broke through the surface and gasped. Her lungs no sooner satiated themselves when an angry wave crashed down, sending her under. She burst back out and sucked in air.

The balloon wavered on the watery surface like a long snake. If she had swum either left or right, she would've been out from under the thing within a matter of seconds. Instead, she had paddled down its length. She couldn't be further away from her brother if she'd tried. "Eideard!" she called.

Another wave crashed down.

She wouldn't be able to keep this up for long.

The silvery material began disappearing, dragged underwater by the weight of its undercarriage.

"Eideard!" she called out.

"Cecilia!" came his distant voice.

"Where are you?"

"Over here!"

She narrowed in on the direction of his voice. "I'm coming!" she yelled.

As fast as the storm had hit, it broke. The wind died down. The clouds separated. The sun brightened the sky. Cecilia spotted Eideard, bobbing up and down. She swam toward him. Every foot in the chilly water felt like a mile. She pushed through the exhaustion.

When she finally reached him, he shoved a firm, square object under her chest. "Here, this will help."

The buoyant device held her weight, offering immediate relief. "This is one of the seat cushions," she said. "Why didn't you tell me they floated? I would've grabbed mine."

"I didn't know. It popped up next to me."

Cecilia shouldn't be surprised. Rabbie may be the smartest, but Eideard by far was the luckiest. As kids, he always found treasure, long-lost trinkets from before the time of the Great War. On one occasion, he'd gone down to the river to fish and came back with a six-inch-high statue of a naked woman. Rabbie's twelve-year-old eyes had widened. "Wow! Where did you get that?" he asked.

"At our favorite fishing spot," Eideard replied.

Rabbie had groaned and complained about life not being fair because he had fished in that very spot only hours earlier. A few days later, their mom found the statue. While she understood their attraction ("The female body holds much beauty," she'd said), she explained that nature did not design the shapely form for young boys to ogle and threw it back in the river. A week later, Eideard caught a massive catfish. He gutted the thing and wouldn't you know, inside its belly lay the statue. This time, he kept it well hidden from their mother. Maybe that sculpture explained why Eideard was yet to have a serious relationship. He had found his perfect woman and no living, breathing human since had come close.

His teeth chattered as he trod water. Cecilia couldn't let him die without first finding a love to rival the one from his childhood. She shoved the cushion at him, then motioned to the inlet. "Come on," she said. "Let's go."

He pushed the cushion back to her. "You keep it."

"I'm the better swimmer."

They settled on the idea of switching as needed.

On Cecilia's long trek with Amalardh, she had kept herself focused by setting mini-goals, like: *Just to the tree. Just to the tree. I just have to make it to the tree.* And when she made it to the tree, she would set another: *Just to the rock. Just to the rock. I just have to make it to the rock.* Sadly, on this occasion, the sheer walls on either side of the inlet had no specific landmarks for her to latch on to.

"I feel like we're not moving," said Eideard.

Cecilia felt the same, only her misery had blunted her desire to say anything. The inlet's opening looked farther away, so they must have been progressing forward, however slowly.

A slippery object brushed against her leg. "Arrrgh! What was that?"

Eideard's eyes locked onto something behind her. His face drained.

Cecilia spun around and gasped at a fin poking from the water. The telltale rocking from side-to-side as it sped her way extinguished any hope that the protrusion belonged to a dolphin.

She fumbled for her knife. Fear, panic, and the icy water turned her fingers to jelly.

The beast rose from the water, bearing its sawtooth fangs.

Eideard's fist connected with its nose. It spun around and shot off.

Cecilia's breath trembled. "How did you know to do that?"

"Amalardh. It was one of the first things he taught me when we went boating."

Warmth swirled through her. Even from afar, Amalardh's Croilar Tier spirit protected her.

A section of wall to their right presented decent outcroppings for hand and footholds. "Let's try climbing," she said. After the near miss with the shark, the sooner they got out of the water the better.

She pushed the floating cushion at Eideard. "Race you," she said, then started swimming.

Eideard chortled. "You are such a cheat!"

A searing pain shooting through her right leg cut Cecilia's joy. She screamed. The same—or maybe different—shark gripped her thigh in its powerful jaws. "Eideard! Help!"

Eideard powered to her. His arm flailed as his knife tore into the beast's gills. The shark's jaws released and the finned attacker drifted away.

Blood pooled around Cecilia. Did it come from her or the shark?

Her heart thumped. Was her leg still even there? She forced herself to wiggle her toes. She bent her knee. Her leg seemed intact.

She pulled herself onto a nearby rock shelf.

Eideard ordered her to lie back so he could inspect. As he guided her right leg to the surface, Cecilia averted her eyes. If the shark had stolen a chunk of flesh, she didn't want to know. "It's just some puncture wounds," Eideard said. The deep concern etched on his face betrayed the lightness of his tone. He pulled off his shirt and wrapped it around the wound. Within seconds, the white cotton turned red.

Puncture wounds my foot. Her lightheadedness confirmed that Eideard had downplayed her injury.

"Cecilia!" he said. "Wake up."

Coldness closed in as she drifted into a dark void.

CHAPTER
30

As Saffron watched Cecilia and Eideard float off in the airship, a red piece of cloth tumbled her way. She picked up the satiny object. Her mother's scarf. It must have fallen from her mother's neck before she died. While items of clothing from the world outside of Terefellia weren't exactly banned, they also weren't encouraged. Most Terefellians didn't care for them. In their minds, anyone outside the Terefellian society was an infidel. Why would they want something that had touched a non-believer's skin? Saffron didn't care. If she spotted something she liked while out exploring, she took it. Her mother had adored the gift and kept it hidden in her buhleycob. The moment she escaped Terefellia, she had tied it around her neck. Saffron held the soft material to her chest. She would cherish this red cloth forever.

"We should get going," said Rabbie.

"Not yet," she said. She tucked the scarf into her pocket and motioned for him to follow her to the precipice. "We should deal with them first." Four Wirador Wosrah had formed from the balls Cecilia had driven into the ocean. The rising tide had pushed the beasts to the steep wall. Because Cecilia had sent the balls off the edge at different spots along the bluff, the climbing warriors spread across fifty feet of the coast. Rabbie and Saffron stood in the middle of them.

Rabbie's eyes shot from one to the other. "They're all going to reach the top at the same time."

On the bright side, Saffron had expected more to have survived the blast.

A few feet to their right, a black, syrupy hand slapped the top of the precipice, as did another to their immediate left. Further down on either side, the other two creatures surfaced.

Saffron pulled two arrows from Rabbie's quiver and handed them to him. "You get that one." She motioned to the one closest to him. "I'll get this one." From her own pack, she grabbed two arrows and dashed to the warrior to her left. The beast grasped her ankle just as she jabbed her weapons into its eyes. Its entire being turned to black rain, which evaporated before hitting the water below.

Rabbie dispatched of his monster and returned to her. His worried face scanned the two remaining beasts as they charged from either side. "Stabbing out the eyes of a breaching warrior is one thing. How do you suggest we fend off two galloping at us at full speed?"

"By not being here when they arrive."

He followed her gaze over the edge and his voice rose an octave. "Are you crazy? We can't jump."

The two beasts drew near.

"That's okay. You don't have to." Ignoring his confused look, she grabbed his hand and pulled him with her as she leaped.

The chilly water sucked out her breath as she plummeted into the ocean. She broke through the surface and turned in a panicked circle. Where was Rabbie?

He burst up beside her, sucking in air. "That was insane." He wiped the water from his face. "I thought you said you couldn't swim."

"I never said I can't swim. I said my people couldn't. As long as we're in the water, the Wirador Wosrah can't get us."

She glanced at the steep wall, expecting to see the two remaining warriors scaling down, but they weren't there. *That's strange. Where did they go?* She couldn't waste time wondering. Her legs already tired under the drag of her heavy, water-logged clothes.

She spotted a submerged rock shelf, the perfect place to rest. She motioned for Rabbie to follow her. Once on top, she crouched to maintain the water level along her upper chest. "Stay low," she said, "or they'll know we're standing on something."

She pressed her palms to the rock's smooth surface to help steady against the undulating swell. "Based on the experiences of the Wirador Wosrah that fell into the stream and the ones that just climbed out of this ocean, they will have the understanding that water either sweeps you out to sea or washes you to land. Since they don't understand how to resist water's will, they won't jump in. But if they see us swimming, they'll figure out the concept and come after us."

She glanced back to the cliff and the hairs on her arms stood on end. A Wirador Wosrah twice as big as a regular beast and with four arms and four legs scuttled down the wall like a giant spider. It stopped, lifted its elongated head, and hissed at her out of its dual mouths. Instead of two eyes, the thing had four (one set on top of the other), and four gargantuan horns. The two beasts, racing at full speed toward each other, must have collided, blending their bodies into one.

"Unbelievable!" said Rabbie. "Is there no end to the freakiness of these things?"

The spider beast made its way to the waterline.

"The tide is rising," Rabbie said. "Soon, we'll get swept off this rock and into its clutches."

Saffron was grappling with the reality that they'd have to fight the grisly beast when Rabbie turned to her. "Can you swim underwater?"

"I've never tried."

"You say it'll copy whatever it sees?" He pointed to the floating clumps of yellowish seaweed that floated along the coast's shoreline. "If we swim under that, it won't see us."

"Explain how it's done."

He described the arm and leg movements.

"Give me a moment." She closed her eyes. Saffron learned

most tasks through visualization. When she could see herself throwing a stone at a target or kicking a practice pell, the mental image flowed through to her muscles. She imagined herself swimming under water just as Rabbie had described, her legs kicking out and back like a frog while her arms pushed forward as if cutting through a field of tall grass.

She opened her eyes and nodded. "Let's do it," she said.

Following his lead, she took a deep breath, slipped off the rock and under the seaweed. The sting of salt water in her eyes soon dissipated. Even though her body moved with precision, no amount of visualization enabled her lungs to hold oxygen for longer than they were willing. She burst out of the water, gasping for air. Rabbie continued another ten feet.

"How can you hold your breath for that long?" she asked.

"I just can. Cecilia's even better. She can hold hers forever."

Determined to improve, Saffron sucked in another lungful of air and dove under. This time, she only went half as far. She burst back up. "This is useless. We're not getting anywhere." She motioned to the beast tracking them along the shoreline. "Every time we break through these weeds for air, it spots us."

"Wait here," said Rabbie. He ducked underwater and swam away.

In the distance, his hand captured a long, floating stick and pulled it under.

What was he doing?

A few moments later, he resurfaced on what looked to be another rock shelf. He waved the stick at her. "Do you know what this is?"

Saffron was certain she didn't.

He beckoned her over. "Come here. I've got an idea."

She surfaced three times before reaching him. Once she saw the sodden head of the three-foot-long yellow stick, she recognized Rabbie's find as feather grass. It grew in abundance along the bluffs. Why was he so excited about this?

With his back to the spider beast, Rabbie pulled out his knife and removed the stick's fluffy head. He then stuck one end into the water and blew through the other. Air bubbles broke through the surface.

How cool. Saffron didn't know feather grass was hollow.

Rabbie explained his plan to take turns breathing through the tube while making their way through the kelp to the other side, where a rocky outcropping would hide them from the beast's line of sight. "Do you think the beast will follow the stick poking out of the water?"

Because Saffron would never think to use feather grass as a breathing tube, she doubted the Wirador Wosrah would either. If the spider beast spotted the moving stick, it would have no reason to follow it. Rabbie's plan sounded solid, except the part about staying underwater, breathing through the thin tube. "I'm not sure I can do this," she said.

"Yes, you can. You're the most amazing person I've met. You can do anything you set your mind to."

Saffron's chest fluttered. Rabbie thought she was amazing? The moment passed and her apprehension returned. Rabbie was right. She could do anything she set her mind to. And there lay her problem. She had tried to imagine herself breathing through a tube while underwater, and couldn't. "You go," she said. "Get yourself to safety. I can stay here as a distraction."

"What? No! I'm not leaving you."

"We don't stand a chance against that eight-legged creature. If we both stay here, we'll either drown or be swept into its clutches. If you go, one of us might survive."

The intensity in his eyes as they locked onto her made Saffron's belly twist. He leaned forward. Her heart thumped. *What was he about to do?* Before she could figure an answer, his soft lips pressed against hers. Her chest hollowed as her breath escaped. She had never kissed a boy before, never even imagined herself doing so. What if she didn't know what to do? But she needn't have worried. Kissing, it seemed, didn't require prior visualization. Her lips responded, kissing him back without even telling them to. As she lost herself in the perfectly divine moment, confusion washed over her. Why the heck was Rabbie kissing her?

She pushed him away. "Why did you do that?"

"The last girl I kissed died the next morning." He shrugged. "I figure, if you're going to die, I should at least get my kiss."

Her jaw went slack. This wasn't the Rabbie she knew. Eideard was supposed to be the toad bucket. She punched him. Hard. "You asshole. I'm not going to die just so you can have some kind of hero's kiss." She'd show him. She snatched the reed from him, ducked under the seaweed, blew through the tube to remove any water, and began breathing. Her anger overrode any thought of panicking. In fact, the more she breathed, the more relaxed she became. Why had she feared trying this?

A bunch of bubbles floated in front of her. They dissipated, revealing Rabbie.

She scowled at him.

His coy smile suggested an element of trickery on his end. Reality smacked harder than a raging beast. Rabbie hadn't kissed her for real. He knew his defiance would piss her off and make her face her fear. She would never forgive him for what he'd just done. But damn. Why did he have to be so charming? She wanted to stay under the ocean with him forever. No more running. No more fighting. No more hating. Just her and this bold young man, who made her heart skip.

He motioned for his turn to use the breathing tube.

Her eyes narrowed. He'd just duped her into a kiss. Two could play that game.

She sucked in a lungful of air and pressed her lips to Rabbie's. Before her passion took hold, she blew the contents of her lungs into his. She broke from the embrace and began swimming. Gosh. Had she really just done that? Kissed Rabbie again? She pushed the moment from her mind. Right now, survival was all that mattered. She sucked in a breath from the breathing tube and handed it to Rabbie. With the fun and games over, they took turns in breathing through the tube until they hit the cliff face on the other side of the outcropping.

Weeds clung to their heads as they slowly surfaced. Had Rabbie's plan worked? It must have, because the spider beast would've been scuttling around the bluff's edge by now.

Saffron glanced up the steep escarpment. Her tired muscles aside, the climb would be relatively easy for her. "Do you think you'll be able to make it up this?"

The swell pushed Rabbie's body against hers. A tingle shot to her toes.

"You don't want to rest a moment?" he asked.

Saffron did not. Resting meant dangling too close to this guy whom she didn't want to feel anything for. He had kissed her out of necessity. She doubted his heart had skipped the way hers had. "I'll rest when it's time to rest," she said.

She clambered up the cliff face. She was about fifteen feet up when—

"Saffron! Jump!" Rabbie yelled.

Why would she want to—

Her throat closed at the sight of the spider beast scuttling her way.

She leaped from the wall but didn't fall. The eight-legged Wirador Wosrah held her tight in its grasp.

CHAPTER
31

Wyndom glanced up at his people toiling away at their daily tasks and the excitement of controlling a Wirador Wosrah, while leading his queen's army into battle, fizzled. What must they think after watching him break down the way he had, wailing like a two-year-old because he'd thought an explosion happening miles away had burned him alive? Had their respect for him lessened? He needed to ensure his standing; make them remember he was still their competent leader.

Leaping to his feet, he thrust his arms into the air and called his followers to prayer. As he danced up and down his rock, his people lapped up his words, confirming that their view of him hadn't changed. So long as Wyndom maintained his role as his people's spiritual guide, they would offer him license to do as he pleased. No matter how bizarre his actions, his loyal sheep would still follow. Wyndom grinned to himself. His outbursts had changed nothing. In the land of goats, he still led a flock of docile sheep.

As a whole, Terefellia possessed a goat's independent nature. The group had broken from the masses who followed the fake Goddess of Light and forged their own path. Within Terefellia, however, leaders—Wyndom included—needed sheep, not goats. Saffron was the perfect example of how little control leaders had against a goat's unruly independence. To prevent a horde of Saffron-like Terefellians breaking through the ranks, the leaders needed to keep their followers docile. And there was no better way to implant submission than shrouding the relationship with their queen under the innocent cloak of a humble shepherd tending her trusting herd. "The queen is our shepherd," leaders would tell the children, "and we are her loyal flock." Beyond providing praise to their queen, the primary purpose of preaching was to reinforce the shepherd-sheep relationship. Wyndom splayed his hands to the sky. "Our queen protects her flock. Submit to her power, give in to her will, and eternal pastures will be yours!"

His people lifted their arms. "We follow our queen's righteous path, so that eternal pastures will be ours."

Smoke wisps slithered out the temple's door and over to the group. "Eifa, we are ready to receive you. We say to you: we are yours!" everyone said.

A plume of smoke shot forth and into Wyndom's chest. Euphoria washed through him.

Do you feel alive? the Maddowshin asked.

Wyndom breathed deep and nodded.

Do you feel invincible?

The pounding of his elated heart certainly did.

Good. Because you need more practice inside a vessel.

The ground in front of Wyndom flipped vertically. The disorienting viewpoint sent him hopping sideways.

Brother Stilton rushed over and steadied him. "Great Leader, are you okay?"

"Yes, son. Take me to my mat so I may lie down. Do not fear. I am engaged in more work for our queen."

Brother Stilton guided Wyndom to the palm tree and eased him to the ground.

"Go now," Wyndom said. "Leave me to my duty."

The sudden shift in Wyndom's world represented the point of view of a Wirador Wosrah clinging sideways to a cliff, a good fifty feet above the ocean. Four black, muscular arms came into view. Confusion overrode his terror. The positioning of the arms made no sense. Was he somehow lying on another warrior?

FLASH. His view changed to a previous moment of a regular Wirador Wosrah rushing along a precipice edge toward Saffron and the annoyingly handsome young man. At top speed, another Wirador Wosrah bolted from the other end. Wyndom's racing warrior reached out to grab Saffron when she jumped, pulling Rabbie with her. Spotting the other Wirador Wosrah, Wyndom flung his arms over his face. He shuddered as a wet, muddy substance smacked hard against him.

I did not know that a high-speed impact could combine two warriors, said the Maddowshin.

FLASH. Wyndom's point of view returned to the Wirador Wosrah clinging to the rock wall. His belly knotted at the sharp perspective change. The beast's gaze turned east. Floating above the ocean, the silver flying craft drifted quietly away.

As you can see, the Treoir Solas has yet again escaped. Our gracious queen is not pleased.

The warrior's focus dropped downward. Several feet out in the water floated Saffron and Rabbie. The beast hissed at them.

Rabbie disappeared under water. Saffron followed.

Wyndom's fingers clawed at his resting mat. What was the fool girl thinking jumping into the water? She didn't know how to swim.

The seconds ticked.

A deep ache ground inside Wyndom's chest. Where did she go? Had she drowned?

She emerged. Saffron could swim underwater? His angst flipped to indignation. The horrid child had always been such a showoff. She could travel beneath the surface all she wanted. Her need for air would betray her location every time. She wouldn't be able to keep this up for long. Eventually, she and Rabbie would tire and be forced to seek rest at the cliff base, where Wyndom's magnificent Wirador Wosrah would be waiting.

The brisk sea air was cold but nowhere near as frosty as the chill that shot down Wyndom's spine. What was that? How dare that cocky lad kiss Saffron! Wyndom lifted his chin in defiance. The brazen young man would get what's coming to him. Saffron would never stand for such contact. He waited in anticipation of her punch to Rabbie's face. But the punch never came. Instead, Saffron returned the enemy's kiss. The audacity of the girl! Beneath his bubbling rage flowed jealousy. Why did she possess the confidence to follow her desires and he didn't?

Saffron pushed Rabbie away. Finally, she had come to her senses. She dipped underwater and Wyndom relaxed. Maybe Saffron was her father's daughter after all. She ran from the person Wyndom knew attracted her, exactly as he would do. Rabbie dove into the water after her, his form utterly perfect. In another time, another place, another world, Wyndom would've loved to welcome this beguiling individual as a son-in-law.

His Wirador Wosrah scanned the undulating seaweed blanket. Seconds passed and still no heads popped up. Terror crept into Wyndom's throat. Saffron and Rabbie remained underwater too long. Had a tangle of weeds trapped them? A sea monster carried them off to a watery grave? *You stupid little girl, Saffron. There is a reason Terefellians don't swim.* He scratched an itch on his cheek. Was that water on his finger? He wiped his eye with the back of his hand. His lashes were wet. The pain in his heart was real. Was Saffron dead?

They are gone, said the Maddowshin. Its voice sounded uncharacteristically sad. *It is for the best.*

As the Wirador Wosrah turned from the ocean, something caught Wyndom's eye.

Wait a minute, he said.

But the eight-legged warrior began its upward climb.

Please. Tell this thing to stop.

The warrior continued.

Rudella! Saffron is my daughter. If she needs my help...

Help is not what you can offer her. It is best for all that you accept no one can survive underwater this long.

Wyndom leaped to his feet. "You will do as I ask. You are just jealous because she is not yours." His people must have become numb to his outbursts because they barely flinched.

The Maddowshin's shiny muscles rippled. *Your belligerence has* disturbed the queen. *Because she has requested me to, I will indulge your folly.*

The climbing beast stopped.

Now, tell it to look around, he said to the Maddowshin.

Wyndom's world became a blur of water, sky, cliff face, rocks, water—

Disoriented, he collapsed to the ground. "STOP!" he yelled.

Searching for a clue while under the visual restrictions of a brainless beast grated as painfully as trying to read a book while a two-year-old turned the pages. *You said the time would come where I would need to control my very own vessel. Well, that time is now. Let me take over this*—what exactly did one call an eight-legged Wirador Wosrah? *Let me control this creature.*

The Maddowshin's grand chest rose and fell as it breathed deep. *In truth, the queen's wish had been for you to take full control right from the start. Based on past experiences, I thought it prudent to give you time to adjust to your additional limbs. I had been ready to hand over the reins, when Saffron disappeared.*

The queen had wanted Wyndom involved? Delight swam through him. He had been correct about his queen needing his superior mind. *If you'd put me in control sooner, then my daughter wouldn't have gotten away. I would've captured Saffron and proven to the queen that her trust in me is valid.*

The queen didn't want you in control solely for the purpose you suggest.

A smile crept over Wyndom's face. He truly was an important part of his queen's grand plan. *What else did our glorious queen need me to do?*

Kill Saffron, said the Maddowshin.

Wyndom's hands went clammy. The queen had wanted him to do what?

Saffron's disobedience is a reflection of you, said the Maddowshin. *Preacher or not, the queen can only take so much. She requested you prove your love for her by killing your daughter. In light of your various conditions, she suggested we give you a beast to help you fulfill this task.* The Maddowshin's eyes—which were Rudella's—held melancholy. *Now that I am giving you full control, you can only hope that Saffron has escaped or has already met her death at the bottom of the ocean.*

Wyndom went cold. Saying he wanted Saffron dead was one thing. Killing her himself? Even under the guise of an eight-legged Wirador Wosrah, would he be able to take her life? The sensation as he squeezed her throat and watched the light drain from her eyes would be exactly as if he killed her with his own hands.

He glanced at the temple door. If his queen wished him to display his love for her by sacrificing his own daughter, he would. He would have to. Saving Saffron's life—if she were still alive—would not be worth giving up his own. Rudella was right. For Wyndom's sake, he could only hope that death had already come for Saffron.

The Maddowshin instructed Wyndom to lie back down. *This time, you will be in control. Do not order what you want. Instead, will the movement to happen.*

Will the movement? What exactly did that mean?

Whoa! Yellow seaweed thirty feet below and him ordering *Eyes on cliff! Eyes on cliff!* helped him understand. Words meant nothing to his vessel. He needed to communicate through his mind. He settled his tension and imagined his own eyes looking in the direction that he needed from his Wirador Wosrah. As the water view transitioned to the rock wall, he stifled an excited yelp.

He willed every muscle in his beast to contract and relax. The warrior felt strong. Powerful. He inched an arm forward. The grip of the remaining limbs remained steady. He scuttled along the cliff face a couple of feet. Exhilaration pounded in his chest. He'd never known such proficiency, such agility with climbing. Falling was not a possibility. Tentatively, he returned his view to the seaweed below.

No palpitations. No chill-sweats. No crippling nausea. So, this was what an utter lack of fear felt like. Wyndom could get used to it. Why had he been so obsessed with wanting to still feel? Emotions were overrated. Besides the euphoria of his sermons, what positive sensations did Wyndom experience? Anxiety, panic, dread, doubt, and dismay ruled his daily life. Giving up seconds of pleasure for an eternity of never knowing fear seemed reasonable. After this little climbing event, he might reconsider taking on his rightful role as the Maddowshin.

You know that even with your control inside a Wirador Wosrah, I can still hear your thoughts, said the Maddowshin.

Yes, my dearest Rudella.

Then you also know that I can never allow you to have that which you think you seek. If you try to attack me, I will kill you.

Wyndom bent and straightened his eight legs, testing his control of the spider beast. *You cannot kill me. Our queen needs my spiritual leadership. Our prayers feed her strength. If you kill me without her blessing, she will destroy you.*

True. Our queen will destroy me if I let you die. But not because of your sermons. Any number of a hundred simpletons can dance on a rock and spout praise to a flock of sheep. My dearest Brother, as I keep telling you, the reason you cannot die is that your purpose is far greater than a preacher. You hold the key to our glorious queen's success. Or failure.

The Maddowshin's words should've sent a rumble of terror to Wyndom's belly. But with Wyndom's current inability to even conjure internal duress, he tuned the Maddowshin out and focused on the yellowish seaweed below. Now, where was that red object he'd spotted earlier? It had looked very much like Sister Esme's scarf.

Wyndom had detested the possession. Not because he believed items previously owned by non-believers unclean. He didn't take the Terefellian scriptures that seriously. He despised the scarf because of what it represented: Saffron cared more for her mother than him. In all the years she'd scavenged through infidel rubble, she'd never brought back anything for him.

He scanned the seaweed-carpeted coast and narrowed in on a red splotch floating just beyond a jutting section of the bluff. He scuttled closer. Yes, the red unquestionably was Esme's scarf. He flexed his mighty warrior's muscles. Their power fed his resolve. How dare Saffron take a keepsake to remember her mother and have nothing to remember him? The girl should've stayed loyal to her father, her leader. If he found Saffron alive, he would crush her. He shot effortlessly along the steep rock and rounded the outcropping.

His nostrils flared. Pinned to the vertical wall was his water-rat of a daughter. The cunning traitor had almost outwitted him.

As he rushed upon her, the terror in her eyes flamed his rage. "Is this what it took for you to finally fear me?" he yelled. If his people heard him, so what? They, too, better know their place. They, too, should fear him.

He grabbed Saffron with the Wirador Wosrah's four hands. She trembled under his grip. He could've just as easily snatched her up with two arms, but since his warrior clung to the vertical rock as expertly with four legs as six, why not terrorize her with an additional set of vice-like grips? He would wring her out like an old towel and her death would be as slow and painful as a burning Quinquagenarian.

His heart was cold. His determination, raw. He prepared himself to squeeze the life out of her when—

"Daddy, if you can hear me, please help me!"

Wyndom froze.

Saffron.

Something climbed onto his back.

"Argh!" A silver blade stabbed his warrior's upper left eye. Seconds later, its upper right view disappeared. Black liquid poured as the eight-legged Wirador Wosrah lost half of its being. Its grip on the cliff failed.

Still clinging to Saffron, Wyndom fell.

A rush of frosty liquid engulfed him as his Wirador Wosrah hit the ocean.

Water and kelp surrounded Wyndom. He couldn't swim.

Cut the feed! he yelled. *Get me out of this beast!*

He let go of Saffron and flailed his arms. His survival was more important than his daughter's death.

A painful sting bit away half of Wyndom's visual field. Another sent it black.

He opened his eyes and gasped for air. He rubbed his hands over his body. He was dry.

The Maddowshin stood over him.

"Go ahead. Gloat," Wyndom said. "Tell me how pathetic I am."

"Words are best left for our queen to say."

A lump caught in Wyndom's throat as a trail of thick, black smoke exited the temple and snaked toward him. He'd had his moment to prove his loyalty and failed. "Will you remember me?" He spoke the words to the Maddowshin, but directed them to Rudella.

Wyndom's fear of being forgotten kept him awake at night. Rudella—whatever remained of her—might not forget him. Saffron certainly would. If she didn't care about him when he was alive, why on earth would she bother remembering him when he was dead? In a matter of minutes, the queen would birth Wyndom as one of five thousand near-identical Wirador Wosrah, and if Rudella couldn't commit to enshrining his memory, then who else would? His people would forget him as quickly as they had all the others who'd departed. In Terefellian lore, the dead were gone. Why bother grieving the past and holding onto fanciful images of those who would never return?

"I will remember you," said Brother Stilton.

Tears filled Wyndom's eyes. What a glorious, loyal, young lad. "Thank y—"

Wyndom jolted as the smoke wrapped around his waist. Like the coil of a powerful spring retracting, the wispy tentacle yanked him across the sandy scape and into the dark temple.

CHAPTER
32

"CECILIA! STAY WITH me," yelled Eideard.

Cecilia's eyes fluttered open. The sky above had darkened from when she last remembered seeing it. How long had she been out? She felt cold and wet.

Wet?

She was still in the ocean, floating on her back. Eideard's arm held her around her chest and they jetted forward, as if pulled by something. Too weak and frozen to care, she let her eyes flutter closed.

"Cecilia! Don't you dare! We're almost to the shore."

A bright light filled her mind as she flipped into the Pass-Over Zone. *Siersha*, she said. *You've come to take me home.*

This is not your time. The Goddess's whisper echoed in her head.

Yes, it was. Cecilia was ready to go. *Carry me to my mother and father.*

Siersha's warm glow enveloped her. Within the light came the image of a giggling toddler running with an uncertain gait toward a man dressed in beige pants and a loose-fitting white shirt, similar to the ones worn by Plocktonian men. Who were these two? Neither man nor child seemed familiar as she watched them both from behind. The man picked the child up and the infant, now facing Cecilia, squealed happily. Her heart fluttered. Alistair—older by several months—peeked over the man's shoulder. He waved his chubby fingers at her.

You must continue to fight for those you love, whispered Siersha. *You must live to see this moment.*

Who is that man? His tightly cropped hair did not resemble Amalardh's shaggy locks.

He is the man that will raise your son.

Show me his face, Cecilia said.

I cannot show you what you yourself are not ready to accept. Your heart lies with Amalardh. Your desire for Alistair's best future lies with Gildas. You question whether Vitus or Plockton is the best place for your son. I know what I want for Alistair, but only you can decide.

Cecilia tried to run toward Alistair, but the grassy surface lifted. She stumbled sideways. She regained her footing and tried again, but the newly formed hill flattened, sending her head over heel. She tried to stand, but the uncertain earth forced her to roll back the other way.

She thought she heard a baby cry. Alistair? But the man and her son had disappeared. She coughed as salty water invaded her lungs. The grass turned to soggy sand. The crying sound sharpened. No longer in the Pass-Over Zone, Cecilia lay on a beach, gasping for air after being knocked about by shoreline waves. A dolphin shrilled and wagged its upper body at her. Was this animal the reason she'd felt as though something pulled her and Eideard through the water? Had it directed them to safety? If so, it certainly couldn't be the dolphin she'd fed days ago, could it?

Eideard dragged her out of the water and dropped to his knees. "Stay with me," he said, wiping the wet hair from her face. He looked up as something distracted him. "People are coming." He waved his hands. "Hey! Over here!"

The sound of feet on creaking sand drew near.

Hold on a little longer, Cecilia told herself. *We are on land. We are safe.*

"Hi," said Eideard. "My sister needs—"

He gasped and fell face first to the sand. A heavy-set, light-skinned man with a bald head pinned him down. Eideard's terrified eyes locked on to Cecilia's fading vision.

"What your sister needs is your silence," said the man. "You got lost in the wrong place."

A pair of dark-skinned feet with a gold ring adorning the left second toe came into view. Strong, unwavering arms picked her up. Snippets of imagery bled into her consciousness: light-skinned feet along with Eideard's black boots crunching on pristine white sand, stone stairs, a hard, cold table, a bright light shining in her face, a man with dark skin wearing a cloth mask over his nose and mouth, a long needle, and someone asking, "Should we cut it off?"

A dank, musty smell tickled Cecilia's nose. She opened her eyes. Rays of sunlight from a small window high in the wall lit up the crumbling ceiling. She rubbed her face. Where was she? She froze as the words, "Should we cut it off?" came flooding back. She slapped her hand onto a coral-colored blanket draped over her. Her right leg remained intact, but... she moved her hand up and down, confirming a large dent in her thigh.

She pulled the blanket back. Someone had replaced her clothes with light blue, wide-legged, cotton pants and a matching short-sleeved top. She pulled the hem of her right pant leg to her crotch. Her fingertips explored the numb and slightly tender indentation on her thigh. Just some puncture wounds, Eideard had told her. Yeah, right. Half her muscle had been eaten. She frowned at the pinkish-purple scar. She'd seen stitched tissue before and knew that flesh wounds took around three weeks to look as healed as hers. As she rubbed her aching forehead, vague memories of previously waking up twirled through her mind. Most of her jumbled thoughts, though, remained a blur.

She swung her legs over the edge of the bed. In front of her, metal bars spanned floor to ceiling. She was in a cell? Why? She stood. Her spinning head sent her back down to the bed. She tried again, this time steadying herself with the cold stone wall.

She grasped the bars and shook them. "Hey!" she yelled. "Is anyone there? Eideard! Can you hear me?"

Silence.

The hallway outside her cell bled into darkness. She shook the bars again and yelled.

Still nothing.

What was going on? Why was she down here? Where was Eideard?

A thick, sticky film covered the inside of her mouth. She scraped her leathery tongue on her teeth and limped to a small, porcelain sink. Yellowish brown rust streaks marred the once alabaster white. She turned on the tap. Pipes banged and rattled. The faucet coughed out a chunk of brown gunk. After a few more splutters, putrid liquid flowed, which gradually lightened in color until it ran clear. She slurped a bit. Aside from the metallic taste, it seemed fresh enough. She cupped her hand under the flowing stream and gulped.

A small toilet bowl sat next to the sink. Despite rust stains, the porcelain surface seemed otherwise clean. Items in this place were old, but not dirty.

She lay down on the thin mattress and pressed her cool palms to her throbbing temples.

Darkness suffocated her soul. Would she ever see her brothers, Amalardh, Alistair, again?

A ray of light burst through a hole in the cloudy sky, illuminating the upper corner of her cell. She squinted at a faded sketch of two serpents wrapped around an elegant, elongated flower. Their vicious fangs seemed intent on piercing the flower's delicate petals. Below the drawing, an inscription read: *GT was here.* Siersha's warmth pulsated in her chest. Did this sketch mean something?

The sound of footsteps startled her. Two broad, bald men, one dark skinned, the other light, approached. Both wore maroon pants and matching squared-off, V-neck pullover tops.

"The Countess will see you," said the dark-skinned man.

Cecilia limped to the cell bars. "Where is my brother? Why are you keeping me down here?"

"I need to open this gate, and to do that, I need your silence," said the light-skinned man. His snarky tone rang familiar. A memory of thick, white hands pressing Eideard face down into sand came flooding back. The gold toe ring on the dark-skinned man confirmed these men were the ones who had found her and Eideard on the beach.

Cecilia understood the dark-skinned man's circumspect look to mean that her cooperation would best serve her interests. She stepped back. The other man unlocked the cell door and motioned for her to come with them.

The stone corridor's damp, musty air clung to the back of Cecilia's throat. She followed the men up a winding stone staircase. Halfway along, her right thigh buckled. She steadied herself against the hard wall. The dark-skinned man's eyes seemed empathetic as he watched her rub her aching thigh.

At the top of the stairs, the other man opened a heavy wooden door and guided her into a broad hallway. The cheery red floor, bright blue ceiling, and patterned yellow walls contrasted her captors' sullen demeanor. Windows with their woven shades mostly drawn lined the left-hand side. A four-inch gap between a curtain and the sill exposed a cloudless sky and a snippet of pristine white sand. Cecilia longed to feel the warm sun on her skin and the touch of something other than cold, hard cement on her toes.

The men stopped in front of a glamorous set of double doors, knocked twice, then led her into a long golden room with a polished floor and burgundy walls. Benches on plush mats ran parallel to each other, forming a walkway to a broad, high-backed chair, which Cecilia supposed belonged to the ruler of these lands. Satin drapes adorned a row of arched windows along the wall behind the throne. The view looked out over a sparkling, round bay.

A dark-skinned woman in a flowing silver and gold dress poured steaming water from a kettle into a glass teapot. A brown object similar to a chestnut tumbled in the increasing water depth. A gold headband held the woman's thick, black hair away from her unlined face. The nut-type object opened and a red flower bloomed.

"Great Countess," said the dark-skinned man, "I present you, Cecilia. Cecilia, this is Countess Kosima of Bayton."

"Thank you, Malek. Thank you, Davian," said the Countess to the dark-skinned and light-skinned men, respectively. "I will see you shortly."

The men nodded. As they exited, Malek's cautious look perplexed Cecilia. Was he concerned for her safety or implying that she had better behave herself?

"Tea?" the Countess asked.

Cecilia glanced at the blossomed bud. She preferred weaving flowers into her hair, not drinking them. "No, thank you," she replied.

The Countess poured the steaming yellow liquid into a glass mug.

"Where is my brother?" Cecilia asked.

The Countess's lips thinned.

Cecilia's tone probably sounded more demanding than it should've, so she softened her approach. "Please. I need to see him. I need to know he is safe."

"You will see him in due time." The Countess motioned to a green couch on the far side of the room. "Come sit with me." Cecilia walked with her to the sofa and sat on its velvet seat. "Your brother has told me his version of events," said the Countess, "and I would like to hear yours."

Cecilia understood the elegant woman's wariness. She had opened her own door to three seemingly harmless Terefellians— Brothers Skylark and Atlas, and Sister Darna. They had professed

270

friendship to infiltrate Cecilia's home. She told the Countess her story, from growing up in Plockton and the raid on her village, to meeting Amalardh and discovering the Prophecy, and all the recent events leading to Malek and Davian finding her on the beach.

The Countess sipped her tea and listened intently.

Cecilia finished by saying, "Eifa is building a black army of monsters. She plans to take over Vitus. When she is done with my city, she'll come for yours. Siersha told me to travel east, where I'd find help."

"And this... Siersha?" said the Countess. "She is the Goddess of Light?"

"Yes," Cecilia said.

The Countess rubbed one of her long gold and silver polished nails. "If this Eifa wins, it would seem grim days are upon us."

Cecilia spied a cord running from one of the floor lamps to a receptacle in the wall. The people of Bayton possessed advances beyond what the folk of Vitus had achieved. "My people are strong and willing fighters," she said. "And your people have access to technologies we are yet to unlock. I believe Siersha sent me here to ask for your help. Will you help me?"

The Countess took Cecilia's hands in hers. "Of course, we will."

Cecilia had expected a certain amount of hesitance and push-back. From the moment she had embraced her role as the Treoir Solas, every step seemed like a mini battle as she fought for belief among a sea of naysayers and doubters. The mental and physical toll of the fight against the Army of Vitus had worn her to the nub. A tear rolled down her cheek. She quickly wiped it away.

"You poor thing," said the Countess. "Please. Don't cry."

"I'm sorry," Cecilia said. "It's just... my life is exhausting. I want everything to go back to the way it was. I don't want another battle or to fight any more monsters."

Empathy washed over the Countess's face as she placed her warm, soft hand on Cecilia's cheek. "You've been carrying too

much on your shoulders. I want to help you end this nightmare."
She stood. Her cheeks glistened as she smiled. "Let's go visit this
brave brother of yours."

Relief flooded Cecilia. She couldn't wait to see Eideard.

As they exited the main doors and walked down a corridor,
the Countess explained that when Vitus formed after the Great
War of two centuries passed, some didn't agree with the plan to
destroy history through the burning of books. They packed what
they could and fled. She pushed open a door leading to the sunny
outside. "And this is what they created."

Bayton folk going about their daily lives looked like a living
rainbow. The women wore splashy, flowing dresses, and the men,
patterned pants with relaxed shirts. Unlike the pretentious former Tower Folk of Vitus, nothing about the Baytonite's clothing
or posture seemed stiff. Nor did they appear to have a class system. Everyone seemed equal and projected a healthy glow.

The Countess pointed to a vivid array of buildings. "Over
there is our institute of learning where our children study science
and chemistry." A garden packed with color lined the path.
"These flowers are not just pretty. Many are the basis for the med-
icines we have discovered. In Vitus, your wounds, severe loss of
blood, and massive infection would've killed you." Her expression
dulled. "Sadly, our advances failed to save my husband. He died
three years ago from the claviceps purpurea fungus. You might
know it as the Black Fire. The infected grains came from Vitus."

Vitus? Cecilia's spine straightened. From what she knew, the
former Senators had stored their harvests inside locked chambers.
"How did your people steal grain undetected?"

"Steal? Goodness, no. We had a trade agreement with Vitus."

Cecilia stopped in her tracks. Under the rule of the former
Senators, the first law of Vitus stated that those who resided
within the great wall were the only true, free individuals of the
new world. All else were enemies.

"Is something wrong?" the Countess asked.

"Why did the Senators destroy my village and so many others, and leave your city alone?"

"I wouldn't call a dozen bags of infected grain leaving us alone. But I understand what you mean." She guided their walk along a sculptured hedge trail. "For many years, the Senators and my husband's father, the former Count, traded goods with each other. The lands around Bayton grow very fine spices, and the Vitus fields produce abundant grain. The relationship worked because we both had something the other wanted."

"Until the Senators broke the trust with the poisoned shipment," Cecilia said.

The Countess's flat look confirmed her supposition. Why was Cecilia not surprised? Everything the Senators had touched turned to salt. The bizarre revelation explained why Vitus's spice stores were so low.

"I'm surprised that I haven't heard of your city," Cecilia said. "Surely someone in Vitus would've remembered seeing foreign trading ships coming and going. No one has mentioned anything."

"Our ships never docked at Vitus's port," the Countess said. "Each side dropped off their goods on an island halfway between the cities."

The explanation made sense. Cecilia supposed the Senators used Blind Prisoners for the loading and unloading, as they would not know what they were carting. The Senators would've limited the number of people who knew about this outsider trading. Those who had known the details, like Aetus—the army captain—and his high commanders, had perished in the Battle for Freedom. But what about Amalardh? From what Cecilia understood, nothing got by him. Had he known about the trade partnership? If he had, surely he would've mentioned something. "When word got to you that the Senators had fallen, why didn't you reach out?" she asked. "We would've welcomed you."

The Countess stopped outside a closed door belonging to an

isolated red brick building. "Vitus had broken our trust once. We were not willing to risk further deception."

Cecilia nodded. The City of Bayton had every right to remain wary. "Had you reached out, I assure you, things would've been very different." She injected levity into her voice. "At the very least, you would've known who my brother and I were and not thought us enemies when we washed up on your beach."

The Countess tilted her head as if processing Cecilia's statement. She close-lipped smiled. "Well, as they say, everything happens for a reason." She pushed the door open.

The pristine white hallway emitted a clean, yet chemical smell with a hint of burned toast. Cecilia followed the Countess to a sizeable room filled with empty tables and chairs. "I believe there is someone over there you are eager to reconnect with," the Countess said.

In the far corner, facing a window, sat a solitary figure. Eideard? Instead of joy, Cecilia felt unease. Why was his hair cropped so close to his scalp? She rushed over and spoke his name. His focus remained glued to the outside world. She pressed her hand to his cheek. "Eideard," she said. His eyes slowly found hers. "It's me, Cecilia." He blinked, then gazed back out the window. Terror ignited in her belly. "Eideard! Look at me."

The Countess stepped up beside her. "He'll be fine. He was very sick. One of the sickest we've treated so far."

"Eideard was sick? What happened?"

"His mind had gone. He was very delusional and tormented by visions. His treatments were harsh. But he's strong. He'll pull through. And so will you."

Cecilia glared at the woman. What did she mean?

Into the room stepped a short, pale-skinned man wearing glasses and a knee-length, white coat. Beside him stood Malek and Davian, the two muscular men from earlier.

"Is the patient ready?" asked the short man.

"She is," said the Countess.

The hair on the back of Cecilia's neck stood on end. What was going on?

"My name is Dr. Dufer," said the short man to Cecilia. "Your room is ready."

"I'm not sick. I don't need any treatment. I'm staying with my brother." Her eyes darted around the room for a potential escape.

"Cecilia," said the Countess, "please don't make this harder than it has to be."

"What did you do to my brother?"

Malek and Davian headed her way. Trapped in the room's corner, Cecilia scrambled onto a table and screamed for them to leave her alone. Malek reached for her. She jumped to another table, narrowly escaping Davian's swiping hand.

She darted from table to table like a mouse evading two cats.

"Cecilia, you must let us help you," said the Countess. "You have experienced great trauma."

Unwilling to go down without a fight, Cecilia threw chairs, turned over tables, and screamed at the top of her lungs. To an outsider looking in, she would have seemed like a crazy person. Exactly what the Countess believed Cecilia to be—only the woman used terms like delusions of grandeur, visual and auditory hallucinations, and confabulations.

What delusions? What hallucinations? And what the heck were confabulations?

With Cecilia backed against a wall, the men captured her.

"This would be easier for all concerned if you calm down," said Davian.

His words inspired her to fight harder. She kicked and screamed as he and Malek dragged her into a small, white room that stank of burned toast and misery.

They wrestled her into a chair and secured her arms and legs with straps. Her rapid-fire questions—"What are you doing? What is going on?"—went unanswered.

"This should make you feel much better," said the doctor. He pressed a sharp needle into her arm. A warm sensation swam to her chest and down to her toes. Had she sprouted wings? Because she felt light and breezy, as though floating in the air. In contrast to her body's featheriness, her eyelids sagged heavily.

The Countess placed her warm hand on Cecilia's. "My dearest child, do not fear. I will help you with your monsters. These gods that you speak of, these visions you are having, they are not real. You suffered severe trauma when the Soldiers of Vitus raided your village. To help you cope, your imagination manifested a spiritual world that does not exist. I will free your mind from its prison."

A buzzing sound.

Strange vibrations ran along Cecilia's head.

Clumps of hair fell to her lap.

Her dopey lips and unruly tongue refused to vocalize the "What happened to my hair?" question tumbling in her mind.

A device created pressure on her temples. Even if her mouth had been willing to cooperate, her brain could no longer form questions about the purpose of the object placed on her head.

Her heavy eyelids dropped.

Someone put an oaky-tasting leather strap in her mouth. "This is to bite down on," the person said.

Bite down? Why would Cecilia want to do that?

A crushing sensation gripped her skull.

A painful jolt shot from her temples to her toes.

Her jaw locked down hard on the leather strap as her muscles tensed.

The vice squeezing her head relaxed.

She fell limp.

All that remained was the smell of burned toast.

CHAPTER
33

AMALARDH GLANCED FROM the dead Prophet to two people standing just inside the same entrance he, Forbillian, and Oisin had entered. Their leather slippers and beige, knee-length tunics appeared as wildly inappropriate for the icy locale as Gaussian's. The small leather packs on their backs seemed sizable enough for a blanket and some food, but not to store thick cloaks. At first, he assumed they both were male, but something about the dark-haired one's more graceful poise made Amalardh question otherwise. The redheaded one wore a familiar-looking sword around his waist. Amalardh's fist tightened. He'd given that blade to Finn.

The man's upper lip curled at Amalardh. "My Siddachet was meant for you."

He was no doubt referring to the spiked disk protruding from the Prophet's forehead.

Forbillian hurled an ax. "Blasted Terefellians."

The woman's hand shot up, catching the spinning weapon.

Amalardh's eyes narrowed. Her reflexes were as sharp as, if not better than, his. He drew his sword. The redhead flung a spiked disk at him. Amalardh swung. The clink of metal on metal reverberated in the vast chamber as he batted the flying disk away.

"The last Croilar Tier," said the man. "How cliché that you choose to fight for your life. How arrogant to think you are better than the seven others that fell."

Forbillian massaged the handle of his double-headed hatchet. "These two aren't regular Terefellians," he said. "They're Wrethun Lof. Croilar Tier hunters." He let his ax fly.

The man twisted sideways, but his reaction had not been quick enough to avoid the hatchet's sharp bite. He slapped his hand to his upper arm. Blood coated his palm. The spinning weapon kept flying and imbedded with deadly force into the icy wall on the other side of the stream. For all of Forbillian's foibles, his strength and aim surpassed expectation.

Oisin barreled into Amalardh, as if unable to stop on the icy surface. "I'm sorry," he said. His apology seemed for something other than the not-so-accidental stumble. He bolted off and hid behind an ice pillar.

The man drew his sword. The blood trickling from his upper arm didn't seem to affect his strength. His wince seemed more from annoyance that he'd allowed the injury in the first place than actual pain. "The Croilar Tier is mine," he said to his partner. "You get the other two."

The woman nodded. Still grasping Forbillian's hatchet, she drew back her arm.

"Watch out, Forbs!" yelled Oisin.

The man lunged at Amalardh.

The woman let her weapon fly.

Rather than blocking the man's swinging sword, Amalardh dove at Forbillian, tackling him away from the spinning ax. Only, the ax never came. Instead, it wedged in the man's spine, sending him face first to the hard ground.

"What just happened?" Forbillian asked.

Amalardh didn't know. Other than—the woman had killed her partner. But why?

She held up her hands. "Please, don't hurt me," she said. "My name is Sister Darna. I mean you no harm. My people, however, do. They aim to conquer your city. I came to warn you."

Amalardh hauled himself to his feet, then offered his hand to Forbillian.

Oisin ran from behind the pillar and sidled up close. "Isn't she cold dressed like that?" he whispered.

"People with hearts of ice don't feel the cold," said Forbillian.

Sister Darna pulled the ax from her partner's back, wiped it clean on his tunic, and handed it to Forbillian. "We must get moving," she said. "More of my people will be coming."

Amalardh remained planted. He did not care to take orders from someone he knew nothing about.

She pulled three spiked disks and two small knives from her pockets. "You are within your rights not to trust me. Take my weapons, if that helps your belief."

Forbillian scooped up her armory and tucked them away in his various pockets. "Words are only as reliable as the lips that utter them," he said. "Arms out." She complied. He patted her down and rifled through her backpack. She had the bare essentials— snow paddles, water, a blanket, a length of rope, and some jerky. He shoved the items back in the pack, keeping the rope. "Perfect. Now we don't have to waste our own when we tie her up."

"No one is tying up anyone," said Amalardh. When he had first met Cecilia, he had treated her like a dog. He had bound her hands and dragged her halfway across the country on a fifteen-foot leash, only to discover her complete innocence. Even though he held suspicions about the Terefellian's motives, he had vowed never again to treat someone as he had Cecilia until they proved a threat.

"You're making a mistake," said Forbillian.

"She is not our prisoner," said Amalardh. "At least, not yet."

Forbillian stared the confident woman down and squeezed the handle of his hatchet. "My hand stays close to my hip."

Amalardh thanked Darna for her help, then motioned to her outfit. "How did you track us dressed that way?"

She side-glanced at Forbillian. "Maybe my heart isn't as icy as some suggest."

Her wit reminded Amalardh of Cecilia's charm. Such distraction, he did not need. Right now, his primary concern centered on whether this Terefellian's threadbare attire would affect his journey. He had enough to worry about with Oisin and Forbillian without adding another frozen body into the mix. "If you freeze out there, you're on your own," he said.

"I can look after myself. My only goal was to stop my people from assassinating the last Croilar Tier."

Forbillian pulled the spiked disk from the Prophet's forehead. He frowned and showed it to Amalardh. "What do you make of this?" he asked.

Amalardh studied the spotless object. The lack of blood was certainly perplexing.

Forbillian removed one of his furry mittens and placed his hand on the Prophet's cheek. "He's cold as ice." He grabbed a knife that he'd sourced from Darna and sliced the Prophet's forearm. Again, no blood.

"I guess someone can live for centuries when they're not really alive," Forbillian said. "At least, alive in the sense that you and I understand." He glowered at Darna. "Is that your deal, too? Is that why you can survive the cold?" He motioned to the dead Terefellian. "Are you and him the living dead?"

Darna's focus remained on the bloodless corpse. "I am very much alive."

Forbillian scoffed. "But that's the endgame, isn't it? Terefellian? Eternal life?"

"Some of us believe that, yes."

Did her expression when looking at the Prophet hold surprise that her people's belief system was true? Or abhorrence at the revelation that life eternal meant existing as the living dead.

"See, I was right," said Forbillian to Amalardh. "They believe in eternal life." He held up his knife and pointed to the dead Terefellian. "Just because that one bled doesn't mean she will. If she's lying about what she is, then she's lying about everything."

"You will not cut—" Amalardh said.

Darna snatched the knife from Forbillian and sliced her forearm. She held up the blood-stained blade and her dripping arm. "Is this enough proof of my life to you? Or do I need to spear an artery?"

Forbillian took the knife from her. "Your people have hunted my family for centuries. Do you really want to give me that choice? Because I'd welcome this knife piercing the throbbing part of your neck."

She stood her ground. "Please, what can I do, what can I say for you to believe me?"

Forbillian backed down. "Fine. Explain how you can survive in this glorious environment in tattered cloth."

"I don't know. I just... I don't notice the cold."

"Wonderful. You're a freak of nature. That makes me feel much better." He glared at Amalardh. "I'm telling you, you're making a mistake trusting her."

"Enough," Amalardh said. He cut a strip of cloth from the dead Terefellian's tunic and wrapped Darna's cut. For someone who could kill Amalardh with a single blow, she seemed to fear his proximity. "Rinse that wound daily and keep it clean," he said.

She nodded.

He led the group across the narrow stone bridge.

Oisin jogged over to the double-headed hatchet imbedded in the ice wall and strained to remove it. The deeply lodged blade held firm. Amalardh stepped over, and although he freed the weapon with one tug, the action required more effort than expected.

Forbillian stowed the ax in his belt. "You seem impressed that an old man like me can wield this thing with such force, when you should be troubled by her ability"—he nodded at Darna— "to catch one spinning through the air."

"I am well aware of her abilities," he said.

"Then you're also aware that her giving up her knives and death disks was a smokescreen. Her actual weapons have eight fingers and two thumbs."

Amalardh glared at him. Did Forbillian forget who he was talking to? Of course, Amalardh knew that an assassin's greatest tools were their hands.

Forbillian gave him a kittenish shrug. "I'm just saying, I would feel safer if we took control of all her weapons."

"You want me to cut off her hands?"

Forbillian's expression perked. "Now that you're suggesting that..."

Amalardh shook his head and motioned for everyone to keep moving to the back stairwell.

"Trust me," Forbillian whispered, "we have fair justification to tie her up."

"No rope. That's final."

"Final, is it? Maybe this will inspire a change of heart." He called out to Darna, who stopped at the base of the stairs. "Since you are being so forthcoming and honest, is it true that Terefellians eat their own?"

Oisin gasped.

Was Forbillian serious? He must have been, because Darna didn't flinch.

"We do," she said. "Is that an issue?"

Forbillian looked at Amalardh squarely. "If you don't tie her up and you wake up without a foot, don't say I didn't warn you."

"Feet are too bony," said Darna. She eyed Forbillian's mid-section. "I prefer large chunks of fatty steaks."

Forbillian lunged at her.

Amalardh held him back. "She's goading you."

Forbillian shook himself free. He jabbed his finger at Darna. "At nighttime, we're tying this thing up."

By the glint in her eye, Darna seemed to enjoy ruffling Forbillian's feathers.

"You are our guest," Amalardh said to her. "If you keep that up, you'll be joining your friend back there." He turned to Forbillian. "And you, a fool who sticks his finger into a wasp's nest deserves to get stung."

"Blast it, the lot of you." Forbillian stormed past Darna and up the steps.

Amalardh nodded for Oisin to follow.

The boy trotted off.

"I didn't mean to cause any problems," said Darna.

"Yes, you did," said Amalardh.

She blinked at him.

Amalardh held her stare. She could look as shocked as she wanted, as long as she got the drift that he would not be manipulated.

Her expression settled to one of acceptance. "Fair enough," she replied.

Amalardh nodded to the dead Terefellian on the other side of the stream. "If you wish for a piece of your companion to take for sustenance, then speak up."

Her eyes flittered from the dead body to Amalardh. Her shoulders curled. She seemed to prefer Forbillian's disdain to Amalardh's forthrightness. "I'd heard stories about you and expected the worst. You're fair and direct and don't judge. What your uncle said about me and my people truly doesn't bother you."

After serving the former Senators of Vitus and their heinous laws for most of his life, very little bothered Amalardh.

"Thank you for the offer, but even if I wanted a pound of Brother Skylark's flesh, which I don't, I must decline. The practice of Notewannes Goi only happens during a specific ceremony and is the ritual of eating one's own. My people consider outside flesh to be unclean. We care about what we put into our bodies. From the looks of your uncle's stomach, he does not. Please assure him he is safe from me."

With his life dedicated to maintaining his own body as an infallible weapon, Amalardh appreciated Darna's stance on what she would and wouldn't eat. As earnest as she seemed, everything about her mannerisms told him she held a secret. And whatever that secret, Amalardh's principles—his very nature—seemed to compound her burden.

He was not being a gentleman when he motioned for her to

go ahead of him up the stairwell. Until he figured out his level of trust, she would remain in his sight.

The icy stairs wound up to a round wooden door hung on a metal track. The shape fit perfectly to the cave's natural exit. Amalardh stepped outside and the chill air stole his breath. He glanced around and compressed his dismay. The bleak snow stretched for miles.

Seated on a rock, Forbillian flashed an irritated look and mumbled that it was about bloody time they arrived. He guided Amalardh off to the side and opened the map from the Croilar Tier Archives.

"We're here." He pointed to the eastern side of the mountain peak with three finger-like protrusions. "From this point on, I'm guessing you have the answers."

His statement must refer to the scroll the Prophet handed to Amalardh. While Forbillian had received a similar offering, he must have already figured out that his gift did not benefit their current situation.

Amalardh unrolled the stiff paper, revealing a long, narrow map, the exact size of the one found in the archives. Its top edge lined up perfectly to the bottom of their current map. No wonder Forbillian had thought the first map had seemed about a third the width of most normal maps. Gaussian must have cut it down from the original. Forbillian's scroll was probably the third and final piece.

A dotted line directed their journey south of their current location to a waterfall on the *Horga River*. The Prophet had said that the answers to life eternal were on this map. The only other pertinent markings were a structure situated atop the *Korfkahn Mountains* (a mountain range running north-to-south) and a circular icon about halfway between the mountain range and the Epona Ocean, named *The Forbidden Pool*. The hairs at the back of Amalardh's neck stood on end. Could this be the pool the Prophet had found? Did its waters provide eternal life?

"The Forbidden Pool!" said Oisin, who had stuck his uninvited curiosity into the mix. "Isn't that—"

"Nothing that we need to concern ourselves with." Forbillian rolled up both maps and handed them to Amalardh. "South it is then," he said.

"Wait," said Darna. "May I have one of my knives?"

"You may not," said Forbillian.

"I don't intend to keep it."

"And I don't intend to give it."

"Fine. We'll leave this door unlocked. Don't blame me when you wake up in the middle of the night with your throat slit by those of my people who are tracking us."

Forbillian's eyes shifted from the woman to the rocky opening. His crumpled brow suggested his inability to figure out how the Terefellian planned to lock the rolling door with a solitary blade. Since he was too proud to expose his lack of understanding, and she was arrogantly set on not explaining her plan, they remained in a silent stand-off. Amalardh snatched one of Darna's knives from his uncle's waistband and rolled the heavy door closed. He inserted the blade between the door and the jamb and hammered it in tight with the rock.

"If she'd meant us harm," whispered Oisin to Forbillian, "she wouldn't have suggested blocking her people from coming after us."

Forbillian huffed and spoke with the apparent intent for Darna to hear. "Or maybe she's preventing our people from coming after her."

Oisin's shoulders straightened. Such a thought would not have entered the trusting kid's mind.

"I came here to help you. I can't force you to believe me," Darna said.

Forbillian looked down his nose at her. "How do you know when a Terefellian is lying?"

By her audible breath, his witless question did not impress her. "Our lips are moving?"

"No. Your hearts are still beating. The only trustworthy Terefellian is a dead Terefellian."

"I am not trying to stop your people from tracking me because they can't. Thomas, Henry, Clarence, and Finn, I believe their names to be, are dead." Her tone remained straight. "Am I lying now?"

Amalardh's heart twinged. When he saw Finn's sword in the other Terefellian's grasp, he had figured an untoward event had befallen his friend.

Forbillian's fist shot forth.

Darna deflected his arm, then kicked him in the belly, sending him flat on his back.

The fight ended before Amalardh could intervene.

Oisin rushed to Forbillian's side. "Forbs, are you okay?"

Forbillian's grunt let everyone know he remained alive.

Grabbing one of Forbillian's axes, Oisin leaped to his feet. "If you don't kill her, then I will," he said to Amalardh.

The kid's words were earnest, but he would hardly survive a fight against the elite Terefellian. Amalardh removed the weapon from Oisin's grasp and handed it back to Forbillian.

Darna tossed her palms in the air. "I'm condemned if I lie, and I'm condemned if I tell the truth. I am sorry about your people, I truly am. I played no part in it. I tried to talk Brother Skylark out of it. I could only do so much. If he suspected that my allegiance lay elsewhere, he would've killed me and all three of you would be dead. What else was I to do?"

"You could've killed him back then," said Oisin.

"And track you on my own?" She folded her arms across her chest. "I guess I should take that as a compliment. I'm good. I'm not that good."

The Terefellian was that good, and if she didn't know it, Amalardh certainly did. He imagined she could survive just fine on her own. Maybe Forbillian's assessment held truth. The young woman's heart still beat, which meant very little about her could be trusted. He hauled his uncle to his feet. "You need to stop provoking her," he said.

Forbillian brushed the snow from his bear coat. "Believe me, I will. When she's dead." He went to walk off, then stopped. "Why are you protecting her?"

Amalardh had no answer, at least, not one he cared to verbalize.

Forbillian flicked his hand at him as if brushing away an annoying bug. He pulled out his compass and set off. Oisin pursed his lips at Amalardh and followed. Darna seemed to know better than to say anything. She offered a polite nod of thanks and joined the march.

Amalardh dragged his hands down his face. Was he doing the right thing in keeping the Terefellian alive? In her own way, she was no different from him. Just as he was meant to kill Cecilia and didn't, Darna was meant to kill Amalardh and didn't. When Amalardh had asked Cecilia why she had saved someone who moments earlier held a sword to her throat, she had replied, "The men who raided my village were ice cold. Wicked. I saw it in their eyes. I didn't see the same in you." As for whether Amalardh saw wickedness in Darna's eyes, he was in no place to judge. Any offense he saw could just as well be a reflection of his own sinfulness. Darna attracted him. Not in the same way Cecilia had. Cecilia had captured his attention because he had never seen anyone look so alive. Darna caught his notice because of her skill.

He pumped his fingers to help warm his numb hands and followed his team's snowy tracks. He could separate a longing of the heart from the lusting of flesh. He would not allow his ache for Cecilia to manifest in a desire to hold someone soft or confuse his awe of Darna's skill with a feeling of attraction to her.

For the next couple of days, Forbillian led the group along a snowy cliff line. At night, Amalardh didn't tie Darna up. And his uncle didn't wake up with a missing foot. How Darna stayed warm was beyond comprehension. The snow beneath her melted as though she produced an excess of heat. Forbillian's bitterness toward her remained, although their arguments lessened, mostly because Darna kept to herself. She tried to strike up conversations with Amalardh, but with her small talk as limited as his, her attempts halted after a couple of stilted comments, a fact which Amalardh appreciated.

Because an emotional connection drove his attraction, Darna's inability to impress Amalardh's mind blunted his body's ache for physical comfort. She seemed to understand this much about him, and for whatever reason, this bothered her. Just last night, she had tried to cuddle close. Upon his rigid rebuff, she had stormed off and mumbled to herself as if arguing with an unseen bystander.

The group stopped for lunch. With the midday sun burning off the morning mist, the impressive view from their precipice trail spanned for miles.

Darna seemed anxious as she engaged in one of her mumble sessions.

Forbillian shook his head. "You know, animals that eat their own have a tendency to go mad."

Amalardh did not suspect insanity. Darna seemed stressed about something.

She walked to the cliff's edge.

His skin prickled. What was the jittery woman going to do? "Get back from there. It's not safe."

"What's the matter? Are you afraid of heights?"

Amalardh wasn't afraid of heights, but the hairs on his legs still frosted at the one-hundred-foot drop. "I'm serious," he said, motioning for her hand.

"Let her fall," said Forbillian. "We can all be put out of our misery."

"He really doesn't like me, does he," she said in a low voice.

"Why do you care?" Amalardh said.

She lowered her head and pressed her hands to her temples. "He would've been so much easier."

"Easier for what? To kill? Instead of me?"

She scoffed and shook her head. "You think that if I had to kill you, I'd have a tough time?"

Amalardh was certain she wouldn't. Whatever bothered Darna, killing Amalardh didn't factor into her concerns. "What about Forbillian would've been easier?" he asked.

She stared into the distance. "If I told you I had voices in my head telling me to do things I don't know how to do, would you believe me?"

Amalardh had read stories about the thin mountain air causing mental disruptions. Was Darna breaking from reality?

The extraordinary heat coming from her melted the snow around her slippers. "Get back here now," he said. "You're sinking."

She looked down and gasped. Her arm shot out. "Help me! Please."

His hand clamped to her hardened palm and his brow furrowed. He'd not expected such roughened skin.

The snow beneath her gave way.

Amalardh's arm jerked. His eyes widened. Did she just pull him?

She fell. And so did he.

Because of the Prophecy, Amalardh knew his death would come. He'd imagined a stabbing, or beheading, or a slow bleeding out, but never a fall. Why had Darna chosen this bizarre way, and why had she waited until now when she could've dispatched of him earlier? Is that what she'd meant about the voices in her head? She'd been sent to kill him, but was arguing with herself, resisting, until that moment where she'd found a way to complete her task while ending her own torment?

As he dropped, peace reigned. Whatever lay ahead for Cecilia, she would achieve her goals without him. Alistair's dimpled smile flashed into his mind. The vision Siersha had shown him of another man raising his son would soon be a reality. Cecilia would defeat Eifa and return to Plockton, where Gildas would guide Alistair to be the perfect Visionary Leader. Amalardh had to believe this because he couldn't die with anguish in his heart.

A white flash shot to the back of his head.

His eyes blinked open. The pearly sky and lustrous grass suggested he lay in the Pass-Over Zone.

He sat up. On a mound surrounded by red sunflowers stood Cecilia with Alistair cradled in her arms.

"They're not really here with me, are they?"

A glowing light drew his attention to Siersha. "They are just your mind creating the perfect memory of your loved ones."

He smiled. Red sunflowers. Of course. Cecilia's favorite.

"Did I fail them?" he asked.

"No."

He nodded. Pure love flowed through his veins as Cecilia and Alistair floated away.

"I shouldn't have trusted the Terefellian."

"You probably shouldn't have. But you did. And do you know why?"

Amalardh didn't.

Siersha's glow brightened. "Because you are no longer the man you believe yourself to be."

Amalardh's constricted chest relaxed. He could live—or rather die—with that. His greatest fear had been opening up his heart and trusting people. As much as the Prophet had been the living dead, so had Amalardh. At least in the moments before his death, he had learned to live; learned to respect others and not tie them up like a dog. He'd shared a joke with his ridiculous and utterly loveable uncle, and he'd let Oisin know how special he was to him.

This wasn't Amalardh's end; it was his beginning. He could enter the Pass-Over World with his head held high and face his father as an equal.

CHAPTER 34

WET AND EXHAUSTED, Saffron hauled herself to the top of the cliff and flopped onto her back. If not for the spider beast faltering when she had called out, "Daddy, if you can hear me, please help me!" she would be dead. The slight pause before it squeezed the life out of her gave Rabbie the additional seconds he needed to stab out its eyes.

"We can't beat them," she said. "We'll never win."

Rabbie collapsed next to her. "Don't say that."

"It's true."

"No. It's not."

She pushed up onto her elbow. "If you honestly believe that we can survive an army of those things, then you're a bigger idiot than I took you for."

His dropped gaze looked hurt.

She flopped back down. She didn't need a soft cotton-puff who took offense at hearing the truth. Rabbie was an idiot, and so was she for kissing him. What was she thinking? She leaped to her feet and winced from the pain of a stupid stone in her stupid boot. She dropped to the ground and pulled the leathery outerwear off. She hadn't really kissed Rabbie, had she? She turned her boot upside down and shook it. The stone landed on the hard dirt with a thud. No. Certainly not. And even if she had kissed him, she hadn't felt anything, had she?

She shoved her foot back in her boot and wiggled her toes. Damn it. What the heck was still in there? She ripped her boot off again. Of course she didn't like Rabbie. Unlike the other

Terefellian girls, Saffron didn't get all gaga over a boy. She crammed her hand inside her boot and felt around until she hit upon the culprit—a sharp, elongated grass seed. She pulled it out and flicked it away. No, Saffron was no mug like Neana, an auburn-haired, swine-regurgitant that lived in the buhleycob next to Saffron's former cave. The ditzy girl gloated daily about how she would have to invoke Gonoh Firth at least a dozen times before finding her husband.

Gonoh Firth was an honor fight where two male suitors wrestled for the right to wed their beloved. The fights were never to the death. A Terefellian soul was too precious to waste on the whims of adolescent love. Neana probably wasn't wrong in believing that at least a dozen saps stood prepared to grapple for her affection. And she planned to make sure every one of them proved their worth. Saffron jammed her foot in her boot and wiggled her toes. Good. No more pain. She found the whole Gonoh Firth ritual disgusting. If a man had the audacity to want to marry her, then he'd have to fight *her* for the honor. If he won, then maybe, just maybe, she would consider marrying him. With her boot free of spikes and bumps, she started marching north along the coastline.

"Wait!" said Rabbie.

She stopped but didn't turn around.

"If we stay on the coastline, we'll be sitting ducks."

Fine. She turned inland.

"Now where are you going?"

"We can't be sitting ducks now, can we? So, we'll go this way and be easy pickings instead."

"All I meant was, we need a plan."

Her jaw clenched. If only Eideard had stayed back instead. Saffron had little interest in Cecilia's eldest brother and wouldn't have felt guilty about her spiky behavior. Rabbie didn't deserve her misplaced rage. But because of a multitude of emotions erupting inside her, she couldn't dial down her snappiness. She hated her father for everything the spiteful man did and didn't do. Her soul ached from her mother's death. She had almost died in the clutches of an eight-legged spider warrior. And why had she so recklessly kissed Rabbie?

"You want a plan?" she said. "This is our plan. We get our butts to Vitus as fast as we can because if my father sends more of those things after us, we're dead. You've got two options: sitting ducks or easy pickings." She pointed north and inland, respectively.

"Which way would you take?" he asked.

Seriously? He can't even make a decision on his own? If he couldn't figure out that the coastline represented the most direct and therefore fastest route to Vitus, then he was more bone-headed than she'd realized. She spun on her heels and directed her trail northward.

"So you think that's the best way?" Rabbie asked.

"I'm walking this way, aren't I?"

"Okay. Just so you know, I'm heading this way."

She turned to see Rabbie pointing inland. She folded her arms across her chest. If he already knew his desired route, why did he bother wasting her time with his questions?

"Are you coming?" he asked.

Her inner turmoil spun at odds with his calm confidence. Maybe he knew something she didn't know. "So, you think the trip to your city is faster by heading inland first?"

"Not by a long shot."

Her arms dropped to her side. "I thought we decided the best way to go was the fastest way."

"We didn't decide anything." He emphasized the word "we." "You decided that 'sitting ducks' was the fastest and therefore best way to go. Because of that, I'm heading inland."

He made his decision just to spite her? She wanted to go left, so he chose right? Fine. If he wanted to go the slowpoke way and get killed by the Wirador Wosrah, he could. She pressed forward with her mission north.

"Saffron, what the heck are you doing?"

"I'm not playing your stupid game. You asked me which way

I'd go. I told you. Then out of spite, you want to go in another direction."

"Is that what you think?" He pressed his hand to his chest. "There is no spite or malice in my decision. Seriously."

Clenching her fists, she stomped in his direction of inland. She no longer cared which path they took, so long as the chosen route put an end to the stupid conversation.

Rabbie shook his head at her as she marched by. "You know, you could've asked me why I prefer easy pickings over sitting ducks instead of assuming things."

Saffron stopped and hung her head. Rabbie was right. After everything they'd been through, why would she think he was deliberately working against her? She jabbed the toe of her boot into the ground. Why was she so useless with her emotions? Rather than deal with feeling vulnerable, she preferred to punch the poor sod who'd dared to make her feel that way.

They walked in silence for a long moment.

"Fine," she finally said. "You win. Why did you decide the longer way was better?"

"Nope," said Rabbie. "You've lost your chance."

"Lost my chance? What do you mean?"

"You don't want to be a team player, that's fine. You don't get to act all snooty, then pretend like everything's okay."

Her spine straightened. Terefellian boys had never defied her. Maybe Rabbie wasn't a cotton-puff pushover after all.

"I hate playing games," he said. "But if I have to, I will. I let you stomp around back there because some terrible things happened. You have a right to be on edge. If you want to yell and scream, that's fine. But I won't let you take it out on me, then act like nothing happened because suddenly you're feeling better."

Rabbie's truthful words stung. Saffron had been so used to looking after herself, she didn't know how to be a partner. He was correct. "We" had not made any decisions together. She had huffed and puffed and let her emotions take over. She kicked a stone from her path. In her defense, he didn't have to be so cryptic about why he chose the long way. He could've said, "Since you chose that way, I think we should go this way because of whatever reason." She sighed and kicked another stone. Saffron had challenged Rabbie to her version of Gonoh Firth. And he'd won.

"I'm sorry," she said. "I don't want to be fighting with you."

He remained quiet, but seemed open to listening to anything she might say.

"You're good at figuring people out."

"Not really," he said.

"You figured me out."

He smirked. "Not to seem rude, but figuring you out was pretty easy."

Saffron bristled. She considered herself somewhat complex. "What was so easy to figure out?"

"Let's just say, with girls like you, I had an excellent teacher."

She scowled at him. Girls like her? What the heck did that mean?

"I mean, you're just like Cecilia," he clarified.

Oh. Her ruffled feathers settled. "How so?"

He raised an eyebrow. "You're both insufferable hotheads."

She laughed and punched his arm. This time, not hard. He feigned pain and rubbed the spot. Their eyes connected and he smiled. She bit her lower lip and dropped her gaze. If he was flirting, which he wasn't, she didn't know how to flirt back.

As they walked in silence, she took in his unassuming profile. At first glance, Eideard seemed the better looking, but his showboat, attention-seeking personality lessened his attractiveness. Saffron admired Rabbie's quiet confidence. Her cheeks flushed as she remembered their first encounter. Rabbie had stripped down naked. Who would've thought that moment would lead to everything that had happened?

Stung by an overwhelming desire to hold his hand, she studied her leathery palms. No one would ever want to hold these ugly things, least of all Rabbie. He'd kissed her as a means to an end. She'd kissed him because... Whatever the reason for kissing him, she'd been a fool for thinking it might lead to something. He'd just told her that she reminded him of Cecilia, which meant he thought of her like a little sister.

The lime-green savannah grasses morphed into a field of crunchy charcoal and blackened stumps, remains from when a fire ravaged the once-wooded area. Saffron had seen the smoke a few months back and couldn't imagine the immense size of a blaze capable of blocking out the sun. Hungry flames had reduced hundred-foot pines to gutted stubs. This travesty represented her people's queen. Destruction for destruction's sake. Or, as was the case in this particular devastation, destruction for stupidity's sake.

No lightning strike or force of nature had caused this blaze. Two imbecilic Terefellians had gone in search of the elusive Nilo, a murderous lion that over the years had mauled at least a dozen sacred goats. If the law forbade Terefellians from gnawing goat flesh, then no lion would either. Saffron's father had set a proclamation: anyone who killed the lion would forever be the Thurang Dern, a ridiculous title that meant grand hunter, which he'd just made up. Along with the vacuous name, the Thurang Dern would keep the lion skin for themselves. Yeah. Right. Her father wouldn't be able to sleep a wink knowing that some lowly sod had such a grand beast's fur in their buhleycob. He would figure a way to manipulate the winner into offering the pelt to him. The decree set forth countless teams of crudely skilled hunters eager to claim their prize. One such team forgot to put out their campfire. That same fire now sent the stink of soot into Saffron's nostrils with every crunchy step.

She stiffened at the charred carcass of what looked like a fawn tangled in a wire fence. She pictured the terrified mother deer fleeing with her baby. Mother had leaped the fence, but baby had lacked the strength. Baby would've cried desperately for its mother as the raging flames closed in. Fear would've kept mother running. Hoping. Believing baby was close behind. When she reached greener pastures, she would've stopped and looked around. Only then would it hit her—baby was gone.

Saffron's breath shortened as a cramping reality hit her. The deer that had run from the terrifying blaze had finally stopped and looked around. Only, instead of momma looking for her baby, Saffron searched helplessly for her mother. But Saffron's mother was gone. Forever.

Rabbie reached out. "Are you okay?"

She smacked his hand away. A glut of emotions hung heavy in her chest. She didn't want to feel any of them. Since her mother's passing, she hadn't had time to fully process. She glowered at Rabbie. If he and his people hadn't come into her life, her mother would still be alive. Her rage returned, and this time, she embraced it full force. She dropped her backpack and shoved him.

He recoiled. "What is wrong with you?"

Saffron had grown up fighting. Expelling emotion through physical blows was the only way she knew how to deal with inner turmoil.

"Fight me," she said.

"What? I'm not going to fight you."

She shoved him again.

"Saffron, stop it."

She couldn't. She didn't want to. Her anger erased her pain. She tackled Rabbie to the ashy ground.

"Saffron. This is not funny."

No. It certainly wasn't. The last thing Saffron felt was humor. They tussled back and forth, Saffron on the offensive, Rabbie blocking and holding her back.

"I want to kill him!" she yelled.

Rabbie pinned her down, his eyes wild with worry. "Kill who?"

She tried to fight his arms, but his muscles out-powered hers. "My father. I hate him. I hate him for what he did to my mother."

Exhausted from a life of constant battling, she burst into tears.

The pain she so desperately tried to ignore escaped and trampled her heart like a thousand wild horses. She coiled into a ball, burying her face in her hands, embarrassed by her own tears. She hadn't cried since her childhood. "Only babies cry," her father had told her. Back then, someone... something, had also died—a piece of her four-year-old heart.

As her tears settled, she went numb. "I used to have a toy," she said quietly. "I called him Glimglob. He was just a rusty tin can I'd found, but he was my everything. The hinged lid was his head. Using sap from a tree, I stuck on two pebbles for eyes, a curved twig for a mouth, and goat fur for hair. I called him Glimglob because that's the noise he made when I'd accidentally kicked him."

Why was she telling Rabbie this story? Did he even care to hear it? He seemed to because his hand softly stroked her hair.

"I carried Glimglob with me everywhere. My father hated it. During a Rite of Quinquagenary, he told me that since my rusty can's life-age superseded fifty years, it, too, needed to retire."

Rabbie's hand paused for the slightest second, as if understanding her pain.

"The laws of Terefellia are for all," my father had said. "Even Glimglob. When I explained he was only five months old, he placed his hands on my shoulders and told me that future leaders of Terefellia didn't play with toys. The children of today who laughed at me would never respect my future role as their leader. He took Glimglob from me and threw him in the fire." She wiped her sniffling nose. "What kind of father does that to a four-year-old?"

She sat up and cuddled her knees to her chest. She must look a mess, but she didn't care. "He told me that when I got older, I would understand and thank him. Well, I got older and the only thing I came to understand was that of the very few kids who poked fun at me, none of them had hurt me the way my father had."

She had never spoken about how much watching her favorite toy burn had hurt. Offloading to Rabbie lifted a heavy weight.

"I watched Glimglob glow red and promised myself I would never, ever let my mom face the Rite of Quinquagenary. I would become the mightiest Terefellian ever, and one day, I would kill my father." Her eyes watered up. "The problem is, I'm the biggest fraud. I failed my mother, and all I want to do right now is run away and hide. My father has all but won. I'm sorry. This mess is all my fault. I should've killed my father when I had the chance."

Rabbie wiped away a lock of hair that had stuck to her wet cheek. "Don't be so hard on yourself. None of this is your fault."

She rested her head on his shoulder and closed her eyes. She felt heavy. Tired. A life focused solely on survival drained her.

Saffron's neck cricked as she woke. She hadn't realized she'd fallen asleep. Although the sky remained dark, the dewy ground signified that sunrise drew near. After sleeping on the plush bench inside her and her mother's hideout house, she had doubted she'd ever experience a comparable rest. Last night's slumber on the ashy ground under the stars proved her wrong. Maybe her tears had drained her so much, her body had no choice other than to shut down. Maybe battling two dozen of Eifa's almost-indestructible Wirador Wosrah exhausted her to the point of uncompromised sleep. Or maybe, for the first time in her life, she could close her eyes and not need to stay half-alert to impending danger because Rabbie, a skillful fighter in his own right, lay beside her.

When Cecilia had shared her tradition of planting a seed to honor the departed and suggested they find a spot with a view of the ocean, Saffron had remained detached because she'd never witnessed daybreak. Curious to understand the fuss, she sat cross-legged and focused on the distant horizon.

Her breath caught as a golden layer grew within the black expanse, separating the dark sky from the nighttime lands. The gold layer rose. In its wake came a brilliant red. The sharp contrast offered a comforting notion that no matter how far evil and destruction tried to reach, there would always be an end—a horizon—upon which beauty reigned. A glowing white arc peeked above the inky lands and the sky burst into bands of gold, orange, and lilac. Cecilia had definitely chosen the right spot for Saffron to lay her mother to rest.

As the sun continued to wink at the waking world, its golden rays painted the sky blue. Engrossed by the magical event, she hadn't realized Rabbie had woken and seated himself next to her. His serene expression suggested the magical sight moved him, too. A young man possessing the strength to fight Wirador Wosrah and the sensitivity to appreciate a sunrise could not possibly be real. Men from Saffron's homeland seemed to only understand beauty of the flesh. They would stomp on a lone desert flower that had bloomed against the odds without a care. Most wouldn't even notice its beauty. And those that did, rather than avoiding it, would trample its delicate head. In their minds, the ignorant flower got what it deserved for having the audacity to blossom in the middle of the Terefellian's path.

Saffron pulled her knees to her chest and sighed. She no longer wanted to simply exist. She wanted to live. The warmth radiating from Rabbie offered hope. Even after experiencing his own horrors, he'd found something in this world worth living for. Saffron had had her mother. Now, she had nothing... except this young man, who accepted her, thorns and all.

Soon, Eifa's Wirador Wosrah army would march on Vitus and thousands of lives would perish, including hers and Rabbie's. If Saffron had had the strength to kill her father before leaving Terefellia, Rabbie, Cecilia, the world wouldn't be in this mess. If she could turn back time, would she change anything? She took in his serene profile and her heart melted.

No. She wouldn't change a thing.

Killing her father would have meant Saffron would have never met Rabbie. And from the short time she'd spent with him, whatever limited time she had left with him was worth a lifetime of never knowing him at all.

CHAPTER
35

BEADS OF TERROR trickled down Wyndom's temple. While in control of a mighty spider Wirador Wosrah, he had faltered and failed to kill his daughter. The queen's smoke had shot out and hauled him into the temple where he stood, trembling in the corner, awaiting his fate.

The queen's globby mass stopped undulating. Wyndom stiffened as a broad tentacle protruded from the rubbery matter and suctioned itself to the hard temple floor. The end separated from the mass, forming an eight-foot-tall column. Its base vibrated. The ripples shot upward, and Eifa's form emerged. Wyndom dropped to his knees. "My Queen! Have mercy." If he could get through this meeting alive, he would never, ever disappoint her again.

She ordered him to stand. He did.

Her shiny liquid mass remained in constant motion. The undulations calmed and mesmerized him. If his queen asked him to pick up a rock and smash it over his head, he would do it. Anything to please her. "Are you mad at your servant?" he asked.

"I am curious," she replied. "Your daughter betrayed you, betrayed your people, betrayed me. You have resented her since the day her lungs first filled with air. She is a weak link that knows too much and now cavorts with the enemy. You lose no sleep over sending loyal souls into flames, yet facing your great adversary, you faltered." Her head tilted, as if genuinely perplexed. "Tell me, what prevented you from killing Saffron?"

Wyndom pressed his hand to his mouth. Of all the things

his queen knew about him, she didn't know the answer to the question that rattled his brain, too. Saffron's insubordination had caused him more aggravation than Cecilia, the queen's most dangerous enemy. Why hadn't he been able to squeeze the life out of her?

"Do you have an answer?" she asked.

His shoulders sagged. Regrettably, he did. "When I looked into her terrified eyes and saw my little girl, I realized..."

"You realized what?"

"That I loved her." No amount of rubbing his own chest could erase the pain brought on by his truth. Wyndom loved his daughter. He always had. He hadn't known how to be a father, especially to a little girl. When he should've felt pride in her talent, jealousy had crept in. A memory of Saffron and her silly tin can battered his mind. Instead of encouraging her imagination and not worrying if the other children poked fun, the mortification he felt from when his childhood peers laughed at him for being too short, too scared, and too uncoordinated took over. Her screams from when he threw Glimglob into the fire still haunted him. As the chasm between father and daughter had grown, denying his love seemed easier. His love had never left. Instead, it lay dormant under crippling layers of regret until she had cried out for his help.

"Do you love me?" asked the queen.

"With all my heart."

"Then prove it."

Wyndom stood tall. "Of course, my Queen. Anything you ask." If she needed more prayer services, then he would do a thousand a day until his dying breath.

"The Maddowshin will send out one hundred of our mighty Wirador Wosrah with the order not to harm Saffron. They will bring her back here, where you will sacrifice her to me."

Wyndom blinked. "Pardon, my Queen?"

"You will kill her with your own hands, your own strength, your own will, not through that of a Wirador Wosrah. You will make a display of it in front of our people." Her twirling surface sped up as if excited. "What better way to express love for a god than for a father to sacrifice a child?"

Wyndom's throat closed.

The queen's shimmering surface stilled. "Is there a problem?"

"No, my Queen."

"Do not disappoint me."

Her form splashed to the ground. The wetness ran along the temple floor and merged with the central mass. The black blob began undulating as the queen returned to her birthing process.

Wyndom shuffled to the temple door in time to spot a horde of Wirador Wosrah galloping into the Terefellian Valley. One hundred warriors against one girl. Saffron stood no chance. And neither did Wyndom.

Days ticked by and no news of Saffron's capture came. For an entity supposedly void of feelings, the Maddowshin seemed empathetic. To help Wyndom take his mind off his murderous destiny, the Maddowshin sent through regular visuals of Brother Skylark and Sister Darna's exhaustive trek in search of Amalardh. The lush eastern lands, mossy forest scent, and distant, snow-capped mountains provided a suitable distraction.

Curiously, when Skylark and Darna hit the snowline, they didn't require additional clothing. Wyndom realized that ever since the two Wrethun Lof had entered the snow region, the Terefellian campfire blazed day and night. His people took turns heating various parts of their bodies under the warm blaze. Because of the collective conscious that the queen had created, the Terefellians were linked to her through the Maddowshin. Just as the Maddowshin had allowed Wyndom to experience Brother Skylark's nausea during the Epona Ocean crossing, the beast could send sensations to the distant Wrethun Lof, including the feel of toasty warm toes.

The queen is brilliant, is she not? The Maddowshin's voice echoed in Wyndom's head.

The revelation that his queen had linked him to his people and her forever, for eternity, sank in. He rubbed his unsettled stomach. He loved his queen. He knew he did. Why, then, did he feel some doubt?

Unplug me, he requested of the Maddowshin. The beast obliged and the visions of the distant lands stopped. Wyndom dropped his face into his hands. Doubts? He couldn't be having any misgivings. Not now. The moment his people birthed their queen into the human realm, Wyndom had sealed his fate. He couldn't jump ship, even if he wanted to. Once connected to the Dark Goddess, no one could sever their tie. He rolled the stiffness out of his neck. He wasn't having doubts. The hours and hours of watching endless snow had simply drained him. The last exciting event had happened days ago, when Brother Skylark had slit the throats of the sailors ferrying him and Sister Darna to the Epona Ocean's eastern shores. Afterward, the bold assassin had attempted to bed Darna. She resisted with ease. "My body is not for you," she had told him. "My body is for the queen. If you spoil it, you will meet with her wrath."

He flopped back against his tree trunk. He needed to snap out of his gloom. An impromptu sermon should do the trick. He stepped onto his prayer rock and called his people to gather. He strutted and danced and did his thing. When he was done, the elation he craved fizzled. His queen's order to make a show of killing Saffron had created an ache so deep, even his people's adulation failed to ease his suffering. He flopped onto his mat and curled into a ball. His soul, which he'd worked so desperately hard to keep alive, seemed as dead as it ever could be. Despite his tethering to close to three hundred Terefellians, Wyndom had never felt more alone.

Do not bother sending any feed, he told the Maddowshin. *Unless, of course, it is a matter of interest.*

Over the next few days, Wyndom ate, gave his sermons, and slept. All the while, his black hole of misery remained. During the day, he spent most of his time napping.

A hatchet piercing Brother Skylark's spine startled Wyndom awake. The image played out from Sister Darna's point of view as she stood inside a cavernous place made of ice. Why had she just killed her Wrethun Lof partner? Wide-eyed, he spun to the Maddowshin.

You said to only bother you for matters of interest, the Maddowshin said. *I determined this to be one.*

Sister Darna's vision shifted from Skylark's splayed, face down body to a man dressed in a wolf coat hunched protectively over another woolly bearded fellow in a bear cape. Sister Darna and Brother Skylark had finally caught up with the Croilar Tier. In a flash, Wyndom immediately knew all that had transpired until this point. Brother Skylark had given Sister Darna the directive to fillet the bearded man and a teen boy dressed in a lynx cape while he took out the Croilar Tier. As Skylark strode with his wielded sword to his victim, Darna had changed her aim from the bear-caped man to her assassin partner, sending her weapon into his back. Rather than defend himself from Skylark's swinging blade, the Croilar Tier had tackled the woolly man to the ground, saving him from an ax that never came.

Wyndom wiggled his numb toes. He'd never encountered such bravery. Such selflessness. The concept of risking one's life for another's did not exist in Wyndom's sphere.

So, this was the man the enemy called Amalardh? A nervous ball lodged in Wyndom's throat. He had not expected the Croilar Tier to be so... intoxicating. The intensity of Amalardh's iridescent blue eyes bore into Wyndom's soul as he wrapped Sister Darna's wound from where she'd sliced herself to prove her living state. What man cares for another's injury with such tenderness? His satin-smooth voice, while commanding, also had a massaging effect. Unlike the ruffian in the bear coat. That brute's husky demeanor grated like fingernails clawing at stone.

Why Sister Darna had killed Brother Skylark, Wyndom still didn't know. The Maddowshin only imparted the information from Darna's memory that it cared to share. *You do not seem concerned by Sister Darna's actions*, he said to the Maddowshin.

I'm sure I will be soon, which is why I woke you. I'll be needing your help.

A chill danced over Wyndom's skin. *You don't want me to kill the Croilar Tier, do you?*

The prospect of slaying your daughter is enough, don't you agree?

Wyndom most certainly did.

When the time comes, I will need your persuasive charm, the Maddowshin said.

Persuasive charm? What on earth did the Maddowshin—Rudella—have planned?

Nighttime fell. Wyndom's skin flushed as Sister Darna sidled up to Amalardh. The Croilar Tier's hard body radiated warmth. *Wrap your arms around him*, Wyndom pleaded. But his communication with Sister Darna was only one way.

"I hope you don't mind," she said to Amalardh. "I am cold."

Amalardh regarded her threadbare tunic and handed over his blanket.

She side-eyed his two companions. Forbillian and Oisin were their names. Snuggled in their fur coats, they both slept soundly.

Wyndom sucked in his breath as she pressed her body against Amalardh's muscular torso.

Amalardh recoiled.

"What?" Darna said. "I'm just trying to get warm."

"Then go lie by the fire."

Darna sprang to her feet.

No! Don't leave him!

She stormed off and launched into a long-winded argument with the Maddowshin, saying things like, *You sent the wrong person; This was a mistake; I told you I couldn't do this.*

Settle! the Maddowshin told her. *And stop moving your lips when you talk to me, or they'll think you're going mad. I have a plan. Soon, you can put an end to all this.*

What is going on? Wyndom said to the Maddowshin. *What do you need Sister Darna to do?*

All in good time, the Maddowshin replied.

The rest of the night, Wyndom barely slept a wink. His thoughts raced with images of Amalardh's glacial blue eyes—fearsome, yet divinely magnetic.

The next morning, Sister Darna and the group continued their trek. At lunchtime, they stopped near a precipice. The view was magnificent.

This is the place, the Maddowshin told Sister Darna. *Walk to the edge.*

A wave of nausea washed over Wyndom as Sister Darna strode to the cliff's perimeter. Don't look down. She did. The drop to the snowy ground below had to be at least one hundred feet. The sound of Amalardh's voice coaxing her from the edge soothed Wyndom's fear. Do as he says, you silly woman. But she stood her ground.

Darna's slippers sank in the snow. Get away from the edge! Wyndom didn't want to drop with her. *Cut the feed!* he begged the Maddowshin. Too late. The ground gave way. Wyndom tensed. Then—

A powerful force gripped his hand. Amalardh. A jolt of electricity shot up his arm and into his chest. He relaxed. Sister Darna wouldn't fall, not while this man held her tight.

Wyndom flinched. Did Sister Darna just deliberately yank Amalardh's arm?

Amalardh lost his footing. As Wyndom felt himself plummet, he gave into the moment. For the first time in his life, he didn't fear death. For the first time since forever, he didn't feel alone. If he could have one wish, that wish would be to die in this moment. Then he wouldn't have to kill his daughter.

But Wyndom wouldn't die. Only Sister Darna and the Croilar

Tier would. But why was the Maddowshin forcing them both to die this way?

As Wyndom fell, the rush of wind buffeting his skin was exhilarating. Images of Saffron flashed through his mind: her perfect chubby baby toes; her balled fist as she punched a young boy for getting too close; her perfect aim as she threw a rock at a distant target; her hardened face as she told Wyndom on the night she left Terefellia, "If you try to stop me, I will kill you."

What a fool he'd been for not loving her the way he should have. *Let me die with them*, he said to the Maddowshin.

You still have a purpose.

I no longer care.

Your queen needs you.

As you said, any one of a hundred fools could take my place.

I need you.

Wyndom's heart skipped. *Rudella? You do?*

A dense impact ended Sister Darna's fall.

A bright light rocketed to the back of Wyndom's eyes.

His world went black.

CHAPTER
36

SUNLIGHT BEAMED OVER a dazzling field carpeted with red sunflowers. Their sweet scent tickled Cecilia's nose. She plucked one and drank in its aroma. Her face scrunched. She sniffed again and recoiled from the smell of burned toast. The flower turned to ash and drifted away in the breeze. Ominous clouds filled the sky. The red field tore apart, revealing charred earth. The sun shrank to a mere speck. Scorched flowers crunched under her feet as she walked toward the diminished glow. *Siersha*, she said, *they want me to deny you.*

The Goddess's tiny light pulsed. *You must.*

Cecilia stopped in her tracks. *You agree with them? But why?* She balled her fist. *You don't know what you're saying. I can't deny you. I won't.*

She seized as a jolt of searing pain shot through to her toes. She collapsed to the ground, retching at the pungent, smoky odor. Drained of all energy, she crawled along the charcoal earth, her hands and knees covered in Eifa's filth. *Siersha! Help me. Please! Take me with you. I can't stand this much longer.*

Cecilia understood the finality of her request and didn't care. This agonizing pain had dragged for far too long. She wanted it to end.

Another jolt. Another seizure. Cecilia flopped onto her back. She couldn't move. What was happening? Who were these voices that kept asking her to deny her Goddess?

Siersha's light engulfed her. Cecilia smiled. Her Goddess had come to take her to the Pass-Over World.

A voice in the distance traveled to the forefront of her mind. Go away, she wanted to yell, but the leather strap in her mouth garbled her words.

"Cecilia," the voice repeated.

Her heavy eyelids fluttered open. A dark-skinned woman in a flowing silver and gold dress swirled and morphed against the backdrop of a white spinning room. Who was this woman?

"This god, this Siersha, is not real," the swirling lady said. "She is a coping mechanism. You cannot move forward with your life until you let her go." She removed the leather strap from Cecilia's mouth. "Now, repeat after me. Siersha is not real."

"No, I won't. I won't say it," Cecilia uttered.

The woman's face hardened. "Turn it up," she said to a short, light-skinned man wearing glasses and a knee-length white coat.

A worried look shot over the face of a bald, dark-skinned man dressed in maroon. She'd seen him before, but where? Her sight dropped to the ground. Toes. Lots of toes as the sandaled feet of the dark-skinned man and a similarly dressed, light-skinned man danced before her. She focused on a gold band around one of the brown toes. Why did it look familiar? She traced from the gold band up to the eyes of the worried-looking man.

The elegant woman stepped into view. "I said, dial it up."

"My Countess," said the man in the white coat, "this one's beliefs run deep. Far deeper than the young man's. We should go slower with her."

These people had been going slow with Cecilia?

The woman gruffly turned a dial. Its arrow moved from the top end of a blue zone into a red area. "We will go at the speed that I instruct. And you will obey my orders."

"To be clear, your order is for this girl to die? Because that is what will happen at that level."

The woman's mouth pulled tight. "Then so be it." Her frigid hand clasped Cecilia's. "Child. Do you hear me?"

Cecilia nodded.

"You heard the doctor. Are you really willing to end your life for your false beliefs?"

Cecilia was. While she couldn't remember much else, she remembered her beliefs. If she let them go, she would have nothing. She closed her heavy eyelids. In the darkness, the light returned. She smiled. The Goddess was waiting for her. *I'm coming,* Cecilia told her. One more jolt of that excruciating pain and her body would fail. The short man had confirmed as much.

A beam of light shot forth and into Cecilia's chest. The light radiated into her lungs and up to her mouth. This is not right. The Goddess is supposed to comfort the dying by wrapping them in her light, not consuming them with it. *What are you doing? Why is your light connecting with me?*

To ensure that what was meant to be will be, said Siersha.

"This is your last chance," said the stern woman. "Admit that your Goddess of Light and everything in your fantasy world is not real. Let yourself be free."

Cecilia tried to yell out, "I will not deny my Goddess," but her lips wouldn't move. She was no longer in control. The Goddess was.

The woman's finger lingered by the switch. "What is your answer?" she demanded.

Forgive me, my dearest Cecilia, for what I am about to do, said Siersha. *You will find me again one day.*

Cecilia's eyes shot open. "Siersha, the one they call the Goddess of Light, is not real."

The woman beamed. "Very good. If you remember one thing after today, remember that thought." She turned to the man in the white coat. "We are done. Let's cement this moment in her mind."

The man lifted a syringe from a silver tray, removed its cap, and jabbed it into Cecilia's arm. Her heavy eyelids closed.

The blackness filled with green. Cecilia once again stood in an open field. Dressed in a brown hooded robe was a man. In his arms, he held a boy. They both smiled at her. Amalardh! Alistair! She waved at them. Appearing from nowhere came a myriad of happy faces: Rabbie, Eideard, Oisin, Marion, Forbillian, Tomkin, Brassal. The vast green field filled with everyone Cecilia knew, including her mother, Analise and Noah.

What a magical, joyous moment.

The sound of children laughing drew her attention. She turned and pressed her hands to her open mouth. Plockton! Her glorious village was just as she remembered: chimneys billowing smoke, window boxes bursting with flowers, and waterwheels turning lazily under the flow of channeled waters. She stepped foot in the courtyard, a protected cove surrounded by an enclave of clay-rendered cottages, and screams of joy rang out. An earth-toned rainbow of young girls swarmed to her side. Each wore a different colored tunic: muted red, tangerine orange, mustard yellow, olive green, dusty blue, and tawny brown, and they all wanted their hair styled just like hers.

Cecilia smiled. This memory was as vivid as the day it actually happened.

Siersha appeared by her side. "This is where it all began," she said.

Nighttime fell. Asher, a Plockton elder with silver hair and a scratchy beard, commanded the bow of his fiddle with the creaminess of melted butter. The courtyard was abuzz as Cecilia's village celebrated baby Jonah's Hinge Celebration.

Cecilia slapped her hands to her cheeks and laughed, mortified at the sight of her two left feet tripping over themselves as she watched herself dance with Leighton.

Daylight broke. Smoke rose around her. Screams rang out as her village burned.

"I don't want these memories!" she said to Siersha.

"You say that now, but these experiences make the person who you are today."

Something pressed down on her shoulder. She turned and came face to face with a set of startled blue eyes. The courtyard where she stood transformed to the mound where she'd dried strawberries and first met Amalardh.

314

Her journey with him flashed by in a series of magical moments ending with... their first kiss. Cecilia pressed her fingertips to her lips. The experience felt as real as if his satiny skin had just left hers.

A cooing sound drew her attention to a basket by her feet. Love welled in her heart as she picked up Alistair and cuddled him.

"These are the memories I want," she said to Siersha.

The Goddess's light dulled. "You cannot pick what you will remember. They all must go."

"What do you mean?" Cecilia asked.

The Goddess nodded to a red dot on Cecilia's upper arm. A faint notion that someone had jabbed that spot with a needle gripped Cecilia.

Heat from the injection site radiated through her.

Alistair was no longer in her arms. He was with... she tried to remember the name of the man who wore the brown, hooded robe. He looked familiar, but she couldn't quite place how she knew him. Next to him stood two young men dressed in toggle button shirts. One had neatly cropped hair. The other wore his shoulder-length locks loose. They waved at her. Out of politeness, she waved back. Who were they? Did they know her?

Other people smiled and made friendly gestures. She wiggled her fingers back at them. Who were all these people? She focused in on the little boy in the hooded man's arm. A moment ago, she knew the child's name. Now? Her mouth twisted. Well, whoever he was, he seemed like a sweet little thing.

Laughing children drew her attention to picturesque cottages nestled amongst tall trees. What a sweet village. Fire ravaged the buildings and Cecilia felt nothing. It was as though the moment never actually happened.

"Where am I?" she asked. "Who are all those people?"

"You are inside your memories."

Next to Cecilia stood a white, glowing entity clothed in silky ribbons.

"Who are you?" Cecilia asked.

A crystal tear slid down the entity's cheek. "I, too, am just one of your memories."

The entity's glow diminished. Cecilia's world darkened. The sweet village and sea of faces disappeared.

"You said I was inside my memories, but I no longer see anything," Cecilia said.

"Exactly," the entity replied. "I must go now. For the sake of humanity, I hope we meet again one day."

The glowing light disappeared.

Cecilia gasped as her eyes popped open.

She lay on a metal-frame bed inside a pristine white room. A soft, lilac blanket draped her body. Sunlight beamed through an open window. Outside, a rainbow of brightly colored flowers waved back and forth in the gentle breeze.

A dark-skinned woman wearing a gold and silver dress took hold of Cecilia's hand. Her touch felt warm and comforting. "You're awake," the woman said.

Cecilia tried to move her gummy mouth, but her muscles wouldn't respond.

"Do you know where you are?" the woman asked.

Cecilia shook her head.

"What about your name?"

Cecilia thought for a moment. Surely, she knew her own name. She couldn't remember.

"It's okay," the woman said. "You have been through a lot. You must not force yourself." She stroked Cecilia's head. "You poor, dear thing. Everything will be okay. My name is Countess Kosima of Bayton. We found you in our bay. You'd been attacked by a shark."

Cecilia blinked. A shark had bitten her?

The Countess guided Cecilia's hand to a large divot in Cecilia's right thigh. "Do you remember?"

Cecilia felt over and around the hard, numb flesh. She shook her head.

The response seemed to please the Countess. "There are some things that are probably best left forgotten." She stroked Cecilia's cheek. "I am so happy to have you back. We will let you rest." She gave Cecilia a white pill and a glass of water. "This will help with your memories."

With no reason to doubt the caring woman, Cecilia swallowed the pill.

"Good girl," the Countess said. She turned to leave.

"Wait," Cecilia uttered. She cleared her throat to help smooth her hoarse voice. "Who am I?"

"Your name is Cecilia. As for who you are, you're just a girl who once had a dreadful nightmare. But you're safe now. Okay?"

Cecilia nodded.

The Countess seemed nice. And this place, wherever Cecilia was, felt comfortable. If she had experienced a nightmare, she didn't want to know what it was. She was happy. She was secure. Everything else didn't matter.

ACKNOWLEDGEMENTS

This journey would not have been possible without the tireless love, support, and encouragement of my wonderful husband, Kurt Oldman. Thank you to my editor, Jennifer Arena, for helping me make my story the best it could possibly be. Thank you to Rosemary Lawton for your keen, grammatical eye. Thank you to my design team: Matthew R. Hinshaw for your creativity with the map, Ivan Cakic for your brilliant cover design, and Phillip Gessert for your patience and attention to detail with the interior. Thank you to my readers. Your requests for more inspired my jumping back into Cecilia's world and creating her new adventure. And to all my friends and family who stood with me, supporting this epic exploit—Thank You!

CONNECT WITH THE AUTHOR

For more information about Sandra and other projects, visit her website at www.SLRostirolla.com

Follow her on Twitter & Instagram @SLRostirolla

http://www.facebook.com/TheCeciliaSeries

We welcome your review of Cecilia—The Order of Terefellian on Goodreads & Amazon

ABOUT THE AUTHOR

Sandra is an Award-Winning author, who grew up in Sydney, Australia. She graduated from the University of Sydney with a BA in Applied Science and has an MBA from La Sierra University, Los Angeles. She enjoys skiing in winter, snorkeling in summer, and hiking whenever she can.

CPSIA information can be obtained
at www.ICGtesting.com
Printed in the USA
FSHW011807240621
82677FS